Hannah Kent is the co-founder of Australian literary journal *Kill Your Darlings*. In 2011, she won the inaugural Writing Australia Unpublished Manuscript Award for her debut novel, *Burial Rites*, the story of Agnes Magnúsdóttir, the last person to be executed in Iceland. Since its publication in 2013, *Burial Rites* has been translated into nearly thirty languages and has received numerous awards and nominations.

ALSO BY HANNAH KENT

Burial Rites

PRAISE AND ACCOLADES FOR *BURIAL RITES*

'A story of swirling sagas, poetry, bitterness, claustrophobia . . . Holds an exhilaration that borders on the sublime.' *Sunday Telegraph*

'A debut of rare sophistication and beauty.' *Observer*

'A remarkably assured debut, takes a tale of crime and punishment in 1820s Iceland and through it opens a window, lit with hard brilliance, on an alien world.' *Independent*, Fiction Books of the Year

'Exceptional' *Sunday Express*

'With language flickering, sparkling and flashing like the northern lights . . . A magical exercise in artful literary fiction.' *Kirkus*, starred review

'Remarkable' *Sunday Times*

'Kent's debut is assured, moving and incredibly well researched and written. It's the perfect mix of literary and historical fiction, giving an insightful and empathetic look at a woman demonised in her lifetime.' *Bookseller*, Books of the Year

'A thrillingly accomplished debut with a powerful sense of place.'
Metro, Books of the Year

'Rarely has a country's starkness and extreme weather been rendered
so exquisitely. The harshness of the landscape and the lifestyle of
nineteenth-century Iceland, with its dank turf houses and meagre food
supply, is as finely detailed as the heartbreak and tragedy of Agnes'
life . . . [A] haunting reading from a bright new talent.' *Booklist*,
starred review

'This is a golden age both of historical fiction and of crime writing.
A rare novel that combines both, this is one of the most gripping,
intriguing and unique books that I've read this year.' KATE MOSSE

'So gripping I wanted to rush through the pages, but so beautifully
written I wanted to linger over every sentence.' MADELINE MILLER,
Winner of the Orange Prize for Fiction

'*Burial Rites* is an accomplished gem, its prose as crisp and sparkling as
its northern setting.' GERALDINE BROOKS

'This compelling, ripped-from-real-life tale reminds me of Margaret
Atwood's *Alias Grace*.' KARIN SLAUGHTER

THE GOOD PEOPLE
HANNAH KENT

PICADOR
Pan Macmillan Australia

First published 2016 in Picador by Pan Macmillan Australia Pty Limited

1 Market Street, Sydney, New South Wales, Australia, 2000

Reprinted 2016 (six times), 2017 (three times)

Cataloguing-in-Publication entry is available
from the National Library of Australia
http://catalogue.nla.gov.au

Typeset in Adobe Garamond Pro by Post Pre-Press Australia
Printed by McPherson's Printing Group
Internal text design by Sandy Cull
Cartography by Pan Macmillan Australia

For my sister, Briony.

There was an old woman and she lived in the woods,
weile weile waile.
There was an old woman and she lived in the woods
down by the river Saile.

She had a baby three months old,
weile weile waile.
She had a baby three months old
down by the river Saile.

She had a penknife, long and sharp,
weile weile waile.
She had a penknife long and sharp
down by the river Saile.

She stuck the penknife in the baby's heart,
weile weile waile.
She stuck the penknife in the baby's heart
down by the river Saile.

Three hard knocks came knocking on the door,
weile weile waile.
Three hard knocks came knocking on the door
down by the river Saile.

'Are you the woman that killed the child?'
weile weile waile.
'Are you the woman that killed the child
down by the river Saile?'

The rope was pulled and she got hung,
weile weile waile.
The rope was pulled and she got hung
down by the river Saile.

And that was the end of the woman in the woods,
weile weile waile.
And that was the end of the woman in the woods
down by the river Saile.

Traditional Irish Murder Ballad, c. 1600

When all is said and done, how do we not know but that
our own unreason may be better than another's truth?
for it has been warmed on our hearths and in our souls,
and is ready for the wild bees of truth to hive in it, and
make their sweet honey. Come into the world again,
wild bees, wild bees!

W.B. Yeats, *The Celtic Twilight*

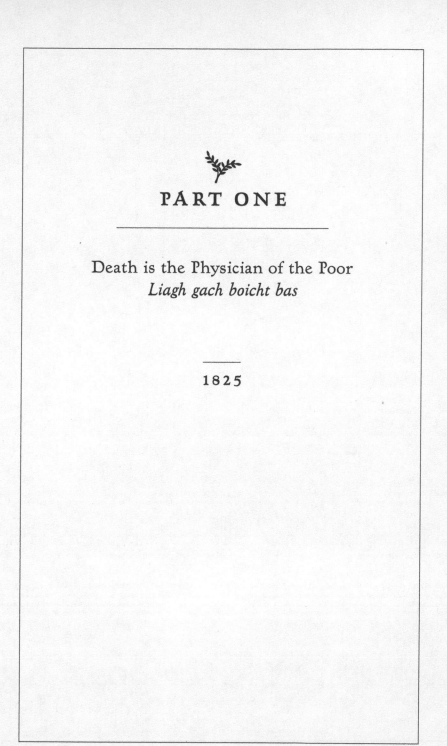

PART ONE

Death is the Physician of the Poor
Liagh gach boicht bas

1825

CHAPTER
ONE

Coltsfoot

Nóra's first thought when they brought her the body was that it could not be her husband's. For one long moment she stared at the men bearing Martin's weight on their sweating shoulders, standing in the gasping cold, and believed that the body was nothing but a cruel imitation; a changeling, brutal in its likeness. Martin's mouth and eyes were open, but his head slumped on his chest and there was no quick in him. The blacksmith and the ploughman had brought her a lifeless stock. It could not be her husband. It was not him at all.

Martin had been digging ditches beside the fields that sloped the valley, Peter O'Connor said. He had seen him stop, place a hand on his chest like a man taking an oath, and fall to the gentle ground. He had not given a shout of pain. He had gone without farewell or fear.

Peter's chapped lips trembled, eyes red-rimmed in their sockets. 'I'm sorry for your trouble,' he whispered.

Nóra's legs collapsed beneath her then and in the fall to the dirt and straw of the yard, she felt her heart seize with terrible understanding.

John O'Donoghue, his thick forearms scar-speckled from iron-work, heaved Martin over his shoulder so that Peter was able to lift Nóra out of the mud. Both men were dark-eyed with grief and when Nóra opened her mouth to scream and found that she had choked on it, they bowed their heads as though they heard her anyway.

Peter wrested the chicken feed from Nóra's clenched fists and kicked the clucking hens from the doorstep. Placing her arm around his shoulders, he led her back inside the cabin to sit by the hearth where her grandchild, Micheál, was sleeping in the unfolded settle bed. The little boy, his cheeks flushed from the heat of the turf fire, stirred as they entered, and Nóra noticed Peter's eyes flicker to him in curiosity.

John followed them inside, his jaw clenched with the weight of Martin's body and his boots tracking mud over the packed clay floor. Grunting with the effort, he laid Martin on the bed in the small sleeping quarter off the main room. Dust from the disturbed straw mattress rose into the air. The blacksmith crossed himself with delib-erate precision and, stooping under the lintel, murmured that his wife, Áine, would be there soon, and that the new priest had been fetched.

Nóra felt her throat close over. She rose to go to Martin's body in the bedroom, but Peter held her wrist.

'Let him be washed,' he said gently.

John cast a troubled look at the boy and left without saying another word, shutting the half-door behind him.

The dark rose.

'You saw him fall, did you? Saw him yourself?' Nóra's voice sounded strange and small. She gripped Peter's hand so tightly her fingers ached.

'I did,' he murmured, looking at Micheál. 'I saw him in the fields and raised my hand, and I saw him fall down.'

'There was a need for those ditches. He told me yesterday there was a need for them to be dug, so the rain . . .' Nóra felt her husband's death creep over her, until she began to shake with it. Peter draped a greatcoat over her shoulders, and she could tell from the familiar smell of burnt coltsfoot that it was Martin's own. They must have brought it back with his body.

'Someone else will have to finish those ditches,' she gasped, rubbing her cheek against the rough frieze.

'Don't be thinking of that now, Nóra.'

'And there will be the thatch, come spring. It needs thatching.'

'We'll all be taking care of that, don't you worry now.'

'And Micheál. The boy . . .' Alarm ran through her and she looked down at the child, his hair copper in the firelight. She was grateful that he slept. The boy's difference did not show so much when he was asleep. The keel of his limbs slackened, and there was no telling the dumb tongue in his head. Martin had always said Micheál looked most like their daughter when asleep. 'You can almost think him well,' he had said once. 'You can see how he will be when the sickness has passed. When we have him cured of it.'

'Is there someone I can fetch for you, Nóra?' Peter asked, his face splintered with concern.

'Micheál. I don't want him here.' Her voice was hoarse. 'Take Micheál to Peg O'Shea's.'

Peter looked uneasy. 'Would you not have him with you?'

'Take him away from here.'

'I don't like to leave you alone, Nóra. Not before Áine is with you.'

'I'll not have Micheál here to be gaped at.' Nóra reached down and grabbed the sleeping boy under his armpits, hauling him into the air in front of Peter. The boy frowned, eyes blinking, gummed with sleep.

'Take him. Take him to Peg's. Before a soul is here.'

Micheál began to squall and struggle as he hung from Nóra's grip. His legs tremored, rashed and dry-looking against the bone.

Peter grimaced. 'Your daughter's, isn't he? God rest her soul.'

'Take him, Peter. Please.'

He gave her a long, sorrowful look. 'Folk won't mind him at a time like this, Nóra. They'll be thinking of you.'

'They'll be gawping and gossiping over him, is what.'

Micheál's head slumped backwards and he began to cry, his hands drawing into fists.

'What ails him?'

'For the love of God, Peter, take him.' Her voice broke. 'Take him away!'

Peter nodded and lifted Micheál onto his lap. The boy was clothed in a girl's woollen dress, too long for him, and Peter awkwardly wrapped the worn cloth around the child's legs, taking care to cover his toes. ''Tis cold out,' he explained. 'Do you not have a shawl for him?'

Nóra, hands shaking, took off her own and gave it to Peter.

He stood up, bundling the bleating boy against his chest. 'I'm sorry, Nóra, so I am.'

The cabin door swung wide after him.

Nóra waited until the sound of Micheál's crying faded and she knew Peter had reached the lane. Then she rose from her low stool and walked into the bedroom, clutching Martin's coat around her shoulders.

'Sweet, sore-wounded Christ.'

Her husband lay on their marriage bed, his arms tucked close to his sides, grass and mud clinging to his calloused hands. His eyes were half closed. Their pearled whites glimmered in the light from the open door.

Martin's stillness in that quiet room sent sorrow pealing through her chest. Easing herself down onto the bed, Nóra touched her forehead against Martin's cheekbone and felt the cold of his stubbled skin.

Pulling his coat over the both of them, she closed her eyes and her lungs emptied of air. Pain descended with the weight of water and she felt that she was drowning. Her chest shuddered, and she was crying into her husband's collarbone, into his clothes reeking of the earth and cow shit and the soft sweet smell of the valley air and all the turf smoke it carried on an autumn evening. She cried like a pining dog, with the strained, strung whimper of abandonment.

Only that morning they had lain in bed together, both awake in the dark of early dawn, the warmth of Martin's hand resting on her stomach.

'I think it will rain today,' he had said, and Nóra had let him pull her close against the broad barrel of his ribs, had matched the rise and fall of her breathing with his own.

'There was a wind in the night.'

'It woke you?'

'The boy woke me. He was crying in fear of it.'

Martin had listened intently. 'There's no sound from him now.'

'Are you digging potatoes today?'

'Ditches.'

'And will you have a word with the new priest about Micheál on your way home?'

'I will.'

Nóra stretched herself out against her husband's dead body and thought of the nights they had slept in company together, the touch of his foot on hers in the unthinking custom of their marriage, and sobbed until she thought she would be sick.

It was only the thought that her cries might wake devils lying in wait for his soul that made her stop. She stuffed her mouth with the sleeve of Martin's coat and shook, silently.

How dare you leave me behind, she thought.

*

'Nóra?'

She had fallen asleep. Through the swelling of her eyes she saw the slender outline of the blacksmith's wife standing in the doorway.

'Áine,' Nóra croaked.

The woman entered, crossing herself at the sight of the body. 'May the Lord have mercy on his soul. I'm sorry for your trouble. Martin, he . . .' She paused and knelt by Nóra's side. 'He was a great man. A rare man.'

Nóra sat up on the bed and wiped her eyes on her apron, embarrassed.

'The sorrow is on you, Nóra. I can see it. And we'd do right to give him a proper wake. Would you be willing for me to wash and lay him out? Father Healy has been sent for. He's on his way.'

Áine put her hand on Nóra's knee and squeezed it. Her face, hanging from wide cheekbones, seemed spectral in the gloom. Nóra stared at her in horror.

'There now. Here are your beads. He's with God now, Nóra. Remember that.' She glanced around the room. 'Are you alone? Did you not have a child . . .?'

Nóra closed her fingers over the rosary. 'I am alone.'

Áine washed Martin as tenderly as if he had been her own husband. At first Nóra watched, clutching the prayer beads so tightly that the wood baubled her skin into welts. She could not believe that it was her husband naked before them, his belly painful-white. It was shameful for another woman to see the pale secrets of his body. When she stood up and held her hand out for the cloth, Áine passed it to her without a word. She washed him then, and with every movement of her hand she farewelled the boned curve of his chest, the sweep of his limbs.

How well I know you, she thought, and when she felt her throat noose tighter, she swallowed hard and forced her eye to the neat cobwebbing of veins across his thighs, the familiar whorl of his hair. She did not understand how Martin's body could seem so small. In life he had been a bear of a man, had carried her on the night of their wedding as though she was nothing more than sunlight.

The dark fur of his chest slicked damp against his skin.

'I think he is clean now, Nóra,' Áine said.

'A little longer.' She ran her palm down his sternum as though waiting for it to lift in breath.

Áine eased the grey cloth from her fingers' grip.

The afternoon darkened and a bitter wind began to blow outside. Nóra sat beside Martin's body and let Áine stir the fire and fix the rushlights. Both of them jumped at a sudden knocking on the door, and Nóra's heart gave a scalding leap at the thought it might be Martin, returned to her by the evening.

'Blessings on this house.'

A young man entered the cabin, his clerical garb flapping in the doorway. The new priest, Nóra realised. He was dark-haired and ruddy-cheeked, with long limbs that seemed at odds with his soft, child's face and pouting mouth. Nóra noticed a conspicuous gap between his front teeth. Father Healy's hat dripped with rain, and when Peter and John followed him inside, their shoulders were wet through. She had not realised that the weather had changed.

'Good evening to you, Father.' Áine took the damp coat he held out to her and carefully arranged it over the rafter to dry by the heat of the fire.

The priest looked around the cabin before noticing Nóra sitting in the bedroom. He walked towards her, ducking under the low doorframe. His eyes were solemn. 'God be with you, Mrs Leahy.

I'm sorry for your trouble.' Taking her hand in his own, he pressed the flesh of her palm. 'It must be a great shock to you.'

Nóra nodded, her mouth dry.

'It happens to us all, but 'tis always sad when those we love go to God.' He released her hand and turned to Martin, placing two slender fingers against her husband's throat. The priest gave a slight nod. 'He has passed. I cannot give the last rites.'

'He had no warning of his death, Father.' It was Peter who spoke. 'Would you not give him the rites anyway? His soul may yet be in his body.'

Father Healy wiped his forehead on his sleeve and grimaced in apology. 'The sacraments are for the living and cannot avail the dead.'

Nóra gripped her rosary until her knuckles paled. 'Pray for him, will you, Father?'

The priest looked from the two men in the doorway to Nóra.

She lifted her chin. 'He was a good man, Father. Say the prayers over him.'

Father Healy sighed, nodded and reached into his bag, taking out a small, used candle and a glass bottle of oil. He lit the candle by the fire in the main room and placed the waxy stub awkwardly in Martin's hand, beginning the prayers and anointing the man's head with a firm touch.

Nóra sank down onto the hard floor beside the bed and let her fingers slide across the beads in blank habit. But the prayers felt empty and cold in her mouth and she soon stopped whispering and sat there, mute.

I am not ready to be alone, she thought.

Father Healy cleared his throat and stood up, brushing his knees of dirt and reaching for his coat and the coin offered by John.

'May God comfort you,' he said to Nóra, shaking the rain from his hat and setting it on his head. He took her hand again and she flinched at the feel of the bones in his fingers.

'May God protect you. Seek His love and forgiveness and keep your faith, Mrs Leahy. I will keep you in my prayers.'

'Thank you, Father.'

They watched the priest mount his donkey in the yard, squinting against the steady rain. He raised a hand to them in farewell, then whipped the animal's flank with a sally rod until the weather closed around him and the valley below absorbed his black, fleeing form.

By nightfall the cabin was filled with neighbours who had heard that Martin had died by the crossroads next to the blacksmith's, falling to the ground on the strike of hammer on anvil as though the ringing of iron had killed him. They gathered around the hearth, taking consolation from their pipes and murmuring condolences to Nóra. Outside, the rain blew against the thatch.

Confronted with a sudden crowd, Nóra concentrated on collecting preparations for the wake with Áine. There was no time to weep while they had *poitín*, clay pipes, tobacco and chairs to find. Nóra knew that death made people long to smoke and drink and eat, as though by tending to their lungs and stomachs they were assuring themselves of their own good health, of the certainty of their continued existence.

When she felt the weight of her grief threaten to press her to the floor, Nóra retreated to the cabin walls and pushed her palms against the cool limewash to steady herself. She took deep breaths and stared at the people in the room. Most of them were from the valley, tied to one another by blood and labour and a shared understanding of the traditions stamped into the soil by those who had come before them. They were quiet, close folk, those who lived on the shadowed side of Crohane, in the fertile crucible formed by the rising rock and hill of Foiladuane, Derreenacullig and Clonkeen. And they were familiar with death. In her small house Nóra could see that her neighbours were making room for sorrow in the way they knew to be best. They piled turf on the fire and built the flames high, filled the air with smoke, and told each other stories. There would be a time to cry, but it was not yet.

Thunder rolled outside, and the guests shivered and drew closer to the fire. As Nóra moved around the room, setting out drinking water, she heard the people whisper stories of divination. The men commented on the weather and the movements of jacksnipes and magpies, seeing in them signs of Martin's death. Much was made of his collapse at the crossroads where they buried suicides. Some spoke of the sudden change in the sky that afternoon, of the great blackening of clouds in the west and how they had surely heralded Martin's passing. Of the storm that was closing in upon them.

Unaware that Nóra was listening, Peter O'Connor was telling the men that, just before he had seen Martin clutch his heart, he had noticed four magpies sitting together in a field.

'There I was, walking the lane, and did those birds move? They did not. They let me pass within arm's reach of them and not once did they startle. "That's mighty strange," I thought to myself, and – I tell you, lads – a shiver went through me for it seemed they stood in conference. "Someone has died," I thought. Then sure, I make my way down the boreen until I reached the crossroads and, soon enough, there is Martin Leahy, lying with the sky in his eyes and the clouds darkening beyond the mountains.'

There was a slap of thunder and they jumped.

'So, 'twas you that found him then, lying there?' asked Nóra's nephew, Daniel, drawing on his pipe.

''Twas. And a sorrow 'twas to me too. I saw that great man topple like a tree. He had not yet the cold upon him, God rest his soul.'

Peter's voice softened to a hush. 'And that's not all of it. When John and I were bringing the body here, dragging him up the slope from the crossroads – and you know the heft of Martin, 'twas slow going – well, we stopped a while to catch our breath, and we looked down the valley, out towards the woods, and there we saw *lights*.'

There was a murmur of intrigue.

'That's right. Lights. Coming from where the *fairies* do be, down by the Piper's Grave,' Peter continued. 'Now, I might not have the full of my eyes, but I swear I saw a glowing by that whitethorn. You mark my words, there'll be another death in this family before long.' His voice dropped to a whisper. 'First the daughter passes, and now the husband. I tell you, death likes three in company. And if the Good People have a hand in it . . . well.'

Nóra's throat tightened and she turned away to seek out Áine. She found her taking chalk pipes and a lump of uncut tobacco from a straw *ciseán*.

'Do you hear that storming?' Áine whispered. She gestured to the basket. 'Your nephew Daniel's woman, the young wife, she's brought some preparations.'

Nóra picked up a small cloth parcel and untied its string with shaking fingers. Salt, damp from the rain. 'Where is she?'

'Praying over Martin.'

The bedroom was crowded, the air blue with the pipe smoke that the older men and women blew over her husband. Nóra noticed that they had turned Martin's body so that his head was at the foot of the bed, so as to avert further misfortune. His mouth had fallen open and his skin had already taken on the waxiness of the dead, his forehead greasy with the priest's oils. The candle stub, unlit, lolled amongst the bedclothes. A young woman knelt beside him, reciting Hail Mary with her eyes closed.

Nóra tapped her on the shoulder. 'Brigid.'

The girl looked up. 'Oh, Nóra,' she whispered, heaving herself to her feet. Her pregnant belly swelled, lifting the front of her skirts and apron so that her bare ankles were visible. 'I'm sorry for your trouble. Martin was a mighty man. How are you keeping?'

Nóra opened her mouth to speak but thought better of it.

'Himself and I brought what you might need.' She nodded to where Daniel sat smoking with Peter. 'I set a basket on the table.'

'I know, Áine showed me. 'Tis kind of you both. I'll pay you for it.'

'A bad year for you.'

Nóra took a breath. 'Do you know who might have the drink?'

'Seán has brought *poitín*.' Brigid pointed through to the main room where Seán Lynch, Daniel's uncle, was setting two clay jars of spirits on the floor. His wife, Kate, was with him, a woman with crowded teeth and a hunched, hounded look. She stood in the doorway, peering around the room in agitation. They had clearly just arrived; their clothes were dark with rain and the smell of cold was on them.

'Nóra, Brigid.' Kate nodded as the two women made their way back into the room. ''Tis a sad evening. Has the priest been? Do we need to hide the drink?'

'Been and gone.'

Seán's face was grim, his eyes and lips set in hard, leathered lines. He pushed tobacco into the bowl of his clay pipe with a calloused thumb. 'Sorry for your trouble,' he told Nóra.

'God save you kindly, Seán.'

'You've a visitor lurking out there,' he said, gesturing towards the door. Taking the offer of an ember from one of the men by the fire, he lit his pipe with the tongs and muttered, 'May God have mercy on the souls of the dead.' Smoke escaped from between his teeth. 'The herb hag. She's out by your dung heap, waiting.'

Nóra paused. 'Nance Roche?'

'Aye, the interfering biddy herself.' He spat on the floor.

'How did she know to come?'

Seán frowned. 'I wouldn't talk to her if she was the last woman alive.'

Kate watched him anxiously.

'Nance Roche? I thought she was the handy woman?' Brigid asked.

'I wonder what she wants,' Nóra muttered. ''Tis a long way for an old woman on a night of tipping rain. I wouldn't put my enemy's dog out tonight.'

'Looking for pipe smoke and drink, it is,' Kate remarked sourly, nostrils flaring. 'Don't go out to her, Nóra. Not that hag, that swindler *cailleach*.'

Night had fallen and the downpour had grown heavier. Nóra pushed out the wooden door of the cabin and peered into the yard, her head hunched under the low awning of thatch. Water poured off the straw ends. At first she couldn't see anything through the rain, only a thin rim of iron grey on the horizon where the dark had not yet suffocated the light. Then, out of the corner of her eye, she saw a small figure moving towards her from the gabled end of the house where the muck of the smallholding lay heaped against the stone wall. Nóra stepped down into the yard, shutting the door behind her to keep out the cold. The mud rose over her toes.

'Who's that there?' she called, her words drowned out by thunder. 'Is that you, Nance Roche?'

The visitor walked to the door and bent her head under the thatch, pulling the cloak from her head.

'So 'tis, Nóra Leahy.'

Lightning flared and Nóra saw the old woman before her,

drenched to the bone, her white hair slick against her skull. Nance blinked away the rain that slid down her forehead and sniffed. She was small, shrunken, with a face as wrinkled as a forgotten russet. Her eyes, fogged with age, looked up at Nóra from beneath heavy eyelids. 'I'm sorry for your trouble.'

'Thank you, Nance.'

''Tis the end of Martin's worry in this life.'

'So 'tis.'

'Your man is on the way of truth now.' Nance's lips parted, revealing the few stray teeth that remained in her gums. 'I've come to see if you will have me keen. Your Martin was a good man.'

Nóra looked at Nance dripping in front of her. Her clothes, heavy with water, hung off narrow shoulder blades, but for all her layers of sopping wool she had a certain presence. There was a sharp, bitter smell coming off her. Like bruised nettles, thought Nóra. Or rotting leaves. The smell of someone who lived close to the forest floor.

'How did you know to come?' asked Nóra.

'I saw that new priest on his ass, beating the dust out of the animal. Only the Devil or a dying man would drive a priest into a wet and dirty night.'

'Father Healy.'

'I had the knowledge then that it was your man, Martin. God rest his soul,' she added.

An icy thread ran the length of Nóra's spine. Thunder sounded.

'The knowledge?'

Nance nodded and reached for Nóra. Her fingers were cold and surprisingly smooth.

Healer's palms, thought Nóra. 'And so you've walked all the way in the wet and wind.'

'No one becomes a worse person for rain on her head. I would do a great deal more for your man.'

Nóra opened the door and flicked the mud off her feet. 'Well, come in so. Seeing as you're here.'

'I will.'

The conversation inside the crowded cabin halted as Nóra led Nance into the room. All eyes looked to the older woman, who stopped inside the doorway and gazed about her, chin raised.

'God save all here,' she said. Her voice was thin, husked with smoke and age.

The men nodded to her in respect. A few of the women looked Nance up and down, noting the thick clag of mud that clung to the hem of her skirt, her weathered face, her soaked shawl. Seán Lynch glared before turning his face to the fire.

John O'Donoghue rose, his blacksmith's bulk suddenly filling the room. 'And you, Nance Roche. God save you.' He moved forward to lead her to the fire, and the other men immediately made room by the hearth. Peter, pipe in mouth, fetched a creepie stool and placed it firmly down by the coals, and Áine brought water for her dirty feet. Daniel offered Nance a small nip of *poitín*, and when she shook her head, the young man mumbled, ''Tis not a drop big enough to fit a wren's bill,' and pressed it into her hand.

Those who had fallen silent resumed their talk once they saw Nance was welcome. Only Seán and Kate Lynch retreated to the shadows where they slouched, watching.

Nance extended her bare toes to the embers, sipping her spirits. Nóra sat beside her, dread unspooling in her stomach as she watched the steam rise from the old woman's shoulders. How had she known Martin had died?

The old woman took a deep breath and raised a hand towards the bedroom. 'He's in there?'

'He is,' Nóra answered, heart fluttering.

Nance cradled her cup. 'When was his hour?'

'John and Peter brought him to me when it was still light. Before evening.' Nóra looked at the ground. The close air of the cabin after the clean night outdoors was making her feel sick. There was too much pipe smoke. Too much noise. She wished she could go outside and lie on the soft slick of mud, breathe in the smell of rain and be alone. Let the lightning strike her.

Nóra felt Nance's hands close around her fingers. The tenderness in her touch was alarming. She fought the urge to push the woman away.

'Nóra Leahy. You listen to me,' Nance whispered. 'For all the death in the world, each woman's grief is her own. It takes a different shape with all of us. But the sad truth is that people will not want your grief a year after you bury your husband. 'Tis the way of it. They'll go back to thinking of themselves. They'll go back to their own lives. So let us mourn Martin now, while they will listen. While they have the patience for it.'

Nóra nodded. She felt like she would throw up.

'And, Nóra, tell me. What's all this muttering about him passing at the crossroads? Is that true?'

''Tis.' It was Brigid who had spoken. She was cutting tobacco at the table behind them. 'Peter O'Connor found him there. A dreadful sorrow.'

Nance turned her head, squinting. 'And who are you?'

'Brigid Lynch.'

'My nephew Daniel's wife,' Nóra explained.

Nance frowned. 'You are carrying. Young Brigid, you ought not to be in a corpse house.'

Brigid stopped cutting the plugs of tobacco and stared.

'You have a right to leave. Before you breathe the death in and infect your child with it.'

'Is that true?' Brigid dropped the knife on the table. 'I knew to stay out of the churchyard, but . . .'

'Churchyard, corpse house, grave mound.' Nance spat on the fire.

Brigid turned to Nóra. 'I don't want to leave Daniel,' she whispered. 'I don't like to go out when 'tis dark. And 'tis storming. I don't want to go alone.'

'No.' Nance shook her head. 'Don't you go alone. 'Tis an uneasy night.'

Brigid pressed both hands against the round of her stomach.

Nance waved at Áine, who was handing out filled pipes to the men. 'Áine O'Donoghue, will you take this girl to a neighbour's? Take her husband too, so he might come back with you. 'Tis no night for a soul to be alone on the road.'

'Take her to Peg O'Shea's,' Nóra muttered. 'She's closest.'

Áine looked between the women. 'What is it? What's wrong?'

''Tis for the good of the young one's child.' Nance reached out and placed her wrinkled hand on Brigid's belly. 'Make haste, girl. Put some salt in your pocket and leave. This storm is brewing.'

By midnight Nóra's cabin was oppressive with the smell of wet wool and the sourness of too many people in a crowded room. The eyelids of Martin Leahy were bright with two pennies, placed there by a neighbour, and there was a crusted saucer of salt balanced on his chest. A plate of tobacco and coltsfoot sat on the dead man's stomach. The air was unbearably close, smoke-rich, as the men nudged their lips with clay pipes, borrowing Nóra's knitting needles to tap out the ashes and wiping them on their trousers.

At the approach of midnight John O'Donoghue recited a rosary for the dead, and the company knelt and mumbled their responses. Then the men retreated to the walls of the cabin and watched the women keen the body by the poor light of the rush tapers, stinking of fat and burning too quickly from their brass pinch.

Nance Roche led the wailing against the muted cracking of thunder. Her forehead was grey with ashes, her hands blackened from where she had smeared cold cinders on the foreheads of the other women. Nóra Leahy felt each powdered cheek split with the hot, wet path of her tears. She knelt on the ground and looked up at the circle of familiar faces, furrowed in solemnity.

This is a nightmare, she thought.

Nance closed her eyes, let her mouth slip open, and began a low lament that vanquished the small conversation of the men like an airless room snuffs a flame. She crouched on the clay floor and rocked back and forth, her hair loosened and thin over her shoulders. She cried without pause, without words. Her keen was hollow, fear-filled. It reminded Nóra of the *bean sídhe*, of the silent, scrabbling death-yawns of drowning men

As Nance keened, the other women muttered prayers for the dead, asking God to accept Martin Leahy's departed soul. Nóra noticed Kate Lynch, brown hair dull in the gloom, next to her kneeling daughter, Sorcha, dimpled and whispering, and Éilís O'Hare, the schoolmaster's wife, crossing herself in a latticework of prayer, one eye open to Nance as she clawed the firelight. Her neighbours and their daughters. The glut of valley women, all wringing their hands. Nóra shut her eyes. None of them knew how she felt. None of them.

It was frightening, to be unbridled from language and led into anguish by the *bean feasa*. Nóra opened her mouth and did not recognise her own voice. She moaned and the sound of her grief scared her.

Many in the room were moved to tears by the *caoineadh* of the women. They bent their damp heads and praised Martin Leahy with tongues loosened by *poitín*, naming the qualities that recommended him to God and man. The fine father of a daughter, gone to God only months before. A decent husband. A man who had the gift for bone-setting, and whose wide hands could always calm horses in a hackle of panic.

Nance's moan dropped to a low ragged breathing. Sweeping up a sudden fistful of ash, she threw her body towards the yard door of the cabin, flinging the cinders towards it. Ashes to banish Those that would restrain a soul's flight into the other world. Ashes to sanctify the grieving of kith and kin and mark it as holy.

Amidst the prayers, Nance slowly dropped her head to her knees, wiped the ash from her face with her skirts, and rose from the floor. The keening had finished. She waited until the words and cries of those in the room subsided into respectful silence, and then, nodding at Nóra, retired to a dark corner. She knotted her white hair at the nape of her neck and accepted a clay pipe, and spent the rest of the night smoking thoughtfully, watching the womenfolk and mourners circle Nóra like birds above a new-shorn field.

The night ground down the hours. Many of the people, dulled and comforted by the heady fumes of burning coltsfoot, lay down to sleep on the floor, plumping beds out of heather and rushes and slurring prayers. Rain escaped down the chimney and fell hissing on the fire. A few kept their eyes open with stories and gossip, taking turns to bless the body and finding omens in the thunderstorm that thrashed the valley outside. Only Nóra saw the old woman rise from her corner, slip her hood back over her head and retreat into the darkness and the howling world.

CHAPTER
TWO

Furze

Nance Roche woke in the early morning, before the fog had eased off the mountains. She had slept in the clothes she had returned home in and their damp had spread to her bones. Pushing herself up from her bed of heather, Nance allowed her eyes to adjust to the low light and rubbed at the cold in her limbs. Her fire was out — only the faintest suggestion of warmth met her outstretched hand. She must have fallen asleep in front of its heat before she could preserve the embers.

Taking her shawl off a hook in the wall, she wrapped herself in the rough wool and familiar smell of hearth smoke, and stepped outside, snatching a water can as she left.

The storm had thrashed the valley with rain all night and the woods behind her stunted cabin dripped with water. The fog was thick, but from her place at the far end of the valley, where the fields and bouldered slopes met the uncleared woodland, she could hear the roar of the river Flesk's swollen waters. A short distance away from her cabin was the Piper's Grave, where the fairies dwelt. She nodded respectfully towards the crooked whitethorn, standing ghostlike in the mist in its circle of stone, briars and overgrown grass.

Nance tightened the shawl around her, joints creaking as she walked to the sodden ditch left by a collapsed badger set. Squatting unsteadily over the edge, she pissed with her eyes shut, her fingers holding on to bracken stalks for balance. Her whole body ached. It often did after a night of keening. As soon as Nance left any corpse house, a great, pulsing headache would swell in her skull.

'Tis the borrowed grief, thought Nance. To stand in the doorway between life and death racks the body and bleeds the brain.

The slope down to the river was slippery with mud and Nance stepped carefully, wet autumn leaves slicked to the bare soles of her feet as she made her way through the brushwood. It would not do to fall. Only last winter she had slipped and hurt her back. It had been a painful week in front of the fire then, but the worst of it was that, injured, she had felt herself crease with isolation. She had thought she had grown used to a life alone, that the skittering presence of birds sufficed for company. But without visitors, without anything to do but rest in the darkness of the cabin, she had felt so violently lonely she had cried.

'If there is one thing that will sink sickness deeper into the body, 'tis loneliness.'

Mad Maggie had told her that. In the early days, when Nance was young. When her father was still alive.

'Mark my words, Nance. That man who came by just now? No wife. Few friends. No brothers or sisters. The only thing keeping him company is his gout, and 'tis the loneliness of him keeping it there.'

Maggie sitting in their cabin, pipe in mouth, plucking a chicken. Feathers in the air. The rain pelting outside. Feathers resting in her wild hair.

That fall was a warning, Nance thought. You are old. You have only yourself to rely upon. Since then she had minded her body with tenderness. Steady steps on grass slippery with weather. No more reckless journeys to cut heather on the mountains when the wind growled. An eye to the fire and its crush of embers. A careful hand with the knife.

The roar from the Flesk grew louder as Nance drew closer, until she could see the white foam of the current teeming at the top of the riverbank through the surrounding trunks of oak, alder and ash. The storm had stripped the trees of their remaining leaves, and the wood was black and tannic with moisture. Only the birch trees, moon-pale, shone in the wet.

Nance picked her way around the broken branches that littered the ground and the tangles of ivy and withered bracken sprawling over the bank. Folk did not often frequent this end of the valley. The women did not come for their water or washing this far upriver because of the Piper's Grave, the lurking fairy fort, and there was a feel of neglect and wildness from their absence. The stones had not been scuffed clean of their moss and the briars had not been cut back for fear of them snagging on laundry. Only Nance came to the water's edge here. Only Nance did not mind living so close to the woods that claimed this part of the river.

The storm had infuriated the current and Nance saw that the stones she usually trusted to take her weight had been dislodged by the high water. The bank crumbled underfoot. The river was not especially wide or deep here, but when in flood the current was strong, and Nance had seen it fatten with swollen-stomached foxes washed out of their holes by fast and violent rains. She did not want to drown.

Taking off her shawl and draping it on a low branch, Nance sank to her knees and crept as close to the river as possible. She lowered her can and the water surged into it, pulling at her arm.

Rubbing her skirts free of leaf litter and soil, Nance shuffled back up to her cabin, trying to clear the fog from her mind. Small wrens swooped the grass and brambles, darting in and out of the mist and its suggestion of light. Mushrooms scalloped out from rotting wood in the undergrowth. The smell of damp soil was everywhere. How Nance preferred to be outside, with the great, wide ceiling of sky and the ground full of life. Her squat cabin, half dug into the ground and slouched in front of the woods with walls of wattle and mud, thatched with potato stalks and heather, seemed ugly and squalid compared to the dripping canopy of trees. She paused and looked down the valley, away from the woods. The whitewashed cabins of the cottiers lay scattered across the curve of the cultivated fields, now stubbled and browning, potato patches with loose-stoned walls beside them. She could see smoke rising from their roofs through the thinning mist. On the bare mountain sides the cabins grew smaller, dug more deeply into the ground to sturdy them against the wind. Their limed walls seemed blue in the morning gloom. Nance cast a look up to where the Leahys' cabin lay on the slope of the hillside. It was the cabin closest to her, and yet even that house seemed far away.

No one lived within calling distance of Nance. Her own window-less cabin, once whitewashed like the others, had flaked and greened with moss and mould over the years, until it looked as though the woods had claimed it as their own.

At least the inside of her little home was as clean and tidy as she could make it, no matter the ceiling crusted with soot and the damp in the corner. The dirt floor was swept and unpocked, and heather and rushes tempered the mustiness of the hay where her goat stood tethered at one end of the room.

Nance stirred the fire into life and left the water pail to settle. The storm had muddied the river and she must be careful not to drink it too quickly.

Never had she felt so weary after keening. Her bones felt rimed with exhaustion. She needed to eat something, a mouthful to feel restored.

The death cry had come on strongly last night. With the ashes on her face, Nance had felt the world shiver apart and had abandoned herself to the wail that rose from her lungs. Dizziness had come upon her, and the room of dark-clothed men and women had spun until all she could see was the fire and, in the smoke, images. An oak tree burning in a forest. A river surrounded by wild iris, yolked with yellow. And then, finally, her mother, hair falling into wild eyes, beckoning her into the dark. She had felt she was mourning the world.

Sometimes, in the company of suffering, Nance felt things. Maggie had called it an inward seeing. The knowledge. Sometimes, as she guided babies from their mothers and into the world, she sensed what their lives would be like, and sometimes the things she sensed frightened her. She remembered delivering a child whose mother had cursed him in her pain and fear, and she had sensed a darkness fall on him. She had cleaned and swaddled the infant, then later, as the mother slept, crushed a worm in his palm for protection.

There were things you could do to answer visions, Nance knew.

She had been troubled by the storm last night. Walking down the mountain slope from the Leahys' cabin under a sky welted with lightning, she had felt movement. Had felt things shifting in the darkness. A summoning. A warning. She had stopped by the fairy fort and waited in the rain with a tug of expectation and portent in her chest, and while the wind blasted the whitethorn, the limestone in the *ráth* flashed purple. She had half expected to see the Devil himself step out of the woods beyond her cabin. Nance did not usually feel afraid to leave a corpse house alone. She knew how to guard her body and soul with ash and salt. But last night, as she waited by the Piper's Grave, she felt vulnerable to whatever unseen presence tremored in the black. It wasn't until she saw lightning strike the mountain high behind her cabin and set fire to the heather that she had understood that something was indeed abroad and had hurried home to her fire and to the company of her animals.

Nance looked over to where her goat stood amongst the nesting hens, impatient in her corner. A drain had been hollowed out of the dirt floor to separate the animal and her leavings from Nance's own quarter, while allowing her warmth to give heat to the room. Nance stepped over the rivulet of waste and water and placed a gentle hand on the goat's head, smoothing the hair on her cheek and combing her beard free of straw.

'You're a good girl, Mora. Faith, what a grand girl you are.' Nance pulled a stool out from the wall and set it beside the goat alongside an armful of beaten furze.

'Is it famished you are? What a great wind there was. Did you not hear it? Were you not afraid?' Nance crooned to the goat, slowly reaching for a tin pail. She leant her forehead on the animal's wiry coat and breathed in her warm odour of dried whin and manure. Mora was skittish and stamped, her hoofs dull against the packed earth and hay, but Nance hummed until she quieted and began to nibble at the dry furze. Nance took hold of her teats and milked, singing softly, her voice cracked from the keening the night before.

When the udder's stream failed, Nance wiped her hands on her skirt and picked up the tin. Stepping to the doorway, she tipped a little onto the threshold for the Good People, and drank the milk, sweet and warm and flecked with the dirt from her own hands, straight from the pail.

No one would come for her today, Nance knew. The valley folk would be swarming the house of the Leahys to pay their respects to the dead and, besides, people did not often come to her at a time like this. She reminded them too much of their own mortality.

The keener. The handy woman. Nance opened her mouth and people thought of the way things went wrong, the way one thing became another. They looked at her white hair and saw twilight. She was both the woman who brought babies to safe harbour in the world, and the siren that cut boats free of their anchors and sent them into the dark.

Nance knew that the only reason they had allowed her this damp cabin between mountain and wood and river for twenty-odd years was because she stood in for that which was not and could not be understood. She was the gatekeeper at the edge of the world. The final human hymn before all fell to wind and shadow and the strange creaking of stars. She was a pagan chorus. An older song.

People are always a little afraid of what they do not recognise, Nance thought.

Warmed and comforted by the goat's milk, Nance wiped her mouth on her sleeve and leant against her doorframe, gazing out to the valley. Above, the sky had unfurled to the grey of dirty fleece, but Nance knew the day would be clear. She would be free to sleep and rest, and perhaps walk the lanes and ditches in the quiet of the afternoon to gather the last of the flowering yarrow and ragwort, the last blackberries and sloes, before winter brittled the world. Whatever remaining rain lingered in the clouds would pass beyond the mountains before breaking.

In all things Nance bent her hours to the sky. She knew its infinite faces.

The wake went on for two days, during which the people of the valley walked the mud-slick path to Nóra's mountainside cabin, some with whiskey bottles held tightly in their hands, rosaries tucked into pockets, others hauling their own stools and rough *súgán* chairs. Rain returned to the valley on the second day. Water dripped off the men's peaked caps and felt hats. They came with cold embers in their pockets and hazel sticks, and sat on wads of bracken amidst the strewn rushes. The air of the corpse house was grey, and people coughed amongst the burning lights of fire and pipe. They knelt and prayed for Martin, touching his sheeted body. The women and children, unused to the draw of a pipe, coughed and blew smoke over the corpse, masking the rough, rising smell of death.

Nóra thought they would never leave. She was sick of their company, the crush of the rushes beneath their feet, the way they sat and spoke of Martin as though they had known him best above all others.

I am his wife, she wanted to spit at them. You did not know him as I knew him.

She could not bear the way the women moved about the walls like shadows, gathering in tight clusters of gossip then disbanding to come and talk of time and faith and God. She hated the way the men spoke endlessly of the whoring October rain, and raised their rough-shod drink in Martin's direction to slur, 'May the Lord have mercy on your soul, Leahy, and on the souls of all the faithful departed,' before returning to their chuckling conversation.

It was only when the rain broke that Nóra was able to leave the cabin to relieve herself behind the house, and to take in great lungfuls of fresh air. She rubbed her hands in the wet grass beside the dung pile and wiped her face, pausing to watch the children play with stones in the yard. Shin-streaked with dirt and bright-eyed with the excitement of an occasion, they piled stones into cairns and took turns to knock them over. Even the shy girls squatted on the ground in pairs to play Poor Snipeen, one holding palms together in prayer while the other stroked their fingers gently. 'Poor Puss,' they murmured, before striking out at the hands in violence. Their slaps and cries of delighted pain echoed through the valley.

Nóra watched them play, a hard lump in her throat. This is what Micheál would be doing if he were not ill, she thought, and she was overcome with a wave of grief so sudden she gasped.

It would be different if he were well, she thought. He would be a comfort to me.

There was a tug on her skirt and Nóra looked down to see a boy of no more than four smiling up at her, an egg in his hand.

'I found this,' he said, and placed it in her palm before scarpering off, bare feet kicking up mud. Nóra stared after him. Here is what a child ought to be, she thought, and pictured Martin holding Micheál before the fire, rubbing his legs to restore the life to them, the boy's eyes closing at the touch of his grandfather's hand.

Nóra blinked quickly to stop the tears from coming and looked out to the horizon.

A curtain of rain was slowly moving across the mountains on the far side of the valley, beyond the low land where the river ran, and the crouch of woods to the east. Other than a few ash trees around the white cabins scattered about the dale on untilled ground, and the tangle of oak and alder beyond Nance Roche's greening *bothán* in the distance, the valley was a broad expanse of fields ribboned with low stone walls and ditches, flanked with bog ground and rough hillside where little else but furze and heather grew amongst the slabs of rock.

Even under the low rainclouds, it was a sight that calmed Nóra. The valley was beautiful. The slow turning towards winter had left the stubble on the fields and the wild grasses bronzed, and the scutter of cloud left shadows brooding across the soil. It was its own world. Only the narrow road, wending through the flat of the valley floor, indicated the world beyond the mountains to the west: the big houses and copper mines, the cramped streets of Killarney bristling with slated buildings and beggars, or, to the east, the distant markets of Cork. Only the occasional merchant headed towards Macroom, his horses' sides laden with casks of butter, suggested that there were other valleys, other towns, where different folk led different lives.

There was a shout of laughter from the children, and Nóra was startled out of her reverie. She turned to see an old woman making her way over the uneven ground from the cabin closest on the hill-side, leaning heavily on a blackthorn stick.

Peg O'Shea.

Her neighbour smiled at the children as she entered the yard, then caught Nóra's eye and shuffled towards her.

'Nóra. I'm so sorry for your trouble.' Her neighbour had the sunken cheeks of the very old, her lips curling inwards from loss of teeth. Her eyes, however, were wren-black and beady. Nóra felt them pass over her face, taking her measure.

'God and Mary to you, Peg. Thank you for taking Micheál.'

''Tis no trouble at all.'

'I didn't want him here. The house is full of people. I thought . . . I thought he might be frightened.'

Peg said nothing, pursing her lips.

'Martin and I, we thought 'twould be best if we kept him from crowds. Kept him quiet with us.'

'Aye, could be.'

'Who has an eye to him?'

'Oh, the house is full of my children and their weans. They give Micheál no mind. And 'tis not as though he'll be wandering off.' She leant closer. 'I didn't know 'twas so bad with him. All these months you've been caring for the boy . . .'

'Martin and I both. We managed between us. The one could mind him while the other worked.'

'How old is he, Nóra?'

'Four.'

'Four. And no more able to speak than a baby.'

Nóra looked down at the egg the little boy had given her, tracing a fingertip upon the shell. ''Tis the illness upon him.'

Peg was silent.

'He has the ability for it. I heard him speak before. When Johanna was alive.'

'Was he walking then too?'

Nóra felt ill. She shook her head, unable to answer, and Peg placed a hand on her shoulder. 'The sky has the appearance of rain. Let's inside to rest our bones. I'll pay my respects.'

The turf fire was at a high blaze inside the cabin, and the conversation amongst the visitors was loud. Laughter spilt from a corner.

'Mmm.' Peg's dark eyes flitted over the company in the room. 'Who brought the drink then?'

'Seán Lynch brought most of it,' Nóra replied.

Peg raised her eyebrows.

'I know. 'Twas not something I expected. Not a generous man.'

'The only thing that man is generous with is his fists.' She cast a sly look to where Kate sat amongst the women, picking at her teeth. 'Seán Lynch would skin a louse and send the hide and fat to market. I wonder what he's after.'

Nóra shrugged. 'We're kin. Don't you forget that my sister married his brother, God rest their souls.'

Peg sniffed. 'Faith, he's up to something. I'd keep an eye to him, Nóra. He'll be wanting something from you now Martin is gone. That one knows the price of everything and the value of nothing.'

They stared across the room to where Seán sat smoking by the fire.

'Believe me, Nóra. An old broom knows the dirty corners best.'

*

They carried the body of Martin to his grave the following afternoon under a colourless sky. The nephews and friends of the man shouldered the rough coffin, followed by other valley men, who would occasionally take turns at carrying the box. It was a long, familiar journey to the graveyard along the road, and the way was slow going. The rains had softened the path into mud and the men trod carefully, anxious not to lose their boots in the suck of it. The women walked behind, sending their cries up into the autumn air, studded with cold. They all knew the way to lead a body to soil.

Nóra gripped her shawl tightly over her head. She could not bear to look at the coffin bobbing beyond the heads in front, and instead cast her eyes to the birds spiralling above the balding branches. She felt strangely dry-eyed, and as she walked through the puddles, glossy with sky, she wondered if some small part of her had died too. The women around her seemed ridiculous in their lamentations, their wet skirts clinging to their legs. Nóra held her tongue still and let her grief sit in her like a stone.

The sight of a funeral drew people from the cabins that sat close upon the road. Children stared with their fingers in their mouths. Men letting their pigs graze on the lane joined the crowd to share a few paces with them, then stepped aside and waited solemnly for them to move on before slapping their pigs' sides with a switch.

Nóra kept her head tilted to the sky, letting the crowd push her onwards. Eagles circled above the hill heights.

The graveyard, slouched next to the little church and shadowed by an old yew tree, was overgrown, green with grass. The men stumbled over the tussocks and carefully set the coffin down beside the hole that had been dug in readiness. Father Healy was waiting for them, slack-jawed and slumped with the spine of a scholar. When his gaze sought out Nóra she pulled her shawl low over her forehead and cast her eyes to the ground.

The service was brief. The priest led the prayers in his halting voice, and Nóra felt the wet ground seep through her skirts as she knelt. She watched as her husband was lowered into the ground, watched as the gravediggers lay sods of grass over the lid of the coffin so that the earth might fall gently upon the wood.

When all was done and there were no more words to be said, and the hole had been filled with the rough black soil of the valley, the people placed their clay pipes upon the grave mound and left. As the crowd followed the curve of the hill down towards the valley, Nóra looked back at the churchyard. From a distance the pipe stems looked like nothing more than a smattering of slender bones, cleaned by birds.

The wind rose as Nóra walked the road after the funeral, at first in a crowd, and then, as people turned off towards their own cabins, in a smaller, silent number. By the time she was hobbling past the ash trees and up the muddy slope to her house, she was alone and the wind was peeling off the mountain crags into the valley, full of bite. A hard rain had started to sting and her knees felt the promise of another storm.

As Nóra approached the cabin she could hear screaming coming from inside. Micheál. The door was ajar, and as she entered she noticed that her house had been cleaned, all evidence of the wake removed. New rushes lay spread on the floor, a bright fire was burning and Peg O'Shea was seated next to it, cradling Micheál and laughing at Brigid, who was wincing at his pitching voice. 'You'd best be getting used to that,' Peg was saying, rocking the red-faced boy. Her smile faded as Nóra walked in.

'Martin is buried, then.'

Nóra sank down on the settle bed next to Brigid, relieved to have the house empty of people.

'And a crowd to bury him too. That's a blessing. Move up to the fire. You'll perish in the cold.'

Nóra held out her arms for Micheál and leant her cheek against his head. The weight of him in her arms, and the ragged, humid cries addressing her skin, made her feel careworn. Her bare toes ached with the cold.

Peg was watching her. 'They're a comfort, children.'

Nóra closed her eyes and pushed her face into the fragile scoop of his neck. His chest tightened beneath her hands as he screamed.

'Thank you for minding him.'

'Don't you say another word about it. I've been praying for you, Nóra. God knows 'tis been a bad and troubling year for ye.'

Nóra released her hold on Micheál, laying him out on her lap. Tears streamed down his face. She began to rub his limbs as she had seen Martin do, straightening his wrists back from where they bent inwards, fingers as stiff as pokers. At her touch Micheál ceased crying, and for a moment she thought he looked at her. His pupils, so dark against the blue of his eyes, seemed to fix on her own. Her heart leapt. Then his gaze slid from her face and he began to howl, his hands buckling back into crooks.

Nóra stopped rubbing him and stared. She was struck with the memory of Martin holding Micheál in his broad hands, spooning cream into his mouth.

How could you leave me alone with this child, she thought.

Peg reached across the hearth and gently smoothed Micheál's hair. 'Sure, he has Johanna's colour.'

Brigid glanced at Nóra.

'I know she was a great loss to you,' Peg continued. '*Is é do mhac do mhac go bpósann sé ach is í d'iníon go bhfaighidh tú bás*. Your son is your son until he marries, but your daughter is your daughter until you die. And now, to lose your man . . . Isn't God cruel, taking those we love most?'

'We all bear our cross,' Nóra murmured. She lifted Micheál higher onto her lap. 'What's troubling you then, little one?'

'Oh, Nóra, he's been squalling fit to wake the dead, the poor cratur. Full of noise and tears, and for what? All these days past too. How do you sleep with him crying so at all hours?'

Micheál screamed louder than before. Tears crawled down his flushed cheeks.

'Did you feed him?' Brigid asked, taking Nóra's cloak from the settle and draping it across the low beam by the fire.

'Did I feed him?' Peg gave Nóra a glinting look. 'I've had five of them myself, and sure, Brigid, 'tis a miracle they all lived to have their own, for I never once fed them but set them to the wind. I'll say, 'tis a good thing you know what you're doing, for the moon looks full with you.' She sucked her remaining teeth. 'Such company you send me, Nóra. This wean and *cailín*. Well, 'twas right to be keeping them away from the trouble.'

'I hope I've kept it out of danger.' Brigid put a protective hand over her stomach. 'Dan wouldn't have me in the house for the pig kill.'

'I knew a woman once,' said Peg. 'She was a doughty thing, had no time for old ways and full of pride. Well, didn't she set herself on catching the blood off the table when the time came for slaughter? And didn't her husband try to stop her? But for all the strong man he was, she had her way. And you can be sure, that child she was carrying came out with a face like raw liver and a mood to match.'

A dull murmur of thunder rolled overhead and Brigid grimaced. 'Is that so?'

'Oh, you wouldn't tempt the Devil. You wouldn't be messing with blood or bodies in your state.'

'It put the fear on me, what that old biddy said. The one with the white hair.'

'The *bean feasa*? Sure, Nance Roche has a peculiar way.'

'I haven't seen her before. I thought she was only a kind of handy woman.'

'Have you not? No, well, she keeps to herself. Until she feels the call on her. Or others go calling for her.'

'Or there's the promise of a warm cabin and a bite to eat,' Nóra added. 'I've never gone to her for the cure, and Martin only once or twice. And yet there she was at the wake. To keen.'

Peg gave Nóra a searching look. 'She has a way of knowing when she's needed.' Her voice was quiet.

'But why have I not heard anyone say she has the knowledge?' Brigid asked.

'Begod, whether you go to her or not, 'tis not something you talk about. People go to her for the things you wouldn't want a priest to know about, or your own mother to see. And well, sure, there's some folk think her name brings misfortune. She puts the fright on them.'

Brigid leant forward, curious. 'And why's that? What did she do?'

'A great crime to be sure.' Peg winked. 'She lives by the woods on her own. That's enough to set tongues going. There's plenty that go to her though. Aye, they do be saying she has the cure. Not like some of them who say they have the charms when all they have is a desire to part you with your whiskey.'

'I knew a Cahill, a cousin of my mam, he had the cure for the shingles.'

Nóra clucked her tongue and rocked Micheál. The exhausted child was finally falling into a whimpering sleep. 'Folk come all the way from Ballyvourney for the charms of Nance Roche. Eight hours hard walking for a man there and back, all for her to whisper something in his ear and look at his warts.'

Peg nodded. 'Musha, Nance of the Fairies, they call her. Nance *na bPúcaí*. There are plenty that will have nothing to do with her on account of it but more who go to her because they believe it so.'

'Do you believe it, Nóra?'

Nóra shook her head dismissively. 'I don't like to talk of it. The world is full of things I don't pretend to understand. They used to say she was going with the Good People, whether 'twas true or not.'

'Peg,' Brigid whispered, glancing to the door as if suddenly expecting it to fly open, 'is she in league with Them? What does the priest say?'

'Father O'Reilly always had a kind word for her when he still walked this earth. Some men of the Church might say she's no person of God, but those who have gone to her say she never performed any cure, only in the name of the Blessed Trinity. Oh, did you hear that now?'

Nóra flinched at the low growl of thunder. 'God be between us and harm.'

'Does she not have a man? Children?'

'No husband I ever heard of. Peg?'

The old woman smiled. 'Not unless she has a fairy man out by the *ráth*. Or that old goat of hers is really her husband, changed by the Good People.' She laughed, as if tickled by the idea.

Brigid was thoughtful. 'The way she came in, her hair all wet and the white lips of her. She looked like a ghost. She looked like someone'd been spending the night trying to drown her in a puddle. And the eyes of her – the fog in them. How can a woman with the cure be going about with eyes like that in her head?'

'You'd do well to keep on the right side of Nance Roche,' Nóra admitted.

Peg chuckled and wiped her gums with a corner of her apron. 'Brigid, all you need to know is that woman was born at the dead hour of night and so has a different way of seeing.'

'Has she always lived here?'

'Oh, long enough now to scare my children and my children's children. But not born here, no. I remember when she came. There were lots of people on the road in those times. Nance was just another poor wandering woman. The priest took pity on her, young as she was then, with no soul to help her. The men built her a *bothán*, just a wee room of mud by the wood. No potato garden to speak of, but she has chickens. And a goat. Oh, she's always put great store by goats. 'Tis all well for a woman to be living off sloes and hazelnuts and *praiseach* in the kinder months, but when she first came we were all expecting her to come knocking and begging for lumpers come winter. But didn't she keep to herself, and didn't she stay that winter, and the next and the next, until folk started saying that 'twas not a natural thing for a woman like her to be living fat off weeds and berries. Some thought she was stealing at night. Others thought she was in league with Himself.'

'The Devil?'

There was a loud clap of thunder. The women jumped.

'What a night to be telling of these things!' Nóra exclaimed.

'Sure, Nance was a queer one from the start.'

'Is it not time to eat? Are you hungry? Peg, will you be staying? 'Tis no night for walking.' For all her desire to be alone during Martin's wake, Nóra suddenly longed for company. The thought of spending the storming evening alone with Micheál made her stomach clutch in dread.

Peg looked around the empty cabin and, as if sensing Nóra's reluctance, nodded. 'I will, if 'tis no trouble to you.'

'Shall I take Micheál?' Brigid offered.

'I'll set him down.' Nóra laid the boy in a makeshift cradle of sally twigs and straw.

'He's a bit too big for that now, is he not?' Peg asked. 'His legs don't fit at all.'

Nóra ignored her. 'I'll go for the milk and then I'll get us a bite to eat.' Another roll of thunder sounded above the rain and the spitting turf fire. 'What a dirty night.'

Peg gave Brigid's belly a gentle pat. ''Tis a good thing you're here with your man's aunt and not out in the dark.' Her eyes narrowed. 'The thunder kills the unhatched birds in their eggs.'

'Peg O'Shea! Don't be frightening her with tall talk.' Nóra lifted a heavy pot of water onto the chain hanging from the hearth wall, squinting in the smoke.

'Go see to the beast, Nóra. She'll be in pieces from the storm.' Peg turned to Brigid. 'The lightning does be taking the profit from the milk. There'll be some fearful churning after tonight, you mark my words.'

Nóra shot Peg a stern look and pulled her wet cloak from its rafter and back over her head. She stepped out into the night with her pail, stumbling in the sudden wind, rain lashing against her face. She lurched towards the byre, eager to escape the downpour.

The cow blinked at her in the dark, eyes round in fear.

'There, Brownie. Easy with you.' Nóra ran her hands over the cow's flank, but when she reached for the stool and placed the pail on the ground, the beast started and pulled at her rope.

'No harm will come to you, girl,' Nóra crooned, but Brownie moaned. There's a fright in her, Nóra thought, and hauled an armful of hay into the bracket. The cow ignored it, panting, and as soon as Nóra took hold of her teats, the cow skittered sideways, leg kicking in its spancel. The pail clattered across the floor. Nóra got up, irritated.

Lightning flashed outside.

'Have it your way, would you,' Nóra muttered, and snatching the pail, she pulled the sodden cloak back over her head. She staggered back through the pelting darkness towards the cabin, pausing under the thatch to scrape the mud from her feet. As she wiped her heel on the step she heard Peg's voice, low with conspiracy, coming from inside.

'Wee Micheál. Would you look at him. He's an ill-thriven thing.'

Nóra froze.

'I heard Martin and Nóra had a cripple child with them. Is it true he hasn't taken a step yet?'

Brigid.

Nóra's heart began to hammer.

'I doubt he ever will! Four years old and the state of him! I knew Nóra was after caring for Johanna's boy, and that there was little keeping body and soul together when he came to them, but one like this? He hasn't the whole of his sense.'

Nóra felt her face flush, despite the chill. Hardly breathing, she pressed her eye to a gap in the wood. Brigid and Peg were staring at the boy.

'Has herself fetched the priest for him?'

'To heal him? I've always believed a priest has the power if he wants to use it. But Father Healy is a busy man. A man from the towns – he's most like spent his life in Tralee or Killarney. And I don't think he will be troubling himself with poor wicker-legged boys.'

Brigid was silent. 'I pray to God that mine is right.'

'Please God he will be. Keep yourself safe and warm. I suspect 'twas only when this one's mother sickened that he began to go soft in the head and his limbs moved to kippeens. I never heard a thing about a strange child while she was alive.'

Nóra's stomach dropped. Her own kin, sitting in her house, blacking her grandson. She pressed her face against the door, feeling her pulse jump in her throat.

'Did Nóra tell you that, so?'

Peg scoffed. 'What do you think? She won't have any talk about him. Why do you think she keeps him here like a clocking hen, and none of us knowing the state of him? Why do you think, with her husband just gone, she made Peter O'Connor bring him to me before there was a crowd in this place? 'Tis a rare soul who has set eyes on him, and for all us being kin, I'd not had a good look at the cratur until these past days. You can imagine the shock I had when I saw the boy.'

'She's shamed by him.'

'Well, something's not right. It must be a great burden. Her daughter dead – God have mercy on her – and now this ailing one to care for all alone.'

'She's doughty though. She'll get on.'

Nóra watched from behind the door as Peg leant back, running a tongue over her gums. 'She's got some spine, that woman. Nóra has always been a proud one. But I do be worried after her. Such a dark season of death and strangeness. Her daughter, and now Martin, and the child blighted with it all.'

'Peter O'Connor was saying he saw a light by the fairy *ráth* in the hour of Martin's passing. Said he thinks there's a third death coming.'

Peg crossed herself and threw another piece of turf on the fire. 'God protect us. Still, worse things have happened.'

Nóra hesitated. Rain dripped down her face, the damp of the cloak soaking into her clothes. She didn't care. She bit her lip, straining to hear what they were saying.

'Did Nance keen for Johanna?'

Peg sighed. 'She didn't, no. Nóra's girl married a Corkman some years back. She's buried there, somewhere out by Macroom. Nóra only heard Johanna had died when her son-in-law came to give her the child. Oh, 'twas a pity. Johanna's man appeared one night at dusk during the harvest just gone, Micheál strapped on a donkey. Told her that Johanna had wasted away and he a widower. Yes, a wasting sickness, the man said. One day she took to her bed with a pounding head and she never got up from it again. She faded day by day until she had gone completely. And he was in no place to care for the boy, and I know his people thought it only right that he be taken to Nóra and Martin. She never said a word like it, but there was a rumour that Micheál was half-starved when he came. A little bag of bones fit for a pauper's coffin.'

How dare she, thought Nóra. Gossiping about me on the day I bury my man. Spreading rumours about my daughter. Tears sprung to her eyes and she pulled away from the door.

'There's no shame in poverty.' Brigid's piping voice travelled over the sound of the wind. 'We all know the price of it.'

'There's no shame for some, but Nóra has always held her head high. Have you ever noticed that she doesn't talk of the dead? My own husband is long gone to God, and yet I talk of him as if he were still here. He remains with me in that way. But when Johanna died, 'twas as though Nóra struck her daughter's name from her tongue. I've no doubt she grieves, but any memories of her daughter she shares with the bottle alone.'

'Does she go the shebeen?'

'Sh. I don't know where Nóra gets her comfort, but if a woman can find peace in the drink, then who are we to grudge her for it.'

It was too much. Nóra hastily wiped her eyes and, jaw clenched, entered the kitchen, her cloak and face slick with rain. She shut the door against the storm and set the pail on the table under the window, packed with straw to keep the cold out.

The women were quiet. Nóra wondered if they guessed she had overheard them.

'Did she give much?' Peg eventually asked.

'She's spooked.' Nóra dragged her cloak off her shoulders and crouched by the fire to warm her hands, her eyes averted.

''Twas a time when we couldn't move for butter in this valley,' muttered Peg. 'Now every second cratur is blasted.'

Micheál murmured and, relieved for something to do, Nóra picked him up out of the cramped cradle. 'You great lad. Oh, the weight in him.'

Peg and Brigid exchanged looks.

'What were ye talking of?' Nóra asked.

'Our Brigid here was asking about Nance.'

'Is that so.'

''Tis. She can't hear enough.'

'Don't let me be interrupting you. Go on with your story, then.' Nóra thought she caught a glimpse of panic between the women.

'Well, now. As I was saying, folk back in the day thought it mighty strange for a woman to be living off thin air and dandelions. And they went to the priest about her. 'Twas not Father Healy, but the priest before him. Father O'Reilly, God have mercy on him. He would have none of their suspicion and gossip. "Leave the poor woman be," said he. Sure, Brigid, Father O'Reilly was a fierce man, a powerful man for those who had no voice or home for themselves. 'Twas he who urged the men to build her the cabin and sent them to her for the herbs and cures. He went to her himself. Terrible rheumatism.'

The water in the black pot trembled. Nóra, lips tight in anger, stared as the rain escaping down the chimney hole hit its iron sides.

'What happened next, then?' Brigid filled the silence.

Peg shifted in her seat, glancing at Nóra. 'Well, not long after Nance had got her cabin she began to get a name for herself. I was on the night-rambling one evening, down at Old Hanna's, and we got to be telling stories about the Good People. And Hanna starts telling us about a fairy bush, a *sceach gheal* that was very near cut down. It was your own Daniel's uncle, Seán Lynch, that was after doing it. Begod, he's some fool. Seán, he was a young man then, and he was up by the blacksmith's with the lads, boasting amongst themselves. Your man Seán was talking of cutting down the whitethorn and the lads were warning him against it. Somehow, word of his daring got back to Nance Roche. Surely you've seen where the tree stands, by the fairy *ráth*? She lives near it. And Nance went to Seán's cabin one night, frightened the life out of him and Kate by appearing in their doorway, and she tells him he'd best leave the whitethorn alone or They would be after him. "That is Their tree," says she. "Don't you be putting a hand to it, or I tell you, Seán Lynch, that you'll be suffering after it. Don't you be putting a hand to anything in violence." Well, didn't he laugh her off, calling her filthy names besides, and didn't he go to cut the *sceach gheal* that very day. Old Hanna said that she saw with her own eyes how Seán took a dirty great swing at the fairy whitethorn with his axe. No word of a lie, didn't Hanna see him miss the trunk completely. Didn't the axe swing through the air, missing the wood and land in his leg. He near cut himself in half. And that is why he has the limp.'

There was a soft gurgle from the floor and the women looked down to see Micheál staring at the rafters, a crooked smile on his face.

Nóra watched Peg lean forward and examine his face, her eyes thoughtful. 'He likes a story.'

'Go on, Peg,' Brigid urged. She was perched on the edge of the settle, the firelight full and flickering on her face.

'Well, that was the start of it. People saw in that axe swing proof Nance had the fairy knowledge, the *fios sigheog*. Folk started to go to her if they thought Them were abroad and at Their tricks. They thought perhaps she used to go with Them, which is how she got her way of understanding.'

'I never met a one who was taken by the Good People. I never met a one who was swept.' Brigid shuddered.

'I'll tell you something now, Brigid. This valley is full of old families. For all the folk on the roads, there's not often room for strangers that don't marry into the blood. Nance planted herself into this soil with herbs and death-cries and sure hands when a woman's time came. There was plenty that feared her after the whitethorn, and there's plenty that fear her to this day, but there's more that need Nance. And as long as they need her, she'll be in that *bothán* by the woods. My man, when he was alive, woke one morning with his eye all swolled up and no seeing out of it. He took to Nance, and she said 'twas the fairies struck him in the eye. Said he must have seen them on the road, and 'twas not his right, so they brought the sight out of the eye that saw them. Said they spat in it when he was asleep. But she had the charm. She put the herb in his eye – *glanrosc*, I think it was – and cured the fairy spite out of it. Now, I don't know whether Nance was ever swept or not but there's no doubting that she has a gift. Whether that gift is God-given or a token from the Good People, well, that's not for us to know.'

'Will Nance be there when my time comes?'

'Sure, 'tis Nance for you.'

Nóra offered Micheál to Brigid, her voice cold. 'Hold him while I fix the tea.'

Brigid settled the boy awkwardly against the curve of her stomach. As if sensing Brigid's strangeness, Micheál stiffened, his arms shooting out from his sides. His mouth crumpled in discontent.

'He likes feathers,' Nóra said, easing potatoes into the steaming pot. 'Here.' She picked up a small downy feather that had escaped from the chicken roost and was blowing about the room in a draught. 'Martin always gave him a tickle.'

Brigid took the feather and stroked the boy's dimpled chin. He giggled, his chest in convulsions. Brigid started laughing with him. 'Will you look at that!'

''Tis a good sign,' said Peg, gesturing to the pair.

Nóra's smile emptied. 'A good sign of what?'

Peg picked up the iron tongs and idly poked the fire.

'Are you a deaf woman now? A good sign of what, Peg O'Shea?'

Peg sighed. 'A good sign that your Micheál might yet be well.'

Nóra pressed her lips together and continued tipping the last of the potatoes into the hot water. She flinched as it splashed her hand.

'We only mean well for the child,' Peg murmured.

'Do ye now?'

'Have you taken him to Nance, Nóra?' Brigid's voice was hesitant. 'I was thinking just now, it might be that he's fairy-struck.'

Silence filled the cabin.

Nóra suddenly dropped down on the floor. She brought her apron to her face and took a shuddering breath. She could smell the familiar scent of cow manure and wet grass.

'There now,' Peg whispered. ''Tis a hard day for you, Nóra Leahy. We had no right to talk of such things. God bless the child and see he grows up to be a great man. Like Martin.'

At the sound of her husband's name, Nóra groaned. Peg placed a hand on her shoulder and she shrugged it off.

'Forgive us. We only mean well. *Tig grian a n-diadh na fearthana.* Sunshine follows rain. Better times will be upon us soon, just wait and see.'

'Faith, God's help is nearer than the door,' Brigid piped.

The rafters creaked in the force of the wind. Micheál continued to laugh.

CHAPTER
THREE

Ragwort

Samhain Eve came upon the valley, announced by a wind that smelled of rotting oak leaves and the vinegar tang of windfall apples. Nóra heard the happy shrieks of children as they traced the field walls and their dressing of brambles, plucking the last bloody berries before night fetched the *púca* to poison them with his breath. They emerged from the ditches in the smoky peace of twilight like a band of murderers, their hands and mouths stained purple. Nóra watched them as they scrambled up the hills to their homes, some of the boys wearing dresses to deceive the fairies. It was a dangerous night to be caught outside. Tonight was a ghost night. The dead were close, and all the beings caught between Heaven and Hell would soon walk the cold loam.

They're coming, thought Nóra. From the graves and the dark and the wet. They're coming for the light of our fires.

The sky was fading. Nóra watched as two young boys were hustled indoors by their anxious mother. It was not the time to tempt the Devil or the fairies. People disappeared on Samhain Eve. Small children went missing. They were lured into ringforts and bogs and mountain sides with music and lights, and were never seen again by their parents.

Nóra remembered, as a very small girl, the fear and talk when a man from the valley did not return to his family's croft one Samhain Eve. They found him the next morning, naked and bleeding, curled into the soil and clutching yellow ragwort in his hands. He was abducted, her mother had told her. Taken to ride with the *sióga* until dawn broke out in feeble light and he was abandoned. Nóra had sat in the shadows, listening to the adults as they spoke in urgent whispers around her parents' fire. Wasn't he a poor soul to be found in such a way. His mother would die of the shame of it. A grown man, shivering and talking of the woods like a poor unfortunate.

'They took me,' he had muttered to the men of the valley when they helped him home, covering him with a coat and bearing his stagger on patient shoulders. 'They took me.'

The next evening the men and women had burnt all the ragwort from the fields to deprive the Good People of their sacred plant. Nóra could still remember the sight: tiny fires burning along the cant of the valley, winking in the darkness.

The brothers had reached their cabin and Nóra watched as their mother closed the door behind them. With a last, long look to the woods and the billhook moon rising over them, she made the sign of the cross and went indoors.

Her house seemed smaller, somehow, after the time outside. Nóra stood by the doorstep and looked at all she had left in the world. How it had changed in the month since Martin died. How empty it seemed. The crude hearth, the smoke of former fires blacking the wall behind it in a tapering shadow of soot. Her potato pot hanging from its chain and the wicker skib resting against the wall. The dash churn by the stopped-up window and the small table under it bearing two miserable pieces of delph and crocks for milk and cream. Even the remaining treasures from her dowry – the salt box on the wall, the butter print, the settle bed with its seat worn smooth from use – seemed dismal. Here was a widow's house. Martin's tobacco and pipe in the hearth's keeping hole were already covered with a film of ash. The low creepie stools were empty of company. The rushes on the floor had dried and powdered underfoot, their freshness long gone with no cause to replace them. There was little sign of life other than the fire's lazy burn, the murmuring of her chickens fluffed in their roost, and the twitching sleep of Micheál as he lay on a pile of heather in the corner of the cabin.

He is like Johanna, Nóra thought, examining her grandchild's face.

The boy looked unbearably smooth in sleep, bloodless and waxen. He had his father's furrow between chin and bottom lip that pushed his mouth out in a wet sulk, but his hair was Johanna's. Reddish and fine. Martin had loved it. Once or twice Nóra had entered the room to find her husband sitting with the boy, stroking his hair as he used to do with their daughter.

Nóra brushed the thin locks from Micheál's forehead, and for one moment, through the stinging blur, imagined that he was Johanna. If she squinted it was as though she was once again a young mother, her little girl sleeping before her. Copper-headed, sighing in sleep. Her only baby to draw breath and stick to life. An uncomplaining child with hair of down.

She remembered what Martin had said the night Johanna was born, swaying with a night empty of sleep and full of whiskey, jubilant and terrified and lightheaded. 'Wee dandelion,' he had said, stroking Johanna's feathery hair. 'Careful or the wind will come and blow you away and scatter you over the mountains.'

A proverb ran through her mind: Scattering is easier than gathering.

Nóra felt a sudden weight on her chest. Her little girl and her husband were gone. Scattered into the air and unreachable. Gone to God, gone to places where she, growing old and already too full of bones, too full of the weight of her years, ought to have gone first. She heard the breath in her throat rasping and snatched her hand away from Micheál.

Her daughter should still be alive. Should be as Nóra had found her when she and Martin had walked the full length of a day to Tadgh and Johanna's cabin in the moors, the first time Nóra had seen her daughter since the wedding. Johanna had seemed filled with happiness, waiting at the top of the lane against the flowering gorse and the sky, wide with light, her son in her arms. How she had smiled to see them. Proud to be a wife. Proud to be a mother.

'This is wee Micheál,' she had said, and Nóra had taken that little boy into her arms and blinked hard at the pricking of tears. How old had he been then? No more than two. But growing and well and soon tottering after the piglet that ran squealing about the damp floor of the cramped cabin.

'By my baptism, but he is the spit of you,' Martin had said.

Micheál had tugged on Johanna's skirt. 'Mammy?' And Nóra had noticed how her daughter swung her son onto her hip with practised ease, how she tickled him under the chin until he shrieked with laughter.

'The years go in a gallop,' Nóra murmured, and Johanna had smiled.

'More,' Micheál had demanded. 'More.'

Nóra sat down heavily on the stool and stared at the boy who now bore little resemblance to the grandchild she remembered. She stared at his mouth, ajar in sleep, the arms thrown up over his head, wrists strangely twisted. The legs that would not bear his weight.

What happened to you? she wondered.

The house was awful in its silence.

Since Martin died, Nóra had felt that she was merely passing time until he returned and, at the same time, was devastated by the knowledge that he would not. She still noticed the absence of sound. There was no whistle as Martin pulled on his boots, no laughter. Her nights had emptied of sleep. She endured their unfeeling hours by curling herself into the depression his body had made in the straw when he was alive, until she could almost imagine that he embraced her.

It was not supposed to be like this. Martin had seemed so well. A man who was ageing, sure, as she was, but a man who carried his winters on a strong back and who had two firm legs wired with the ropey muscle of a farmer. His had not been a sour body. Even as their hair had greyed, and she had seen Martin's face shaped by time and weather – mirroring her own, she imagined – he had seemed quick with life. She had expected him to outlive them all. She had envisioned her own death at his patient, watchful side. Had sometimes, in a gloomy mood, imagined him at her own funeral, throwing clay onto her coffin.

During the wake, the women had told her that the grief would subside. Nóra hated them for it. There was a void there, she understood now. How had she lived her whole life and not noticed it! A sea of loneliness that sang a siren song to the bereaved. What a gentle thing it would be to give into it and drown. What an easy keel into the abyss. How quiet it would be.

She had thought she'd never surpass the grief of that summer afternoon when Tadgh arrived, his eyes blank and his hair littered gold with the harvest chaff.

Johanna is dead, he had said. My wife is dead.

Johanna, dandelion child, gone like clocking seed on the wind and, as she felt the field of oats rise up about her, the scythe falling from her hand, there came the thought: This is it. The tide is come and I will let it take me.

Had it not been for Martin . . . He had found comfort in Micheál, that now-motherless foundling brought by Tadgh in a turf basket. He had urged her to care for the boy, to dribble milk into his piping, empty mouth. He had loved him. Found reason for happiness in him.

'He looks as though he is dying,' Nóra had said that night as they sat, drowned in grief. It was evening. The harvest sun had fallen and they had left the half-door open to allow the pinking dusk to spread throughout the room.

Martin had lifted the boy from the basket, holding him as though he were an injured bird. 'He is starved. Look at his legs.'

'Tadgh says he does not talk anymore. Has not spoken for six months or more.'

The griping boy calmed in the embrace of his grandfather. 'We will fetch the doctor for him, and we will make him well. Nóra? Do you hear me?'

'We cannot afford a doctor.'

She remembered Martin's wide hands, the kindness in the way he stroked the boy's hair. The dirt under the rough callouses of his skin. He had petted Micheál in the same way he soothed spooked horses, speaking with a calm tongue. Even that night, stabbed through with grief for their daughter, Martin had been calm.

'We will fetch the doctor, Nóra,' he had said. Only then had his voice broken. 'What we could not do for Johanna we will do for her son. For our grandson.'

Nóra stared at the empty stool that had held her husband that summer night.

Why could God not have taken Micheál? Why leave an ill-formed child in the place of a good man, a good woman?

I would throw this boy against a wall if it would bring me back Martin and my daughter, Nóra thought. The notion horrified her no sooner than it had crossed her mind. She glanced at the sleeping boy and crossed herself in shame.

No. It would not do. To sit slumped by the hearth, thinking dark thoughts, was no way to welcome the dead. This was no home for her daughter's spirit, or the returning soul of her man, God have mercy on them.

While Micheál slept, Nóra rose and filled the pot with water from her well bucket, dropping in as many potatoes as she could spare. With those set upon the fire to boil, she arranged stools around the hearth: Martin's place, closest to the flame, another for Johanna beside it. They might be gone, she thought, but with God's grace she could welcome them again for one night of the year.

When the lumpers had softened, Nóra drained them onto the skib and placed a noggin of salted water in the middle of their steaming flesh. She ate a few, slipping them out of their skins as quickly as she was able and dipping them into the water to cool and flavour the potato. Then she took Martin's pipe out of the nook in the hearth wall, wiped the dust out of the bowl and blew through the stem to clear it. She set it on his stool.

As she went about the room, snatching cobwebs from the low rafters and straightening the cross by the window, Nóra allowed herself to think again of when her daughter was little and when they were all together as a family. She remembered the first years, when Johanna was still soft-cheeked, playing with nuts gathered from wild trees: hazelnuts, acorns, chestnuts. She thought of the potato lamps they made, hollowed out by Martin and handed to Johanna to scrape out faces. Holes for eyes. Gaping mouths.

By the time Nóra finished the Samhain preparations, the usual evening sounds of lowing cattle and the cries and calls of men returning inside from work had long ceased, and all was still and silent except for the crackle of the fire and Micheál's quiet breathing. Nóra poured out piggins of buttermilk for Martin and Johanna, starting at the sudden screech of a barn owl outside. She placed the wooden cups beside the stools and knelt to say her evening prayers. Leaving the rushlights burning and her grandchild sleeping, Nóra went to bed with a small bottle of *poitín*, and sipped at it until she felt herself dissolve with the heat of the liquor. The high fire that had been burning all evening had dried the air in the house and, in the warmth of it, Nóra fell into a deep, exhausted sleep.

It was midnight when she heard the noise. A muffled thump, like a fist against a chest. Nóra sat up in bed, her head throbbing. It wasn't Micheál. The sound had come from outside. She had not imagined it, surely.

Looking out to the main room and the hearth, she could see her grandson's sleeping form. The turf burnt red. All was wine-dark.

Nóra heard the sound again. Someone was outside. Someone wanted to get in. There was a noise on the thatch, like a stone thrown against the house.

Her blood darted through her veins.

Was it Martin? Johanna? Nóra's tongue was dry with fear. She placed her feet on the ground and rose, glancing around the room, swaying. She was drunk.

There was another sound – a clinking, like a fingernail tapping on a tin bucket. She made her way into the main room of the cabin. There was no one there.

Another thump. Nóra let out a soft cry. She wished she hadn't been drinking.

Laughter sounded.

'Who's there?' Her voice sounded feeble.

Another muffled laugh. A man's laugh.

'Martin?' she whispered.

'Hallowe'en knock!' growled a low voice.

Nóra's breath caught in her throat.

'Hallowe'en knock! A penny a stock. If you don't let me in, I'll knock. Knock. Knock.' There was a sudden pounding against the mud wall of her cabin.

Nóra flung open the door. In the light of the high, slender moon she could see three men standing in front of her, their faces covered in masks of rough cloth. Holes had been cut out for their eyes and mouths, giving them an expression of menace. Nóra stepped backwards in fear as the young man in the middle skipped forward into the cabin, laughing.

'Hallowe'en knock!' He did a clumsy jig, rattling the long string of hazelnuts that hung around his neck. His fellows started giggling behind him, but their laughs faded as Nóra started to cry. The dancer stopped and pulled the mask from his face, and Nóra saw that it was John O'Shea, Peg's grandson.

'Widow Leahy. I'm –'

'Damn you all!' Blood drained from her face.

John glanced back at his companions. They stared, slack-mouthed.

'Get out, John,' Nóra hissed.

'We didn't mean to give you such a fright.'

Nóra gave a short, barking laugh. The other boys took their masks off and looked to John. Valley boys, all of them. Not her husband. Not her daughter. Just bold, masked boys.

'Taunting widows are you now, John?' She was shaking like an aspen.

John looked uncomfortable. ''Tis Samhain. We're after soul cakes.'

'And money,' his friend mumbled.

''Twas just for a laugh, is all.'

'And are ye laughing, lads?' Nóra raised her hand as if to slap them and the boys shrank back against the open door. 'Ye spalpeens. Stalking new-made widows in the dead of night! Waking good folk from their sleep with your unholy ways!'

'You won't say to *mamó*?' John twisted his mask in his hands.

'Oh, Peg'll be hearing of it. Away with ye!' Nóra picked up a stool and flung it at them as they ran out of the cabin into the night. She swung the door to, fastened the latch and leant her head against it. For one tender moment she had thought it was Martin and Johanna at her door. Stupidly, she realised that she had been anticipating their faces. The shock of the lads and their awful masks had shaken her, but it was the ruined expectation that had hurt the most.

I am a drunk old woman crying over ghosts that do not come, Nóra thought.

Micheál had woken. He wailed in his bed of heather, eyes round and dark. Nóra staggered over to where he lay and slumped to the ground. She stroked his head and tried to sing to him as Martin had done, but the tune was mournful and her voice broke on the words. Eventually she rose and fetched her husband's greatcoat from her bed. Wrapping it around her and breathing in his old scent of burnt coltsfoot, Nóra eased herself to the ground next to Micheál.

~

'God and Mary to you, Nance.'

Nance looked up from her knife to see a shawled figure in the doorway.

'Old Hanna?'

'And getting older with every passing day.'

'Come in and God welcome.' Nance helped her visitor to a stool by the fire. 'Is it for yourself you're come?'

The woman grunted as she sat down, shaking her head. ''Tis my sister. She has a fever.'

Nance passed Hanna a cup of fresh milk and nodded at it. 'Drink. Tell me, how long has she been sick, and does she eat?'

'She eats nothing, but takes a little water. The sweat pours from her and she shivers as though she is bitter cold. But we have the fire high, and 'tis warm as you like in with her.'

'I can give you the cure.'

'Praise be.' Hanna took a sip of the milk and pointed to the knife in Nance's hand. 'I've come and stopped you from your work.'

''Twas only thistles I was cutting. For my hens. Musha, curing fevers is my work.' Nance put the blade down and walked to the corner of the room, taking a little cloth bag from it. She untied the leather string of the bag and, using her fingertips, carefully sprinkled the herb from it into the neck of a brown glass bottle, muttering under her breath.

'What is that?' Hanna asked, when the bottle was filled and Nance had finished her charm.

'Meadowsweet.'

'Will it cure her?'

'Put the dried flowers drawing on the boil as soon as you get home to her. Give her three drinks off the top of it and she will be as well as she ever was.'

'Thank you, Nance.' Hanna was relieved.

'But don't be looking behind you until you've reached the lane. Don't be looking at the Piper's Grave or the whitethorn, or the bottle will empty.'

Hanna looked grave. 'Very well, so.'

'Finish that milk now, and God be on the road with you.'

The woman drained the cup and, wiping her mouth on the back of her hand, stood up and reached for the bottle.

'Remember what I said: don't look back.'

'Very well, Nance. And God bless you.'

Nance walked Hanna to the door, farewelling her with a wave. 'Close your fist around that bottle there.' She waited in the doorway and watched the woman walk from the woods towards the settled valley, her eyes down and her shawl pulled firmly about her head, as though to blinker herself against even a passing glance at the fairy *ráth* and the whitethorn, red haws glistening upon the branches, blood-bright.

It was not so often that women came to her for herbal cures. Most women in the valley knew enough to tend to the daily blights and bruises of living: wild honey for the inflamed and crusted eye, comfrey for pained bones, yarrow leaves pushed inside the nose to make it bleed and relieve the pounding head. Nance knew the people visited John O'Donoghue for brutal surgery, trusting his blacksmith's strength to pull the rotting teeth from their mouths or slip the dislocated shoulder back snug into its joint. They came to her only when their own poultices of gander dung and mustard or their teas of king fern failed to halt the infection or smother the cough. They came to her only when their panic had begun to fight the bridle, when their children continued to lie slack in their arms, or they knew that whatever illness plaguing them was more powerful than red dandelion or penny leaves or the salted tongue of a fox.

''Tis something else this time,' they would say, extending a twisted foot or breathing through a congested lung. ''Tis the evil eye,' they said. ''Tis the Good People.'

It was mainly the men who came for herbs. Those who worked in the fields and were less used to the sight of their own blood. Those who did not trust the doctor or could not afford his labelled tinctures. Men of the earth, they took comfort in seeing their sores stemmed by plants they had played with as boys, by a hand as wrinkled as the grandmothers they remembered by the fires of their childhoods.

But Nance knew that most of her patients did not come for herbs at all. Those with broken bodies came in the light of day in the company of family. Those who sought other advice, who found something deeply amiss, who could not lay a finger on the origin of their suffering, came in the shifting hours of dawn and twilight, when there was time for secrecy and they would not be missed. They came alone, wrapped against the cold, their faces ashen with anxiety. Nance knew that, for all her stoppered teas and mixtures of fat and ragwort, it was these visits that allowed her to remain in her cabin. They wanted her time. They wanted her voice, and her hands holding their own. They saw in her age and loneliness the proof of her cure.

What woman lives on her own with a goat and a low roof of drying herbs? What woman keeps company with the birds and the creatures that belonged to the dappled places? What woman finds contentment in such a solitary life, has no need of children or the comfort of a man? One who has been chosen to walk the boundaries. One who somehow has an understanding of the mysteries of the world and who sees in the clawing briars God's own handwriting.

Nance took a deep breath of the crisp autumn air and, nodding towards the fairy *ráth*, returned inside to her thistles.

⚹

Nóra set out to the Killarney fair early, a skiff over her arm to carry her shoes and save them from the mud of the road. The dark dawned to a white-knuckled day as she walked, the jackdaws shrieking at the November morning.

How odd to think that she would be returning with a stranger. Someone to live with and talk to, and who would share the heat of her fire. Someone who might help whittle the long winter days away until spring came with its comforts of birdsong and work.

It had been Peg O'Shea who had given her the idea to hire a maid. After Samhain Eve, Nóra's grief had sharpened into righteous anger and she had stormed into Peg's cabin.

'I've a mind to make a harness out of your boy, John,' Nóra had announced. 'Running around after dark, putting the fear into widows and children and disturbing my sleep. Here I am with no husband, himself fresh in the grave, and only myself and my nephews to work the ground, and now I have John and his spalpeens battering down the door in masks.'

Nóra winced as she walked along the road, remembering her words to Peg.

'He's gallows-bound with that larking. Do they want to be seeing me in my grave? Is that what they were after with their badness?'

'Ah, that's not it at all.' Peg had taken one of Nóra's hands and held it lightly in her own. 'I tell you, them boys scare more than widows. 'Tis a good thing they had their masks on or you would have been crying louder. Have you seen the face on our John? Like a flitch of bacon on the turn. You should see the girls running from the sight. Ah, Nóra. Come now. We're kin and all. I'll have a word with him.'

It was then that Peg had gently advised Nóra to find some kind of company. When she had pulled a face at Peg's suggestion that she move in with Daniel and Brigid, the older woman had encouraged her to look for someone at the November hiring fair.

'Get a girl, just to see you through winter,' she had said. ''Twould be a grand help to you, what with Micheál and all. 'Twill be hard looking after a wee cripple on your own. Was it that your man was in the fields and running errands, and you in the house with the boy? Well, what when you're off to sell your eggs and butter?'

'I can sell eggs and butter to those who come collecting for it.'

'And when you're in the fields in the summer? Doing the work of two to keep the thatch over your head?'

'I can't be thinking of summer yet.'

'Well then, Nóra, do you think it best to be sitting the dark hours through on your own? There are girls from up north, their families are starving. Would it not be a comfort to know you're taking one in? Would it not be a comfort to have an extra soul about the place this winter?'

There had been sense in what Peg had said. Later that day, sobbing to ruin on her bed while the child howled by the dying fire, Nóra understood that she was slipping. She was not like Martin. Her grandchild was no comfort to her; he was burdensome. She needed someone who might quiet the shrieking wean, who might help her resurface after she was hit with the waves of her grief. Someone who was not from the valley, who would not spread knowledge of Micheál's withered legs amongst her neighbours, would not say he was astray in the head.

It was a ten-mile walk to Killarney through coarse, moory land, brindled in autumn, past small mud cabins huddled by the road-side, the sound of cocks and hens from within, waiting to be let out. Open, flat-boarded carts pulled by donkeys clattered past Nóra on the lane, and she shrank back against the briars and holly of the ditches to let them pass. The men nodded to her, reins in hand, while their sleepy-eyed, shawled wives, stared out across the morass to the mountains in the distance: Mangerton, Crohane, Torc, their familiar mass towering purple against the sky.

Nóra was glad to leave her own house, glad for the hours of walking to clear her head and breathe in the air. Since Martin had died, she had kept to her cabin, refusing to join the night-visiting for stories and song as she once had. Nóra didn't like to admit it, but she felt bitter towards the other women of the valley, found their sympathy cloying and insincere. Some had come to her door with food and offers of condolence and distraction, but Nóra, ashamed of Micheál, had refused to invite them inside to sit at the fire. Since then, in that cruelly imperceptible manner of grown women, the valley wives had slowly closed their company to her. There was nothing overt about their exclusion. They still greeted her when she met them at the well most mornings, but there was a way they had of turning in amongst themselves that made her feel unwanted. They did not trust her, Nóra knew. Those who stayed inside their cabins had something shameful to hide: bruises, poverty, sickness.

They must know about Micheál, Nóra thought. They must suspect something is not right with him.

She felt suffocated by the constant neediness of her grandchild. He made her uneasy. The night before she had tried to encourage him to walk, holding him up so that his feet brushed the ground. But he had thrown his red head back, exposing the pale length of his throat and the sharp ridges of his collarbone, and screamed as though she was pressing pins into his heels. Perhaps she ought to fetch the doctor again. There were plenty of doctors in Killarney, she knew, but accustomed as they were to the deep purses of tourists who came for the lakes, she doubted they would consider looking at Micheál for what she could afford. It was not as though the first doctor had been able to do anything for him. She would be taking food out of their mouths and for no good.

No. In the valley the sick were faced with the usual crossroads of priest, blacksmith or graveyard.

Or Nance, said a small voice in her head.

Killarney was alive with noise and smoke. New Street and High Street bristled with paupers and children begging halfpennies, and the buildings along the many filthy lanes were close and oppressive. Those who had come to sell their produce jostled for space beside the arbutus shops and cooperages and tanneries, carts wheeling close to jaunting cars, barrels and sacks. While most farmers had come to hire help for the winter term, there were people selling their autumn pigs and small, horned cows that lumbered slowly through the street, stirring it into mud. The unpaved roads were pocked, puddle-shined, and the air was clear. Men hauled creels of turf on their backs, cut from the black bogs beside the mountains in summer, and women sold potatoes, butter and salmon from the rivers. There was a crisp promise of winter in the air and a gravity to the fair's atmosphere. All must be sold, must be bought, must be piled and stacked and stored and buried, before the earth ground its teeth in frost and wind. Better-off farmers swung their sticks of blackthorn and bought themselves shoes, and young men, drink-taken, trailed their coats behind them, eyes and ashplants eager for fight. Women counted eggs from straw baskets, fingers loose around the creamy shells, and all along the lanes and in the dark corners, those advertising themselves as labourers waited silently.

They stood apart from the carts and produce, casting their eyes quickly at every man and woman walking past. There were more boys than girls, some as young as seven, shivering next to one another in attitudes of hope or reluctance. Each carried a small item to show that they were seeking work: a parcel of clothes or food, or a bundle of sticks. Nóra knew some of those parcels were empty. Mothers and fathers stood behind the smaller children, their eyes jumping from one farmer to another. They spoke with the hirers on behalf of their sons and daughters, and, although Nóra could not hear what they were saying, she could tell from the fixed smiles that they spoke of honest workers, hardy constitutions. The mothers folded their lips into narrow lines, their fingers tightly gripping their sons' shoulders. It would be a long time until they saw each other again.

Nóra noticed one grey-skinned woman standing beside a girl of twelve or thirteen. The girl was hunched over, coughing the sticky wheeze of the ill. Nóra watched as the mother, seeing a man approach, gently covered her daughter's mouth with her hand to muffle the sound and ease her upright. The sick did not get hired. No one wanted to bring badness into the home. No one wanted to pay for a stranger's coffin.

Nóra's eye was suddenly drawn to a tall, thin-faced girl standing apart from the other children, holding a parcel under one arm. She was leaning against a cart, frowning, watching a farmer inspect the teeth of a young redheaded man for hire. There was something appealing about the girl, in the thickness of the freckles on her face and the slight stoop of her back, as though she was reluctant to grow any taller. She was no beauty. Nóra felt a strange pull towards her.

'Good morning to you.'

The girl looked up and immediately pulled away from the cart, standing straight.

'What's your name?' Nóra asked.

'Mary Clifford.' The girl's voice was low, husked.

'Tell me, Mary Clifford, are you looking for work?'

'I am.'

'And where are you from? Where are your people?'

'Not far from Annamore. By the bog.'

'And how old are you?'

'I don't know, missus.'

'Fourteen by the looks of you.'

'Yes, missus. Fourteen, I'm sure. And fifteen next year, please God.'

Nóra nodded. She had thought that the girl might have been older, given her height, but fourteen was a better age. She would not be thinking of marriage yet.

'Have you brothers and sisters?'

'I have, missus. Eight of them.'

'You're the eldest, are you?'

'Eldest girl. That's my brother there.' She pointed across the lane to the redheaded boy. The farmer with him was now lifting his cap and inspecting his hair. They watched as the farmer ran rough hands across the boy's scalp, pushing his head this way and that, looking for lice. Her brother's cheeks were flushed with humiliation.

'And is your mother or father here?'

'My brother and I walked the road ourselves.' She paused. 'Mam and Da are at home with the young ones and the work.'

'Are you well? Has there been any sickness in your house?'

The girl blushed. 'I'm well, missus.' She opened her mouth to show Nóra her teeth, but Nóra shook her head, embarrassed.

'Can you milk and churn then, Mary?'

'I can. I've a good hand for it.' She held out her palms as though Nóra might be able to see evidence of ability in her swollen knuckles, the hard skin on the pads of her fingers.

'And you are used to minding children?'

'I've always helped Mam with the babies. There being eight of us, so.' The girl took a little step forward, as if afraid she was losing Nóra's interest. 'And I'm a fair spinner. And an early riser, too. I wake before the birds, my mam says, and I do her washing and card and I've a strong back. I can be beetling clothes all day.'

Nóra couldn't help but smile at the girl's solemn eagerness. 'Have you been hired before?'

'I have, missus. I was hired at a place north of here for a term this summer gone.'

'And did you like it?'

Mary paused, running her tongue over dry lips. ''Twas a hard place, missus.'

'You didn't care to stay on, then.'

She shook her head. 'I'm after a different farm.'

Nóra nodded, fighting a sudden headache. Martin had always hired what help they needed, and she was unused to so baldly interrogating a stranger. The men Martin had brought home had been quiet, hard workers who were uncomfortable indoors, holding their arms close to their sides as if afraid they would break something. They ate quickly, skinning a potato with their eyes already on the next. They mumbled the rosary, slept on the floor and woke before dawn; rough-nailed, yoke-backed men who smelt of hay and mayweed and rarely showed their teeth. Some came back every year, others did not. There had never been any need to hire a girl.

Nóra allowed herself a moment to study Mary's face and the girl looked back at her, clear-eyed, jaw clenched against the cold. Her clothes were thin and too small for her – her wrists extended well beyond the cuff of her blouse and the seams were tight around her arms and shoulders – but she seemed clean. Her hair was cut to her chin and combed, with no sign of lice. She seemed anxious to please, and Nóra thought of the eight other children at home in whatever damp *bothán* her parents had raised her in. She thought of Johanna, the whispers that rippled back to her about her daughter begging food off neighbours. This girl had the same hair as her. The same as Micheál. A light copper – like a hare, or pine needles drying out on the ground.

'Will you come for a term with me then, Mary? I have my daughter's child to care for. How much do you want for the six months?'

'Two pound,' Mary said quickly.

Nóra narrowed her eyes. 'You're too young for that money. One and half.'

Mary nodded and Nóra placed a shilling in her palm. The girl quickly tucked it into her parcel and cast her eyes to her brother, giving him a solemn nod. He had been abandoned by the farmer who had examined him and now stood alone amidst the crowd and the smoke. He watched them leave, and at the last moment raised a hand in farewell.

The journey back to Nóra's house was a quiet one. The sun emerged and the bright splatter left by cartwheels and footprints was clear on the road. The district's tramping to Killarney with hoof and flock had left the path churned. Mud glistened.

Nóra and Mary made slow work of the journey, but Nóra didn't mind. She was relieved to have the business of hiring done with. She walked close to the lane ditches, stooping now and then to pull starry clusters of chickweed for her hens. Mary, noticing, began to look too. She stepped carefully between the mud and rocks, avoiding the toothed leaves of nettles.

'Were you not afraid of coming such a long way in the dark?' Nóra asked.

'I had my brother,' Mary answered simply.

'You're a brave girl.'

She shrugged. 'There's so many of us. I didn't dare move for fear I'd miss a job. I would have stood there all day.'

They followed the road in silence then, through moor ground and small swathes of trees, already bare in the steady approach of winter; past the dark, lacquered shine of holly. The grass by the roadside was browned and long and beyond, in the distance, the mountains patched with heather and rock stood silent against the sky. Spirals of smoke from turf fires accompanied them as they walked.

It was late afternoon by the time the two women reached Nóra's cabin, and the sun had started to falter. They stood for a moment in the yard, panting after the trudge up the slope, and Nóra watched the girl assess her surroundings. Her eyes passed over the two-roomed thatched dwelling, the small byre beside it and the scattered hens. Nóra wondered whether Mary had expected something more, perhaps a larger home thatched with wheat straw rather than reeds. Perhaps the stumping mass of a pig in the yard or signs of a donkey rather than a quiet home with one tiny window stuffed with straw, the whitewashed walls greening with moss and a stony scoreground of potato.

'I have a cow. She keeps us in milk and dirt.' Nóra led Mary to the byre and they stepped into its warm darkness and its smell of flank and piss, the dark outline of the cow on the straw at their feet.

'You're to water, feed and milk her in the mornings and churn the butter. Once a week, you'll churn. I'll do the evening's milking.'

'What's her name?'

'Brownie, we . . . I call her.'

Nóra watched as Mary brought her chapped hands down to the cow's head and stroked her ears. Brownie slowly shifted her weight, her bony haunches rolling.

'Does she give much milk?'

'Enough,' replied Nóra. 'God keep her well.'

They stepped back into the soft light and walked the wet path to the house, the chickens running towards them over the yard. 'Decent hens,' Nóra said. 'Here, give them the chickweed. Sure, they're mad for it. They're not laying as much now, but I have my faithful few and they give their eggs right through the winter.' She shot Mary a stern look. 'You're not to take any. No eggs or butter. You'd be eating the rent. Do you eat much?'

'No more than I can help.'

'Hmm. Follow me now.'

Nóra pushed open the half-door and greeted Peg O'Shea, who was sitting by the fire with Micheál in her lap.

'Peg, this here is Mary.'

'God save you and welcome.' Peg gave Mary an appraising look. 'You'll be a Clancy girl, with the red hair of you.'

'Clifford. I'm Mary Clifford,' the girl said, eyes flicking to Micheál. Her mouth slipped open.

'Clifford, is it? Well, God bless you, Cliffords and Clancys alike. Is it far you've come?'

'She set out to the rabble fair in the dark of this morning,' Nóra said. 'Annamore. Twelve mile or more.'

'And the walk all this way too? Musha, you'll be dead on your feet.'

'She has two strong legs.'

'And two strong arms from the look of things. Take him, will you? This is Micheál. I expect Nóra's told you about him.' Peg gathered the boy up and motioned for Mary to come closer.

Mary stared. Micheál's nose was crusted and spittle had dried in the corner of his mouth. As Peg held him out to her, he began to groan like a man beaten.

She took a step back. 'What's wrong with him?'

There was silence, broken only by Micheál's guttural moaning.

Peg sighed and placed the boy back down on her lap. Casting a knowing look at Nóra, she scraped the dried saliva from the boy's face with a fingernail.

'What do you mean, "What's wrong with him?"' Nóra's voice was dangerous.

'What ails him? That noise he's making. Why is he carping like that? Can he not talk?'

'He's delicate, is all,' Peg said softly.

'Delicate,' Mary repeated. She edged backwards until her hands were resting on the doorframe. 'Is it catching?'

Nóra made an animal noise in the back of her throat. 'You're a bold girl to ask a question like that.'

'Nóra –'

'"Is it catching?" Do you hear her, Peg? The cheek of it.'

'No, I don't mean. Only, he does not seem . . .'

'Seem what?'

'Nóra. She has a right to ask.' Peg spat on a corner of her apron and scrubbed at Micheál's face.

'Only . . .' Mary pointed at his legs, exposed where the dress bunched up about his midriff. 'Can he even walk?' Her lip trembled.

'She's just a girl, Nóra,' Peg said quietly. 'Come here and see for yourself, Mary Clifford. He's not got a catching sickness. He won't harm you. He's just a child. Just a harmless child.'

Mary nodded, swallowing hard.

'Go on. Take a peep at him. He's a dear thing, really.'

Mary peered over Peg's shoulder at the boy. His eyes were half shut, gazing down the length of a snub nose, and his mouth was slack. Gurgled breathing came from his throat.

'Is he in pain?' Mary asked.

'He's not, no. He can laugh, and he can sit up a ways by himself, and he can move his arms sometimes to play with things.'

'How old is he?'

'Well, now,' said Peg. 'He'd be four years now, isn't that so, Nóra?'

'He likes feathers,' Nóra breathed. She sat down unsteadily on the creepie stool opposite Peg. 'He likes feathers.'

'Sure, four it is. And he likes feathers. And acorns. And knuckle bones.' Peg's voice held a forced liveliness. ''Tis just the legs of him.'

'He can't walk,' Nóra croaked. 'He used to be able to, but now he can't.'

Mary eyed the boy with apprehension, her lips pressed tightly together. 'Micheál? My name is Mary.' She glanced over to Nóra. 'Is he shy?'

'He can't talk to tell us.' Nóra was silent for a moment. 'I should have told you.'

Mary shook her head. Her hair had curled in the damp air of the walk back to the cabin and she looked young and frightened. Nóra felt sudden self-loathing. She is just a girl, she thought. She is just a child herself, and here I am shouting at her. A stranger.

'Well, now. You've come all this way and I've not even given you a drink. You must be thirsty.' Nóra stood and replenished the pot of water on the hearth from the well pail.

Peg gave Mary a little squeeze on the shoulder. 'Let's set him down there. On the heather. He won't go far.'

'I can take him.' Mary sat down next to Peg and lifted the boy onto her lap. 'He's all bones! He's light as a bird.'

The women watched her as she pulled the cloth of Micheál's dress down around his legs, then took off her own shawl and used it to swaddle his feet. 'There now. Now you're easy,' she murmured.

'Well. 'Tis a pleasure to have you amongst us, Mary Clifford. I wish you well and God bless. I'd best be on my way.' She gave Nóra a meaningful glance and shuffled out the door, leaving them alone.

Mary tucked Micheál's head against her collarbone, her arms awkwardly clasped around his body. 'He has a tremor in him,' she remarked.

Nóra poured out two piggins of buttermilk and began to prepare potatoes for their dinner. There was a tightening in her throat, as though a rope had been pulled against her neck, and she did not trust herself to speak. Several minutes passed before she heard Mary's quavering voice behind her.

'I'll do my best for you.'

'I'm sure you will.' Nóra choked on the words. 'I'm sure you will.'

Later that evening, once Mary and Nóra had finished their quiet meal and called the hens in for the night, they turned out the settle bed, placing a rough mattress of woven straw and a blanket down.

'You'll be warm here, by the fire,' Nóra said.

'Thank you, missus.'

'And you'll have Micheál to keep the heat in the bed.'

'Does he not use that cradle?' Mary pointed to the rough cot of woven sally twigs.

'He's grown too big for it. It cramps him. Now, mind you tuck him in well or he'll kick his bedclothes off in the night.'

Mary looked at Micheál, who was propped up against the wall, his head rolling on one shoulder.

'Tomorrow I'll show you a little of the valley, if 'tis fine. You'll need to know where the well is. And I'll show you the best place to wash clothes in the river. It might do you good to meet a few of the other girls about here.'

'Will Micheál come with us?'

Nóra gave her a sharp look.

'I mean, do you leave him here, or do you take him about with you? A boy like him, who hasn't the use of his legs . . .'

'I don't like to be taking him outside.'

'You leave him alone?'

'I won't have folk splashing water on drowned mice.' Nóra picked up the pail of dirty water they had washed their feet in. Easing the door open, she cried a warning to the fairies and threw it into the yard.

CHAPTER
FOUR

Ash

'Are you of the living or the dead?'
Peter O'Connor opened the door to Nance's cabin and ducked his head under the low frame, a bottle of *poitín* in his hand. 'Dead from dry-thirst.'

Nance beckoned him in. 'Sit down, will you. Grand to see you, Peter.'

''Twas a fine wake they gave Martin, and a fine *caoineadh* from you, Nance.' Peter lowered himself down by the fire and fussed with his pipe, taking Nance's crude pair of tongs and lifting an ember to light it. 'Lord have mercy on the souls of the dead,' he whispered. He sucked on the pipe until the tobacco flared and a coil of smoke rose.

'What brings you today, Peter? Is it the shoulder of you?'

Peter shook his head. 'The arm is alright.'

'Is it the eyes?' When the man didn't respond, Nance settled herself more comfortably on her stool and waited patiently.

'I keep having these dreams,' Peter said finally.

'Ah, dreams, is it?'

He clenched his jaw. 'I don't know what's bringing them on, Nance. Powerful dreams, they are.'

'And are they troubling you?'

Peter took a long draw on his pipe. 'Ever since I found Martin lying dead by the crossroads.'

'Full of trouble, are they?'

'Full of badness.' Peter looked up from the fire and Nance saw that his face was dark. 'I can't shake the feeling that something terrible is coming, Nance. I dream of dead animals. Their throats slit and them bleeding into the ground.' He cast a look at Nance's goat. 'Or I dream that I'm drowning. Or a hanged man. I wake choking.'

Nance waited for Peter to continue speaking, and when the man remained silent, his knees drawn up to his chest, Nance gestured to the bottle he had brought. 'Will we have a drink?' She pulled the cork out and passed the bottle to him.

He took a deep gulp, winced and wiped his mouth.

'Powerful *poitín*,' Nance muttered, taking a swig of her own. She sat back down by the fire. She was prepared to wait. Sometimes a listening ear was all that was needed. Just silence and time in a cabin where there was no chatter, or stories, or neighbours. Where there was nothing but a fire and a woman. A woman they didn't desire. A woman whose tongue didn't slip secrets to other wives. Just an old woman with an ear and a taste for the smoke and the drink. That was worth slipping out of their cabins for, worth the walk between the lazy beds and the mossed walls to visit her in the fading hours. Nance knew the power of silence.

The fire burnt. Peter smoked the bowl of tobacco down to ash and rapped it out against his knees. They passed the bottle of drink between them, until the damp night air seeped under the door, making Peter restless.

'Did I tell you about the four magpies I saw before our Martin passed, mercy on his soul?'

Nance leant forward. 'You did not, Peter.'

'Four of them. There's death coming, isn't there? I saw lights by your Piper's Grave. By the ringfort. And that night I had the first of these dreams.'

'I saw lightning strike the heather on the mountain,' Nance muttered.

'The night Martin died?'

'The very same. There's a strange wind blowing.'

'They're abroad. The Good People. Do you think that's why I've been dreaming the things I have, Nance?'

She reached out and patted his shoulder, and saw, briefly, his narrow cot against the wall in his cabin, the long hours spent smoking while the night pressed down. 'Weren't you born with a caul on your head, and isn't it truth that such a one has eyes for things that are beyond the knowing of most? Still, Peter, let you remember, a lot of fears are born of sitting too long alone in the dark.'

Peter picked his teeth with a dirty fingernail and gave a short laugh. 'Faith, what does it matter? I'd best be on my way.'

'Sure, Peter. Go on home.'

He helped Nance to her feet and waited as she used the tongs to pluck a coal from the fire, dipping it, hissing, in her water bucket to cool. She dried the dead ember on her skirt, spat on the ground and passed it to him. 'You'll see no *púca* tonight. God save you on the road.'

Peter put it into his pocket with a curt nod. 'Bless you, Nance Roche. You're a good living woman, no matter what the new priest says.'

Nance raised an eyebrow. 'The priest has been wasting words on me, has he?'

Peter chuckled. 'I didn't say? Oh, you should have heard him at Mass. He was trying to open our eyes to the new world, he said. 'Twas our duty to slough off the old ways that keep Irishmen at the bottom of the pile. 'Tis a new age for Ireland and for the Catholic Church. We're to be paying our pennies to the Catholic campaign, not to unholy keeners.'

'Slough off the old ways. He has a pretty mouth on him, then.'

'Not so pretty, Nance.' Peter shook his head. 'I'd give him a wide berth. Let him settle in. Learn how we do things around here.'

'I suppose he thinks I am one for those "old ways".'

Peter's face grew solemn. 'Heathen ways, Nance. He said he knows that people come to you and that we're not to anymore.' He paused. 'He said you're full of devilment and tricks to be keening for the money.'

'So. The new priest is against me.'

'Father Healy may be. But here I am, Nance. And by my soul, I see no devilment in your home.'

'The Lord protect you, Peter O'Connor.'

The man gave her a smile and set his hat on his head. 'We still have need of you. We still have need of the old ways and knowledge.' He paused, his smile fading. 'It reminds me, Nance. There's a boy, you know. Up with Nóra Leahy. A cripple boy. I thought you should know, in case the widow has need of you.'

'I saw no cripple when I was up there for the keening.'

'No. She had me take him away.'

'What ails him?'

'I couldn't tell you, Nance.' Peter looked out into the encroaching dark. 'But 'tis certain there's something terrible wrong.'

Nance spent the rest of the evening hunched close to her fireside, her tongue worrying the teeth in her gums. The night felt restless. She could hear the croak of frogs and a small scratching that might have been a burrowing rat, a jackdaw on the thatch.

In the unbusy hours, time lost traction. Often, as Nance sat quietly carding wool or waiting for her few potatoes to boil, she imagined that Maggie sat in the room with her. Marked, terrifying, calm-eyed Maggie, drying her herbs, skinning her rabbits. Maggie with her pipe clamped between her teeth, keeping her fingers busy. Showing Nance how to listen to the secret, knocking heartbeat of the world. Teaching her how to save others, if she could not save her mother.

How quickly the air thickened with ghosts.

'Some folk are born different, Nance. They are born on the outside of things, with a skin a little thinner, eyes a little keener to what goes unnoticed by most. Their hearts swallow more blood than ordinary hearts; the river runs differently for them.'

A memory of them sitting in her father's cabin, washing the road from their feet. Nance's heart thrilling in her chest at delivering her first baby into the world – the seventh son of a jarvey's wife. The first sight of the hair, the waxen slip of the child into her hands. How she had trembled at the sound of the infant's cry.

Maggie smiling at her, settling on the stool, lighting her pipe. 'I remember when you were born, Nance. Your mam was in some froth of pain. Colliding with nature, so she was. I came and all was chaos – your da was in a fit because you were showing a mighty reluctance to be dragged into the world. I loosened every lock. I unbarred the door and pushed the straw from the window. I untied the knots from my shawl and your mam's clothes, and told the men to set the cow free. They kicked her into the night. Only then, when everything was slack, did you slip amongst us like a fish from a loose net.'

'Did you know I was different then?'

Her aunt had smiled. Tapped the ash from her pipe. 'You came as children sometimes do, Nance. In the small, sliding hours of the night. Fists clenched. Already brawling with the world.'

There was silence.

'I don't want to have the difference upon me. I don't want to be alone like that.'

Maggie leant closer, eyes fierce. 'What is in the marrow is hard to take out of the bone. You'll learn that soon enough.'

Mary woke with a start, a weight of panic on her chest. Sitting up in a sweat, she gazed about her, taking in the rosy glow of the hearth and the unfamiliar walls of the cabin. A moment passed before she remembered where she was.

I am in the widow's house.

Mary looked at the sleeping child lying beside her, the thin buckle of his spine pressing against her leg.

I am in the widow's house, she thought. And this is the child I must care for.

She lay back down and tried to sleep, but the smells of the cabin were strange, and there was a gnawing at her chest. A desire to be back in Annamore, lying beside her brothers and sisters, the whole tangle of them in front of the fire on the sweet-smelling rushes, made her eyes fill with tears. Mary blinked them away, tucked her wrists under her chin and pushed her face against the makeshift pillow of rags.

Her stomach groaned. She had eaten too much. At least I will not go hungry here, she thought, for all the widow's warnings about eggs. There were worse places she could be. David had told her about the farm he had been hired to last autumn, a smallholding out on the peninsula where they spent the days cutting and carrying seaweed for the fields. Long days of standing in salt water, back bent to the cold, and the heavy trudge to the fields. The weed had soaked his clothes through the loose weave of the basket and turned his skin raw.

Pray to God you are hired to some place where they feed you well, he had said.

It wasn't the work David had minded. All the men and women of the place had taken their fair share of labour. But it was a poor thing to have your body trellised in salt, your feet bleeding from hidden rocks, and a belly full of sea air and little else.

Her brother had not told her these things in front of their mother. She would have worried herself sick with it, and it was hard enough to see her fretting over the children at home, with the coughs, and the potatoes too few in the ground and the bodies too many, and the rumour of evictions and the middlemen's crowbars that passed from cabin to cabin like a dark shadow. Her brother had waited until they were outside, looking for stray eggs in the tufts of grass.

Find yourself a place where they feed you, David had said. No matter the dirt. Sure, some families that do be hiring have nothing more than we. They lay down on rushes every night just the same as us. But find yourself a farmer who will see to it that you're fed.

They had fed her at the northern farm over the summer. Lumpers. Stirabout. But only after the family had eaten; she was left to drain the piggin of buttermilk and scrape the pot clean of meal.

Mary turned on her side. It could be worse, she comforted herself. One woman and a child, rattling around in a house with a cow and a bit of scoreground. But there was a strange feeling in the place, something she could not quite make out. Perhaps it was the loneliness of the woman. The widow, Nóra Leahy. Hollow-cheeked and hair greying about her temples. She looked as though she had been thrashed by womanhood; her ankles were swollen and her face threaded with deep lines. Mary had studied her at the fair, noticing the sun's trace on her skin, the expanse of furrows that suggested a life well lived.

David had warned her to take a good look at their faces. If a man has a red nose, he's a man in liquor and you'd best avoid his house because you can be sure all the money goes on the drink and not on those under his roof. The women with puckered mouths? Mary, gossip is sour. They'll be watching your every move. Best find a face where there's little shadow of a frown and their eyes are all crow's feet. They've either been staring into the sun all their lives, or they're a kind soul, and you can be sure that whether 'tis work in the field or smiling that gave them such a face, you'll be better off with them.

Nóra Leahy had crow's feet. She had seemed kind enough at Killarney, her clothes neat and her face open. But she had not told her that she was a widow, and she had lied about the boy.

What was it she had said?

I have my daughter's child to care for.

No word about a scragged boy with a loose, mute jaw. No suggestion of a house of illness, or death, or the need for secrecy.

Mary had never seen a child like Micheál before. Asleep he could almost be any skinny wretch, a little boy like any other, although stunted and pallid. But awake, there was no doubting that something was gravely wrong with him. His blue eyes seemed to slip unseeing over the world, passing over her as though she were not there at all. It was unnatural, the way he folded his wrists against his chest, the sloping angle of his mouth. He looked old, somehow. His skin was tight and dry, and there was a thinness to it, like the pages in a priest's holy book. He had nothing of the round-cheeked softness of the children Mary knew. When she had stepped through the door of the cabin and seen the old woman holding him on her lap, she had thought at first that it wasn't a child at all but some strange scarecrow. A baby's plaything, made from sticks and an old dress, like the effigy of St Brigid carried on the saint's holy day: shrivelled head, hard angles hidden by discarded cloth. And then, as she had drawn closer and seen that it, *he*, was alive, her heart had dropped in fear. Thin and flared with a disease like those that sucked the sap from a plant and shrivelled it to withered stalk. She had been sent to a home touched with sickness, and she would be tainted with it.

But no. He was not sick, they said. Only slow. Only struggling to grow as other children did.

A copperheaded, snub-nosed, wasting runt. A pattern of sally rods bound by skin and rash and groaning like a demon.

Mary brought a gentle hand to Micheál's forehead and pushed the hair back from it. He was drooling: a watery line of spittle ran from the corner of his mouth across his face. Mary smoothed it away with the back of her hand and wiped it on the blanket.

The widow must be ashamed of the boy. That is why Nóra had not told her.

What had her daughter done to deserve such a child?

If a woman could bestow a harelip on a baby by meeting a hare in the road, what ill thing was met with to turn a boy ragged and skew the bones in his skin? It must have been a grave sin, to thwart a child in the womb so.

But he had not been born this way, the widow had said.

Perhaps something had struck him down.

There was nothing for it, Mary decided. She could not go home. This farm, this valley – like a pock in the skin of the earth, sunk between the height of rocky mountains – was hers to know for the next half-year. She would have to bite down on her lip and work. She was earning real money for her family, and as long as she and David were out and gathering shillings, there would be no eviction. She could stand six months with a hard, contrary woman and a bone-racked boy. Then she'd be back on the rushes with her brothers and sisters, and her father's low voice saying the rosary, and they would all fall asleep by the warmth of their fire and not even the whistling wind would wake them.

Nóra woke with restless excitement. There was a stranger in the house. The girl, Mary. Throwing on her outer clothes, she dressed quickly and entered the main room.

The girl wasn't there.

The settle bed had been turned back in so that it resembled a bench once more, and the fire had been raked and was burning high. In the corner of the room, Nóra saw that Micheál had been placed in an empty basket and that the heavy iron tongs from the fire had been laid across it, inches from his unmoving head.

Mary was nowhere to be seen.

The chickens were no longer in their roost, and Nóra reached a hand in for the eggs. There were four, still warm. Placing them carefully in the egg basket, she heard the creak of the yard door and spun around. Mary stood there, bundled against the bright cold of the morning, a steaming pail of milk in one hand, covered with a cloth.

'Mary,' Nóra gasped.

'Good morning to you.' Mary lifted the milk onto the table and began to strain it through the cloth into a crock.

'I thought you had gone.'

'Just an early riser, missus. Like I said. And you asking me to milk mornings and . . .' Her voice tapered off. 'Have I done something wrong?'

Nóra laughed in her relief. 'Never mind it. 'Twas only because of last evening and, well . . .' She paused. 'Where is the spancel?'

'I couldn't find one.'

'You milked Brownie without it?'

'I did. She's a gentle dear.'

'The spancel is here. In that corner. I keep it inside so no butter stealer can use it against me.' Nóra pointed at the tongs resting over the basket. 'I've not seen that for some time.'

Mary reddened and picked them up, setting them back down by the fire. 'They're for the fairies, missus. So he isn't taken. 'Tis what we do in Annamore.'

'Well, I know what they're for and 'tis the same here. It has been a long time since I had to be worrying about the fairies taking my child.'

Mary pinked. 'Micheál . . . Well, the doty child wet himself in the night. I wanted to clean him but there's no water.'

'I'll show you the well.'

The morning was clean and damp and filled with a brightness that glanced off the wet moss on the field walls, turning them a vivid green. It was cold, but the early sunlight was soft and golden, and lit the haze of smoke that drifted from the cabins. Mist pooled in the bottom of the valley.

'The river is down there,' Nóra said, standing with Mary in the yard. They had left Micheál in the cabin, walled in the potato basket, safe from the fire. 'The Flesk, as we call it. You can go fetch water there if you like, but 'tis a long walk back with the pails and 'tis all uphill. Slippery too, in the rain. When the weather turns you'll go there to beetle the clothes. 'Tis a longer walk to the well, but 'tis steady and kinder on my knees. All the women go to the well for their water. 'Tis clearer.'

'Are there many that live in this valley?' Mary asked.

'Women? Just as many as the men, although there's a few unmarried farmers. See that house closest to us? That's where Peg O'Shea lives, the woman you met last night. She has a fine and full family. Five children and their children besides.' Nóra pointed down the valley, where the lane dipped around the mountain to the flatter plain, as they began to walk. 'And that place way down there – do you see the two buildings and the lime kiln a ways off? There, in the middle of the valley. That's the blacksmith's. John O'Donoghue and his wife Áine. 'Tis a great house for *cuaird*, for night-visiting. They've no children at all though they've been married ten years. People don't speak of it. My nephew's home is just beyond that, along the valley, though you can't see it for all the mist. Daniel Lynch is his name. His wife is expecting their first child. You might see him and his brother about the place. They'll help with the labour some. My husband died not long ago.'

'Sorry for your trouble, missus.'

There was the sound of laughter, and Nóra, suddenly fighting tears, was grateful to see two women come around the slope with water pails in hand, joining them on the lane.

'God bless you, Nóra Leahy,' said one of them, pulling her cloak off her face so she could better see. Curly wisps of fair hair escaped from her braid.

'And you too, Sorcha. Éilís. This here is Mary Clifford.'

The women looked at Mary with interest, their eyes narrowed. 'To the well, are ye?'

'We are.'

'Mary, Éilís is the wife of the schoolmaster here, William O'Hare. He takes the children for their lessons by the hedgerows. And Sorcha is the daughter of my brother-in-law's brother's wife.'

Mary looked confused.

'Don't worry, you'll meet them in time. There's no hiding. Everyone knows everyone here.'

'We're all tied together, whether we like it or no,' Éilís added, raising an eyebrow. She was a short bull of a woman with dark bags under her eyes.

'Did you hear about Father Healy, Nóra?'

'What about him?'

Sorcha puffed out her cheeks. 'He heard about your man Martin's wake. Didn't it fire him up?' She laughed. 'You should have heard him speak at Mass. Oh, he had the anger up.'

Nóra shook her head irritably. 'What are you saying?'

Sorcha leant in closer, swinging her water pail against her leg. 'He had the word against your keener, Nance Roche. Preached against her, like. Said she's not to be brought in for *caoineadh*. Said it is not in line with the Church.'

'And what sort of wake would it be without keening?' Nóra exclaimed. 'Did you ever hear of such a thing?'

'Oh, he was fit to be tied,' Éilís added. She was enjoying the scandal. 'He was spitting all over everyone. I had to wipe my face.'

'We've a new priest,' Nóra explained to Mary. 'Father Healy.'

Sorcha stooped to pick up a dandelion and put it in her mouth, chewing on the leaf. 'He doesn't stand for much. I wonder how he knew Nance was at your cabin? He'd already left. 'Twas pissing down that night.'

'Someone must have told him,' Éilís suggested darkly.

The well was cut into the slope of the valley where the mountain met the level ground, a rough hole, surrounded by bushes of furze and heather. An ash tree grew nearby, to mark the place and to make the water sweeter, and tattered ribbons flapped from its trunk and lower branches in the breeze. There were already a group of women talking by the well, pails of water by their feet. They looked up at the sound of Éilís and Sorcha's voices and greeted Nóra, eyes flashing quickly to Mary and glancing over her ill-fitting clothes. Some spat on the ground. 'God be between us and harm,' whispered another.

''Tis your red hair,' Nóra muttered to Mary.

'My red hair?'

'Do you not meet with the spitting in Annamore?'

'Never on my life.'

'Well, don't mind them.' She nodded to two of the women. 'This is Mary Clifford. She's come to work for me. I'm showing her the well. Mary, you've met Sorcha and Éilís. This here is Hanna and Biddy.'

The women murmured greetings, then turned back to the huddle, intent on their conversation. They were also talking of Father Healy.

'He thinks heathens are amongst us,' said one of those gathered.

'He didn't say that! He thinks the old ways are just a superstition. He won't give in to it.'

'A priest should believe it more than anyone,' Hanna remarked.

'Those were his words. He thinks the Devil's amongst us in more ways than one.'

As Nóra bent to draw the water she noticed that several women looked at her anxiously. A few patted her on the back as she pulled the bucket from the well, but few offered her little more than a greeting. When Nóra joined Mary with the filled pails, they began to walk the path back to the cabin without farewell.

'Are they your friends?' Mary asked.

'They're blood-tied to me, if that's what you're asking.'

'Why did they spit on the ground when they saw my hair?'

'They think you might have the evil eye.'

Mary shifted uncomfortably, but said nothing.

'Don't be vexed over it. 'Tis just the way of it here.'

'Sorcha seems a lively girl.'

'Sorcha? What that one knows at cow-time the whole countryside will be repeating before moonrise.'

'Is it true what she said about your priest giving out to the keener?'

Nóra snorted. 'I don't know what they be teaching them in the towns these days. What's the good of stripping us of our ways? They're as Christian as the both of us.'

'Has your man, the priest, seen to Micheál?'

'You're yet to learn a few things about the people around here. But you may as well learn now that a priest is not often in the homes of the people without a palm of money.'

A putrid smell met them as they opened the door to Nóra's cabin. Mary looked in the potato basket and saw that Micheál had shat himself. He sat upright in his own filth, hands sticky and eyes wide, as if surprised.

''Tis in his hair,' Mary exclaimed, pinching her nose with one hand.

'Take him outside and wash him then.'

Mary hauled the basket with the boy still inside out into the yard. The shit had already started to dry on his skin, and the dried ball of peck heath she scrubbed him with did little to loosen the dirt. Nóra brought out a scrap of grey soap made from fern ash and fat, and eventually Mary managed to clean the boy. The chill of the well water and the scraping of the heath on his skin made Micheál scream, and it was some time before Mary could soothe him. She paced the length of the yard, the chickens at her feet, bundling Micheál up in her shawl and singing to him. By the time he fell asleep, she was exhausted.

'Bring him here to me,' Nóra said, returning outside with her arms extended as soon as his cries had softened. She noticed the emptied pail. 'Did you not use the barrel water?'

'The what?'

'The rain water.' Nóra pointed to an old barrel standing by the byre. 'Go back to the well, would you, and get us more drinking water. If anyone asks you why you're back so soon, don't tell them the reason. Say you're a mighty one for cleaning. Don't mention Micheál.'

Mary lugged the water pail back to the well, trying to ignore the smell of shit that lingered on her clothes and hands. She hoped that the clearing beside the ash tree would be empty of people, but as she rounded the corner, she saw that Éilís O'Hare was still there, talking to another woman she had not seen before.

''Tis the maid again,' Éilís sang, noticing her at once and raising a hand. 'Kate, this is . . . What's your name again there, girl?'

'My name is Mary Clifford.'

'Mary Clifford. That's the one I was telling you about. The Widow Leahy has help in.' Éilís raised her eyebrows at the other woman, who stared at Mary with cold intensity.

'I'm Kate Lynch,' the woman said. 'Éilís here was saying that you're new to the valley. That you're a hired girl.'

'That's right,' Mary said. 'I'm from Annamore. Up north.'

'I know where Annamore is,' Kate said. 'Full of red-haired girls, is it?'

'Only some,' Mary said. She made to kneel down by the well to fetch her water, but Kate took a step in front of her.

'We know why you're here,' Kate said. 'I'm a relation of the widow's and Éilís here is my sister. My man is the brother of Nóra's dead sister's husband.'

'I'm sorry for your troubles,' Mary murmured.

'You're here because of the child, are you not? The widow's grandchild left after her daughter was swept.'

'Swept?'

Kate took hold of Mary's water pail. Her knuckles were red, swollen. 'That boy is no ordinary wean, is he?'

'I don't know what you mean.'

Éilís laughed. 'The widow keeps him safe in her cabin, but we know. We know.'

Kate leant down and looked Mary in the eye, still gripping her water pail. 'I'm going to tell you something now, girl, and you'd best be listening to me. Martin Leahy was a well man before the widow's daughter was taken, and before that child came to this valley. But no one drops down at a crossroads and dies in good health without some kind of interference. As soon as that changeling was delivered . . .' She stopped to spit on the ground. 'As soon as that blasted cratur came into Nóra's house, all manner of powerful trouble started, and now Martin is dead.'

'You're new to this valley, and I don't expect you to understand what is going on around you. Not yet,' Éilís said. 'But there's people here who are conspiring with Them, and it has caused a shadow to drop on us.'

'That child Nóra keeps away from the eyes of us? I ask you, do you think that's a natural boy?' Kate hissed between her teeth.

'He's a cripple,' Mary stuttered. She pulled at her water pail and Kate let it go with a grimace.

'A cripple, is he?'

'You've a lot to learn, Mary Clifford. The widow had no right bringing in a strange girl to care for that boy. Not after what he did to her daughter and husband.'

'Has she told you about her daughter?' Éilís asked.

'I know she died.'

Kate slowly shook her head. 'No, Mary Clifford. No. She did not die. She was swept. Taken. Carried away by the Good People. Oh, you're laughing at that, are you?'

Mary shook her head. The woman's breath was hot in her face.

'How well it is that you are not afraid,' Kate said. 'But you should be. If I were you, I would go on back home to Annamore.

No good will come of your work there, not in that house. Let you go on back to the widow and tell her that I know what that boy is, and that she ought to take remedies to banish him before someone does it for her.'

CHAPTER
FIVE

Alder

When **Nóra heard the knock** on her half-door she
thought it was Peg. 'Come in,' she cried, not looking
up from where she was dressing Micheál. She knotted
the cloth about the boy's hips, then, not hearing any movement,
looked up. At first she could not see the visitor – the sun outside
cast their face into shadow. But as the door creaked open a man
stepped inside, taking off a ragged felt hat, and her heart clutched
in recognition.

Tadgh.

Nóra stood, her breath suddenly sharp. Her son-in-law had
changed since she had last seen him, when he had arrived bearing his
starving son on the donkey. Tadgh had always been small and wiry,
but now he seemed shrunken. He had grown a beard, but it was
patchy and thin. He seemed untended.

Grief has withered him, she thought.

'I heard Martin died,' Tadgh said. 'I'm sorry for your troubles.'

'Tadgh. 'Tis good to see you.'

'Is it?' he asked.

'How have you been keeping?' Nóra showed him to the settle bed and sank down on a stool. She felt weak.

Tadgh shrugged. 'Times are hard,' he said simply. 'How is the boy?'

'Grand, so he is.'

Tadgh nodded absently, gazing about the room. ''Tis a fine place you have. I saw the cow. He has milk, then.'

'Micheál? He does. There's enough for him.' Nóra pointed to where the boy, now cleaned, lay on a clump of heather.

Tadgh stood and regarded him from a height. 'He's unchanged then,' he said suddenly. 'There's still that queer look to him. Is it illness, do you think?'

Nóra swallowed hard. She said nothing.

'When he stopped walking Johanna thought he was ill. She thought he had caught something off her.'

'Faith, 'tis nothing that time won't heal, so I think,' said Nóra, trying to maintain a steady voice.

Tadgh scratched his head, the sound of his fingernails loud against his scalp. He looked troubled. 'He was such a bonny child. Such a fair little babby.'

'So he is still, for all the difference.'

'He is not,' Tadgh said decisively. He stared at Nóra. 'For two years he was well. Then . . . I thought it might be the hunger, you know. I thought 'twas our doing. The place was so awful cold, and there wasn't a lot we could give him. I gave him all I . . .' His voice broke. Nóra could see that he was fighting to speak without emotion. 'I thought I'd done it,' he whispered finally, glassy-eyed.

'Tadgh,' Nóra breathed. 'Tadgh.'

'I thought he might be better here. That's what they said. That it was just want of milk and things to eat.'

'I'm taking good care of him, Tadgh. I have a girl in with me now.'

'But he's the same, isn't he?' He squatted beside Micheál and extended a hand out over the boy, waving it in his face. Micheál took no notice of it. 'Do you think 'tis his mind, like?'

Nóra said nothing.

'Johanna didn't think 'twas the cold. Or the hunger.'

'She thought it was the bug.'

Tadgh nodded. 'At first. She thought it had gone into his legs like it had gone into her head. Stopped him from walking, like. Just as it stopped her from . . .' He bit his lip and lowered himself to the ground, sitting cross-legged next to Micheál. 'My little man. Your da is here.'

Micheál arched his back and shot a thin arm out in an aimless punch.

'Look at him fighting.'

'He does that of a time. He can move.'

Tadgh gave a sad smile. 'But he is not walking.'

'I try, sometimes. I set him up with his feet on the ground. Hold him, like, with the wee soles of him on the clay. But he can't seem to put the weight of him down.'

They both looked at Micheál. He was staring at something on the ceiling, and as they looked up to see what had captured his attention, he let out a pitching squeal of laughter.

Tadgh smiled. 'A laugh for your da. Maybe he'll be talking next time.'

''Tis awful good to see you, Tadgh. You seem changed.'

Tadgh looked down at his hands, as if considering the black crescents of dirt under his fingernails. 'I have been meaning to come.'

'You have been busy.'

'No. There is no work.'

'You have been grieving, then.'

'I have been afraid to come, Nóra. I have been afraid of what I would see. 'Twas not until I heard that Martin had passed, Lord keep him, that I knew I needed to visit you.'

'Tadgh? You're scaring me, the talk of you.'

'I wasn't going to say a word about it, Nóra.' He looked at her with the darkling, lowered stare of a hunted man.

'Johanna. 'Twas in the last days. She was in the bed, and the cloud was on her mind, and she was fighting it best she could, but the pain was awful on her and it made her say some things.' He frowned. 'She said some awful things, Nóra.'

'What did she say?'

'I don't want to tell you.'

'Tadgh, tell me. For God's sake, you're frightening me.'

'One time, she was lying abed, her eyes closed. For all of me I thought she was sleeping. And then I hear a queer muttering coming from her, and I says, "Are you awake, Johanna? Is it the pain?" And she shook her head, slight, like this . . .' He turned his head slowly from side to side, his eyes never leaving Nóra's. 'And I says, "What is it?" And she says, "Bring me Micheál." So I pick the lad up and put him on the bed next to her, and she opened her eyes a wee bit and took a look at him, and a queer expression crosses her face. Like she's never seen him before in her life. "That's not my child," she says. She's looking at me, shaking her head. "That's not my child."'

Nóra's mouth was dry. She swallowed thickly.

'"Sure, 'tis," says I. "He's your own son, so he is. Do you not know your own son?" And she tries to sit up and looks at him again. "That's not my boy," she says. "Bring me my boy." Sure, I didn't know what to do, so I keep telling her 'tis Micheál, and her strange way of talking was scaring me that much that I put him on her lap, and that was it. She started screaming. "That's not my son! Bring me Micheál!" And she's pushing Micheál off the bed, and were I not there to catch him he would have had a tumble.' Tadgh was breathing heavily. 'I didn't know what to do, so I took Micheál away, out of her sight. But all that night long she was like it. "My son has been stolen from me. My boy has been stolen." She was clawing at me to go and get the police, raise a watch, like. She wanted to put Micheál out the house. "Get rid of it!" she was saying. "Put it on the dung pile and bring me back our son!"

'That was it then. That was the last of it, before she fell asleep. 'Twas the last thing she said to me. In the days after, she was not herself. She was halfway to God.'

Nóra stared at Tadgh, feeling like she would choke.

'I didn't want to tell you, Nóra,' Tadgh said, pressing his fingers into his temples. 'But I see him now, Micheál . . .'

Nóra looked down at the little boy. He was jerking his head, as if stabbed by something unseen.

'I see him now and I wonder. I wonder at what she said. I see him and I know he's my son, but I don't recognise him at all.'

'I know why.'

They turned to see Mary in the open doorway, her apron wet and dripping, clutching the pail of water to her chest. Her face was chalk-white.

'He is a changeling,' she whimpered. 'And everyone knows it but you.'

The dark unpainted forge of the blacksmith's sat in the heart of the valley, by the crossroads that divided the community into quarters. On most days the patterned ringing of hammer on anvil could be heard in all directions, and the constant smoke from the forge proved an easy marker for those who required ironwork, or sought to have their teeth pulled. At night, once the day's labour had been done, people often gathered at the blacksmith's, the forge becoming a rambling house for the men and the small cabin beside it one for the women. It was a place of frequent company. On nights when the moon gave a clean, clear light to the valley, it was not uncommon for the young people to step outside and dance at the crossroads above the buried bones of suicides, the very place Martin Leahy had died.

Nance did not often come to the blacksmith's. There was little she owned that needed the attention of pumping bellows and sweaty-faced men – she preferred the quiet skill of the travelling tinkers. It was also a place where she felt her difference. It was often busy with farmers and labourers bringing workhorses to be shod or to be treated for spavins or farcy, and, despite her years in the valley, Nance had never become accustomed to the way conversation stopped in her presence. It was one thing to enter a wake house and have the company fall into respectful silence. It was another to move through a crowded yard in the prickled air of others' wary regard and to hear laughter at her back. They made her feel like nothing more than a strange old woman plucking herbs, her eyes clouded with age and the smoke of her own badly fired hearth. No matter that some of these men came to her with their carbuncles and congested lungs, or lay their wheezing children by her fire. In the broad light of day, amidst the noise of industry, their stares made her feel scorned and feeble.

'God bless your work, John O'Donoghue,' Nance said, standing in the doorway. She had lingered on the road until she saw that the yard of the smith's was clear of people, then clenched her teeth and made for the forge.

John paused, his hammer raised in the air. 'Nance Roche,' he said simply. A local boy, charged with pumping the bellows, gaped in Nance's direction.

'I was wondering if you would let me take some of that water there. Your iron water.'

John put down his hammer and wiped his sweating face with a greasy, blackened cloth. 'Iron water,' he repeated. He stared at Nance, breathing hard. 'How much do you need?'

Nance pulled her water pail out from under her cloak. 'As much as I might carry.'

John took the pail and lowered it into the bucket where he cooled the iron. 'I've filled it to half. Will that do you?'

'It will. It will. I thank you, John. Bless you.'

John nodded, then returned to the anvil. As he raised his hammer he motioned towards the cabin. 'Go see the little woman, Nance. She'll give you something to eat.'

The cabin of the O'Donoghues was built from the same mountain rock as the forge, but was thickly whitewashed, its thatch of heather and oats rising high over a cavernous ceiling. Both half-doors were open to admit the light, and Nance could hear a woman's voice singing inside.

'Bless you, woman of the house.'

Áine O'Donoghue was kneeling in front of the turf fire, scrubbing a shirt in a wide wooden tub. She looked up, squinting. 'Nance Roche?' Her face eased into a smile. 'Come in and welcome. 'Tis not often I see you here.' She rose to her feet, wiping her wet forearms on her apron. 'What's that you have?'

'Only a little forge water, Áine. Your man was good enough to give me some.'

'Did he now. I suppose I shouldn't be asking what you want that for?' Áine gave a wry smile and patted the stool beside her. 'Sit you down. Would you like something to eat?'

'Go on with your washing, Áine. I don't mean to stop you.'

'Sure, 'twould be a poor thing if I did.' Áine picked up a cold potato and gave it to Nance. 'How are you keeping?'

'I'm still alive, which is enough.'

'Are you prepared for the winter? Isn't it awful bitter out? And not even December.'

'Pure bitter. I see you and John are well.'

'Well enough.'

Nance gestured to the bucket of forge water at her feet. 'Protection. I thought Brigid Lynch might be in need of it. Her time is coming.' She peeled the potato and glanced at Áine. The woman was looking intently at the puckered skin on her fingers, leaning forward with her elbows on her knees.

'Why don't you come see me?' Nance heard herself asking.

Áine feigned surprise. 'See you, Nance?'

'I can help you.'

Áine blushed. 'And for what? The mouth sore is gone from me now. You gave me the cure and I thank you for it.'

'I don't mean the sore.' Nance took a bite of the cold potato and chewed it thoughtfully. 'It can't be easy, seeing the women of this place full of children and you having none yourself.'

Áine gave a strange, wan smile. Her voice was soft. 'Oh, that. Sure, it can't be helped, Nance.'

'There are ways, Áine. For every ill thing set upon this world, there is a cure.'

Áine shook her head. '*An rud nach féidir ní féidir é.* What can't be done, can't be done. I have made my peace with it.'

'You poor unfortunate.' Nance dropped the rest of the potato in her lap and took Áine's hands. The woman smiled at her, but as Nance continued to hold her fingers Áine's face tightened and her chin trembled.

'Have you truly made your peace with it? With your quiet house?'

'Don't,' she whispered.

'Áine.'

'Please, Nance. You're a good woman. Don't be upsetting . . . Please.'

Nance pulled Áine closer to her, until their foreheads were almost touching. 'Children are the curse of this country,' she whispered, gripping Áine's hands. 'Especially when you don't have any.'

Áine laughed, but pulled away to hastily wipe her eyes.

'Come and see me,' Nance whispered. 'You know where I am.'

Shuffling back to her cabin, the narrow handle of her water pail cutting into her hand, Nance thought about what had come over her. She didn't normally like to pry into others' business. Maggie had always taught her to stay away until she was summoned.

'The cure will always work best for those who seek it,' she had said. 'Those who look are those who find.'

But in that moment Nance had felt a quiet summoning to speak to Áine. There was a hesitation. A look of raw longing. That's how it was with most people. All that private pain kept out of sight, but sometimes, in the space of one breath, something opened and you could see the heart of things before the door was shut again. It was as good as a vision. A murmur of vulnerability. A tremor in the soil, before all was still.

How hidden the heart, Nance thought. How frightened we are of being known, and yet how desperately we long for it.

Father Healy was waiting for Nance outside her cabin, his stark figure cutting a black line against the rising alder. He stood still, watching her walk the path with his arms folded in front of him, and then, noticing the heavy pail she carried, stepped forward and took it from her.

'Thank you, Father.'

They walked in silence to the muddy ground before Nance's cabin, where he set the pail of forge water down and faced her.

''Tis Nance Roche they call you?'

''Tis.'

'I want time with you, then.'

'Time with me, is it, Father? What an honour.' Nance bent her aching fingers back. 'And how can I help you?'

'Help me?' He shook his head. 'I've come to tell you to help your-self, woman. I've come to tell you to stop your ways.'

'My ways, now. What ways would they be?' Nance put her hands on her hips and tried to catch her breath. Her chest felt dry and tight from lugging the water across the valley. All she wanted to do was return inside and rest.

'Word has travelled that you were keening at Martin Leahy's wake.'

Nance frowned. 'So I was. And what of it?'

'The synod forbids professional keeners wailing at wakes as an unchristian practice. It is a heathenish custom and abhorrent to God.'

'Abhorrent to God? I find it hard to believe, Father, that God does not understand sorrow. Sure, Christ died on a cross surrounded by his keeners.'

Father Healy gave a tight smile. ''Tis not the same at all. I have been told that you make it your *trade* to cry at burials.'

'What is the harm in that?'

'Your sorrow is artificial, Nance. Rather than comfort those who are afflicted, you live upon their dead.'

Nance shook her head. 'I do not, Father. That's not it at all. I feel their sorrow. I give voice to the grief of others when they have not a voice for it themselves.'

'But they pay you for it.'

''Tis not money.'

'Food then. Drink. Payment in kind for immoderate, false sad-ness.' The man gave a sad laugh. 'Nance, listen to me now. You can't be taking money – or anything like it – for keening. The church won't stand for it, and neither will I.' He raised an eyebrow. 'When I heard about the keening I asked about you.'

'Is that so, Father?'

'People tell me that you drink. You take the pipe. You don't come to Mass.'

Nance laughed. 'If you're after visiting all them that don't go to Mass, you'll be out on that donkey of yours the whole week long.'

Father Healy pinked a little. 'Yes. I mean to correct the lack of religious feeling here.'

'But the people here do be having a spiritual temper, Father. Sure, we all have faith in the things of the invisible world. We're a most religious people. Come now, Father. Would you not care for a drink? Look, the sky is turning.'

The priest hesitated, and then followed Nance into her cabin, glancing around the dark room in uncertainty.

'Be so kind as to sit yourself down on that creepie there. Make yourself easy. I'll have the water on the boil now.'

Father Healy lowered himself down on the stool, his knees sticking out at angles. He gestured to the dried herbs hanging from the rafters. 'William O'Hare tells me that you act the charlatan.'

'The schoolmaster? What would he know? He's never visited me in his life.'

'Aye, him. He says you live by keening and quackery. That you lure the people of this parish with false promises of healing.'

'Some folk here . . . Well, we don't agree together.'

'So, 'tis not just the money-taking for the false bawling, but you act the *bean leighis* too?'

'Act?' Nance handed the priest a steaming cup. He regarded it with suspicion. 'Father. People come to me of their own accord and

I use the knowledge that has been given me to help them. They leave me gifts in thanks for it. I am no thief.'

'Well, now, see, this puts me in some state of confusion!' The priest ran a hand through his hair. 'For Seán Lynch tells me you prey on the trust of others and try to get something for nothing.'

Nance sucked her gums. 'I help them. I am a doctor to them.'

'Oh yes, so I have heard. Like the Dublin doctors, so you are. O'Hare said that you forced a gander's beak down his wife's throat when she came to you for thrush.'

'Ah, Éilís? 'Tis an old cure. Did it not heal her?'

'William did not say.'

'It healed her alright. Éilís O'Hare might be thinking she's above herself now, married to a Killarney man. But she's a liar if she says I never healed her. That woman would be in the ground if it weren't for me.'

'No one dies of thrush.'

'I healed her all the same.'

The priest peered at his tea and put it firmly on the ground. 'Can you not see that I am trying to help you?'

Nance smiled. 'I respect you, Father. Sure, you're a good and holy man with a heart for the people. But you should know that Father O'Reilly, God rest him, saw I had the gift. He sent folk to me. Drink your tea.'

'I won't, if 'tis all the same to you.' The priest looked up again at the herbs. 'I know the likes of you. I know the poor turn their hand to whatever living they can make. The vulnerable.' His voice dropped to a whisper. 'There's still a need in this parish for the . . .' He looked uncomfortable. '*Handy woman.* For the mothers. Give up the keening and the herbs and charms and all the pagan superstitions, and make an honest living by that.'

Nance sighed. 'Father, as little as the wren needs, it must

gather it. 'Tis by the cures and keening or my heart would break in hunger, but 'tis more than that. I have the *knowledge* given to me by the Good People and I must use it for the people here or 'twould leave me.'

There was a moment of silence. The jackdaws disturbed the trees outside.

''Tis not the fairies you're talking of. No, I won't have that.'

'Do you not believe in the Good People, Father?'

The priest rose to his feet. 'Nance Roche. I take no pleasure in being here. I take no pleasure in harsh words. But do you think of your stomach or your soul?'

'Ah, you're no believer. But I tell you, Father, 'twas the Good People that led me out of my misery on the roads and led me to this valley and to Father O'Reilly. 'Twas the Good People who saw me safe and not starving in Killarney when my family were gone and I alone with no man or money to my name. 'Twas Them that gave me the knowledge to cure folk and bring the fairy dart out of them and –'

''Tis pagan to say they exist at all.' The priest's face suddenly took on a look of pity, and Nance felt a wave of anger at the condescension in his expression.

'Well, God be praised. A priest who is against the curing of the sick. God knows 'tis hard I work for the bit I have, and 'tis poor I am and always have been, but never have I begged from any Christian in this valley, and haven't I always meant well? And haven't I cured the priest before you, and him always seeing the good in all?'

Father Healy shook his head. 'And to the bad he turned his eye. You know what they say, woman? The road to Hell is paved with good intentions.'

'And the road to Heaven is well signposted, Father . . .' Nance smiled. 'But badly lit at night.'

The priest snorted. 'I'll not have keening, and I'll not have women seeking to swindle the sick with talk of fairies. By all means, be a handy woman to those in need, but I'll not have this parish riddled with superstition by those who mean to profit by it.'

'Oh, you're a wonderful great man, taking our money and counting out sins in exchange, and not letting an honest woman have her bit in return for all the good she does.'

'I've tried to do right by you, Nance Roche. I came here to lead you to the better path. But if 'tis stubborn you are, I would see you leave this place.'

'The people would not let you drive me out. They need me. You will see that they need me.'

'Well, now. I don't think it will go well with you, Nance Roche, despite what you think.' The priest ducked his head under the cabin door and strode to his donkey, which was grazing beside the woods. Nance followed, watching as he mounted and gave it a hearty kick with his heels. He looked back at her as he rode towards the lane. 'Go on, Nance. Stop it with the keening and the fairy talk. You want a long spoon when supping with the Devil.'

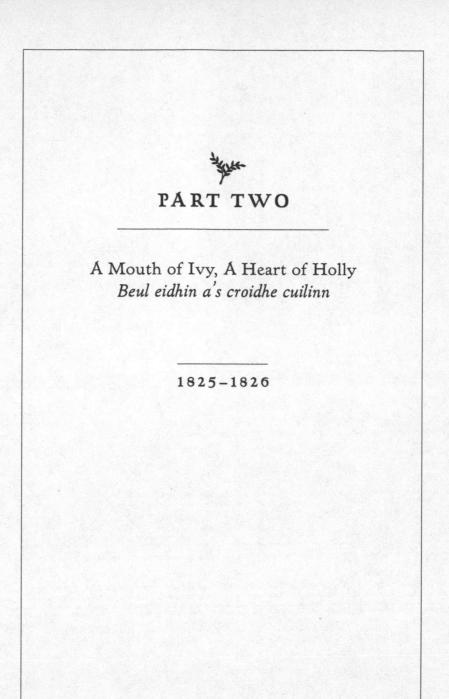

PART TWO

A Mouth of Ivy, A Heart of Holly
Beul eidhin a's croidhe cuilinn

1825–1826

CHAPTER
SIX

Nettle

December arrived and bled the days of sunlight, while the nights grew bitter, wind-rattled. The water that pooled outside beneath the doorstep was tight with ice by morning and starlings lit upon the thatched roofs of the valley, circling the smoking chimney holes for warmth.

Micheál became restless in the cold. When the heat of the fire died away at night and the chill crawled into the room, he woke Mary with whimpers, arms jerking, fingernails sharp in her back like a kitten fighting a sack and a swift-flowing river.

Anxious to warm him, Mary wrapped him in their blanket, pressed his pointed chin to her shoulder and, sitting up, lumbered his shivering bones against her chest until he surrendered to fatigue. Sometimes she traced his eyebrows and the delicate skin of his eyelids with a gentle fingertip to encourage him to close his eyes, or opened the front of her clothes to place his cheek on the bare skin of her neck and re-assure him with her warmth. She fell asleep with him upon her chest, slumped against the wooden corner of the settle, and would wake in the grey of morning with a stiff neck and her legs dead and unfeeling.

She had never felt so tired. Mary had thought that the winter days, with their lull in labour and their quiet, unfriendly weather, would be easeful after her term of working through harvest. Those days had been unceasing. She had fetched and flailed and stooped until she felt she would die, until she was spangled with chaff and her hands bled from handling flax. But the child exhausted her in a different way. He tortured her with constant, shrill needfulness. Sometimes it seemed that he screamed his throat raw and no amount of soothing would quiet him. She fed him and he ate like the starved, swallowing thick mouthfuls of potato mixed with milk, and yet he was as thin as winter air. He would not let her sleep the night through. Mary woke every morning with her body aching to rest, her limbs cramping from long hours of holding the boy close to her, her eyes as raw as if someone had tried to pluck them from their sockets. She would stumble in the half-light to uncover the embers from their blanket of ash and set water to boil, before lurching into the shocking blue of the yard, the air so cold it seized her lungs.

Her one moment of peace each morning was in the cramped, shit-stained byre, when she was able to lean her forehead against the dusty comfort of the cow and milk her, singing old songs to calm herself and the animal. Sometimes she cried from weariness, without caring. She pressed her face into the cow's belly and felt her eyes grow hot with tears, and as her fingers encouraged the teats, she let her song give way to sobs. The milk hardly came, no matter the sound from her.

Ever since the visit from the widow's son-in-law, Nóra had withdrawn into herself. Mary knew she had spoken out of turn, had let the fear of being cornered by the women at the well have the run of her mouth. As soon as she had spoken in the doorway she had flinched at her own accusation. She had thought she would be sent back to Annamore with empty pockets. But Nóra had simply looked at her with the preoccupied, inward stare of someone who is told there is a ghost in the room. The man, Tadgh, had reacted even more strangely. He had gazed at Mary with curiosity, then reached out and touched her hair, stroking the cropped ends between his fingers as though she was an angel and he could not decide whether to kiss or fight her. Then, just as quickly, he had recoiled. 'May the Good Lord protect you,' he had said to her before stepping out into the pale afternoon and stumbling down the lane, a hand over his mouth. He had not looked back and they had not seen him since.

Nóra, Mary noticed, had watched this without feeling. After Tadgh left, she had sat still and breathed deeply and steadily, as if asleep. Then she had beckoned Mary to the fire. 'Sit down.' When Mary had hesitated, Nóra's voice became edged with impatience. 'Sit down.'

As Mary sat on the creaking straw-seat, Nóra had fossicked in the nook of the hearth. Mary heard the squeak of a cork being pulled from a bottle, and when Nóra brought her forearm to the wall to hide her face, Mary had guessed she was drinking.

'People are calling Micheál a changeling, are they?' She turned and her eyes were bleary.

'They were speaking of him as changeling at the well.'

Nóra had begun to laugh in a wild panic, like a woman who finds a lost child and is split by anger and relief. Mary watched as Nóra bent over, shaking, tears spilling from her eyes. Micheál, attracted by the noise, had squealed, mouth wide. His shrieks brought her flesh out in goosebumps.

It was all too strange. The sight of Nóra laughing when there was nothing but dread, heavy and rolling in her stomach, made Mary's heart thud. She had been brought into a home where everything was on the point of collapse, where ill fortune and sorrow had eaten into the timber of this woman and she was breaking down in front of her.

Unsettled, Mary had wrapped her shawl about her head and had gone out to sit in the byre.

Mary had stayed beside the comforting warmth of the cow until the day faltered and she could hear the wind whistling through the stone wall. She wished that she could leave the widow to her mad laughter, and walk the rocky road back to Annamore that night. Were it not for the thought of her empty-bellied brothers and sisters, and the weariness pulling at the corners of her mother's mouth, she would have walked the whole night long to return home.

When she went back inside, Nóra had acted as though nothing had happened. She asked Mary to begin preparing their dinner and had sat with her knitting, fingers plying the needles furiously. Only once did she raise her head and address Mary, her face inscrutable. '*Briseann an dúchas trí chrúba an chait*. The true nature of the cat shows in the way it uses its claws.'

'Yes, missus,' Mary had replied. She had not known what the woman meant by the proverb, but it seemed ominous and had not comforted her.

Since then, neither of them had spoken of Tadgh's visit, nor the gossip at the well, nor what had happened after, although Mary thought that Nóra was not as attentive to Micheál as before. More and more it fell to her to bathe and feed him and to rise in the night to console him from the unseen terrors plaguing his soft, mysterious mind. Mary became used to the shadows that emerged in the ill-lit witching hours. She woke and tended the child like a mourner over a corpse.

One night, rasping awake at Micheál's scraping cry, Mary wriggled away from his grasping arms and buried her head under the rag-pillow, too tired to sit and warm him or rub the soles of his feet. She fell back into the blissful arm of sleep, until the smell of sour piss roused her and she woke to soaked hay, the boy wet-backed and freezing beside her, screaming like the murdered.

It had become cold in Nance's *bothán*. In the late autumn days she had spent many hours gathering what fuel for her fire she could find, cutting the prickled gorse from the mountain slopes and wild land with a black-handled knife and taking what dung had not already been gathered from the fields by the children. Some of the valley folk had brought her small baskets of turf in exchange for her cures, but she knew those few, precious scraws would not be enough to last her the winter. The cold would stalk her, threaten her, if she did not find some way to keep her fire alive through the months of biting wind. Always, the need to find ways to survive. No lingering children to take care of her. No parent living to help. Every year, this battle to keep on. Every year the fight to remain. It wearied her.

When did I become so old? Nance wondered as she huddled over her fire. My bones are becoming as fluted and hollow as the skeletons of birds.

How slippery time had become. When she was younger the days had seemed unceasing. The world had felt infinitely full of wonder.

Yet the more she aged, the more the mountains shrank against the sky. Even the river seemed colder than when she first arrived in the valley, those twenty years ago. Seasons came and went with staggering swiftness.

Nance remembered the woods of Mangerton when she was small. Walking through them with her cans of goat milk and *poitín* for the tourists, and the hard, clinking purse she brought back to the grateful hand of her father, she had felt that she was a child of the trees. The moss on the forest floor comforted her bare feet, and she had felt protected by the canopy of leaves, had felt the wind to be a voice that rushed through her hair for no other purpose than to speak to her alone. How well she had known God, then. How unknotted her soul. How easy to be.

Nance remembered walking the mountain, plucking snagged wool from the thorns of briars and gorse, waiting for ponies carrying tourists on their way to the Devil's Punch Bowl, only to be overwhelmed by the beauty of the sun lighting on the water of the lakes. Lough Leane golden, and the surrounding mountains bearing down in holy indigo. The shifting, unfurling clouds passing the sun like pilgrims past a saint. Nance remembered walking, only to be winded by the grace of the world.

'Why are you crying?' her father had asked her once, caulking his boat on the shore of the lough.

How old had she been? The summer before Maggie came with her herbs and visitors and mysterious ways of being. A child still. A bud unblossomed. A lifetime ago.

'Nance? Why are you crying?'

'Because everything is too beautiful.'

Her father had understood the profundity of her love. 'Nature is at her best in the morning and the evening. Sure, 'tis no bad thing to cry over. Most people go through their days without ever acknowledging her.'

Perhaps it was then that he began to teach her the language of the sky with his boatman's eye for weather. Before the slow disappearing of her mother, before Maggie came, when they were all together and they were whole and well.

'The world isn't ours,' he said once. 'It belongs to itself, and that is why it is beautiful.'

It was her father who had showed her the high mackerel clouds that brought rain and fish, and the deceitful emptiness of summer days which hid the sign of storms at night. The sky, he taught her, could be an ally, a messenger of warning. When it brought them the wheeling screams of seagulls, they knew not to stray too far from shore or cabin.

Sometimes, before the gentle-blooded tourists flocked to spend their money on the strawberry girls like Nance and boatmen like her father, and jarveys to the crumbling Muckross Abbey with its towering heart of yew, or when her mother had suffered through another terrible night, her father took her out onto the lakes and bid her look up.

'Can you see the clouds there, Nance?'

Nance remembered lifting her face to the sky, squinting against early sun.

'What do you make of them? Are they not like a goat's beard? A combed goat's beard?'

Even now, she could almost smell the clay and water.

'Do you see where the beard turns black, there?' He would haul an oar into the boat and raise his arm. 'That's where the wind'll be coming from today. Faith, a strong wind. And that black tip of his beard is full of rain. What do you think we're after doing with a beard such as that in the sky?'

'I think we should be going home.'

'That goat will bring us no good. No gentlemen and their ladies today. Let's get back to your mam.'

He had loved the lakes, her father. And the sea. Raised near Corca Dhuibhne, he had spoken of the ocean as some men speak of their mothers – with reverence and a great, choking love. 'When good weather is on its way, the sea will make a sweet and quiet sound. The sea will be settled and calm and you may trust in her. But gannets in the harbour in early morning and you know she's warning you to leave her alone. The cormorant on his rock shows you the wind and, depending on where he is facing to, where it is likely to come from.

'Most people don't see the world. But you've got the eye, I think, Nance. You've got the eye.'

There was a cough at the door and Nance started. The fire had gone out and there was a man standing on her threshold. She had not heard him approach.

'Who's there?' Nance croaked, bringing her palms to her cheeks. They were wet. Had she been crying?

''Tis Daniel Lynch, Nance.' He sounded nervous. 'I've come to see you about my wife, Brigid.'

Nance peered in the low light and saw the young man who had been smoking at the wake of Martin Leahy.

'Brought you a hen,' he said, nodding to the struggling chicken he held pinned under his arm. 'She's stopped laying, but I thought it might be good for your pot. I didn't know . . .'

'That's kind.' Nance beckoned him in with a trembling finger. 'Come in, son, come in and God welcome.'

Daniel ducked his head under the door and Nance noticed him take in the small cabin with its tethered goat, the drain of waste and the dead fire in front of her. He pulled the chicken out from under his arm and offered it to Nance, holding it by its legs. The bird flapped, sending the bunches of herbs swaying on their strings.

'Set her on the floor, there, good man. She can stretch her legs. Grand so.' Nance prodded at the fire and blew on the embers. 'Would you pass me some of that dried furze? Ah, I thank you. So, you've come about your young wife, your Brigid. The one with child. Is she in good health?' Nance nudged a stool towards Daniel and he sat down.

'She is. Only . . .' He let out a short laugh, embarrassed. 'I don't really know why I'm here. 'Tis nothing, only the little woman's taken to walking at night. In her sleep.' He watched the hen jump the drain and begin to scratch in the hay.

'Walking at night, is she? Not a thing for a woman in her state to be doing. Will you have a drink?' Nance reached for an empty piggin and poured out a liquid, tinctured yellow, from a pot near the fire.

Daniel regarded the cup with a frown. 'What's this, then?'

''Tis a cold tea. 'Twill calm you.'

'Oh, I don't have a need for calming,' Daniel said, but he took a tentative sip. 'It tastes like weeds.'

'Go on, Daniel. Tell me about your Brigid.'

'I don't like to make a fuss, only, begod, 'tis a strange thing she's doing and I have no wish for people to talk of it.'

'You say she's walking in her sleep.'

He nodded. 'A few evenings back I woke in the night and she wasn't to be seen. Her side of the bed was cold empty. My brother sleeps by the fire and we have the wee room to ourselves. Well, I woke up and thought to myself, "She's maybe after getting a sip of water," and so I waited. But a good time crept past and there was no sign of her. I went out and there's my brother, sound asleep, except the door is wide open and there's a fierce cold coming in. I look for Brigid's cloak and 'tis there, where she normally sets it on the rafter, but her shawl is missing. Well, I was frightened for her then. I didn't know if someone had taken her, or what. You hear stories . . .' His voice broke off and he took another sip of tea. 'I woke my brother and asked him had he seen her and he hadn't. So we set out to look for her and thank God for the bright moon! After a time we find her shawl lying on the ground and perhaps we walk on for another mile, and I see a flash of white, and . . .' Daniel frowned, pulling at his lip. 'Well, 'twas her. Lying down, asleep.'

'She was safe, then.'

'That's why I thought to come see you, Nance. She wasn't just lying any place. She was asleep in the *cillín*. Near the fairy *ráth*. Hardly a stone's throw from where we're sitting now.'

Nance felt the hair on the back of her neck stand up. The *cillín* was a small triangle of land next to the fairies' whitethorn. The grass grew long there, around a standing stone guarded by a ragged copse of holly trees. The thin slab of rock stood perpendicular to the soil like a tombstone, the vestige of an etched cross upon its surface. Surrounding it, like stars without pattern, were white stones marking where clusters of limbo-bones lay in the soil. Sometimes the people of the valley buried unwed mothers there, and sometimes those who had died in sin. But mostly the *cillín* was for children. Stillborns. It was not a place people visited unless they had an unchristened baby to bury.

'The *cillín*?'

Daniel rubbed at the stubble on his chin. 'You see now why I've come? She was lying there amongst the stones. Amongst all the poor dead, buried babies. I thought she was dead herself until I shook her awake. I've heard of folk that do be wandering in their sleep. But to a *cillín*?'

'Who knows of this?'

'Not a soul besides my brother, David, and myself. And I made him swear to keep it quiet. 'Tis the kind of thing to get tongues moving faster than a middleman to tithe day. Especially with all the goings-on in this place.'

'Tell me. What goings-on?'

Daniel grimaced. 'I don't know, Nance. There's just an uneasy feeling about the place. Cows are not giving the milk they once did.' He pointed at the chicken fussing in the straw. 'Hens have stopped laying. Folk are still talking of the way Martin Leahy died. A fit man in the full of his health, dying at a crossroads? People are saying 'tis unnatural. Some are getting on with nonsense about the evil eye. Saying he was blinked, like. Others keep talking about a *changeling* child. A changeling, like! We all know Nóra Leahy has a boy in with her. When her daughter died, the son-in-law came with a child in a basket. We saw him in the fields. But when no one saw the boy afterwards, we thought perhaps he was sick. Ailing, like. But Brigid has seen him. And she told me that there's something woeful wrong with him. Woeful wrong.'

Nance remembered the cripple Peter had spoken of. 'Not a sick child, then.'

'Sure, he's got no health about him, but it seems to be more than that. Brigid says the boy is a wee raw thing, all bones and no sense in his head. Not like any child she's seen before.'

'Have you seen him yourself?'

'Me? I've not seen him, no. But I'm thinking that perhaps . . . Perhaps if that boy has been touched by the Good People, then they're after touching others. Or maybe he has the evil eye and he blinked Martin Leahy, and now he's after blinking my wife.' Daniel pressed his thumbs to his temples. 'Holy Jesus, I don't know, Nance.'

Nance nodded. 'I think it best to keep this to yourself, Daniel. People here have enough troubles without finding cause for fear in things they do not understand.'

'Would explain it if the boy was changeling, though. The more I think of it, the more I wonder whether the Good People are abroad, and if they're after sweeping folk for themselves. Only, you hear the stories, about the women who are carrying. About them disappearing into ringforts.' He leant closer. 'I remember the stories. The old folk still tell them. The Good People have a need of women who are carrying, to take the human child for their own, and keep the woman to feed theirs . . .' He took a deep breath. 'Begod, I know there's plenty that laugh at those who believe every wind they meet with is a *sigh-gaoithe*. But I thought you might know, Nance. People say you go with Them. That they gave you knowledge and the eye to see Them.'

Nance dragged more furze onto the fire and the flames leapt up, casting wild light across their faces. 'How was your Brigid when she woke?'

'Her face was all white and washy when she saw where she was. She had no memory of walking out the cabin, nor down the lane.'

'And has she walked in her sleep before?'

'She hasn't. Well, not that she can remember, and not since she's been my wife.'

Nance cast him a sharp look. 'And is all well between ye? Are you great with each other? There's no reason for your wife to be wanting to go with the fairies, now?'

'Not on my life.'

'Naught to flee from, then. Well now, Daniel. Sure, 'tis a dangerous time for a woman when she's carrying. 'Tis a time of interference. Your wife is on a threshold and can be pulled back and forth. Either into the world we know, or the one that we don't. And 'tis true, what you say about the Good People. They are much given to taking young women. I've never known a woman to be swept into the fairy *ráth* by here, but 'tis not to say they won't or haven't.'

'They say 'twas the fate of Johanna Leahy by Macroom. That 'twas not to God she went, but to the fairy fort by there. That when she saw they'd changed her own son for fairy, she let them sweep her to be with her boy.'

Nance leant closer, her face growing flushed in the rising heat of the fire. 'The Good People are cunning when they are not merry. They do what pleases them because they serve neither God nor Devil, and no one can assure them of a place in Heaven or Hell. Not good enough to be saved, and not bad enough to be lost.'

'Are you saying that the Good People are abroad, then?'

'They have always been here. They are as old as the sea.'

Daniel had grown ashen. His blue eyes stared at hers in the firelight.

'Have you ever gone walking at the changing hours by the woods or in the lonesome places and felt Them watching you? Not so wicked as a man waiting to beat you, but not so gentle as a mother watching her children sleep.'

Daniel swallowed. 'I believe it. I do. I am not such a fool to say that there is no more to this world than what I can see with my own two eyes.'

Nance nodded approvingly. 'The Good People watch us with a kind of knowing that can undo a man. Make him want to turn heel. Sometimes they wish to reward him, and he finds he has fairy skill with the pipe, or that his sick cow is well again, and there's no accounting for it. But sometimes they punish those who speak ill against them. Sometimes they repay good with good. Bad with bad. Sometimes 'tis all unreason and no knowing why things are as they are, except to say 'tis the fairies behind it and they have their own intentions.'

'And so why are they after taking Brigid? What has she done to the Good People that they might like to steal her away?' He paused for a moment. 'Do you think 'tis something *I* have done?'

'Daniel, your Brigid is a dear one. There's no use in you believing she has some hand in this, or that she's astray. There's no fault on her. When They are here, watching us, they know the human of us and an envy comes upon them and there are some who will have of our kin, of our blood. I have seen them sweep a woman in front of my eyes.'

'Sweet Christ. 'Tis as folk are saying. There's some awful mischief about and 'tis the Good People behind it.' Daniel's face was pale. 'What must I do?'

'Is your Brigid changed at all? Does she eat? Is she injured in any way?'

'She eats. She was frightened to wake and see that she was sleeping in the *cillín* and her feet were bloodied from hard walking, but she is not changed.'

Nance leant back, satisfied. 'She was not abducted, then. She is still your wife.'

'Begod, what is happening in this valley, Nance? Moves my bones to powder. The priest said 'tis no reason for the cows and hens and Martin but the will of God, and all will be well, but he's a man from town.'

Nance spat on the ground. 'Perhaps someone has offended Them.'

'There is talk that one of Them is amongst us.'

'Aye, that boy your Brigid speaks of. With Nóra Leahy.'

Daniel looked at the floor. 'Or another,' he mumbled.

Nance gave Daniel a hard look. 'Do you know something? Has that Seán Lynch been swinging his axe at whitethorns again?'

'He has not. He'll have no talk of the Good People, and he spends his nights on ramble driving us all to tears with his talk of Father Healy and Daniel O'Connell. The priest has been in his ear about the Catholic Association. A penny a month and O'Connell will have us all emancipated, so says Seán. We all think he's on the drink and bouncing the boot off his wife again, but he has not been interfering with the fairy trees.'

'That one has trouble coming to him,' Nance said. 'Cheating the Devil in the dark, so he is.'

Daniel picked up his tea and drank it, avoiding her gaze. 'He has the hard word against you, Nance.'

'Oh. There's plenty that have the hard word against me. But I know what I know.' She lifted her hands in front of Daniel's face and he flinched, leaning away from the reach of her fingers. 'What do you see?'

He gaped at her.

'My thumbs. Do you see how they're turned?' She showed him her swollen knuckles, the crooked angle of her joints.

'I do.'

''Tis Their mark on me. 'Tis how you may know that whatever
Seán Lynch and Father Healy say about me, I have the knowledge
of Them and there is no lie in it. Whatever lies they tell about me,
there is no lie in this.' She fixed him with a kindly look. 'Do you
trust me?'

'Aye, Nance. I believe you.'

'Then let me tell you that all will be well if you do as I say. Your
wife must rest until her time comes. She is to get what sleep she can
and she's not to walk at all. Is she still up and about the house?'

'She is.'

'No more. You must do all the chores, Daniel. Churn the butter.
Feed her hens. Cook your praties. No fire must be taken out of the
house when she's in it. Not even the flare of your pipe. Not even a
spark. Do you understand?'

'I do.'

'Not a single flame nor ember, Daniel, or you'll be taking the luck
out of the house. You'd be breaking all that which serves to protect
her and keep her in the world. And give her these.' Nance shuffled
to the corner of her cabin and fetched a parcel of cloth tightly bound
with straw. She unknotted the ties and shook some dried berries into
Daniel's palm.

He peered at them nervously. 'What are these?'

'Bittersweet. They will urge her into a deeper sleep. So deep she
will not have the strength or wherewithal to rise at night. Let her take
them in the evening and I will hold the charm for her in my mind,
and I will think on protection for her.' She patted his arm. 'All will
be well, Daniel.'

'I thank you, Nance.'

'God bless you, and may you have a fine, long family. Come
back if she keeps at her walking. Wait . . .' Nance put a hand on
Daniel's arm. 'There is something else you may do. If 'tis the Good

People that are luring her out of doors, let you make a cross from birch twigs and nail it over your sleeping place. Birch will guard her.'

He hesitated by the door. 'You're a good woman, Nance. I know Father Healy preached against you, but I think he's a blind-hearted man.'

'Do you feel better, Daniel?'

'I do.'

Nance watched Daniel begin the slow walk home, holding the berries safe between his hands like a man in prayer. The sky soared with late-afternoon light, hemming the clouds with bright bloodi-ness. Just before he disappeared from view, Daniel turned around and stared at her, crossing himself.

The first snow arrived in the valley. Staggered winds blew white upon the fields until, from the height of Nóra's cabin, the stone walls dividing them looked like the whorls of a fingerprint. Men planted themselves by the fire, coughing up the season, and the women carded wool and kept company with their spinning wheels, as though compelled to wrap themselves and their families in more layers of homespun. It was a quiet, waiting time of year.

Nóra woke in the grey throat of morning and blinked in the feeble light. She longed to sleep. The nights were shattered with the boy's screaming, and it was all she could do to hang on to the balm of sleep's senselessness. How lonely waking in an empty bed had become.

Her head throbbed from the *poitín* bottle. Lying on her back, Nóra stared up into the thatch and listened for some sign that Mary was awake. Most mornings she waited until she heard the scuff of the girl's footsteps as she readied the fire and set water to boil, or her voice murmuring to the child as she bathed the piss from his legs. Then, Nóra would close her eyes and imagine that it was not Mary but Martin moving about the room, unlatching the door and letting the hens out to scrounge along the wall of the byre amidst the frost and dirty straw. She could picture him perfectly. His lips as he whistled the old songs, his nail pulling away the skins of his morning potatoes, and the careless way he threw them aside. She could hear his usual wry complaint that her hens were tearing into the thatch, and remembered the crinkle of his eyes when she, flustered, defended them. She allowed herself this lie, even when the disappointment on seeing not Martin but the long-limbed maid, puffy-eyed, by the fire was almost too painful to bear.

Nóra could hear nothing. Tying her shawl tightly around her, she went out and saw that the fire had been lit, although there was no sign of Mary. The settle was unfolded and Micheál lay in its corner. Not wanting to rouse his attention, Nóra crept slowly to the side of the bed before peering at him. The boy was listless, his hair sticking to his head with sweat. Nóra watched his mouth slowly undulate, his lips pert and softly wet. Who is he talking to? she wondered.

'Micheál.'

He ignored her, raising his eyebrows and grimacing at the wall.

'Micheál,' Nóra repeated. The boy's arms were stiff and turned inwards, like the broken wings of a bird pitched from the nest. She called his name for the third time and he finally fixed her with an unblinking stare. His lip curled and she could see the glisten of his teeth. For a moment he seemed to bare them at her.

Micheál had begun to scare her. Everything he did – his quick, unpredictable movements, his calls and shrieks at things she could not see – reminded her of Mary's words.

He is a changeling. And everyone knows it but you.

'What are you?' Nóra whispered.

Micheál looked up to the rafters and blinked. His chin was flaked with a tidemark of dried saliva. He was snot-nosed, his eyes fringed with pale lashes, slick with moisture. Nóra placed a firm hand on his forehead. She could see his jaw grind under his skin.

'Are you child or changeling?' Nóra whispered. She felt her throat jump with the pulse of her panicked heart.

Micheál closed his eyes and let out a pealing, wet shriek, bucking his spine against the straw bedding. Before Nóra could snatch her hand away, Micheál reached up and grabbed a fistful of her loose hair. She tried to uncurl his fingers but he jerked his arm backwards and the pain came, hot and searing.

'Micheál!'

Nóra winced and tried to twist herself free, but the boy's small, sticky fingers were knotted in her hair. He pulled harder. Tears sprang to her eyes.

'Let me go. Let me go, you bold cratur!' Hair ripped from her skin, and in the sudden glare of pain she lashed out and tried to slap Micheál across the face. The angle was awkward and she missed him, cuffing the top of his head instead. In her anger she released his fingers and, holding his jaw firmly with one hand, slapped him again with the other, hitting his cheek. Her palm stung.

'The badness in you!' she shouted, slapping him again. His face was pink, his mouth wide and bawling. Nóra wanted to stuff it shut. Wanted to push his soiled linen in his mouth to stop up his screams. 'You wicked thing,' she hissed, holding her smarting scalp.

'He can't help himself.'

Nóra turned and saw Mary standing by the door, the milk bucket resting on her hip.

'He was pulling the hair out of my skull!'

Mary closed the door against the white brilliance of snow. 'Are you alright?'

'I can't sleep for him! He screams all night.' Nóra could hear the hysteria in her voice.

The maid nodded. 'I think 'tis the cold. And he has a rash on his back. From the way he soils himself.'

Nóra sat by the fire, her hand against her throbbing skin. 'You could wash him, you know.'

'I do,' Mary protested, and her voice was so thin that Nóra felt ashamed.

'Well. How is Brownie milking?'

''Tis not a lot, missus. You said she's a good milker, but . . . I've been singing to her because I know they like the singing. But she's going to the dry.'

Nóra closed her eyes. 'The way we're going, we'll be short for rent.'

'Shall I churn today?'

'Is there enough?'

Mary lifted a corner of the cloth covering the crock of settled milk on the table. 'Sure, well. There might be just enough to churn. Just enough. Should I give Micheál the buttermilk? It might soothe him. I don't know whether 'tis the bitter cold or perhaps he's dreaming things that wake him so and lead him to screaming. I can't sleep for his screaming either.'

'Well, the road to Annamore is where you left it.'

'I don't mean that,' Mary said, anxious. 'Not that I want to go home, like. Only there seems to be a change coming over him and I don't know how to keep the peace in him. He's suffering, I think.'

'Have they been telling you this at the well?'

'They've not, no,' Mary protested. 'The women there have not been talking to me at all. I go and fetch the water and come back again, and I don't stop to gossip or talk about you or Micheál. I promise you.'

Nóra realised that the maid was near tears.

'One of the women sees me coming down the road and takes three steps backwards. On account of my red hair. Kate. Kate Lynch.'

'She's got an awful fear of the evil eye. Don't you mind her. She'll cross herself when meeting with anything in the road. Hare, weasel, magpie.'

'She spits on the ground and says, "The Cross of Christ between me and harm!"'

Nóra rolled her eyes. 'Kate'll be crossing herself at me soon, in fear of a widow's curse.'

Micheál took a shuddering breath and began to scream louder. 'Look at the legs of him,' Mary said, pointing. 'He's hardly kicking. Do you not think they look broken? Like he's no feeling in them at all.' She bent down to the crying boy and lifted his dress to show Nóra. 'Look.'

Micheál's legs were as thin as the winter-bare striplings outside. His skin clung to the bone, streaked with marks. Nóra felt sick at the sight.

Mary chewed her lip. 'He's being smoked up by some kind of sickness. I know he's not had the walking in them for some time, but now he has hardly the twitch in his toes.'

Nóra hastily pulled the cloth back over Micheál's thighs. 'I wonder, Mary,' she murmured. 'How much suffering can a person bear without something turning in them?'

The girl was silent.

Nóra combed her tangled hair with her fingers and stared at Micheál. When she slapped him she had felt on the brink of something dark, something she knew she would not be able to come back from. There was no knowing what she might have done had Mary not come inside at that moment, and it frightened her.

What has happened to me?

Nóra had always believed herself to be a good woman. A kind woman. But perhaps, she thought, we are good only when life makes it easy for us to be so. Maybe the heart hardens when good fortune is not there to soften it.

'Do you think we ought to send for the doctor?' Mary asked.

Nóra turned to her with weariness. 'The doctor, you say. Are there doctors on every lane up in Annamore? Do they come and tend you for nothing?' She nodded at the crock on the table. 'That's all the money I have there and precious little it is too. Do you think I have coins buried about the place? Do you think I am a rich woman? Cream and butter and eggs – that's what stitches body and soul together.' She began to plait her hair with quick roughness, tugging at the grey strands. 'I don't know how you all live up in Annamore, but down here, in this valley, we grease the landlord's palm with whitemeats. How do you think I keep the three of us out of the rain? Turf on the fire? And now the blessed cow is on the dry and you would have me fork out a fortune for a doctor to come and condemn my grandson! When next summer I'll have no man to go and work the fields and earn the keeping of the cabin, and 'twill be the crowbar and the lonely road for me!'

Mary was solemn. 'Have you not your nephews to work the ground for you?'

Nóra took a deep breath. 'Aye. Aye, I've nephews.'

'Perhaps it won't be as bad as you say.'

'Perhaps not.'

'And perhaps there is a doctor who will see to Micheál for nothing. Or maybe for a hen.' Mary's voice was soft. 'Your wee hens are good layers. You said so yourself. Would a doctor not come for a hen?'

Nóra shook her head. 'The hens are not laying as they did. And what do you think a hen is worth to a doctor who lives in town and eats eggs every morning like he laid them himself?' She sighed. ''Tis the priest we want. 'Tis the priest for folk like us.'

'Shall I fetch him then?'

Nóra stood and pulled the shawl over her head. 'No. Get on with your churning, Mary. If anyone is after summoning the priest for Micheál, it should be me.'

Nóra set out down the lane across the face of the valley slope. The air was cold and clean, and the snow on the ground stung her bare feet as she walked. There was no one else on the road. All was still, except for the circling of rooks above the empty fields.

The priest's house was a small whitewashed building set at the corner of the valley where the heather sprawled and the road bent around the mountain, leading the way to Glenflesk. After being admitted inside by a thickset housekeeper, Nóra waited in the parlour where the fireplace lay unlit, before the priest joined her. He had been at his breakfast. Nóra noticed egg yolk dribbling a fatty line down his clerical shirt.

'Widow Leahy. How are you getting on?'

'Thank you, Father, I'm well enough.'

'I'm sorry for your troubles. As they say, "'Tis a lonely washing that has no man's shirt in it."'

Nóra blinked back a prickling of irritation. 'Thank you, Father.'

'Now, how might I help you?'

'I'm sorry to be disturbing you. I know 'tis dreadful early and you a busy man.'

The priest smiled. 'Tell me why you've come.'

''Tis my grandson. I've come because his mother, my daughter, is dead and I was hoping you might be able to heal him.'

'Your grandson, is it? What sickness does he have?' Father Healy's face grew sombre. 'Is it the smallpox?'

''Tis not the pox, or a sickness like that, no. 'Tis something worse. I don't know what.'

'Have you sent for the doctor?'

'I haven't the wherewithal. Not now.' Nóra could feel herself blushing and it embarrassed her. 'What means I have is spent on a live-in girl to help with him.'

'Begging pardon, Widow Leahy, but perhaps that is the problem.' Father Healy's tone was gentle. 'Getting a girl in when you could get the doctor and have him well again.'

'I don't think he can be made well again by a doctor,' Nóra said.

'Then why have you come for me?'

'He has a need for a priest's healing. He hasn't the full of his mind.'

'Ah. Is he soft-brained?' Father Healy asked.

'I don't know. He's hardly a child at all.'

'Hardly a child? What an odd thing to say. What are his symptoms?'

'He has not the use of his legs, Father. He won't say a word, although not two years ago he was talking like any other little boy. He is forever awake and screaming. He does not thrive.'

Father Healy gave her a look of pity. 'I see.'

'He was born well. That's why 'twould be a kindness for you to come and see him. Why I'm asking you to call, Father. I think . . . perhaps something has happened to him.'

'Such as?'

Nóra clenched her jaw to stop her chin from trembling. 'People are saying he is a changeling.'

Father Healy looked at her from under lowered brows, his face colouring. 'That is superstitious prattle, Widow. Don't be listening to talk like that. A woman like yourself – you've more sense than that.'

'Father,' Nóra added hastily, 'I know there's plenty folk who don't believe in a happening like that, but if you were to come and see the boy . . .'

There was silence. The priest looked apprehensive. 'If the boy is afflicted with a suffering of the usual kind, or if he is dying, I might attend to him. I would be glad to help. But if he is an idiot . . .'

'Would you not pray for him? Heal him?'

'Why do *you* not pray for him, Widow Leahy?'

'I do!'

Father Healy sighed. 'Ah, but you do not attend Mass. Ever since your husband died. I know 'tis a troubling time for you, but believe me when I tell you that it is at Mass where you will find your comfort.'

''Tis no easy thing to be widowed, Father.'

The priest's expression softened slightly. He glanced out the small window, clicking his tongue. 'Is the boy christened?'

'He is.'

'Has he had the Holy Eucharist?'

'No, Father, he is only four.'

'And no doctor has ever seen to him?'

'Once. This summer gone. Martin fetched a man from Killarney, but he did nothing. Just took our money.'

Father Healy nodded, as though he had expected as much. 'Widow Leahy, I think perhaps that it is your duty to care for this child and do the best you can.'

Nóra wiped her eyes. She felt lightheaded with frustration. 'Would you not come and see him and make the sign of the cross over him, Father? A priest such as yourself has the power to banish –'

'Don't be saying fairies, Widow. I'll have no talk of fairies.'

'But Father O'Reilly –'

'Acted the fairy doctor? Presumed to act the fantastic ecclesiastical? Father O'Reilly, may God bless his soul, had no right to engage in these vestiges of pagan rites. And not without leave in writing from the bishop of the diocese would I do the same.'

His face was earnest. 'Widow Leahy, 'tis my responsibility to raise the people of this valley to a morality that corresponds to the requirements of our faith. How can we insist on the rights of Catholics when the valleys are full of the smoke of heathen bonfires and the wailing of hags at wakes? Those who are after keeping us out of parliament need only point to the Catholics pouring beestings at the foot of whitethorns, dancing at crossroads, whispering of fairies!'

Nóra stared as Father Healy pulled out a handkerchief to wipe the spittle that had gathered at the corner of his mouth. Her feet ached from the cold. 'Forgive me, Father, but your shirt is dirty with egg,' she said. Without waiting to see the priest's reaction, she stood and left the room.

Nóra turned off the lane by the parish house and walked a mile down a little-used path, her face hot with anger. The river could be heard in the distance and soon Nóra reached a ditch where a slow trickle of water had melted snow to mud. She sank to her knees beside a tumbled stone wall to which nettles clung in a thicket.

It was true, what she had said to the priest. Martin had gone for the doctor, though they could not afford it. Borrowing a horse down at the blacksmith's and rising in the mist of the following morning to ride into Killarney and fetch that man. How strange he had seemed, trotting beside Martin. The doctor had been tufted with white hair that clung to his balding scalp and covered the back of his hands like down, and his small wire spectacles had slipped down the greasy length of his nose with every jolt of his horse. When he had stepped into the cabin, he had glanced up at the ceiling as if he expected it to fall upon his head.

Nóra had been so nervous her teeth had chattered. 'God bless you, Doctor, and welcome, and thank you for coming, sir.'

The man had set his satchel upon the ground, nudging the fresh rushes with his foot.

'I'm sorry to hear you have a sickly child. Where is the patient?'

Martin had pointed to where Micheál lay, listless in his cot.

The doctor stooped over the bed and looked down at the boy. 'How old is he?'

'Three years old, sir. No, four.'

The doctor puffed his cheeks, his whiskers fluttering as he exhaled. 'Not yours?'

'Our daughter's child.'

'And where is she?'

'Passed, sir.'

The doctor had squatted awkwardly on the ground, the cloth of his trousers tight around his knees. The leather of his boots squeaked. He dragged his satchel towards him, opened the clasps and took out a long instrument. 'I'm going to listen to his heart,' he explained, glancing up.

The doctor had worked silently. He had pressed the silver stop of his instrument to Micheál's chest, before discarding it and bending down and placing the hairy whorl of his ear directly on the boy's white skin. Then he had tapped Micheál's chest, bouncing his fingertips along the ridges of the boy's protruding bones as though the child was an instrument he had forgotten how to play.

'What is it, Doctor?'

The man had brought a finger to his lips and shushed her with a solemn eye. He pressed the fat pads of his fingers under the boy's jawbone, lifted his arms and examined the milky hollows of his armpits, prised his lips apart and studied his tongue, then fitted his hands around the back of the boy and, gently, as though he were handling glass, turned Micheál onto his stomach. He had clucked at the sight of the rash upon the boy's back, but said nothing, then ran his fingers down the ridges of the child's spine, turning his legs and arms this way and that.

'Is it the pox, Doctor?'

'Tell me, have you known this child from birth?'

Martin had answered. 'He is just come to us. He was born well. There was no sickness upon him then. We saw him once and he seemed a normal, healthy lad.'

'Did he ever speak?'

'He did. He was learning his words same as any other.'

'And does he ever speak now?'

Martin and Nóra glanced at each other.

'We know he is dreadful thin. Hungry, sir. Always hungry. We knew at once there was a wasting on him, and we thought 'twas the hunger. We think his mouth is so full of hunger he has no room for words.'

The doctor hauled himself to his feet, sighing, brushing his clothes down. 'He hasn't spoken a word since you took him in, then? Nor taken a step neither?'

Silence.

The man ran a hand over his shining scalp and glanced at Martin. 'I might have a word with you.'

'What you have to say you may tell to the both of us.'

The doctor took his spectacles off and polished their glass with a handkerchief. 'I don't have good news, I'm afraid. The child does not have the smallpox, nor is he consumptive. The rash on his back is no sign of disease; rather, I think it is caused by the wearing of his skin. On account of him being unable to sit up by himself.'

'But will he be well again? Will it pass? What have we to do for him?'

The doctor put his spectacles back on. 'Sometimes children do not thrive.' He returned his instruments to his leather case.

'But he was born well. We saw it ourselves. And so he may be well again.'

The doctor straightened, lips pursed. 'That might be, but *I* believe he will remain ill-thriven.'

'Do you not have something in your bag to give him? 'Tis not right that a healthy boy becomes this way.' Her tongue had dried on the words. 'Look. Look there. Hungry. Bawling. Not saying a thing. He was cold, he had not enough in his belly, and he is mouldered with it all, I know.'

'Nóra.' Martin's eyes had been soft.

'He was well. I saw him walk! There is surely something in your bag, some medicine. Would you not give him some medicine? All you've done is prod him like a piece of meat on the turn.'

'Nóra!' Martin had gripped her wrist.

'I think you should prepare yourself for the worst,' the doctor had said, frowning. 'It would be remiss of me to encourage hope when there is none. I'm sorry.'

'You cannot tell us what ails him?'

'He is cretinous.'

'I don't understand.'

'He is malformed.'

Nóra shook her head. 'Doctor, he has all his fingers and toes, I –'

'I'm sorry.' The doctor had pulled on his coat, spectacles slipping down his nose again as he shrugged the cloth over his shoulders. 'The boy is a cretin. There is nothing I can do.'

The day had turned querulous, the horizon blurred under far-off snowfall. Nóra felt a bone-deep longing for Martin, for his calm reassurance. Even when the doctor had departed, and Nóra had felt anger throb through her, Martin had drawn her into the warmth of his chest and murmured, 'For what cannot be cured, patience is best.'

For what cannot be cured, Nóra thought, leaning against the rough stones. I am burdened with a dying child who will not die.

She wished Micheál dead, then. She wished that he would fall asleep and never wake up, but be taken into Heaven by the angels or into the ringfort by the fairies, or wherever a mute soul went. Better that than to grow old in a body that could not accommodate the years. Better that than to suffer the bridle and bit of the world.

There was no use in denying the truth of it, she thought. 'Twould be a kind of grace if he died.

Nóra shuddered. She knew women sometimes did kill children. But the stories she heard were always of unwed mothers who gave birth in dirty private places, and who bore their anguish out in lapses of guilty violence. Sometimes they were caught. When the bloodstain was found, or the stones shifted from the river floor and the little sacked body rose to the water's surface to the shrieking surprise of those at their laundry. There was a woman who had drowned herself and her unborn child in Lough Leane and people said that a mist shrouded the water on the anniversary of their deaths every year since.

But I am no murderer, Nóra thought. I am a good woman. She wiped her swollen face with muddy fingers. I will not kill my own daughter's boy. I will save him. I will restore him.

A light snow began to fall, and a rook, feathers sweeping the still air, landed on the stones. 'I am alone,' Nóra said plainly.

The rook ignored her, wiped his grey beak on the wall. As Nóra watched him, marvelling at the bird's closeness, she felt a sudden weight to the air, a prickling at the nape of her neck.

Then she saw the nettles.

A memory came to her. Martin shouldering the door open one spring evening filthy with rain, his hand clutched to his chest. He had a dreadful cold in it, he said. As though there were no blood in it at all.

Nóra had examined the swollen fingers. 'Looks to be plenty of blood in there,' she'd said. 'Too much blood.'

But the hand had remained that way all night and the following day too, and the next evening Martin had said he would go to Nance Roche for a cure. 'Sure, hadn't she brought the worm out of Patrick's guts, and the lump out of John's arm, and no harm done?'

'She's an odd one,' Nóra had said, but Martin replied that anything was better than living the rest of his life with his hand a block of ice, and so he had gone.

Martin returned from Nance's the following morning with his hand swollen still, violent pink, but supple, moving.

'She's marvellous skill, that woman.' He was relieved, filled with wonderment. 'You'll never guess how she did it. Nettles,' he said. 'She returned the blood to it with nettles.' And he raised his hand to Nóra's cheek to show her how his warmth had been restored.

Now, wrapping the cloth of her dress around her hands to keep the leaves from stinging her fingers, Nóra tugged the nettles from the ground, heaping them in her apron. She knew that she must look like a madwoman, a hooded figure nettling in the snow. But her heart thrilled in her chest. She would cure him.

It will work, she thought. It worked for Martin and so it will work for Micheál.

'Sweet Mother of God, make this work.' The words folded under themselves and became a circle of prayer. 'I will warm the life back into him. It will work. Virgin Mother, I beseech thee.'

Nóra returned to the cabin, her apron filled with nettles, their toothed leaves dampened by snowmelt. Shutting the door behind her, she found Micheál on the ground and Mary in the middle of the room, lifting the heavy dash of the churn and whispering, 'Come butter, come butter, come butter, come.' She stopped as Nóra entered, panting from the exertion and rubbing her shoulders.

'What did the priest say?'

'He'll have none of it. So, I went nettling.'

'You went nettling? In the snow?' Mary frowned.

'I did, and what of it? Go on with that churning, then.'

As Mary resumed heaving the dash up and down, Nóra threw her cloak over the hearth beam, shook the nettles into a basket and knelt by Micheál. She dragged the boy gently towards her by his ankles, then lifted his dress to expose his legs. Wrapping her hand in a corner of her shawl, she picked up a nettle, and with her other hand lifted Micheál's bare foot. She tickled his toes with the plant, brushing the edge of the leaves against his skin.

The sound of the dash stopped. Nóra knew Mary was watching her, but she said nothing.

Micheál's foot sat in her palm, oddly heavy. There was not so much as a flinch from the boy. Nóra wondered how Nance might have laid the nettles upon Martin's ice-struck, immobile hand. She imagined her husband sitting in the dark of Nance's hovel, holding his palm out as she whispered words over it, rubbed the stinging into his skin.

Nóra lifted the plant up and brought it down on Micheál's lower leg, more firmly this time. A long stroke to drag the leaves from knee to ankle.

Micheál pointed his chin into the air in a weird expression of defiance and then, as the smart settled on his shin, his eyes closed and he wailed.

Mary cleared her throat. 'What are you doing?'

Nóra ignored her. She lifted the nettle again and brought it down on Micheál's crooked knees in a light slap, on his ankles and bare feet. His skin pinked under the stinging plant, welts rising.

He must feel it, she thought. If he cries, he must feel it.

Mary stood still, her grip tightening on the dash.

Nothing. His legs, blotched, did not move. Nóra felt desperation rising in her. It had worked for Martin. Her husband's hand was restored to him with nettles. Yes, it had hurt, he had said, but when the sting subsided he found that his flesh had been flooded with warmth. Martin, holding her face to prove that he was well again. The rough thickness of his thumb rubbing her cheek, soothing her. As good as new, he had said. It takes a lot more than that to bring me down.

Nóra thought she saw Micheál's toes curl and, heartened, brought the nettles down harder on his knees.

'Please stop that,' Mary whispered.

We will make him well again, Martin had assured her. We will care for him together, for Johanna. He will be a comfort to us. Our own grandchild.

The boy began to scream harder and Nóra paused to look at him. His face was scrunched. He seemed like an angry, bucking imp, red in hair and face. His eyes were crimped shut, tears streaming from them, and as he jerked he smacked his fists on the floor. Nóra winced as he struck the clay.

This is not my son, Johanna had said.

And at once Nóra, her heart fluttering at his screams, saw that the boy was not, could not be the child she had seen in her daughter's cabin. Her eyes began to water, and she saw plainly the puckish strangeness that people had been speaking of. All those months she had thought there was a shadow of Johanna about the boy, a familiarity that anchored him to her. Martin had seen it, had loved him for it. But now, Nóra knew that nothing of Johanna ran through this child's blood. It was like Tadgh said. She had not recognised him as her own because there was nothing of her family in the creature. He was a cuckoo in the nest.

There is nothing of them in him, Nóra thought. He is not Micheál. And she turned the boy over and brought another nettle down on his calves.

He wailed, his face against the rushes on the floor. Crumbs of mud spattered off the plants, dirtying his clothes and her apron.

'Stop!' Mary cried.

He is fairy, Nóra thought. He is not my grandson.

Mary rushed to the floor and attempted to rip the nettle out of her hand.

'Leave me,' Nóra said through clenched teeth. She yanked her hand out of the girl's grip.

'He doesn't like it,' Mary whimpered.

Nóra ignored her.

Without warning, the girl suddenly grabbed the basket holding the remainder of the nettles and tried to fling it across the room. Nóra snatched the woven edge in time, and hauled the basket back towards her, her mouth in a determined line. She refused to look the girl in the eye. Mary got to her feet and tugged at it, crying openly now, her mouth open and wailing, as pink as the boy's. They wrestled with the basket, each heaving it back and forth, jerking the other, until, finally, Nóra wrenched it out of Mary's grasp and sat it down beside her, stony-eyed.

''Tis a cruelty!' Mary sobbed.

The child was bawling so hard he had begun to choke. His head rocked from side to side.

Nóra continued to whip him with nettles.

Mary bent down and snatched the rest of the plants out of the basket with her bare hands, throwing them onto the fire. The embers blackened under the damp weight of the nettles. Then, before Nóra could say anything, Mary bolted for the door, flinging it wide and running into the snowy yard.

CHAPTER
SEVEN

Dock

'What is all this madness?'

Peg O'Shea stood in the doorway, gaping at Nóra and Micheál. Nóra was sitting on the floor, shoulders shaking, clenching her fists until her nails dug into the flesh of her palms. Micheál, half naked, was shrieking with pain. As he screamed, he lifted his head and let it fall on the floor in a repetitive, sickly knocking. His face was covered with dirt from the nettles.

Peg hobbled in and quickly picked him off the ground. 'Oh, come now. Oh, little one. Shush now.' She sank onto a stool next to where Nóra lay slumped. 'Nóra Leahy. What in God's holy name have you done to this boy?'

Nóra shrugged and wiped her running nose.

'That maid of yours, Mary, she comes running into my house in pieces, crying you're after whipping the boy with nettles. Are you turned in your mind? Does the boy not suffer enough already?' Peg watched Nóra closely then stamped her foot on the ground. 'Enough! Stop your crying and talk sense to me.'

'Father Healy,' Nóra gasped.

'What about himself?'

'He will not heal the boy. I asked him. He said he has surely turned idiot and there's nothing to be done. He said I'm not to be talking of the Good People, and that 'tis all superstition.' Nóra's chin trembled. 'Where is Mary to now?'

'I sent her to the Flesk for dock leaves. Pull the shirt of him down, Nóra. Here, I'll do it then. The wee lad is screaming like you've burnt him alive.'

Peg lay Micheál on her lap and bundled him in her shawl. 'You've a right to be telling me what is happening.'

'People are saying he is a changeling.' Nóra's face scrunched in despair.

Peg was silent. 'Well. There might be something in that. *Is ait an mac an saol.* Life is a strange son.'

'If you believe he is a changeling, then why do you touch him?' Nóra spluttered. 'Why do you care if I nettle him?'

'You are as cold as a holy trout, Nóra Leahy. Do you not know yourself that if the wee one is a changeling, your own good grandson suffers the ill you inflict on his stock? If the Good People have him, they will not take kindly to you treating one of their own like this.' Peg lifted Micheál's dress and examined his legs, turning them in her hands. 'You did a good job of it. What on earth were you hoping to do?'

Nóra hauled herself up onto the settle. 'I thought 'twould restore the quick to his legs. I thought the sting might give him cause to move.' She took a shuddering breath.

'That is some dreadful quackery if I ever heard it. Quite the herb woman, you are.' Peg clucked her tongue.

''Twas what Nance Roche did to Martin when he was alive and with me. Nettles brought the quick back to his hand.'

'Nance Roche has the knowledge. Some pride you have there,

Nóra, thinking you've the same skill as that one. 'Twould be better if you made a tea of the nettle and gave it to him, the doty child.' She pulled Micheál's head back against her skinny throat and held him tightly, murmuring into his ear. 'What have we to do with you, then? From what wild place have you come to us?'

'Peg, I know what they are saying of me,' Nóra said, her voice cracking. 'They say my own daughter was not called away by God, but by Them in the *ráth*. They say her own son is with her in the hill, and I am left with the fairy child. They say the misfortune in the valley is *his* fault and will be on my soul. They say . . .' Her voice broke. 'They say Martin died because of him being here. And I look at him, and I wonder, Peg.'

'Nóra Leahy. Hold your head up and not care a tinker's curse what anyone says to cheapen ye,' Peg replied. 'Night will come again, please God. You should be glad this one is a changeling, for then you bear no blame for him. There are ways to restore Micheál to you.'

'I know what they do to banish changelings,' Nóra spat. 'Put him on the dung heap in the night for the fairies to claim! Threaten him with fire. Would you have me put that one on a hot shovel and roast him? Would you have me smack him with a reddened poker and bring the eye out of him?'

Peg's face was serious. 'Enough. Enough with all your mad cures dreamt up out of despair, and enough of all this dark talk. You have a need to talk with one who knows of these things.' She looked Nóra in the eye. 'You have a need to speak with Nance.'

Mary ran down the grassy slope as fast as she could, briars snagging her skirt and the skin of her legs as she went. Her blood sang at the sudden pain of it, but she did not stop until she could see the riverbank beyond a tangle of fallen tree branches. The flowing water looked as dark as a nightmare. By the time she reached its edge, her shins were scraped bloody by brambles.

Taking jagged breaths, Mary kept her head down, searching for the long leaves of water dock amidst winter's ruin of dead grasses and the snap of withered bracken. She found a clump of dock growing on the side of the crumbling bank, and crawled towards the water on her belly to reach it without the soil giving way. Tugging at the leaves with an outstretched hand, she looked into the water and saw her own warped reflection staring back at her. She was shocked to see the fear on her face, and the urge to cry swelled again. She wiped her streaming eyes and nose on her sleeve.

Seeing Nóra whip the boy with nettles had unsettled something within her. There was an ugliness there that she had only seen a few times before in her life. Once she had seen a man sneer at a madwoman who had taken to wandering in her undershirt, contempt crowning his face in a dark halo. Another time she had seen a group of older girls crawl backwards, naked, through a briar on May morning. There was something about their pale bodies writhing against the grass, flinching at the prick of thorns, that had deeply disturbed her. At the time she had not known what it was they were doing, and had buttoned the secret sight of them deep down in her chest. It was only later that she heard of the powers of double-rooted briars, understood that the girls had been crawling through the Devil arch to curse someone. She had never seen those girls again. But the memory of them had clawed its way back to her mind at the sight of the muddy widow lashing the legs of the child.

It was not the beating. Mary had seen children younger than Micheál smacked into yesterday by their mothers in Annamore. She had felt the weight of a man's swinging arm at the northern farm.

It was the cruelty in the blows. The widow had looked demented. She had brought the nettles down on Micheál's skin like he was nothing more to her than a stubborn nag, or a carcass to be flensed. It turned the pulse of her heart.

The nettling had not looked like a cure. It had looked like punishment.

The slope was greasy with snow and mud and Mary found her feet sliding on her way back to the cabin. More than once she had to use her hands to scramble up the hillside, and she felt the smear of mud on her face when she wiped her swollen eyes. On the way to the river she had taken the path leading from the lane, but in her haste to return she had run towards the woods where the ground was most steep. The air burnt in her lungs. Suddenly, the soil beneath her left foot gave way, pain flared through her and she fell to the ground.

Mary let go of the dock leaves and gripped her ankle in both hands. She blinked back tears and sat there rocking in the mud, chest heaving.

I want to go home.

The thought ran through her like a thread, drawing tightly, until she felt puckered with longing.

I want to go home.

Clenching her teeth, Mary tried to stand. It was no use. The tendons in her ankle sprang with pain. Sitting in the mud she let the tears come. She hated the valley. She hated the brittle, unnatural child, and the damp loneliness that hung off the widow like a mist. She hated the broken nights and the smell of piss that clung to the cripple's clothes, and she hated the pity in the face of the old neighbour. She wanted her brothers and sisters. She wanted the feel of the younger ones' fingers combing her hair by the fire. She wanted the cheerful noise of the babies, and their red-cheeked faces, and their little hands on her shoulder, waking her in the morning. She wanted David and his solemn understanding.

'Tis too much, Mary thought. Why is the world so terrible and strange?

'I never saw anyone cry so bitterly.'

Mary flinched. An old woman stood behind her, wrapped in a tattered shawl, dragging a broken branch.

'Are you hurt?' The woman bent down, concerned. Mary, too surprised to move, stared back. The woman's skin was creased and her eyes were clouded, but there was softness in her voice. She reached out and placed her ancient hand on Mary's bent knee.

'You're hurt.' The woman answered her own question. 'Sit still for a moment now.' She fussed with the broken branch and Mary saw that she had been using it as a sled. It was piled with lumps of turf, dung and plants. The woman carefully took these off, placing them on the ground beside her, and snapped off the smaller twigs. She soon had a rough stick, which she gave to Mary.

'Try standing, girl. Take this.'

Mary hauled herself upright onto her good foot, and planted the stick firmly into the waterlogged ground.

'Now, put your other arm about my shoulders. I'm taking you to my home. I can do something for you there. See, that's my cabin.'

'What about your turf?' Mary sniffed. She could feel the thin ridge of the woman's shoulder blade against her arm.

The woman grimaced under her weight. 'Never you mind that. Can you hobble along, so?'

Mary leant heavily on the stick and held her sore foot aloft. 'I don't want to hurt you.'

'I'm as strong as an ox.' The woman smiled. 'That's it. This way.'

They stumbled back down the slope until they reached the dirty clearing beside the woods. A small mud cabin stood against a wall of alder trees, their bare branches knotted with the old nests of birds. There was no chimney, but Mary could see smoke listing from one end, where a gap in the thatch admitted it to the open air. A tethered goat grazing on the grass at the woods' edge looked up at their voices. It stared, gimlet-eyed, at Mary.

'You live here?'

'I do.'

'I thought this cabin was abandoned.' Mary could hear the river in the distance.

'I've lived here twenty years or more. Come in, girl. Come in and sit by the fire.'

Mary grasped the doorframe of the cabin and hopped inside. From the clearing the *bothán* had looked crude and damp, but the room was surprisingly warm. The floor was covered in cut green rushes, which gave off a clean, sweet smell, and a turf fire burnt upon a large hearthstone, away from the wall. There was no window to admit the light, but the fire's glowing heart prevented the darkness from gloom. Mary, glancing up, saw a vast number of St Brigid's crosses, blackened by years of smoke, fixed against the rafters around the low ceiling. In the corner of the room stood straw baskets, some filled with ratty, uncarded wool.

'Are you a *bean leighis*?' Mary asked, gesturing towards the drying herbs dangling from the rough-hewed crossbeams.

The woman was washing the mud off her feet and hands on the threshold. 'Have you not seen a one with the charms before?'

Mary shook her head, her mouth dry.

'Sit down on that stool there.' The woman shut the door and the room became darker, the firelight throwing long shadows against the walls. 'My name is Nance Roche,' she said. 'And you are the maid with Nóra Leahy.'

Mary paused. 'I am. I'm Mary Clifford.'

''Tis an unhappy house you're in.' Nance sat beside Mary. 'Nóra Leahy is an unhappy widow.'

'Aren't all widows unhappy?'

Nance laughed and Mary noticed her bare gums, the few teeth bunkered in them. 'Not every dead husband is mourned, *cailín*. Nor every wife.'

'What happened to your teeth?'

'Ah, there was time enough for me to lose them when I'd nothing for them to do. But here, let me take a look at you.'

Mary extended her bare foot in front of the fire, feeling the warmth of it against her sole. ''Tis my ankle.'

Nance examined the swelling without touching her. 'Musha, so 'tis. Will you let me give you the cure?'

Mary's eyes were wide in the dark. 'Will it hurt?'

'No more than it does now.'

Mary nodded.

Nance spat on her hands and lay them gently upon the ankle. 'Christ upon a cross. A horse's leg was dislocated. He joined blood to blood, flesh to flesh, bone to bone. As He healed that, may He cure this. Amen.'

Mary crossed herself in imitation of Nance, and as she did so she felt a slow rising of heat against her skin, as though she had drawn too close to a flame. But the pain faded, and she exhaled at its lessening. She tried to stand, but Nance shot out a finger in warning.

'Not yet. You'll need a poultice.' She stood and, as Mary watched in curiosity, filled a chipped earthenware bowl with plants from a basket covered with a damp cloth.

'What are those herbs there, then?' Mary asked.

'Oh, that's my secret.' Nance picked up an egg and cracked it sharply on the bowl's rim, straining the white through her crooked fingers. When the egg had separated, she slipped the remaining yolk into her mouth and swallowed it.

'Do I have to eat that?' Mary asked, pointing to the bowl.

''Tis for your skin and not your belly. Royal fern, watercress, nettles.'

'Nettles?' Mary couldn't keep the panic out of her voice.

'They'll not hurt you. I've soaked them and that takes much of the sting out.' Nance pestled the plants with a worn wooden beetle.

Mary closed her eyes and remembered the angry welts on Micheál's legs, the widow's wrapped hand bringing the nettles down on his skin. Her stomach clenched and she suddenly vomited, the splatter hissing on the fire.

'I'm sorry,' she gasped, and vomited again.

Mary felt hands smoothing the hair off her face, Nance's bony fingers rubbing her shoulder.

'There now,' she said. 'There now.'

A dipper of cool water was brought to Mary's lips.

'I'm sorry,' she stuttered. She spat out the acid bile and felt the sting of it in her nostrils.

'Ah, you poor thing. You've had a shock.'

''Tis not my ankle.' The touch of the old woman reminded Mary of her mother. Wiping her mouth with the back of her hand, she felt the residual sting of the nettles on her palm and sobbed.

Nance picked up Mary's hands and turned them over, studying the welts. Her brow furrowed. 'Is she hurting you?'

There was a long silence.

'Mary Clifford. Is it Nóra Leahy that did this to you?'

'Not me,' Mary finally blurted out. 'Him. Micheál. She's after hurting him.'

Nance nodded. 'The cripple boy.'

'You know about Micheál?'

Nance released the girl's hands and tucked her shawl firmly about her. 'I'm hearing a lot of talk about that child. A lot of rumour.'

'He's not natural,' Mary hacked. 'And she knows it. She hides him! She has me hide him because she's frightened of what people will say of him. But they already know, and they say he is a change-ling and to blame for everything, and she is punishing him for it.' Mary felt the words tip out over her tongue. 'She whipped him with nettles. She drinks and she has a look in her eye that puts the fright on me. They're astray, the both of them. I'm scared of what is going to happen.'

Nance held her smarting hands tightly. 'There now,' she soothed. 'You've found me, now. You've found me.'

Micheál had finally stopped crying. Nóra offered to take him from Peg's tight clutch, but the older woman simply stared her down. 'Sit you there by the fire and breathe some sense back into your head.'

'I wish Martin were here,' Nóra gasped. She felt as though her soul was grinding itself into powder under the weight of her own unhappiness.

Peg's voice was stern. 'Of course you do. But Martin is with God, and you've a right to be getting on with life in the best way you can.'

'I wish Martin was here,' Nóra repeated. She could feel the blood beat in her face. 'And I wish that it was Micheál who was dead.'

Peg sucked her teeth.

'I would carry Micheál to the graveyard and bury him alive if my daughter would come to me!' She fell from her stool onto all fours. 'I would!' she screamed. 'I wish it were Johanna with me!'

'Enough!'

Nóra felt two rough fingers pinch her chin and pull her head upwards.

'Enough,' Peg hissed. Her grip was firm. 'Nóra Leahy, you think you are the only mother to lose a daughter? Five children I have buried in the *cillín*. Five.' Her voice was calm. ''Tis a great misfortune to lower two coffins in one year, but 'tis no reason to let your heart and mind go to the dogs and to be crying and crawling about the house like a man senseless with drink taken. And don't you be screaming of murder for the valley to hear. Don't you be threatening worse things to this child than what has already befallen him.'

Nóra pushed Peg's fingers away from her face. 'Who are you to tell me what shape my loss can take?'

'Nóra, I want to help you.'

There was the sound of voices in the yard outside. The women exchanged looks.

'Who is that?' Nóra hissed.

'Is it Mary with the dock leaf?'

''Tis not her voice.' Nóra got to her feet and fixed the bolt on the door, then waited by the wall, her ear craned to the gap in the doorframe.

There was a sharp knock.

'Who is it?' Nóra cried.

'Nóra Leahy, you'd best be opening to me. I've your Mary here, and a sorry state she's in too.'

Peg's eyes widened. 'Nance? In God's name, Nóra, let the woman in.'

Nóra wiped her eyes on her sleeve and undid the latch. Light flooded the cabin.

Nance stood before her, the old woman's eyes swimming in their clouded, bleeding blue. She was bundled against the cold, a straw basket over one arm. 'You're in a bad way,' she murmured. 'Secrecy does not agree with you.'

Nóra felt Nance take in her tear-stained face, the scratches on her wrist, fingernails bitten down to the painful quick. 'What are you doing here?'

'Your girl rolled her ankle by the river and I found her there. I've come to see her home safe, but I think . . .' Nance peered past Nóra to Peg and the boy at her chest. 'I think, Nóra Leahy, that you have further need of me.' She placed her free hand on Nóra's shoulder and, pushing her out of the way, stepped inside.

Mary followed, giving Nóra a wary glance as she limped over the doorstep.

'Are you badly hurt?' Nóra asked, pointing at the rough bandage.

The girl shook her head. Said nothing.

'So this is the nettled child. There now. Let me take a look at him, Peg O'Shea. This hidden boy.' Nance pulled the hood off her head, and took two dock leaves from her basket. Rolling the cloth away from Micheál's legs, she wrapped the leaves around his calves. 'You've marked him like a cat, Nóra Leahy.'

'I didn't mean to harm him. I only wanted to see him well.' She took a sharp breath. 'You did the same to Martin. He told me. You brought the life back to his hand.'

Peg passed Micheál into Nance's outstretched arms. The woman held him for a moment, gazing into his unspeaking face.

'Your Martin was not as this child is.'

Nóra saw the boy as Nance saw him then. A wild, crabbed child no heavier than the weight of snow upon a branch. A clutch of bones rippling with the movement of wind on water. Thistle-headed. Fierce-chinned. Small fingers clutching in front of him as though the air were filled with wonders and not the smoke of the fire and their own stale breath.

She watched as Nance ran a single fingertip over his forehead.

What had happened? What had her daughter done to lose her son? Had she not crossed his face with ashes? Not bit his fingernails until he was nine weeks old? Not sprinkled his mouth with salt, or barred his cradle with iron? All women knew how to protect their children from abduction. A hazel stick by the door. Milk spilt after stumbling.

Nance lay Micheál down on the rushes by their feet. 'He is very thin,' she said quietly.

'I'm not starving him, if that is what you are saying. He eats and eats.'

'Whist now. That is not what I'm saying.' Nance regarded her with a gentle eye. 'Mary tells me you were given this child when your daughter died, God have mercy on her soul. Did he come into this world a natural child, or has he been changed?'

'He was a fine boy at his birth, and in the two years after it. But when my daughter began to sicken, he became ill-favoured.' Nóra swallowed hard. 'They thought 'twas the cold and the hunger that did it. But my daughter thought her boy was gone from her. She did not see her own son in him. She asked . . .' Nóra took a deep breath. 'She asked that he be put outside in the last days of her life.'

Peg looked at her with curiosity. 'You never said a word of this to me, Nóra.'

''Twas no sin on her,' Nóra protested. 'She was a good mother.'

'Tell me.' Nance interrupted. 'Tell me how he is unnatural.'

'Do you not see it yourself? Look at him. Nothing of him is natural.'

There was a heavy silence. A gust of wind blew ice under the gap in the door.

'He screams at night,' Mary whispered. 'He will not rest, and he will not lie still in my arms. He kicks and bites me.'

'There is nothing of my family in that boy.'

'Sore-wounded Christ, Nóra.' Peg pressed her fingers to her temples. 'Faith, I don't know, Nance. He does not walk. He does not speak.'

'He tried to pull the hair out of my head!'

Nance studied the boy closely. 'Fetch me a thread, Nóra,' she said. 'I have a need to measure him.'

'Why?'

'It may well be that he is full of fairy, or that he has been overlooked.'

'By the evil eye?' Mary asked.

'Aye. That he has been blinked.'

Nóra reached for her knitting and pulled roughly at the wool. She bit a length off with her teeth and passed it to Nance, who pulled it tight between her fingers and held it to Micheál's toes and hips with a practised thumb, measuring each leg. The wind blew.

''Tis as I thought. He is not evenly grown,' said Nance, 'and sure, that can be a sign of strange things.'

'Sweet Christ. Not even the Killarney doctor saw that.'

'You're wanting a reason for his being changed, Nóra. You're wanting a reason for the unnatural in him.'

Nóra's face pinched in grief. 'I am afraid . . . I am afraid he is a changeling.'

The old woman straightened her back. 'Now, that he might be, or he might not. There are ways to see whether the Good People have merely blasted him and taken the growing and thriving out of his legs, or whether . . .' Nance lay a hand on the boy's ribcage. His hair had cotted about his temples and his face was flushed.

'Whether what? Nance?'

'Nóra, the Good People may have struck your grandson and left him a cripple, or it might be that they've taken him altogether and left this changeling in his place. This cratur here might be fairy-born.'

Nóra put her hand over her mouth, nodding tearfully. 'Mary, you saw it. You saw it the first time you stepped foot in here.'

Mary cast her eyes to the sputter of a rushlight.

'Johanna. She must have known. A mother always knows her own child.' Nóra took a shuddering breath. 'I knew it too. That first time I saw him. I knew because I expected to love him and . . . I thought something was wrong with me. That my heart . . .' She clutched at her shawl, piercing its weave with her fingers. 'But this – this would explain it. 'Tis the truth of it. There is no sin in my hard heart against him.'

Peg sucked her gums. She was sitting back, her face in disquiet. 'And how might we see if he is one of Them or merely suffering the fairy blast?'

'A change-child is ever eating, never growing. And silence in a child is a sign of the Good People's spite to us when They have been offended. It is by Their never talking that they might be known. His crying at all hours, that too is a sign of the changeling.'

'But Nance, surely a child's cries are no great sign of it belonging to Them. Were that the case, my own children were more fairy than human,' Peg said.

Nance gave her a sharp look. 'But your own children have had the use of their legs all their lives, Peg, and even I, in my little house, hear their prattle on the wind.'

''Tis the sound of his cry too,' Mary added. 'There is a strangeness to it.'

Nóra closed her eyes. 'Like the scream of a fox.'

Peg reached for the poker and stirred the fire, frowning. A constellation of sparks rose above them.

'There are ways in which we might ask the fairy to reveal its nature. To see if it is a changeling,' Nance said.

'I have heard of those ways,' Nóra said, a tremor in her voice. 'Heated shovels and burning coals.' She shook her head. 'I don't want to kill it.'

Nance sat back on her heels and gave her a long look. 'Nóra Leahy, we are not talking of murder. Only threatening the changeling to banish it. I would have your true grandchild restored to you.'

'My brother told me that those by the sea, they leave their change-lings below the high-water mark on the shore when the tide is out.' Mary's face was as pale as milk. 'When the child's crying can no longer be heard, they know the changeling has fled. 'Tis true,' she whispered, blanching at Peg's expression. 'He heard the story himself.'

'Many have lost their children to the fairies over the years,' Nance said. 'Their wives and mothers too. Nóra, you should know 'tis powerful difficult to recover one taken by the Good People. There are those who have chosen to care for the changeling instead, although they be contrary craturs.'

Mary nodded vehemently. ''Tis what I heard in Annamore.' Her voice dropped to a whisper. ''Tis a dreadful shame to lose a baby to the fairies, but 'tis best to care for the wee stock they leave behind and hope they bring the child back in time.'

'I would have Micheál restored to me,' Nóra said flatly. 'How can I love this one when I know the wished-for child is with Them? When I might yet see his face?'

'You would not live with his fairy likeness?'

A stillness passed through Nóra. She sat awkwardly, scrunching her clothes, hardly breathing. 'I have no family. My husband and daughter are passed, God have mercy on them. I have only my nephews, and this . . . cratur. This changeling, if that is what he is. Folk are talking about him. They are blaming him for Martin's death, and the omens they see, and the way the winter has dried up the hens and cows. And if what they say is true . . . I must do something,' Nóra whispered. 'I must try to have my grandson returned.'

Nance inclined her head to one side. 'There is a possibility, Nóra, if 'tis fairy interference here, that your daughter and her son are together under hill, in the *ráth*, dancing. They are fed and kept and happy together.' She waved her hand towards the door. ''Tis an easier life.'

Nóra shook her head. 'If I cannot have Johanna . . . If there is a chance I could have her true son, Martin's true grandson, instead of this . . . I will have her true son.'

The fire spat. Flames crept over the broken embers. Nance closed her eyes for a long moment, as if suddenly overcome with weariness, and lifted her palm from the boy's body. Nóra watched as he snatched at her retreating fingers, catching the back of Nance's hand with his nails. A tiny scratch opened on the old woman's papered skin.

'So it is, then, Nóra Leahy,' she murmured, glancing at the little bead of blood. 'Come to me at the turn of the year and we will begin. We will put the fairy out of him.'

CHAPTER
EIGHT

Yarrow

December moved slowly. The women sang to their cows against the heavy-clouded skies, their voices ringing out in vapour. They slipped their hands inside their clothes to warm their palms against their skin and take the shock out of their touch, and milked their beasts with fingers firm and pleading. They pressed their cheeks against the flanks and sang and milked, and prayed to God it was full of butter.

But the milk came meagre, and across the valley only a long churn would bring the butter against the dash. When at last it broke, the women, relieved, took a small ball of the fat and smeared it on the walls of their homes. They twisted the staff three times and placed it across the mouth of the churn, and some tied twigs of rowan on the dash. Others salted the wooden lids.

At night, under a gibbous moon, the women left their infants in the arms of older daughters and walked the frosted path to the cross-roads on *cuaird*. They lit around the fire of Áine's rambling cabin like moths, faces shining.

'Have you tried a horseshoe?' Áine was saying. 'Sure, himself can find you a shoe of one heating and if you tie it to the churn it will bring the butter.'

'Faith, just a nail would do it.'

'Or three sprigs of yarrow in the pail when you milk.'

'And don't be singing or drinking while you churn. Or starting something with your man. Butter will never come if you're combing and carding each other.'

The women nodded in agreement. There were six of them gathered, crowded around the heat of the hearth. They scuffed their bare feet on the cobbles.

'Did you see the ring around the moon tonight?' asked Biddy.

There was a murmur of assent.

'Sign of rain.'

'And all this fog. Fog on mountains, foul weather.'

''Tis no weather to be out in, that's for sure.'

'I've been seeing Nance Roche creeping about the fields these mornings, so I have.'

Several eyes glanced to where Kate Lynch sat huddled by the fire, her arms cosseted around her body.

'Not even daylight, and she's shuffling through the mist going from place to place, cow to cow. Cursing them. Putting the blink on them.'

Sorcha gave a nervous smile. 'Mam, I bet she was only bleeding them.'

'Aye, she'll be getting powerful hungry now Father Healy has preached against folk going to her for the cure or the keening. How else does she fit food to her mouth?'

'I often see her about,' said Hanna. 'She walks the long field by the road, gathering herbs at dawn or dusk for the cures. She has the knowledge of what herbs to gather, where and when, and how to keep the power in the plant. And what harm if she's also after taking the wool from the brambles, if there's any to be had? Sure, I wouldn't think anything of it.'

'Well, I mind her bleeding animals, Hanna, if that's the mischief she's up to, and the winter weakening the cows as it is.' Éilís sighed. 'Faith, there's no butter to be had in the milk. There's no profit at all in the churn. If that one is creeping about in the dark with her knife, plugging the necks of the beasts and boiling their blood with ill-gotten oats, well, I think that's something the priest should know about.'

'Aye, and the constable.'

'She'd steal the eye out of your head,' Kate hissed.

'She never did a thing against you, and here you are, heaping mud on her name.' It was Áine who had spoken. There was an awkward silence.

Hanna nodded to where Áine had risen to her feet, face flushed. 'She's right. 'Tis a disgrace. That woman gives out the knowledge, and you have cause to believe it, for didn't Nance cure my own sister of the fever not a few months back? My own sister, sick and sweating in her bed with a fever I thought would leave her dead and cold. And if it weren't for the cure that *bean feasa* gave me, 'twould be nothing for my sister but six feet in a graveyard.'

'Maybe 'tis that your sister would be well, charm or no.'

'You'd be a fool to think it. Nance gave me the cure in a bottle, and she told me not to be looking at the fairy *ráth* on my way home but to go straight back to my sister. Well, I did as she said, but – and God knows I tell no lie – as I walked passed that whitethorn, I felt the cure being pulled from my hands. I gripped it tight, and I kept my eyes to the ground, but the Good People were fighting me for it. 'Tis only that I didn't see them that I had the power to get home to my sister. I boiled the herb and gave her three drinks from the drawing of it, and she was out of bed and spinning by my side that very night.'

'You were always one for the stories.'

Hanna bristled. 'Have you no respect for the old amongst us, Éilís?'

'We're only having a laugh, like, Hanna,' Sorcha muttered.

Éilís's face twisted. 'I'm not laughing. The way I see it, Father Healy has a right to be calling her a pagan.'

Hanna sat up straight, indignant. 'Father O'Reilly credited her with the powers. He went to her himself. A priest. As did you, before you married that schoolmaster of yours. I remember when Patrick's cow was sickened, and she told him 'twas the blast and found the fairy dart about it too. The ice was dripping off the cow house though 'twas freezing outside. Such was the heat of the cure, so says Patrick.'

'My man says Father Healy will preach against her every Mass, if that's what it takes.'

'He'll learn to change his tune,' Hanna said darkly. 'There's good reason Father O'Reilly spoke for her. You'd best be listening to me, Éilís. Before Nance Roche lived here, she lived many places. She was no sooner in one place than in another, it used to be said, selling her besoms and dyes on the road, and giving out the cure for the afflictions of those she met.

'It happened that she passed through this valley, walking the long road to Macroom, and she stopped a while. She was sleeping under the furze, out in the open, poor woman. Bone-tired.

'Then who should go past her on the road but Father O'Reilly, and without even looking at him she said, "I know that you've a swelling in your hand, and I tell you, Father, I can give you the cure." Well, the priest asked her, "And what cure might that be?" And Nance said, "You walked past the fairy place and you took a stone from there, and 'tis the hand you took it with that has the swelling." Well, she was right about that, and Father O'Reilly couldn't say a word, he was so surprised. Nance said, "Now you've been shown that I have the knowledge and the healing and no harm in it." And Father O'Reilly, quick as a whip, said, "I see you've the knowledge, but you've given me no healing." And Nance said, "You're standing in it." And sure, the priest looked down and 'twas yarrow he was standing in. And he let her cure him with the yarrow, and all of us saw the swollen hand of the priest cured.

'That is why, until the day he died, Father O'Reilly never had the hard word against Nance, only praised her and gave her as much help as he was able, and assisted her in her living. That is why she has the *bothán* by the woods. He had it built for her, and she selected the site herself, for 'tis close to the Good People and those who gave her the knowledge. Close to the woods and the herbs that grow in them. Close to the boundary water. Sure, 'tis a place for a wise woman, and 'tis wisdom Nance Roche has.'

There was laughter from Éilís. 'Will you listen to that? Your tongue collects no rust, Hanna, with all the stories you tell.'

'That's the truth of it as it were told to me, and the one who told it was no liar!'

'I heard nothing about Father O'Reilly picking up a stone from the *ráth*, though my mam said he had the rheumatism,' mused Biddy.

'Sure, 'twas rheumatism and no fairy in it at all,' said Éilís. 'Nance is an old woman and she's soft in the head, and those who believe she has the cure are softer still.'

Hanna pursed her lips in anger.

'There's no doubting she's a strange one, Hanna,' Sorcha said sheepishly.

'Have you ever met one with the charms who had not the strangeness? It comes with the gift. You can't be expecting one who knows the things she does to be taking part in your almighty cackle every morning at the well. If you're looking for a friend without fault, you'll be looking for a friend forever.'

'Ah, but is that gift you speak of God-given, or is it from the Devil?'

''Tis nothing to do with the Devil at all, Éilís,' Hanna scoffed. ''Tis from her travelling with the fairies. 'Tis no Devil about it!'

'Father Healy says the fairies are for the pagans, and what is not for God is for the Devil.'

'Pssh, the Good People are for themselves alone. They belong to the water and soil and *ráth*. Devil! They're in the Piper's Grave with the whitethorn, not in Hell.'

'Don't you let the priest catch you saying that.'

There was silence. Hanna shook her head.

'Well, this has put you all in each other's hair combs,' Áine mused.

'Do you not see that Nance is after some badness? The priest would have her out. He has the word against her, and sure, she's living hand to mouth and the promise of a hungry year is upon her. Next thing the profit has been stolen from the milk?' Kate bit her lip. 'I saw her creeping about in the fog. God's truth, there are women who turn themselves into hares to suck milk from the cows at night.'

There were some raised eyebrows. Áine rolled her eyes.

'Faith, 'tis true with God as my witness. Once, there was a Corkman. He saw a hare drinking from his cow – suckling it, straight from the udder! – and he got his gun and shot it with a bullet made from sixpence. He followed the blood trail and sure, if he didn't find an old woman sitting by her fire, her leg bleeding.'

'Shame your Seán has such bad aim,' Hanna murmured. There was tittering.

'He sure never misses me!' Kate cried.

The women glanced at one another, their laughter snuffed.

'Kate, do you not . . . Yourself and Seán. Do you not agree together?'

Kate flushed red, her eyes fixed on the fire in front of them. She said nothing.

'Is that the truth of it? Is he after beating you again?' It was Hanna who spoke.

'Kate?'

Kate shrugged, her jaw clenched. 'To the Devil, all of you,' she muttered.

The smirk left Áine's face. She stood and gave Kate a pat on the shoulder. 'The cows will be in butter again. You'll see.'

'What's to be done?' Kate whispered to herself. She shook off Áine's hand. 'What's to be done?'

'It can't stay raining always. As soon as they calve, they will be back in butter.'

The women nestled closer around the fire, exchanging looks. Outside, the hungry wind keened.

The smooth whiteness of the fields melted to mud and dying grass, and the valley felt darker for it. It rained constantly, and the people stayed close to their smoking fires and the inconstant dripping from poor thatch. They muttered, 'A green Christmas leaves a full graveyard,' as they lit their candles and asked the Virgin to stave off winter sickness.

Nance spent the holy day inside her cabin, passing the quiet, rain-filled hours cutting besoms by the fire and dying the scrags of wool she had removed from thorns and brambles and carded into use. Seeing that change-child, that bony marvel nettle-welted in the cabin of Nóra Leahy, had plated her mind with disquiet. It had stirred embers of memory she had thought long dead. Things she had willed herself to forget.

Nance paused in her work to stretch her fingers and checked the simmering pot of stirabout on the fire. She had woken that morning to find turf and a bag of yellow meal lying in her doorway, protected from the rain by a square of oilcloth. There was no knowing who had left the sacks there, although Nance suspected the quiet generosity of Peter O'Connor and his habit of silent, unannounced kindness. Or the gifts might have been a gesture of gratitude from someone who had lately come to her with the winter lying in their lungs; one of those who continued to bring their complaints to her despite the priest's warning. The parade of sickness to her door had thinned since Father Healy had preached against her. No doubt her patients' concern for their souls was now greater than their anxiety over chapped hands or the fevers glittering through their children.

Her days had emptied. It reminded Nance of when she had first fled Killarney and gone to the quiet stretches of rock and moor in her grief. When she had climbed the dry stone walls and walked the fields and slept by the fires of strangers. Those hard years of grinding hunger after the death of her father and the disappearance of her mother and Maggie. Long years of wandering every road between Killorglin and Kenmare, smoking rabbits from their warrens and waiting with fast hands, poisoning rivers with spurge and collecting the rising bodies of dead fish under nightfall. Selling besoms, selling dyes of alder catkin, blackberry and birch. Bog myrtle for yellow. Dark green from briar root. Gathering galls for schoolmasters, some as poor as her, so they might make their ink. Nance of the Herbs, they called her, Nance of the Fairies, and she did as well as she could until her teeth began to fall out of her mouth, and she woke some mornings under hedges, bones aching, not knowing whether she could face another day of walking hungry, walking cold or sunburnt, walking thirsty.

It had been grief and fear that had driven her from Mangerton mountain, but it was hunger that called her back. There was always a living to be scraped off the Killarney tourists if you knew how.

Nance did not remember how she fell into begging, but she remembered the boredom of it. Ten years of crowding the inns, thrusting herself upon the coaches the minute they stopped, blocking shop doors if the shopkeeper was busy and unable to deliver a swift kick and threat.

'Oh, my lady, look at the poor who can't look at you. Heaven be your bed and give us something, blessings be with you on the road. Oh, help the poor cratur whose heart is broke in hunger. Charity, for the love of God.'

Nance shuddered. It was a good thing she had left that town again. It was a good thing she had heard the Good People summoning her to the valley and the priest who protected her, who saw the fairy in her skill, and who let her lay her hooked hands on his own troubled flesh.

She hoped never to go back to Killarney.

For all of Father O'Reilly's welcome, it had taken time before people walked the path to Nance's door. They had built her the *bothán* and left her there. Weeks had gone by without visitors, and she had thought she would go mad from the solitude after the noise and crowds of the town. Younger, then, she had scrambled up the bare shoulders of the mountains to find company in the clouds that brooded on the hilltops. There, in the presence of something ancient and immutable, she found her comfort. She could crouch on the wind-whipped grass and dig the stones from the ground and fling them down at the suspicious cottiers and their fear of any woman who was not tethered to man or hearth. There, upon the mountain, her difference – no matter its great weight, its sharp and restless ache upon her heart – was, in the face of such unyielding beauty, a small and passing shadow in a greater story.

Those days on the mountains had prevented her from turning mad with loneliness. She had climbed until her breath beat in her lungs, and she had watched the rain sweep across the valley below in its slow, grey veil, or the sun track its benevolence across the fields, and she had understood, finally, Maggie's words. Solitude, her difference, would make her free.

But those were younger years, and now Nance felt her age like a millstone around her neck. In the absence of company, without the distraction of boils and rheumatism and heavy coughs or stubborn, bleeding wounds, the past rose up around her like a tide of water, and there was no retreat to higher ground. There was no fleeing the slow flood of remembrance that came. She was an old woman condemned to sit by the fire, bones singing with weather.

Nance carded her stolen wool and her mind filled with her father and his smell of leather and river weed. The timber of his boat creaking, his stories of the Chieftan O'Donoghue rising out of the lakes on May morning. She tried to remember the weight of his hand on her shoulder.

But it was so long ago. And, as always, when she thought of her father, unbidden dark memories of her mother came also.

Nance could almost see that sallow face, looming over her like the moon in the midnight hours.

Mad Mary Roche.

She could almost hear her mother's voice again.

'They're here.'

Teeth bared. Hair uncombed over her face. Her mother waiting by the cabin door while she dressed. Quietly, so as not to disturb her father. Her mother leading her into the night.

Nance struggling to keep up with her mother's long stride. Walking out of the small yard beside their cabin, out past the potato bed, down the lane where the other cabins of the jarveys and lakemen and strawberry girls stood in slum, absorbed into the nightscape at the foot of Mangerton mountain.

Ten years old and pleading in fear, following her mother's dark back past the silver, slender trunks of birch and the sprawl of oak branches.

'Mam, where are we going?'

The water suddenly before them, balancing a fine cloud of mist. The lakes holding their dark mirror to the sky, holding the moon and the stars, until the startled flap of a duck in the reeds disturbed the water and the reflected night rippled. How the lakes had pulled the breath from her in their beauty. Staring at their silvered surface on that first night had felt like stumbling across a rare vision of holiness. It filled her mind with terror.

Her mother stopping. Turning. Face suddenly wide-eyed in fear, like a pig that sees the knife.

'They're here.'

'Who is here?'

'Can you not see Them?'

'I can't see at all.'

'You won't see Them there.' One cold hand against her chest. 'Here. You'll see Them here.'

That first night in the woods by the lake. Crying, curling herself into a nook of mossed limestone, watching her mother dart from tree to tree, muttering to herself, scratching patterns into the soil.

Her father, sitting by the fire when they returned at dawn, his head in his hands. Grabbing Nance, squeezing the breath out of her lungs. Stroking her dirty face as he put her to bed.

'Please, Mary.' Voices in the tremble of early morning. 'People will be making a fairy out of you.'

'I don't mean to do it.'

'I know.'

'I am not myself. I have been away.'

'You are here now.'

Heavy-lidded, watching him comb leaves out of her mother's hair with his calloused fingers.

'Am I? Am I here? Am I my own self?'

'You are my Mary Roche.'

'I don't know. I don't feel I am myself.'

'Mary . . .'

'Don't let Them take me again.'

'I won't. I won't.'

Was that when it all began? Was that when Nance first began to learn about the strange hinges of the world, the thresholds between what was known and all that lay beyond? That night, at ten years old, she had understood, finally, why people feared the darkness. It was an open door, and you could step through it and be changed. Be touched and altered.

Before then, Nance had loved the woods. In the daylight hours, waiting for tourists with cans of milk and *poitín*, the morning rain left the moss vivid underfoot, and the leaves cast their dappled shadow on the clay and stone and leaf. Birds rustled the berried briars. The sight of the forest floor carpeted with the beetled backs of acorns had rushed her with happiness. But afterwards, she understood that the woods changed at twilight; that they grew intolerant of strangers. The birds stopped cheeping and blinkered themselves against the dark, and the fox began to search for blood. The Good People claimed the darkling shadows for their own.

So many years gone and time stretching until she was thin with it all, and still Nance remembered that night in the woods, and the nights that came after. Shaken awake by a mother already half-swept, dragged to the woods where the branches creaked unseen and she choked with fear until piss ran down her leg.

*

She was older when her father began to fix the door at nights, winding rope about the latch. She had helped him. They thought it might stop her mother from leaving. Might stop her eyes from glinting wild, stop her trespass. But still, her mother was swept – on the wind, with the lights – and the strange woman left locked in their cabin, scratching at the walls and dirt floor until her nails broke and bled, was not Mary Roche. The woman They left in her place was a likeness who threw her food against the wall and would not eat, who did not recognise Nance, and who fought her father when he would see her safe in bed.

'I miss Mam,' Nance had whispered once, when the woman who was no longer her mother slept.

'I do too.' Her father's voice was soft.

'Why does she not know me?'

'Your mother is away.'

'She's there. She's sleeping.'

'She is not. Your mammy is away. With the Good People.' His voice had broken.

'Will she come back?'

Her father had shrugged. 'I don't know.'

'Who is the woman in there?'

'She is something left. A trick. They have hoped to trick us.'

'But she looks like Mam.'

The look on his face was one Nance had seen on the faces of other men many times in the years since. The shine of a man in desperation.

'Yes, she looks like Mam. But she is not her. She has been changed.'

What might have happened had her mother never gone with Them? If Nance had been free to marry the son of a jarvey, had lived amongst the people of her childhood all her life long? If Maggie had never been needed. If Maggie had never come in crisis and marked out the difference in her.

Her mother swept, Nance grown in her absence, and then a tall woman in the house, cheek marred by a long purple mark like the burn of a poker. Even in the streets of Killarney, spilling as they were with pockmarked children and men who hung a life's hard living off their cheekbones, the woman had seemed hard.

'This is your aunt, Nance. She brought you into this world.'

The woman had stood still, staring down at her. 'You've grown.'

'I'm not a child anymore.'

'Maggie's come to get your mam back from where she's been taken.'

Nance had looked over to the dark bundle lying in the corner of the cabin.

''Tis not your mam. Not there.' Maggie's voice was solemn. Deep.

'How will you get her back?'

Her aunt had slowly stepped forward and bent to her, until their faces were level. Nance had seen that, up close, the skin of the mark was tight, like scar tissue.

'You see that mark of mine, do you?'

Nance had nodded.

'You know about the Good People?'

Yes. Nance knew about the Good People. She had felt Them in the woods, by the lake, where her mother gave herself up to them. Where she, as a child, had curled into a nest of exposed roots and the moonlight made the world seem strange and the air was thick, occupied.

Her aunt smiled, and at once Nance's fear left her. She looked into the woman's grey eyes and saw that they were clear and kind, and without thinking she brought a finger up to touch the scar.

Dear, dark Maggie. From that first day when they cut bracken for her bed, Maggie began to show her the way in which the world was webbed; how nothing lived in isolation. God Himself signed the stalks of ferns. The world was in secret sympathy with itself. The flowers of charlock were yellow to signify their cure for jaundice. There was power in the places where the landscape met its own, in the meeting of waterways or the crucible of mountains. There was strength in all that was new: the beestings, the dew of the morning. It was from Maggie that Nance learnt the power in a black-handled knife, in the swarthy, puckering mix of hen dirt and urine, in the plant over the door, the garment worn next to the skin. It was Maggie who – in those years when they fought for her mother's return – had shown her not only which herbs and plants to cut, but when, and which to pull by hand and which to set a knife to, and which were made stronger by the moist footprints left by saints as they walked the evenings on their holy days, blessing the ground beneath them.

'There are worlds beyond our own that we must share this earth with,' Maggie told her. 'And there are times when they act on one another. Your mam bears no sin for being swept. Don't you be cross at her for being away.'

'Will you cure her?'

'I will do what I can with what I have, but to understand the Good People is to know that they will not be understood.'

The other families were all a little afraid of Maggie. Her father was too. Her aunt carried a presence, a stillness like that which precedes a storm, when the ants pour over the ground and the birds find shelter and stop singing to wait for the rain. No one dared speak out against her for fear she knew how to set curses.

'She's a queer one,' they said. 'That Mad Maggie. She who does be in it.'

'I never cursed anyone in my life,' Maggie told Nance once. 'But it never does any harm to let folk think you know how.' Her eyes had sharpened. 'People will not come to me if they don't respect me; if they don't fear me, just a little. Oh, there are curses to lay, you can be sure of it. But 'tis not worth the breath you spend. *Piseógs* are fires that flare in the face of those who set them. In time, a curse will always return.'

'Do you know the curses, Maggie? You have no hand in *piseógs*, do you?'

That glinting look. The slow stroke of the purple mark on her face.

'I never say either way to them that come.'

And the people did come to her. Despite her strange blemish, despite her pipe-smoking, and her manly hands, and her cold way of looking at you longer than was comfortable, they decided she had the charms and they came. During the long length of the year the door would be opened to faces waiting out in the cold; shawled, hopeful faces nodding at the sight of Maggie's broad back.

'Is the one with the knowledge in?' they'd ask, and it fell to Nance to meet them at the door and ask loud questions of their ailments, so that Maggie, greeting them under lowered brows, a pipe smouldering in her mouth, might know a little of what she was to treat and surprise them with foresight.

Her father did not remain at home when Maggie took her visitors. His wife was absent, and his home overrun. He spent long hours with his boat, and with the other boatmen, coming home to take up the *poitín* gifted to Maggie for her juniper, her sheep droppings boiled in new milk, her blistering rubbings of crowfoot, her worsted socks filled with hot salt.

'Mind you don't let Nance too close to them that come,' he'd say. 'Full of sickness as they are.'

'She's learning fast,' Maggie said. 'She has a hand for it. Isn't that true, Nance?'

'What's the smell in here?'

'Gladding root. Stinking Iris,' Nance murmured.

Maggie pointed to the bottle. 'Let you don't take too much drink. That's powerful drink, and you on the water.'

'Aye, I know. I know. "Drink makes you shoot the landlord."'

'Worse than that, it makes you miss,' Maggie chided.

The sacred days past and Nance stayed close to her fire. She did not go to hear Mass, and no one came to see her with the priest's word so recently upon them. She wondered what he said of her.

Only the wren boys, faces hidden behind tapering masks of straw, ventured out into the dark fields close to her cabin on St Stephen's Day to beat their *bodhráns* of cured dog skin. She watched them march the muddy fields, bearing the wet-feathered body of the dead bird on a branch of holly. Their cry travelled on the winter wind: 'Up with the kettle, down with the pan, give us some money to bury the wren!'

The wren boys did not come near her cabin for alms or coin. They never had. Nance knew that most of the children feared her. She supposed she was now what Maggie had been to the children under Mangerton. A *cailleach* lurking in her cave of a cabin, able to whistle curses up from spit and hen shit.

In the early days, when Nance knew they believed in her power but did not know its kind, the valley people came to her for the working of badness against others. *Piseógs*. One hazy morning she had opened her door to a woman with her eye black and tooth loose in her gum, and words spilling out of her in fear. She had brought Nance money.

Kate Lynch. Younger then. Fear-filled. Raging.

'I want him dead,' she had said, shaking greasy curls out of her face and showing Nance the glint in her sweating palm.

'Will you sit down with me?' Nance had asked, and when Kate grabbed her hand and tipped the coin into it, she had let the money fall to the ground. 'Sit down,' she said, as the woman gave her a look of bewilderment and scrabbled for the rolling silver. 'Sit down and talk.'

'Why'd you drop it?' Kate demanded, on her knees. 'That's good egg money. I earned it myself. 'Tis honest, not stolen. I earned it with my own hens, and 'tis not his neither. I hide it from him.'

'I cannot take your money.'

The woman stared, her mouth a torn pocket in a pale face.

'I'll not be taking payment in coin. I'd lose the gift.'

Understanding had smoothed the furrows in Kate's brow. She counted the coins and, satisfied, slipped them into her pocket. 'You have the gift though.'

'I have the cure. And the knowledge.'

'The kind of knowledge that would see a bad man buried?'

Nance nodded at her bruise. 'Is that his badness I can see there?'

'You don't know the half of it.' Kate had bitten her lip, and then suddenly, before Nance could stop her, undressed, ripping at her outer clothes and lifting her shift to reveal a body pummelled into spoil beneath.

'Your husband?'

'I sure didn't fall.' She pulled her clothes back down, her face taut with determination. 'I want to be rid of him. You can do that. I know you can. They're saying you're in league with Them that does be in it, and that you have the power.' She lowered her voice. 'I want you to curse him.'

'Even if I wanted to, I don't know the ways.'

'I don't believe you. I know you're not from the valley, but I might show you a blessed well. Where you might walk against the sun. Where you might turn the stones against him.'

'An evil curse does no good to the one who lays it.'

'I would do it myself, but I don't have the skill. Look.' The woman had bent down and picked up the hem of her skirt, and with scrabbling fingers drawn out the slender flash of a needle. 'Every day I set it in my clothes to protect myself from him. Every night I wake and point the eye of it to his damned heart. To give him ill luck.' She waved the needle in Nance's face. 'But it does nothing. You have to help me.'

Nance had put her hands up, guided the needle away from her. 'Listen to me now. Whist now. Curses come home to roost. You do not want to be laying curses on your man, no matter how he rakes you.'

Kate shook her head. 'He's going to kill me. There's no sin in it if he's after killing me.'

'There are other things you might do. You might leave.'

Kate gave a sharp laugh. 'And bundle all my children on my back and take to the road and feed them on mushrooms and *praiseach*?'

'Long loneliness is better than bad company.'

'I want him dead. No, I want him to suffer. I want him to suffer as I have. I want his body to rot, and I want him to sicken, and I want him to wake each morning and spit blood as I have done.'

'I will give you mallow for the bruises.'

'You will not set a curse against him?'

'I will not.'

Kate sank onto the stool. 'Then you must tell me what *I* may do to curse him. Tell me how I might lay a *piseóg*.' Her face contorted. 'I have walked the well. I have turned those cursing stones at twilight. I point my needle at his chest and I pray to God that he be damned. But nothing. Nothing. He thrives. He bounces his fists off me.'

'I cannot tell you the ways.'

'But you know them. And there are other ways. I know there are. But no one will tell me.' Her voice cracked. 'Tell me how to lay a *piseóg* upon him, or do it yourself. Or I will turn the stones against you.'

CHAPTER
NINE

Selfheal

The eve of the new year returned the snow to the fields in whirling winds, the flakes sticking to the thatch and sweeping against the outer walls, hiding the mud spatter and the damp fingers of mould that stained the limewash.

Nóra kept glancing from her spinning to where Micheál lay sleeping in the settle bed, twitching like a dog.

'Is it time, do you think, Mary?'

The maid looked up from where she was slowly winding the wool and peered at the slant of light that fell in from the half-door that hung ajar. 'I think perhaps 'tis not yet twilight. 'Twas twilight she said to come.'

'I thought perhaps 'twas growing dark.'

'Not yet. Perhaps we might wait until the chickens return. Hens keep the hours.'

'Yes, I know that,' Nóra snapped. She wiped her waxy fingers on her apron. 'You pulled the herb? Where is it?'

Mary, hands busy, nodded to the bunch of mint lying in the corner of the room, the leaves a little wilted.

''Tis straggly. Where did you fetch it?'

'The well.'

'Did anyone see you? Were the women there? Éilís? God forbid Kate Lynch saw. She'll cry devilry.'

'No one was there.'

'I don't see why Nance Roche didn't cut the mint herself.'

Mary shrugged. 'Perhaps there is no mint down by the woods. She's an old woman. 'Tis a long way to go, just for some herbs.'

Nóra pulled a face. 'Nothing stops that one, old or no.' She hesitated. 'Did she say there was a danger in pulling it?'

'Not if we cut it in the name of the Trinity.' Mary looked at Micheál as he stirred, his hand lifting in the air and then falling back behind his head. 'I blessed the mint before I put the blade to it.'

Nóra pursed her lips. 'I don't understand it. Mint. Mint is good for fleas and moths. How is mint going to bring a child back from Them?'

'I always tied it around the wrists of my brothers and sisters,' Mary said.

'And why was that?'

'Keeps away the sickness.'

'And did it work?'

Mary shook her head, her eyes fixed on the wool before her. 'Two are with God.'

Nóra's fierce expression softened, and she looked down at the spinning wheel. 'I'm sorry for your troubles.'

''Twas the will of God, but He took a long time in taking them.'

'They suffered?'

'All day and all night they'd cough. They gave up their lives a little cough at a time. But now they are gone to the angels.'

There was a long silence. Nóra glanced at the girl and saw that she was clenching her teeth, her jaw working furiously under her skin.

'But you have many other brothers and sisters.'

Mary sniffed. 'I do.'

'My daughter was the only child I had,' Nóra said. 'Her death was a great loss to me. I have lost my parents, and my sister, and my husband, but 'tis Johanna that . . .' She looked at Mary and, suddenly unable to speak, placed her fist on her chest.

The maid's face was unreadable. 'She was your daughter,' she said plainly.

'She was.'

'You loved her.'

'The first time I saw Johanna . . .' Nóra's voice was strangled. She wanted to say that with Johanna's birth she had felt a love so fierce it terrified. That the world had cleft and her daughter was the kernel at its core. 'Yes,' she said. 'I loved her.'

'As I loved my sisters.'

Nóra shook her head. ''Tis more than love. You will know it some day. To be a mother is to have your heart cut out and placed in your child.'

The wind groaned outside.

'Perhaps I will light the candle now. Just in case.' Nóra got up and closed the half-door, then stoppered the window with straw against the rising draught. The room fell into low light. The fire climbed. Dabbing at her eyes, Nóra lit a candle and set it on the table to guard the house from the coming night and its unseen swift of spirits. The flame whipped on its wick.

'Did you fetch water when you were at the well, or was it only the mint you took?'

'The mint,' Mary replied.

Nóra frowned. 'And what will you have us drink tomorrow when the new year is upon us?'

Mary looked confused. 'I will return to the well. As I do every morning.'

'You will not. I'll not have anyone sleeping under this roof going to the well to draw water on the first day of the new year. Don't you guard yourself up there in Annamore?'

'I fetch the water same as always.'

Nóra pushed the candle to one side and pulled out a small cloth bag filled with flour. 'I'll tell you how it is. There'll be no throwing of the ashes tomorrow. The feet water, you leave that be. From sun-up to sundown, you'll not be parting with anything of this house. And don't be sweeping the floor and all the luck from it either.'

Mary rose to her feet. 'What harm is there in well-going?'

Nóra pulled a face, added milk, water and soda to the flour, roughly mixing it with her hand. 'There's no good in drawing first water from a well on new year's day and that's all I know. Don't be questioning the old ways.' She cast an anxious look to the sleeping boy. 'Especially not now.'

The two women were silent as the new year bread baked. Nóra moved between the fire and loaf in its pot to the door, remarking on the slow descent of light outside, while Mary woke the boy and rugged him in the blanket for the journey to come. Nóra nipped the bread when it was cooked, breaking a corner to let the Devil out, and they ate it before the fire, Mary sopping the crust with milk and easing wet morsels into the child's maw with her fingers. He ate ravenously, chewing at her knuckles. His cries for more continued long after the bread was finished.

'Always hungry, never satisfied,' Nóra sniffed. 'Is that not what Nance was saying? The sign of the changeling?'

'There's a bonfire on the mountain,' Mary said, licking her thumb and sponging crumbs off her clothes. 'I saw some boys piling furze and heather and dead branches up there this morning. Do you think there'll be dancing?'

Nóra picked her teeth with a nail. 'You've a right to come with me to Nance. I don't pay you to go dancing.'

Mary glanced at the boy. 'Are the Good People abroad, do you think?'

''Tis as Nance said. Just as day is joined to night, so does the year have its seams.' She got up and opened the half-door, peering across the valley. 'And that is when They come. That is when They change their abode. Through the stitching of the year. Which way do you think this wind is blowing?'

The light was fading. Beyond the swathes of fast-falling snow, the glow of a fire could be seen on the hill. A dark plume rose from it, tracing the air with the heady smell of wood smoke.

Mary joined Nóra by the door, Micheál on her hip, his head resting on her shoulder. He was oddly quiet. 'I think 'tis coming from the west. Are we in for a storm?'

Nóra brushed her shoulders of snowmelt and shut the door fast again, sliding a wooden bolt against the wickerwork. 'They say there's portent in the direction of a new year's wind.'

'What does a wind from the west bring?'

'Please God, a better year than last.'

Nance sat in the dark of her cabin and, through her open door, watched the dying year surrender to snow. The night was falling holy, as though the glory of God was in the changing of the light. Sitting in her ragged shawls, she felt the silence ring in her ears as loudly as a monastic bell.

It would begin that night. The cures. The mysterious pleading. The unpicking of old magic.

Nance felt the sly pricking of dread.

The boy was not the first child she had seen who had the mark of the Good People. Back when she was new to the valley, after years of cold begging, long after Maggie and the woman who was not her mother had gone, a woman had come to her door, dragging a small, scrunched child behind her. The girl, five years old, had not smiled since the summer before, and while at first she had whispered to her brothers and sisters, she now refused to utter a word. Her mother had wrung her hands, picked at the chapped skin between her fingers.

'She does not answer to her name. She has no interest in playing. In going anywhere. In helping me about the house. And our house is full of strange strife over it.'

Nance had regarded the mute carefully. She was a tiny, folded bird of a child, knees grey with dust from the road. She sat watching them without expression, shoulders cowed.

'When did this begin? Did something happen to her?'

The woman shook her head. 'I blame myself. I left her to the care of her older sisters. I had to go haying . . . She is changed. Deep in my heart I feel that she is not my daughter. She will not respond to her name.'

The woman said that she had left the girl at the crossroads to recover her own daughter from the custody of the fairies. She did not have the heart, she said, to hold her over the fire, for she resembled her own child. The mother had tied her to the post but she had somehow escaped and wandered home. Put herself to bed in her daughter's place. The woman's husband was saying they must now beat the changeling and brand it on the forehead with the sign of the cross. He said they must anger the fairies and force Them to come collect Their own.

Nance had asked the woman to return to her seven times with the changeling. If the power in fire might not be used, they would use the Good People's own plants against Them.

***

Seven mornings of *lus mór*, the great herb. Nance had collected the foxglove at dawn, and given the changeling three drops of juice from the leaves on the tongue, three in the ear. When the fairy child's pulse dropped and she knew that the plant had gripped the blood, she and the mother had swung it in and out of the door with the words she had heard Maggie use, all those years ago.

'If you're a fairy, away with you.'

Seven days she plied the mute imp with foxglove. Seven days the heart of the changeling slowed. Seven days her skin broke in cold sweat.

'Does she suffer?' the mother asked.

'She resists her return to her own people.'

The day after the seventh treatment, the woman had returned alone, her face shining. 'She speaks! She speaks!'

Two fat roosters and a noggin of butter. But as soon as the mother had left, Nance curled up on the rushes of her floor and wept until she thought she would be sick. She could not tell if she was relieved, or terrified.

It was proof of her ability beyond the herbs. It was proof in her knowledge, proof that there was power in the soil, in the raving. All that Maggie had said was true. She was different. She straddled the river and its sorcered current. She left footprints on both banks.

Too late for her mother.

In the weeks after, her thumbs turned. Nance woke and saw the knotting of her knuckles, and saw that They had marked her. Gifted her, and ransomed her.

I have done it once, so I will be able to do it again, Nance thought.

She got up to close the door to preserve the warmth of her fire. She could see flames on the hilltops through the silent drifts, and shadows of dancing bodies flickering. She thought she could hear the beating of a drum.

A good night for ritual, she thought, and saw, then, two dark figures making their way down the path to her cabin.

'Nóra Leahy. Mary Clifford.'

The women were breathing hard, the maid gripping Micheál to her chest, slipping a little under his weight.

'Did anyone see you?'

'They are all atop the mountain.'

'Good. Come in from the cold. 'Tis turning bitter.' Nance led them into the cabin, pointing to a bucket of warmed water. 'Wash your feet there, so.'

Mary hesitated. 'I have Micheál – I mean, I have the . . . Where should I set him down?'

'Is he sleeping?'

Mary pulled away the blanket that swaddled the boy to her chest and shook her head. 'His eyes are open. He squalled to be taken outside, but I think the fresh air has settled him.'

Nance noticed that Nóra lingered by the doorway, shaking the ice from her cloak. 'Come in and bless you, Nóra. 'Tis right you are here. Sit down and take the cold off you.'

The widow pinched her lips and took a tentative step inside, glancing around the room. She started as a rustle came from the dark corner.

''Tis just Mora. My blessed goat. Did you bring the mint with you?'

Mary gently placed the child down by the fire and rummaged within the shawl crossed against her chest. She pulled out the mint and offered it to Nance.

''Tis nine sprigs you have?'

Mary nodded. 'They're a little wilted.'

'You need to chew them.'

Nóra looked confused. 'You're making her eat them?'

'Not eat. Chew. Chew the leaves into a pap. We will be needing the juice.' Nance opened her mouth and pointed to her dark gums. 'I'd do it myself, but . . .'

'Go on then, Mary.' Nóra was impatient.

The girl hesitated, studying the mint in her palm. 'I don't want to.'

''Tis only mint. Don't keep us waiting all night.'

Nance smiled. ''Tis nothing I'm asking you to do that I wouldn't be doing myself. Musha, 'tis only the mint you picked yourself.'

Mary reluctantly tugged the leaves from a stalk and slipped them into her mouth.

'Don't swallow the juice of them,' Nance warned. She fetched a wooden bowl and held it under Mary's chin. The girl, face stricken, spat the green pap into it and wiped her mouth with the back of her hand.

'All the leaves from the nine sprigs,' Nance said, nodding to the remaining stalks. She glanced sideways at the widow and saw that Nóra was staring at Mary, brow furrowed.

Mary crammed her mouth with the remaining mint and chewed it into a paste, her eyes averted. When she finally spat the wet mush into the bowl, her tongue and teeth were stained green.

Nance peered into the slaver, swirling it, then poured it into an old handkerchief to strain the liquid. Mary picked remnants of chewed mint from her lips.

'What is all this for, Nance?'

Nance gave the bowl to Nóra and shuffled to the corner of the room. She returned gripping a thimble.

'There is wisdom in beginning with small charms.' She motioned to the boy. 'Sit down on that stool there, Mary, and hold the child still for me. Aye, that's it. Now, hold his head.' She turned to Nóra. 'You don't want to hold him over the fire? Well, we've a right to be seeing if the cratur isn't struck with an illness of the plain kind.' She thrust the thimble in her face. 'Juice of mint in each ear, and we'll soon know if he's fairy or if the fairies have only made him deaf.'

Mary held Micheál across her lap and turned the fragile round of the boy's skull in her hands to expose the curl of his ear.

Nance dipped the hollow of bone into the bowl and spooned its fill into the boy's canal.

'And now the other?' Mary asked, grimacing as Micheál struggled under her grip, moaning. She turned her hands, exposing the other ear for Nance.

The air was fragrant with the herb. They watched as the liquid spilt into the boy's copper hair.

'What now?'

'Now you wait until morning to see if he has been cured, if he listens to your voices. Perhaps tries to speak. Or if he is unchanged.'

'Is that all?'

Nance shook her head. "Tis a powerful dark night out there. The hours are more powerful for the changing in them.' She wiped a little of the mint from the rim of the boy's ear, then stooped and drew a cloth off a basket by the fire. 'Selfheal.'

Nóra peered inside. 'For sore throats?'

'And for the fairy blast. For the sudden stroke.' She knelt on the floor and, uncovering the boy's feet, kneaded the leaves of selfheal into his soles. Mary and Nóra's eyes bore into her as she smeared the herb into his skin. Nance thought she could feel the glower of Nóra's desperation, the tussle of her hope and her fear.

The child lay still, spumed with mint, blinking into sleep.

"Tis enough, now. Enough for tonight.'

Mary sniffed the bruised selfheal, nostrils flaring.

'When will we know if it has worked?' Nóra plucked the leaves from Mary's hands and cast them on the floor.

'By morning,' Nance murmured. 'You may wake and find your grandson, or you may not. There are other charms, other rituals . . .' Her voice dropped away. 'You will see. All will be well.'

'Do you believe so, Nance?'

'I do, Nóra. In time, all will be well.'

The fires on the hills smouldered orange as the women left, pockets charged with ashes to guard them from the night. Watching them fade into the grey fall of snow, Nance thought she could hear Maggie's voice. A whisper in the dark.

If you don't know the way, walk slowly.

She had chewed the mint herself that night. That first night of the many nights spent in trying to send the changeling woman away and force her mother back. Her father had gone on *cuaird*, and it was just Nance and Maggie, sitting on stools next to where the woman who was not Mary Roche lay. The cratur had not even stirred when they poured the herb into her ears.

'I don't think she will come back,' Nance had said miserably. They were sitting by the fire, staring at the embers, waiting for her father to return.

Maggie was pensive. 'I promised your father I'd do what I could for him.' She hesitated. 'But 'tis not often one who is swept is returned.'

'Why won't the Good People return her?'

''Tis hard to give up what is precious.'

'Maggie?'

'Yes, Nance.'

'How do you know all the things that you know?'

'Some folk are forced to the edges by their difference.' Maggie brought an unthinking hand up to her scar. 'But 'tis at the edges that they find their power.'

⚔

That night Nóra dreamt she was by the Flesk, washing Martin's clothes with the heat of the sun on her back. It was summer. The banks of the river were thick with grass and the wide high stretch of fern. She dreamt she held the wooden beetle in her hand, bringing it down again and again in a rocky pool to pound the dirt from the sopping laundry. As she thumped the beetle for the last time, a bloodstain erupted in the cloth. Curious, she beat at the clothes again, and the blood circled wider, creeping through the weave.

Dread searched her.

Nóra put down the beetle. Something moved under the shirt. Skin prickling, she ripped the wet clothes away.

It was Micheál, his skull stoved in. Drowning in the pinking water of her laundry.

Nóra woke in sweat. First light crept under the cabin door. Uneasy, she padded out to the settle bed where Mary lay snoring. The boy was beside her, a blanket over his head.

Nóra felt her heart stumble over its beats. She reached out and pulled the blanket from the child's face.

He was alive, blinking at her with gummed eyes.

Relieved, Nóra unwrapped the boy from his swaddling and examined his stained feet, the green crust in his ears.

'Are you Johanna's son?' Nóra asked. 'Are you Micheál Kelliher?'

The boy lifted his hands and clawed at her hair, and in mouth-thick gibber he made his answer.

CHAPTER TEN

Hogweed

'Nóra Leahy sent me. She says to tell you that the cratur is unchanged and still spitting and screaming and the cretin he was when we came to you.'

Nance looked up from where she sat in her doorway, skinning a hare. Her hands ran bloody. 'Is that so, Mary Clifford?'

''Tis. There was no cure to be had in the leaves. In the herbs.' The girl hesitated, standing with arms folded and her shawl tightly gathered around her head. 'But in case you're thinking 'twas me that sent the charm out of the mint . . . I promise. I pulled it in the name of the Trinity. And the dew was on it. I did all as you said.'

Nance wiped her hands on her skirt and held the hare out to Mary. 'Take this for me now.'

Mary took it. Nance noticed the girl examine the raw stretch and sinew of the skinned animal.

'Don't you have a fear of eating this?'

'Why is that?' Nance picked up the swimming bowl of guts beside her.

'All the magic that does be in it.'

Nance motioned for Mary to follow her inside the cabin and

shut the door. 'I don't have a fear of eating anything that makes a mouthful. Hares, rabbits, eels.'

Mary pulled a face. 'My brother says an eel can travel the county in a day. Says it takes its tail in its mouth and rolls like a hoop.' She shuddered. 'I don't like anything as cunning as that.'

'I like them well enough if I can catch them.'

Mary sat down by the fire and pointed to the hare skin laid out on the floor. 'Will you be selling that? I've seen boys with caps of hare. The ears still on.'

Nance took the skinned hare from Mary and set it in the empty crock. 'I sell what I can. Dyes mostly, but also skins and besoms. Peck soap.'

'I like the black there,' Mary said, pointing to a loose ball of wool in a basket.

'Alder catkin. Or the roots of spurge. I make them from crottle lichen, bogwater. Sell them. Even heather can wring out a dye. Oh, there's colour to be had from even the humblest of what grows in God's soil.'

'You know a lot.'

'I've lived a long time.'

Mary regarded Nance in the gloomy light. "Tis not the years in a person that gives them knowledge, is it? 'Tis Them that belong to the wilds. They say you speak with Them. You know where the fairies do be, and you speak with Them, and that is how you know these things.' She lifted her chin to the dried plants hanging from the ceiling. 'Is that true? That you learnt it from the fairies and that is why you will return the widow's grandson to her? Because you know Their ways and tricks.'

Nance washed her hands, greasy from handling the hare innards. There was more than youthful curiosity in Mary's voice. There was suspicion there. A sharp-shouldered wariness.

There was a sudden thump of boots outside and Mary stood up quickly, knocking her head against a bunch of St John's wort and sending dried flowers scattering to the ground.

'Here! Here!' It was a man's voice. 'She's here. There's smoke, there's a fire lit. Come on with you, David.'

There was a scuffle outside and three heavy knocks on the cabin wall. Silt fell from the ceiling. 'Nance Roche!'

'Open the door for me, Mary.'

The girl got up and pulled the wicker door ajar.

'May God and Mary and Patrick bless you, Nance Roche, for you must come with me.' It was Daniel Lynch, his face shiny with sweat, chest falling heavy in laboured breathing. He entered and another man, a stoop-shouldered youth that looked much like him, followed, clearly embarrassed by their intrusion.

'Daniel. God save you. What's wrong?'

'We have need of you. The little woman is in the straw. Brigid. My wife.'

'What hour did it begin?' Nance asked.

'Dawn. Her face is all chalk and the pain is on her. I told her I'd come for you.'

Nance turned to Mary, who was gawking at Daniel, slack-jawed. 'Mary, run home to Nóra. Tell her to bring women with her to the Lynches' cabin. Brigid's cousins, her aunts, if she has any other kin. Ask them to bring what clean cloth they have. Milk, butter. Bless yourself as you set out, and bless them before they step inside the Lynches' cabin. I will be there, waiting for them.'

The girl nodded furiously, then pelted out of the door, long legs running, shawl slipping off her head. The brothers watched her flee up the path, mud flicking from her bare feet.

Nance asked them to wait outside while she filled her basket with what she might need. She pulled handfuls of dried herbs from the ceiling and wrapped them in rags. Dried ox-eye daisies and water-cress. Yarrow. She gathered a hazel stick, black threads, and the pail of forge water she had kept covered with a cloth.

'I'm ready,' she said, handing the heavy pail to Daniel. 'Take me to your wife.'

When Nance walked in the Lynches' cabin she knew immediately that all was not well. Brigid lay on a heap of broom and heather by the fire, and the blanket she had placed under her was soaked with blood. Nance turned back outside and held up her hands to stop the brothers from following her inside.

'You did well in fetching me. Now, go on and don't be hovering about this door like horseflies. I'll have you told when there is news to tell.' She spat on the ground. 'God be with you.'

Brigid's eyes were screwed shut with pain. At the sound of the door closing she threw her head back. 'Daniel?'

'God bless you, child, 'tis Nance. Your man's gone and fetched me for you.' She knelt on the floor beside the woman and pushed a folded blanket under her back.

Fear rose off the girl in waves. She is a spooked mare, Nance thought.

'I'm frightened,' Brigid choked. 'Is it supposed to feel like this? It doesn't feel right.'

'I'll see you safe.' Nance bent over the girl and began to whisper a prayer in her right ear.

Nóra arrived at the Lynches' cabin with Éilís O'Hare, Kate and Sorcha. She hadn't wanted to ask the women to come at all, so bitter did she feel towards them and their constant spluttering of gossip, but they were the only women bound to Brigid through her marriage, and if blood could not be fetched to mind her, it was right that a kind of kin be in the room. She had sent Mary to Peg with Micheál.

Nóra opened the door and found the room full of smoke and smell. Brigid was moaning in protest as Nance insisted that her hips face the fire. The heat inside the cabin was insufferable. Brigid's face rolled with sweat, and the old woman's hair was damp against her skin.

The women stopped in the doorway, staring as Nance urged Brigid to lay still and not kneel as she was trying. The young woman's thighs were slippery with blood.

'Sorcha, come in and help your cousin settle. I need her to face the fire, so.' With her help, Nance picked up Brigid's feet and hauled her closer to the hearth, blazing it with dried furze until the darkness peeled back to the corners of the room.

Brigid's pupils were dark and wide and unseeing. Éilís stood by the wall gripping a jug of water, her jaw set, tense. Kate hovered beside her daughter, taking a long red ribbon from the neck of her crossed shawl and holding it out in her left hand.

'What are you doing with that ribbon there, Kate?' Éilís asked. 'What's that for?'

Kate didn't answer, but began to knot and unknot it over Brigid's heaving form.

'What are you doing?'

'To ease the birth,' Kate muttered. Nance cast her a long look but said nothing.

'Nance, how are you getting on?' Nóra asked.

'There is watercress in that basket. Pound it to a poultice, will you. And you two can make yourselves useful. Take the black thread in there and tie it where I tell you.'

Éilís and Sorcha glanced at each other.

'Quickly! You need to arrest the flow of blood. Tie that thread there on her wrists.'

The two women heard the urgency in her voice and bent closer.

'Bite it if you must, and tie it on each ankle, each finger. Each toe. Tightly, mind.'

There was a light tapping on the door, and Mary's face peered inside, eyes growing wide at the sight of the blood on the ground.

'Nance.' Nóra gestured at the girl with the pestle.

'Send her away. For pig dung. Try the blacksmith's.'

'You heard her,' Nóra said.

Mary disappeared outside and the women continued their slow work on Brigid. She lay still, teeth bared. Nóra passed Nance the poultice and knelt behind Brigid so that she might rest her head on her lap.

Nance's lips pressed tightly together in concentration as she lifted the girl's damp dress, exposing the swell of her belly. She smeared the pounded watercress on Brigid's thighs, skin and pubic hair.

Blood rippled out of her. All the women saw it.

An hour dripped by. Mary returned from the blacksmith's, her hands dirty with pig dung. Áine was with her, gripping a rosary and woven cross.

Nance looked up at the sound of their entrance. 'Áine,' she cried. 'Bless you, but I can't be letting you stay.' She stood, her apron as bloody as a butcher's, and took Áine by the shoulders.

'I want to help,' Áine protested.

Nance whispered an apology and walked Áine outside, shutting the door firmly behind them.

'Why can't Áine come in?' Mary whispered to Nóra. 'What has she done?'

Nóra clucked her tongue and continued to sponge Brigid's temples with forge water.

'She only wanted to pray over her.'

'Everyone knows Áine's barren,' Kate spat. 'She might cast the evil eye over the child.'

'She would not! She's a good woman.'

'Whether she's good or not has nothing to do with it. Most of them with the evil eye have no knowledge of when they cast it.' Kate licked her lips. 'You could be casting it for all we know. The redheaded girls do be with the evil eye. Unlucky.'

Nóra had just opened her mouth to protest when Nance returned inside with a small clay jug. A stink of ammonia filled the room.

'What is that?' Mary gaped.

'The water of the husband,' murmured Nóra.

Using a heather besom, Nance began to dash the urine around the room and on Brigid's face, stomach and lower body, flicking the last of it on the small wicker cradle in the corner.

'An old and holy blessing,' Nance muttered.

The women said nothing.

Throughout the day they tended to Brigid under Nance's direction. They mixed the pig dung with forge water and pasted it over her abdomen with their bare hands. They took turns knotting and untying Kate's ribbon ceaselessly over her until their arms ached and the ribbon grew stained with the grease of their fingers. They watched Brigid's toes and fingers seize and swell with trapped blood under their ties of thread, and dribbled ox-eye daisy boiled on new milk into her open mouth.

It was only as the day eased back into darkness that the child came.

It was dead, its lips dark.

Brigid, weak as water, tumbled into unconsciousness.

Daniel was ushered into the cabin and shown the tiny body of his son. The women stood around him, faces grey with exhaustion, too tired to grieve. He looked down at his unconscious wife and brought a hand over his mouth as if afraid of what might come out of it. Mary stepped aside and watched as he walked back out into the cold blue of the evening to fight his grief out with the sky.

Nance told Sorcha to wrap the baby and cover its face.

'Is Brigid dead?' Kate asked.

'Not yet.' Nance took a small piece of paper from her basket, unfolded it and shook something into an earthenware bowl. 'Fetch a light,' she muttered.

Mary raked over the smoking fire to uncover the belly of embers and carefully pincered a live coal with the tongs.

'Set it here.' Nance held out the bowl, and Mary saw it was full of hogweed seed and dried horse dung. She placed the ember in the bowl and smoke uncurled from the mix. 'Let her breathe of it,' Nance said.

Mary crouched beside Brigid and placed the smoking hogweed beneath her nose.

'Does she stir?'

'I can't be sure she's breathing.' Smoke covered the woman's face like a veil.

'Pull her chin down for me, girl.' Taking the bowl from Mary, Nance blew the smoke into Brigid's open mouth.

Nothing happened.

'Shall we say a prayer?' Mary asked.

Brigid's nostrils flared and she began to cough.

'Praise be,' Nance said, wiping her hand across her forehead. It left a trail of blood. 'She's life in her yet.'

The evening was a strange, silent one. Brigid woke and wailed for her child and for her husband, and clamped her mouth against

Nance's insistent hand offering her berries of bittersweet. She fell asleep only when exhaustion overtook her. Then the women rolled her body to remove the bloody heather and replace it with fresh straw. Nance shoved the afterbirth on the fire, where it hissed and gave off a meaty smell.

'Where is her man?'

'Outside,' Mary said. She peered out the door. 'He's on his knees in the field.'

Nance was sitting on a stool, her head in her hands. 'He must be fetched.'

Nóra's face was white. 'Let him grieve, Nance. Let him sit in the soil.'

'No. The young have weak spirits. They are hard put to defend themselves against the devils that hover all places.'

'Give him a moment alone.'

'Mary Clifford,' Nance said. 'Go and bring Daniel back in. He has a right to protect the soul of that child.'

Sorcha looked down at the little bundle in her lap. 'I . . . I blessed him. I crossed his forehead with the forge water. Is that not a christening? Is that not enough to get him to Heaven?'

Kate sniffed. ''Twas dead afore it came out.'

'Still,' Sorcha protested. 'A blessing is a blessing.'

'Go get Daniel, Mary,' Nance repeated. She pushed herself to her feet and staggered over to the chicken roost against the wall of the Lynches' cabin. Peering at the line of blinking hens, Nance reached in and grabbed one, pinning it underneath her elbow to prevent the bird from flapping. It struggled against her grip. 'Fetch Daniel,' she said.

Mary ran out into the field, her ankle jarring on the uneven ground. Mud splashed up her dress.

Brigid's husband was kneeling amongst the lazy beds, his head on his knees. Áine, Peter, Seán, John and his brother, David, stood around him, keeping him company in silence. Above them the clouds had vanished and the sky was bright with emerging stars.

'Leave him be, girl,' Seán said.

'Nance says she needs him.'

'He's done all he can.'

'She's worried about the devils.'

Áine's brow creased. 'What now?'

Mary bit at her nails. They tasted of dung.

Peter nodded. 'Nance is right. That child is not gone to God. Brigid is ill protected. There is evil that would seek to enter your house, Daniel.'

Seán spat on the ground. 'Peter. Don't be talking of this now.'

Daniel looked up and Mary flinched at the sight of his red-rimmed eyes, the raw look of his mouth. 'She wants me?'

Mary nodded. 'She's taken one of your chickens and asked me to fetch you.'

Seán groaned and placed a hand on Daniel's shoulder. 'She's done enough, nephew, don't you think?'

Daniel shrugged him off angrily.

'Go on, Daniel,' Peter urged. He turned to Seán. 'Let the man do something for his child.'

Nance met Mary and Daniel by the open door and passed the hen over the threshold. 'You know what I need from you,' she said, placing a knife in his hand. 'I'm sorry for your trouble. Kill it.'

Daniel didn't look at her, but accepted the chicken and, in one swift movement, cut its head off. He gave it to Nance and she threw it on the fire, where it smouldered. The women inside brought their hands to their faces as the smell of burning feathers filled the air.

Nance took the dead bird, which jerked wildly in death throes. Holding it firmly by the feet, she turned the hen upside down and dripped its blood on the floor of the cabin by the entrance. She returned it to Daniel, wiping her hands on her skirt. 'Circle the cabin with blood. Protect your wife.'

Mary stepped inside and sat next to Nóra, who was watching over Brigid, her eyes swimming. 'Missus. What was that for?'

'For the wee babby's soul,' Sorcha answered, crossing herself. 'Protection.'

Éilís stood up suddenly. 'If spilt blood can waylay the Devil, then sure this place is holy, for Brigid's blood is burning with the straw on the fire and the air is full of it!' She spat on the ground and stormed out the open door without looking back.

Mary noticed that one of the Lynches' farm dogs had appeared outside. It stood on the threshold of the cabin, crouched close to the ground, sniffing the chicken blood.

Before Mary could say anything, Nóra rose and kicked it from the door.

Nance returned home from the birth reeking of blood and shaking with exhaustion. No food had passed her lips since that morning and, walking the narrow path home in the starred night, she felt overcome with dizziness. The night was cold but clear, and the full moon cast pure over mist that lingered on the ground, unmoved by any wind. The air seemed impossibly damp and sweet after the heat and smoke of the cabin.

Suddenly Nance stumbled sideways to the stone wall that bordered the lane, falling against thorny briars and dropping her basket of soiled linen and the remains of her herbs.

How she wished the child had been born alive.

She had delivered a generation of children in the valley, it seemed. She saw them every day: small, shrill children who buried their snotty faces into their mothers' skirts, scraped their knees on the walls, and grew strong scarpering along the fields. But amongst the children she delivered who stuck to life like burrs were others who came too still, too small, knotted with cord. There were those who did not catch to the fabric of the world. It happened. She knew it happened.

So why did the death of Brigid Lynch's child fill her with such dread? She had done all that was needed. She had done all that Maggie had taught her to do.

The besom of broom and the piss of the husband.

The heat of the fire set to the slope of the hips.

The thread, when the blood came, and the pig muck on the abdomen, and the forge water and watercress, and even Kate's relentless unknotting of the blessed ribbon.

Nance remembered then. She had not brought her cloth. The white swaddling cloth that she had dragged through the dew of every St Brigid's morning to be blessed by the saint, to be wrapped around the mother if the labour was long.

Would that have saved the child?

Nance slowly picked up her basket and pushed herself from the wall. The brambles snagged her clothes. It no longer mattered. She had done everything in her power, but the child was not meant for the world.

The woods and her small cabin before them looked cold and empty in the deep blue of the night. Her goat, a ghost in the distance, stood looking at her, waiting to be led indoors.

She reached the cabin and threw her arms around the animal, comforted by the round heat and smell of her.

'Truth, you are a patient girl,' she murmured, nuzzling her face into Mora's wiry coat. She led her indoors and tethered her to the hook in the wall, then lit the fire. She drank some milk, scattered groundsel and a little yellow meal to her chickens, some already roosting, and lay down wearily on her bed.

But sleep did not come. Nance lay on the heather, cradled by her own exhaustion, her mind uneasy. Again, she had the sense that something terrible was happening. That in some irreparable way the world was changing, that it spun away from her, and that in the whirl of change she was being flung to some forsaken corner.

The fire cracked as the turf sods slowly disintegrated into ash.

What would her father say to her now, if he were alive? He who understood the strange winds that blew, who understood the anatomy of storms.

'The cod swims in deeper waters,' she remembered him murmuring, pulling her head to his shoulder. 'There's a mighty peace in the deep, and that is all the cod is after. The untroubled deep. But a storm will toss the water about like a devil. Fish, weed, sand, stones, even the old bones and bits of wrecked ships, 'tis all tossed feathers when the storm hits. Fish that like the deep are thrown into the shallows, and fish that have a need of the shallows are pushed into the deep.'

His hands stroking her hair. The smell of boiling potatoes as they waited for their dinner.

'Begod, I tell no lie. But what does the cod do when he senses a storm in the water? He swallows stones. Faith, 'tis true or I'm not your da. Your cod will fill himself with stones to stay out of the mighty swell of the sea. He will sink himself. All fish are afraid of thunder, but only some know how to keep themselves out of the way of it.'

Nance closed her eyes and her heart clenched in pining for her father.

The dead are close, she thought. The dead are close.

*

Sometime before dawn Nance heard a noise outside. Rising to her feet, she took a dead ember from the fire for protection against the fairies and peered into the uncertain night. The sound came from the Piper's Grave. Nance set out in the direction of the *ráth*.

The moon had listed to the horizon, but its light still cast a varnish over the valley and Nance could see a man standing next to the great slab of stone in the *cillín*, his hand resting on its slender edge. He was praying, it seemed. His head was lowered.

Daniel.

Nance stole closer and watched him from beyond the low wall that marked the sacred space from the surrounding fields. A small box lay by his feet.

Nance wondered whether Daniel had made the coffin himself, nailing together what poor, unhallowed wood he could cobble from his home, or whether a neighbour had, in generosity, made one to accommodate the unbaptised child.

She watched as Daniel wandered the *cillín*, his eyes to the ground, then having decided on a place and retrieved a spade, began to dig a grave. The soil was cold and hard, and for many long minutes all Nance could hear was the rasp of the spade's iron edge against the untended ground. Nance watched as Daniel fetched the tiny coffin and placed it gently into the earth on his knees. He stayed there for some time before wearily rising to his feet and filling the grave in with clay.

It was only when he walked to the wall to lift a large white stone to mark the unconsecrated grave that he saw Nance. He stopped and stared at her in the moonlight, holding the rock in both hands as though he could not trust his eyes. Then slowly, without a word of greeting, he turned, placed the stone on the disturbed soil and walked away, his arms holding the spade across his shoulders like a man crucified.

Nance stood there in the unfolding dark until the crow of a cock-
erel broke the stillness of the valley. Casting one long look to where
the stillborn lay in the silent, eternal soil, she crossed herself and
returned to her cabin.

CHAPTER
ELEVEN

Foxglove

Brigid's terrible labour and the dead child were all the women seemed to talk about in the days after the birth. Mary noticed that they came to the well in greater numbers than was usual, standing in dark clothes like the jackdaws that clustered in the fields. Some wore expressions of sympathetic sorrow, mothers who had lost their own children and who understood the woman's loss, but some seemed, to Mary's ears, more interested in finding fault with what Brigid had or had not done to secure the life in her child.

'David said she did not visit John O'Donoghue to blow the bellows.'

'Sure, I've done that six times and 'tis six fine children I now have in this world.'

''Tis a powerful way to promise safe delivery, the bellows.'

'She was at the wake of Martin Leahy. I saw her. She knelt by his dead body. Do you think there's something in that?'

'Ah, but she was not there when the body was coffined.'

'No,' said one woman with an air of conspiracy. 'But where *was* she? Was she not with Peg O'Shea, who, I hear, was minding Nóra Leahy's grandson?'

There was a murmur of incredulity.

'I would not be easy in my mind to stay in the same room as that cratur.'

'Now, tell me. Do you know what illness is upon him? I knew Nóra was brought the child when her daughter died, but I've never seen her with him. I've not seen the child at all.'

'She hides him.'

'Because he is a changeling! He's no child at all!'

'Begod, I've heard he will not walk in company, but dances and sings when alone.'

'And how would you know that, if no one's with him to spy all that dancing?'

There was laughter, then someone nudged the woman who had spoken and gestured to Mary.

'You're the maid of Nóra Leahy, are you not?'

'Mary Clifford is her name.'

Mary looked up from her well buckets and saw a kind-faced woman sizing her up.

'Is it true, *cailín*? What they say about that boy? Is he a changeling?'

Mary swallowed hard. The women were all looking at her. 'Nance Roche will have him restored.'

The woman chewed the inside of her cheek thoughtfully. 'You know, I saw a changeling child before.'

'Hanna!'

There were some surprised chuckles. The woman spun around. ''Tis no thing to laugh at. Terrible sorrow for the mother. How would you feel if your own son was stolen and you were left with a bawling withered root sickening in your own child's cradle?' The laughter subsided and she clucked her tongue. 'Good, well. Nance knows what she's doing.'

There was a cry, and Mary saw Kate Lynch storming through the group, her empty water pail banging against her leg. She was scowling. 'You should be asking yourselves what hand Nance had in Brigid's trouble!'

'What are you saying, Kate?'

One of the women, her throat flushed with excitement, raised her voice. 'I always knew she was a baby-dropper.'

'What do you mean by that?'

The woman's voice fell to a whisper and the others shuffled into a tighter circle. ''Tis the word for them. After what they do.' She glanced at the women, her eyes narrowed. 'I heard 'tis why she came here, all those years ago – to escape those who would see her hang.'

'Faith, I've always thought she came here running from something.'

'She's a baby-dropper. She knows all the ways.'

'And what ways might they be?' asked Hanna, staring at the others with distaste.

The woman rolled her eyes, lips moist with scandal. 'Truth, they call them baby-droppers as they know how to let the baby, when it comes, drop straight into a pail of water.' She stopped to see if the women knew her meaning. 'Sure, if the baby drowns in that pail before it takes a breath, then no judge could say it was done intentional.' She shuddered. 'Or, soon as the baby is born, she wraps the cord around its neck. Quick, like. Strangles it with its own cord and says it came that way, the poor misfortunate.'

'Are you saying that Brigid Lynch asked Nance to kill her own child?'

The woman blushed. 'I'm not. I'm saying you don't ask a fox to mind the hens.'

Mary had heard enough. She stood up and, thrusting her chin down, made to force her way through the group.

''Twas the herbs she gave her.'

Mary paused.

It was Kate Lynch who had spoken. She stood there with her arms held out from her body, her shawl pulled down past her eyes, face shadowed.

'Daniel told Seán he went to see Nance a few weeks ago. Brigid was wandering in her sleep. He found her in the *cillín*.'

There was a gasp. Several women crossed themselves.

''Tis not the half of it! He asked Nance for a cure for the sleep-walking and Daniel told Seán she gave him berries of *bittersweet*.'

'And what is the harm in bittersweet?'

''Tis nightshade!' Kate threw her pail on the road and it rattled over the stones. ''Tis poison. Nance Roche is corrupting her own cures. Don't you see it? You're blind, the lot of ye. She's summoning illnesses so she might put food in her mouth.'

⚛

'What do you think it was, then?' Mary was sitting on the floor with Micheál while Nóra strained potatoes for their morning meal.

''Tis just the way of it with some children.'

'Do you not think 'twas Nance's herbs that did it?'

'Herbs?'

'The bittersweet. Kate Lynch said Daniel went to Nance for a cure to stop Brigid from walking the fields in her sleep, and now they're saying 'twas the berries Nance gave him that killed the child in her.'

Nóra frowned. 'We were there. You saw with your own eyes Nance Roche doing all she could to bring that child forth whole and living.'

Mary sighed and absently brushed the hair from Micheál's forehead. 'Do you not think there's some danger in us taking Micheál to her for the cure?'

Nóra glanced sideways at the boy. ''Tis not Micheál.'

'Still, 'tis not likely to hurt him, the herbs, do you think? If 'twas the bittersweet that killed the wee baby . . .'

Nóra slapped the skib of potatoes on the pot. ''Twas only a mush of mint, and it did nothing at all! No good. No bad.' She drew back away from the cloud of steam.

'Not the mint,' Mary mumbled. 'But whatever she'll be using next. Sure, Nance'll be using a mighty herb next. Might be a danger in that.' Micheál gurgled beneath her, and she smiled, gently batting at his swinging fists.

'What would you have me do, then? Raise that fairy as my own? Have him crying like a *bean sídhe* every night with no stopping him? Your eyes look like two burnt holes in a blanket, and mine feel the same.' Nóra picked up a hot potato and dropped it back on the wicker, sucking her fingers.

Mary's smile fell. 'I just worry for him, is all.'

'There's no point worrying about that cratur. Look.' She pointed to the boy, her lips pincered. 'See? It smiles.'

Mary gave the child a tickle on his chest and he squirmed in pleasure.

'It has you wrapped around its wee finger.'

'Why do you call him *it*?'

Nóra pretended she hadn't heard.

'When he's not after crying or screaming or sleeping he almost looks like a real boy, don't you think?' Mary tapped him on the chin and Micheál shrieked in laughter.

Nóra watched them, frowning. The maid looked younger when she smiled. Mary's face was so often solemn, so often puffy and red-eyed with weariness, that Nóra had forgotten how young she was. How far away from home she was. With the cold sunlight from the open half-door lighting on the red of Mary's hair, and the girl's laughter softening her face, Nóra was reminded of Johanna.

'You must miss your family,' she said suddenly.

Mary looked up, her face twisting. 'My family?'

'Well?'

'I do.' The girl looked back at Micheál and ran her hands through his hair. 'I miss them mightily. All the little ones. 'Twas me that looked after them and I worry for them with me gone and my mam with no time on her hands to be giving them.'

'You think of them, from time to time.'

Mary hid her face, and Nóra saw that she was pinching the skin on the back of her hand.

She's trying not to cry, she thought, and a little of the hardness she had felt towards the girl at the sight of her playing with the boy crumbled away. Without saying a word Nóra rose and walked into her bedroom. Lifting the mattress from the bedstead she felt around the rough boards until she found a parcel. She unwrapped it, her heart beating rapidly.

It was as she had left it. A clipping of her daughter's hair. Rust-red. Bound together with string with the curl of childhood still at its ends.

A comb with only a few of the teeth missing, a stray hair still caught in the bone.

An arbutus carving from Killarney, their initials carefully marked amidst a tangle of carved roses. The mirror it had held had long broken and fallen out, but the wood remained. A wedding present from Martin.

Nóra brought the lock of Johanna's hair to her nose, searching for the smell of her child, but it had faded. All was straw bedding and dust. She put it back in the cloth with the carving, casting a gentle thumb over Martin's initials, and returned the parcel to its hiding place.

The comb she picked up and took with her back to the fireside. Before she could change her mind she handed it to Mary. 'Here.'

The girl frowned, not understanding.

Nóra picked up the maid's hand and pressed the comb into it. ''Twas my daughter's. She had the same hair as you. Pretty.'

Mary held the comb lightly in her hand and ran her thumb over the fine teeth of bone.

''Tis a gift.'

'I've never had a comb before.'

'Well, now you do.'

'Thank you, missus.' Mary smiled, and Nóra brought a hand to her chest at the sudden aching she felt there.

'Your daughter must have been beautiful.'

Nóra pressed her fingers to her ribs, but the ache deepened. 'Well, its own child is bright to the carrion crow.' Her voice shook. 'You'll be a mother one day, Mary Clifford. You'll know.'

Mary shook her head. 'I won't be married.'

'You don't want children of your own, then?'

'There's enough children in this world for me to look after.'

'Ah, but they'll grow up. Your brothers and sisters will grow and then you'll be lonesome for your own.' Nóra picked up a cooled potato and passed it to Mary. 'Feed it, then. Go on.' She began to peel a lumper for herself, watching the way the maid fed the mewling boy. Rather than break off small pieces for the child, Mary took bites of potato flesh, then spat the chewed mush in her hand to slip into Micheál's mouth.

She caught Nóra's glance. 'So he doesn't choke,' she muttered.

'You dote on it.' Nóra bit into her potato and chewed, watching.

'That mint. It has done nothing for it. I've been thinking. We'll be taking it back to Nance's tonight.'

Mary blanched. 'Do you not want to wait to make sure that the selfheal –'

'Tonight. There's no fixing in the boy. There's none of my grandson returned. How can you sit there feeding the fairy, knowing it has not even enough blood in it to earn its place in Heaven? Knowing that Johanna's poor Micheál is out with the fairies when he ought to be in here with me?'

'He has to be fed, still.'

Nóra shook her head and swallowed. 'I can't be waiting for the selfheal.' She shivered, stood and fetched the bottle of *poitín* from the keeping-hole in the hearth wall. She could feel Mary's eyes on her.

'Now, you're not to be thinking 'tis mine. The drink was Martin's and 'twas only for the men who came for a night of company.' Nóra grimaced as she pulled the cork. 'But I've a need to calm . . . I've a need for . . .' She took a tentative sip, closing her eyes, and a vision of her daughter's hair in its cloth shivered through her. She coughed on the fumes of the drink and offered the bottle to Mary.

The maid shook her head, picking up the comb.

Nóra sat, clutching the bottle. 'We will take the changeling back tonight, Mary. I can't be waiting like this. Hearing it scream, waiting for it to change. I can't be waiting.' She took another sip. 'Ever since Nance pronounced it fairy, I can't help but think on what Johanna's son will be like. Her true son. He will have grown. I can almost see him . . .' Nóra lifted the bottle to her lips and took a deeper draught. 'I dream about him, Mary. I see her boy. A right natural little lad, laughing. I hear him. His voice speaking to me. Just as when I first saw him in his mother's arms. And I hold him and I tell him of his mother. How good she was, how . . . how beautiful. Oh, she was a beautiful child, Mary. Every night I combed her hair with that you've got now. Combed it till it shone. She loved that. I dream of combing her hair, Mary. I dream of the both of them, Johanna and Micheál, and them both alive and with me, and . . .' She shut her eyes and her voice grew bitter. 'But then that one starts up with its screaming.'

Mary was silent. She brought a hand to her mouth and spat a gob of chewed potato into it.

Nóra waved the *poitín* in the boy's direction as Mary fed him, his body jerking. 'That one has no love for me. It knows nothing like that. All it is . . .' She pushed the cork back into the neck of the bottle. 'It's all need and no thanks for it.'

Mary wiped her hands on her skirt and eased the child up onto her chest, tucking his head against the side of her chin.

'But Johanna's true son . . .' Nóra took a deep breath. 'Even in my dreams he is a consolation. He is a gift. Something left for me.' She looked across at the maid and saw both Mary and the boy watching her. The changeling was quiet, his eyes sloping over her face.

'Do you know, Mary, in my dreams he looks like Martin.'

Mary glanced at the *poitín* bottle in Nóra's hands and began to brush the fairy's hair. He blinked at the light pull of Johanna's comb.

Nóra shuddered.

'Tonight,' she said, tugging the cork and taking another swift sip. 'We'll take it at dusk.'

They returned to Nance's cabin that evening, the boy bundled in rags, pale legs dangling against Mary's thin hip. The sky was crowded with clouds threatening rain, but as they reached the end of the valley the horizon broke clear, letting in a late sun. Light fell on the puddles in the fields until they seemed like pools of gold amidst the mud. Mary glanced at Nóra and saw that she had seen the sudden seams of light on the ground too. A good omen. They smiled, and Mary thought the widow seemed calmer for the drink. She had seen Nóra tuck the bottle safely into her shawl before they left.

Nance was sitting on a stool in her doorway, smoking the evening hours. She waited until Mary and Nóra stepped into her yard before rising and greeting them. 'God and Mary to you.'

'You knew we'd be coming.' Nóra's words were slurred.

'Your Mary Clifford there told me that there was no change in him. I thought you'd be here one of these nights.'

'There's no change in him at all.' Nóra reached out to take Micheál from Mary's arms, but her grip was weak and she stumbled, nearly dropping the boy. Mary quickly grabbed the child and hoisted him back onto her hip. He began to squeal.

Nóra righted herself, blushing. 'There, see.' She pointed to the way his legs fell useless, toes pointed inwards. 'Do you see, Nance? No kick at all.'

'Mmm.' Nance narrowed her eyes at Nóra, then took a drag on her pipe and blew smoke over the boy's face. He needled the air with his cries. 'Best come in then.' As they stepped into the cabin, Nance caught Mary's arm. 'Has that one liquor taken?'

Mary nodded and Nance ran a tongue over her gums. 'Right so. Well, put him down.' She pointed to her bed of heather in the corner. 'Nóra Leahy, I'll not be lying to you. The cure of mint and selfheal was a small thing but it proved the child changeling as we suspected. Now, to banish the fairy calls for stronger stems.'

Nóra sat down on the stool by the fire and looked at Nance expectantly. Her face was flushed, her hair dishevelled from the walk outside. 'What is it you'll be trying next?'

Nance waited until Mary had settled the boy on her bed. '*Lus mór*. The great herb.' She showed the women some green leaves, slightly crumpled.

'Foxglove,' Mary whispered, her eyes flashing to Nóra. ''Tis poison.'

'Fairy blasts calls for fairy plants,' Nance chided. 'And no plant is a poison to the one who knows how to use it.'

Mary's heart began to pound in fear, as though the current of her blood had changed direction. 'You'll not be giving it to him for the eating, will you? Just for the soles of his feet like before?'

Nance regarded Mary with a smoky eye. 'You have a right to trust me.'

Nóra nodded absently in agreement.

Mary bit her lip. She felt sick. The cabin air was hot and stuffy, and she could smell the goat waste lying in the drain. She closed her eyes and felt sweat break out on her upper lip. In his dark corner, Micheál was bleating like a lamb separated from its mother. A strained wavering cry sounding over and over.

''Tis a bath we'll be giving him tonight,' said Nance, and she placed the foxglove leaves in a large pot of water. Nóra rose to help her lift the black crock directly on the embers of her fire.

'We'll wait until 'tis warm enough for the water to take on the power of the *lus mór*,' Nance said, settled back on her stool.

'There's no need to have the boy on the bed when I might hold him,' Mary said. Without waiting for the women to respond, she rose and stumbled to the child. His eyes darted over her face as she approached. Mary picked him up, her eyes averted from his lolling head, the quiver of his face.

'She's forever holding it,' Nóra muttered to Nance.

'It keeps him from crying,' Mary said.

'Well, there's truth in that,' murmured Nance. 'Not a sound from him now.'

Nóra frowned. 'But sure, aren't you holding it the whole night long, and it screaming like you're about to cut the throat of it?'

Mary tucked Micheál close against her chest, and arranged his legs so that they fell neatly over her knees. 'I think it does calm him some. To be held.'

Nóra blinked slowly, staring. 'It screams and screams.'

Nance was thoughtful. ''Tis no harm in the girl holding the changeling, Nóra. Sure, 'tis right that she be kind to it for the sake of your Micheál with Them.' She picked up a piece of knotted rag and soaked it in goat's milk, handing it to Mary. 'Here, give the cratur this to suck on.'

They waited for the water to take hold of the plant. Nóra sat staring at the leaves floating in the crock, her hands trembling. When Nance handed Nóra a small cup of *poitín* the widow drained it in silence.

When the water had warmed, Nance and Nóra hauled the pot off the embers and Nance motioned to Mary. 'Take the wee dress off him now. We'll put him in the bath.'

Mary's mouth was dry as she lay Micheál on the floor and began to unwrap the clothes from his body. She could feel the women's eyes on her, feel the fragile neck of the boy cradled in her hand as she lifted his skull off the floor to slip the cloth over it. As she took the last of the rags off him, his white body purled in gooseflesh.

'The water won't burn him, will it?' she asked.

Nance shook her head, reaching for the boy. Together they eased his dangling legs into the crock. 'Down into it now. That's it, girl. Hold his arms. Don't be getting the water on your skin. Dip him in so.'

The boy's eyes widened at the heat of the water, then fixed on the shadows moving against the wall.

'He's too big,' Mary gasped, breathing hard. 'I don't think he'll fit.'

'Sure, the fairy's all bones. We'll get him in there.'

Water lapped over the side of the pot as they folded the boy's arms across his chest and slipped him into the crock. His knees bent high about his neck.

'Let go of him now.'

Mary hesitated. 'If I let go of his head he'll knock it on the side of the pot.'

Nóra's voice came out in a husk. 'Do as Nance said, Mary.'

Mary took away her hand and the boy's head dropped to the side, his ear close to the water. The women stepped back and watched him.

'The fairy in him is suspicious,' Nance muttered, and Mary saw the truth of it as soon as the words were spoken. Micheál's head lolled back above the water, his chin pointed to the soot-stained rafters. A shudder went through him like wind rippling over water and he yelped, tongue stretched.

'That's the fox cry of him,' Nóra whispered.

Mary felt her stomach cramp and she could not tell if it was from fear or excitement. The darkness seemed to hum around them.

'Now we must give him the juice of it.' Nance leant forward and reached for the boy's chin. At her touch his jaw snapped shut, hinges of muscle suddenly tense. Glancing back at Nóra and Mary, Nance tried to slip her finger between his lips and behind his teeth, but the boy jerked his head, struggling.

'Mary. Open his mouth for me, would you?'

''Tis as though it knows,' Nóra marvelled. 'It knows we're after banishing it.'

'Mary?'

Mary knelt by the crock and reached for Micheál's mouth. He groaned as she touched him, his arms wresting and splashing the water from the pot. She recoiled, waiting until the boy had stilled and she wasn't in danger of the liquid spilling on her. Then she reached for him again and gently inserted the tips of her fingers between his lips. Micheál looked at her from the corner of his eye, his head slumped towards his shoulder. The pink gleam of his inner lip sat beneath her fingers. She could feel the hard press of his teeth.

'Will this hurt him?' she asked.

'Not at all,' Nance reassured her. 'Remember, girl, we're only after sending him back to his kind.'

Mary felt for the gap in the ridge of teeth and, quickly pushing her fingers into the wet of Micheál's mouth, pressed down on his molars. His jaw dropped open. Nance pinned one crooked finger on his tongue and squeezed the juice of foxglove leaf down his throat.

'There. 'Tis done.'

Mary pulled her fingers from the boy's mouth as though she had been burnt. When she glanced down at them she could see the vague imprint of his teeth on her knuckles.

'What do we do now?' Nóra asked. Mary turned and saw that the widow was swaying behind them, grey hair sticking to her forehead in sweat.

'We wait,' Nance said.

Micheál sat scrunched in the crock, moaning, disturbing the water like a fish in a pail. Mary thought that perhaps the warm bath comforted him, had lifted the chill from his marrow and soothed the flaking rash on his back. His eyes were glazed and his cheeks flushed red, and she thought that, for the first time since she had seen the child, he was peaceful. She exhaled in relief.

Then, slowly, so that at first it was almost imperceptible, a shaking rose in him.

'So it begins,' Nance murmured.

The shaking grew stronger. He tremored like the crushed catkin of birch, like the fluttered seed of an ash tree, and within minutes the convulsions grew so violent that he seemed to be shivering out of his skin.

Panic flared in Mary's chest. 'Nance?'

'The herb is doing its work.'

Water splashed from the pot as the convulsions turned to thrashing. Micheál's head swung forward, his chin suddenly tight against his throat. Water swallowed his face.

'He'll drown,' Mary whispered. She reached for Nance's shoulder, but the woman gently pushed her back.

'Nóra. Lift him. Help me lift him.'

Nóra, looking bewildered, drunk, did as Nance said. Together the older women lifted the convulsing boy, wet-skinned and dripping, from the bath of boiled leaves. He shook in their grip like a rabid dog, his mouth rent open in a terrifying gape, arms rod-straight and trembling, and his head shaking from side to side as though in terror of what was being done to him.

'Mary! Open the door for us.'

She held her breath in horror, unable to move.

'Open the door!'

A strange noise began to come from the boy. A shrill gasping, as though there weren't enough air in the world and he was struggling to breathe.

'Open the door! Mary!'

Mary, fear sparking through her, did as she was told. She ran to the door and pushed the wicker open to the night, then shrank back against the wall. Outside the night sky was gripped with stars.

Nance's face was solemn, intent. She looked at Nóra with her clouded eyes, trying to catch her attention. 'Help me swing him,' she said. Nóra nodded, jaw clenched in concentration. Holding the shaking boy firmly about the ribs and shoulders they staggered to the doorway.

'I'll say what must be said, and you'll help me swing him. Don't let go, only swing him out the door. Back and forth with him.'

Nóra nodded, mute.

'Mary! Get the shovel from the corner of the room. There. Quickly now!'

Mary, a plummeting in her bowels, did as she was told.

'Set it under his legs. Under him, as though he were sitting on it. Nóra, hold tight of him. Now we'll swing him.' Nance closed her eyes and took a deep breath. 'If you're a fairy, away with you!'

Following Nance's direction, Nóra swung the boy out towards the darkness. Her fingers gripped the sinewy knot of his shaking shoulder.

'If you're a fairy, away with you!'

Mary grasped the shovel tightly, holding it under Micheál's swinging legs, stretches of bone heaving out towards the woods, the flare of his rash dull in the firelight.

'If you're a fairy, away with you!'

They swung him towards the night and its harbour of sprites; the crouching, waiting cunning of the unseen world. Mary held the shovel and they swung him like a body from a scaffold as he shook under their hands. And when they lowered him to the ground, she cast the shovel aside and picked him up and wrapped her shawl against his clammy, trembling nakedness, his skin now pricked with cold, and as she held him to the warmth of her chest by the fire, she felt the pulse of his unnatural heart slow, until it seemed to pattern out into a beat she no longer recognised.

CHAPTER
TWELVE

Germander speedwell

O ne week after she had delivered Brigid of her still, unbreathing son, Nance returned to the Lynches' cabin with her arms full of germander speedwell. She had dreamt of Brigid every night since the birth. Had felt the painful pull of her breasts, full of unsuckled milk, and had woken, wild, turning to the woods to hunt down milkwort, speedwell and watercress, and all the green that might calm the summoning on the girl's body.

When first light spilled in haze over the mountain summits she walked into the valley and knocked on the Lynches' door.

Daniel answered, his face gored with lack of sleep.

'What do you want?' he asked.

Nance heard the gravel in his voice and simply showed him what she carried in her basket.

'What's that for then?'

'To ease her pain, so it is.'

'She needs more than herbs,' Daniel said, leaning against the doorframe with crossed arms. When Nance peered past him into the room, he blocked her view. 'I think you've done enough here, Nance.'

'Let me see to your wife, Daniel.'

'She's not been churched yet.'

'I know. Let me see her. I can help her.'

'More bittersweet, is it?' Daniel's mouth twisted and he leant forward and stared Nance hard in the eye. 'I told you,' he spat. 'I told you she went walking to the *cillín*, and you did *nothing*. And now our baby lies buried there.'

Nance held his eye firm. 'It happens, so it does, Daniel. No one bears the fault for it. We did all we could for it, I promise. 'Tis just the way of the world. 'Tis just the will of God.'

Daniel ran a hand over his unshaven chin, his blue eyes hard. 'Who is to say that those berries didn't kill my son?'

'The bittersweet was to help her sleep and nothing more.'

'So you say.'

Nance straightened her back. 'Daniel, I've lived long years upon this earth. I've delivered more children than I can count. Do you think I'd turn murderer upon babes in my late hour?'

He laughed, his breath vapour in the half-light. 'Yes, well. Can you blame a man?'

'Will you let me tend to her?'

'Like I say, Nance, she's not been churched. You're the one always talking about spirits. Are you not afraid she'll poison you with her unclean breath? The sin of the birth is on her.'

'I have no mind of churching. That's the priest's business. That's the Church, so it is. I'm here as her handy woman.'

'Aye, her handy woman. Some handy woman.' He nodded to the lane. 'Off with ye.'

'Will I leave the herbs with you then?'

'Off with ye!' His voice rang out in the early morning. A flock of starlings lifted out of a nearby ash tree.

Nance eyed him, then placed the basket of herbs on the ground.

'Use them as a poultice,' she said, but before the words were out of her mouth, Daniel stepped forward and kicked the basket clear off the ground. He was breathing hard, his anger two pink spots in his cheeks.

Nance froze, her heart suddenly crossways. She looked to the ground, stared at her toes, their yellow nails.

The air was charged. Neither of them moved.

There was a slight creaking by the cabin and both Nance and Daniel turned at the sound. The door was pushed out, and Brigid stood there in the gap, her head resting on the doorframe. She was pale, her dark hair undone and tangled about her head. She cast a long look at Daniel, and Nance thought that something passed between them. Then, without saying a word, she retreated back into the house, closing the door behind her.

'I can help her,' Nance said.

Daniel stood with his head bowed, and then tramped across the yard to where the basket had rolled to a stop. Nance watched as he stooped and picked her herbs out of the mud in clumsy handfuls and threw them back into the basket. He wiped his hands on his trousers and offered her the creel. 'Go on home, Nance.'

'Would you not give her the herbs yourself?'

'Please, Nance. Go on home.'

'All you need do is wash them and press them into a poultice.'

'Please. Nance. Go on home!'

Nance silently accepted the soiled herbs, her tongue dry. Without meeting Daniel's eye, she turned and walked back to the lane.

A change had come over the boy, although it was not as Nóra had hoped. Every morning, while it was still dark and the cock had not yet crowed, she woke, bleary-eyed, and fumbled her way out from the bedroom to stand over the sleeping maid and the changeling beside her. Nóra hovered above the settle bed, draped in Martin's greatcoat, trying to make out the child's features. Each morning he seemed to be neither asleep nor awake, but in a strange, slit-eyed daze. At times he moved, but there was little of the vigorous jerking of before. Instead he seemed to list between loose-limbed stillness and an eerie trembling, like the tremor of an aspen tree. She examined his mouth, wondering if it lay slack as any normal child's would in sleep, or whether it was the slung yawn of the fairy. Sometimes she saw the boy's tongue slip out over his lips, and her heart would pound in anticipation of hearing him speak, of the return of language.

Nóra stood like this over the settle bed one morning, thinking that perhaps the foxglove had worked, that the breathing coming from the boy was the beginning of words, when Mary gasped awake. She shrank from the sight of Nóra hunched over, staring.

'You frightened me.'

Nóra hunkered down over the child on her knees, inclined her ear towards his mouth. 'I thought I heard the shape of a word.'

Mary sat up, her hair mussed from sleep. 'You heard him talking?'

'Not talking. But a sound. A breathing. As though he were about to whisper something to me.'

They listened for a moment, but Micheál's lips were sluggish, unmoving.

'He was sick again in the night.'

'Sick?'

The maid gestured to a pail beside the bed, a cloth swimming in the dirty water. 'Retching up over himself. All over with the sick of him, the piss of him.' She drew closer, her forehead crinkled in concern. 'He trembles.'

Nóra stood up, fingers pulling at her bottom lip. 'Surely that is a good sign.'

Mary picked up one of Micheál's limp hands, considering it. 'He is not as he was before.'

'The *lus mór* is working in it.'

Mary stroked the little hand. 'He is as my sisters were before they died. All loose. No sound coming from him at all.'

Nóra acted as though she had not heard. ''Tis cold, Mary. Get up and unrake the fire, would you?'

The girl placed the boy's hand back under the blanket. 'You don't think he'll die, do you?'

'God willing, the fairy will die if that's what it takes for Micheál's return.' Nóra opened the door and peered out into the fog of the morning.

Mary stilled. 'You want him to die? The fairy?' She joined Nóra at the door. 'Missus, sure, is there not sin in that? The foxglove poisoning him like that?'

''Tis no sin if 'tis the fairy banished. 'Tis no matter. No sin in seeking to rid the fairy and save Micheál.' She turned and gripped Mary about the shoulder. ''Tis a good thing, what we're doing for it. Can you not see that the scream is gone from it? The kicking and punching and all the fighting in it? If we can banish the fairy and fix it to leave, the Good People will have Their own back, and I will have mine. The foxglove will work and God be praised for it. Now, would you not light the fire? The cold is on me.'

The girl obeyed, retreating to the hearth where she began to fuss amongst the coals.

Nóra turned to the view of the misty valley. Through the gloom she could see the shifting of cows already turned out of byres, hear the clank of empty milk pails and the voices of women. The brief glimmer of new-lit fires as doors were opened and closed. And down by the river, the dark mass of evergreens and the hatched outline of bare branches. Nóra thought she could see the whitethorn of the Piper's Grave and, as she stared, a flitting light in the murk around it. Like a candle flame quivering, held by someone moving in and out of the darkness. Like a rushlight lit and blown out into smoke, and lit and blown out again by the breath of someone unseen.

A shiver went down Nóra's back. She thought of what Peter O'Connor had said the night of Martin's wake.

I saw a glowing by that whitethorn. You mark my words, there'll be another death in this family before long.

Then, just as suddenly as the lights had appeared, they vanished.

'Missus?'

Mary was watching her, the iron poker in her hand, the flames quickening in the hearth.

'What?'

'The cold is coming in, and you said you were feeling it, so.'

Shaken, Nóra shut the half-door and returned to her place by the fire. Wrapping Martin's greatcoat firmly about her, she felt a hard bump in her side and, sliding her hand into the coat's pocket, pulled out an irregular jag of charcoal. It sat in her palm, light and crumbling.

Mary placed a scraw on the fire. When Nóra remained silent, she glanced up.

'What's that?'

''Twas in Martin's coat.'

Mary peered at it more closely. 'Ashes?'

Nóra shook her head. 'A dead ember.'

'Protection.'

'Protection against the *púca*.'

'Did Nance give it to you, then?'

'She did not, no. 'Twas here, in Martin's coat.'

The girl nodded absently and tucked the blanket in more firmly around the boy's shoulders. 'His hair is growing long.'

Nóra stared at the ember in her hand. Martin had never mentioned it, had never gone to Nance for anything other than the cold swelling in his hand. It was to the blacksmith's for the teeth that troubled him, the broken rib all those years back when he fell from a horse. Never Nance.

'And his nails too,' Mary was saying. 'Missus?'

Nóra turned the ember in her fingers. Had he gone in secret? Had he gone for something to protect the boy? Or had he gone for protection against him?

'Missus?'

'What?' Nóra snapped, shoving the ember back into the coat pocket.

'Micheál's nails. They're too long. He might scratch himself with them.'

''Tis not Micheál!' Nóra reached for her shawl and began to wrap it around her head.

'The . . . boy. I meant –'

'I'll milk the cow this morning.'

'Shall I cut his nails?'

'Do what you like with it.'

Nóra slammed the door behind her and paused in the yard, letting the damp of the morning cool the burning of her cheeks. She gripped the handle of the milk pail until it pinched hard against her skin, swung it against her leg until she could feel the lip bruising her thigh.

Nóra looked down towards the Piper's Grave where the white-thorn was emerging in the gathering light. She would have burnt it down, stuffed their clothes full of ashes had they been able to help against the fairies and their slow malevolence.

Let it tremble, she thought. Let the foxglove shake the fairy out of my house, and give me back my daughter's son. Please, God, rid the fairy.

'Nance Roche, are you in there?'

It was a man's voice, coloured with impatience. Nance paused and put the eel she was skinning back in its bucket of river water.

'Are you of the living or the dead?' she asked.

'Mercy woman, 'tis not one of your patients come to be tricked. 'Tis Father Healy. I've come to speak with you.'

Nance rose and went to the door. The priest was standing outside with his feet apart, his coat flapping in the wind.

'Father. What a pleasure.'

'And how are you keeping, Nance?'

'Still alive.'

'You didn't hear the Mass on the holy days?'

Nance smiled. 'Ara, 'tis a long way for an old woman.'

'But you got your meal and turf?'

Nance paused, wiping her bloody hands on her apron. 'That was you, was it?'

'Did you think 'twas a gift for the quackery?' Father Healy peered past her. 'Are you alone in there?'

'Not if you count the company of goats.'

'I don't.'

'Come in to the warm, so. Let me make you welcome in thanks for the meal. Sure, 'twas kind of you to be thinking of an old woman like me, alone on the day of our Lord.'

The priest shook his head. 'No, thank you, I'll not be coming in.'

'Have it your way then, Father.'

'I will.'

Nance waited for the priest to speak. The eel blood had started to dry to a rusty stain on her skin. 'Well now, Father. Say what you've come to say. Constant company wears out its welcome.'

He crossed his arms tightly over his chest. 'You should know, Nance, 'tis with a heavy heart I come to you today.' He shifted his weight. ''Tis a serious matter I've come about.'

'Best say it and be done with the saying of it, then, Father.'

Father Healy swallowed. 'I've had good word that it was by your hand that Brigid Lynch lost her baby. There is an accusation against you. Some folk came to me saying you sought to poison Brigid Lynch.'

Nance looked at the priest. 'That is quite an accusation.'

'Did you or did you not give her berries of bittersweet?'

'Bittersweet is no poison. Not when taken as it should.'

'I'm told 'tis nightshade.'

'Her man came to me looking for a cure. She was walking in her sleep and he was afraid for her. I am no murderer, Father. The herbs I pull are taken with prayer. In the name of the Lord.'

Father Healy shook his head. 'Well, I can tell you now, Nance Roche, that herb-pulling like that . . . 'Tis an abuse of God's holy ordinance. I can't stand for it. There's people here in this parish who have had enough of you bringing misfortune down on them with your pagan, unmeaning practices.'

'Say what you will about my practices, Father, but they are full of meaning.'

'They've had enough of your bawling.'

'Aye, you're against the keening, so you said.'

Father Healy fixed her with a grim look. 'No, Nance. No. This has gone beyond keening. This is about nostrums and *piseógs*.'

Nance's body ached and she fought a sudden desire to lie down on the grass and turn her face up to the sky. *Piseógs* and curses.

That was what it was about. *Piseógs* and the dark things people did to one another when their hearts blacked with anger and the edges of their souls curled in bitterness. *Piseógs*. Muttered supplication to the Devil before the sun rises on a feast day. Curses wrought out of the wellbeing of another. The shifting, secret trade of vengeance and ill intent.

'Aye. *Piseógs*. And 'tis not just Brigid Lynch I've come about. Seán Lynch found a wreath of mountain ash on his gate,' Father Healy continued.

'Did he now?'

'And he is saying 'tis a *piseóg*.'

'Now, Father, I know a few things about this world we're in, and a wreath of ash is no *piseóg*. A good, clean fire, a hurley and a fence – that is what the quicken tree is for. 'Tis not useful for any kind of *piseóg*.'

Father Healy's eyes lit up. 'Oh, you know what is good for a *piseóg*, do you, Nance?'

'I have no part in *piseógs*. I don't lay curses. I have no hand in that.'

'Then would you tell me, Nance, why there are plenty coming to me now saying 'tis your custom? They're saying 'tis how you survive here, Nance. Taking people's money for wickedness. Stealing the butter profit from the milk. Cursing churns. Setting neighbour against neighbour and cursing those that would not let you steal from them.'

'Is it stealing the butter, I am?' Nance gestured to her *bothán*. 'Rolling in riches, am I?'

'Nance, whether 'tis people thinking you're stealing with curses, or whether you're stealing by plugging the necks of beasts . . .' He paused as if to note her reaction. 'I can't be standing for thievery. I'll be fetching the police for that. Sure, the constable will take you in if that is what you're after doing.'

Nance lifted her stained hands to the priest. ''Tis eels that fill my belly, not stolen butter.'

'Look at you, red-handed as the Devil.'

'You know as well as I that no one is bothered by a bit of eel catching.'

'Nance, go on and catch as many eels as you like. You're right, 'tis no bother to anyone who knows. But don't be stealing the blood out of beasts, and don't be putting the fear on the valley with your *piseógs*!'

Nance laughed in exasperation.

''Tis not a thing to be laughing at!' The priest took a step towards her. 'Nance, I tell you, my patience is mighty thin with you. If keening is unholy, then laying mountain ash and giving herbs to women in a delicate state to earn your place here is devilry.'

'Father –'

'Nance! I warned you to be a handy woman to those who need and no more.' His face softened. 'If bittersweet be a cure, and the death of Brigid Lynch's baby the work of God, then no more about it. But . . .' He pointed a finger of warning at her chest. 'Don't be laying curses.'

Nance threw her hands up in the air. 'Father, I have no hand in *piseógs*! I have no hand in curses.'

'Just a hand in with *Them that does be in it*. I know 'tis your mouth that's been spreading the word about fairies.' Father Healy turned his palms upwards in ecclesiastic habit. 'Nóra Leahy came to me begging magic, gabbling superstition. Saying the poor boy she has in her care is the talk of the valley, that he's fairy. That wouldn't be your worm in her ear, would it, Nance? Sure, folk will pay handsome when they're desperate. No harm in claiming cures when they bring food and turf to the door.'

Nance felt anger rise in her. 'That boy is not natural.'

'And you are doctor to the unnatural?'

'I am.'

'And you plan to cure him.'

'I plan to banish the fairy and bring Nóra Leahy back her grandson.'

Father Healy gave her a look of weary frustration. ''Twould be a kindness for you to tell Nóra Leahy that she has a right to care for the cretin, and to expect nothing more.'

'There's no kindness in helplessness, Father.'

'But there is in false hope?' The priest sighed and looked out to the valley. 'People are suffering, Nance.'

'Yes, Father.'

'They're worried about the butter. About being forced on the road. About having no money to pay the rent with. About neighbours turning on them, wishing them ill. Wishing sickness and death on them.'

'Yes, Father.'

He looked back at her, his brow furrowed. 'If I find out that you do have a hand in it, I'll not be as kind as I have been, Nance. I will see you out on the road. I will see you out of the valley.'

CHAPTER
THIRTEEN

Devil's-bit scabious

St Brigid's Eve came to the valley and with it the assurance of spring. Winter-weary, the eve of the holy day lured people out of their stuffy cabins down to where the field rushes grew and tremored in the wind.

Mary thought she could almost feel the swelling of the earth beneath her feet as she escaped the confines of the widow's cabin and ran down the mountainside to the grassy stretch of moor. It was cold, but the sun was bright, and she felt that the waterlogged fields carried the promise of growth. Even in the gloom of dipped soil, where old snow lay patterned with the midnight flight of rabbits, early daffodils had emerged. She watched the robins, blood-smocked against the sky, and imagined they were leading her to the rushes, that they were pleased to know that warmth would return to the light.

It was a relief to be in the open air. A relief to leave Nóra and her constant crouching over the boy, watching him like a cat staring at a dying bird. A relief to leave the sight of the child fitting and moaning like the Devil was inside him, fighting for purchase. The very air of the cabin seemed leaden to Mary. She suffocated in the weight of the widow's expectation.

As Mary walked towards the clumps of rushes, she took deep breaths to clear the dust from her lungs, to take in the smells of the trembling fields. Wet grass, cow shit, turf smoke and clay. Golden discs of coltsfoot and the raggy flowers of groundsel clustered against the dun and green. The day was fresh, slapped with cold, and Mary's eyes watered in the light.

She had left the child in Nóra's care, so eager had she been for a minute to herself outside without the twitching weight of the boy against her hip. She had suggested to Nóra that she take Micheál into the yard. Wrap him against the cold and let the sun fall on his pallid skin, while she went for the rushes and made the St Brigid's cross for the house. But the widow, eyes red-rimmed, had said that she would be keeping it out of sight, and for Mary to hurry and not dawdle but come straight back to the cabin.

Mary's brothers had always made the St Brigid's crosses at home. They would walk miles of bog to find the best rushes, pluck out the tangled grasses and wipe them clean of mud, before returning to sit and twist the plants while Mary and the younger children watched.

'See, 'tis important to pull them, not cut them with a knife. That's how you keep the holy in the reed. Sure, you fashion the cross with the sun.'

Mary pictured David sitting in the yard, the green rods over his knees, tongue inching from his mouth in concentration as he folded the rushes around each other.

'What happens if you make the cross against the sun?'

David had frowned. 'What would you be doing that for now? That's some contrariness there, Mary. Faith, 'tis with the sun you do be making it, to keep the power in the charm.'

They would watch his quick fingers work the tapered stems until they could see the green pattern take shape. A four-legged cross made in the name of the saint, to bless and hang above the door in protection against evil, fire and hunger. It would keep them safe even as the shine of the green rush dried to straw, and the smoke from the fire blacked it with soot.

Mary wanted a cross to hang in the widow's house. She wanted to know that she was guarded anew by a nailed blessing. The sight of the boy under the power of the foxglove filled her with a horror so deep and unsettling that she felt calcified with it. There was something evil in his fitting, she knew. Something that made her stomach drop every morning on waking, knowing that she would have to hold the child while his body shook with the supernatural.

Nóra was hunched over her knitting when Mary returned, her hand gripping the bunch of bright rushes. But the boy was no longer in his place by the fire. Mary stood in the doorway, her eyes flitting around the cabin.

She has done something to him, she thought suddenly. She has set him on the mountain, or buried him, or left him at the crossroads. Her stomach knotted with dread.

'Where's Micheál?' she asked.

The widow sniffed and inclined her head to the corner of the room. Mary saw then that the boy lay on the heather Nóra kept for kindling, on his back, unmoving. Her relief, on rushing to him and finding him alive, finding his little bracket of bones still lifting and falling in breath, was overwhelming.

She wedged the rushes under her arm and used her free hands to lift him onto her hip.

'I'm taking him out for the air,' she said to Nóra, snatching at the blanket hanging over the settle bed. 'I'll watch him while I make the cross.'

Nóra's eyes followed her as she left. 'You see anyone coming, you bring it right back inside.'

With the sunlight on his face and the breeze stirring his hair, Micheál seemed to rouse from the limp half-sleep he had lain in since the bath of foxglove. Mary settled him down on the blanket by her feet and, as she perched on a stool and began to weave the rushes, she noticed that his eyes widened, their blue reflecting the sky above him.

''Tis a fair day to be out in,' she murmured, and he blinked, as though he heard her and agreed. She paused to watch him, smiling at the tiny flare of his nostrils, the pink slip of his tongue. He wants to taste the air, she thought.

For all the years' growing in him, Micheál seemed newborn lying in the daylight. The foxglove had left him pale, as though his skin had never seen the sky. Lying in the light, the sun caught the fragile cartilage of his ears and Mary saw how they grew pink, how they blushed transparent. She noticed the fine blond hairs on the side of his face.

''Tis St Brigid's Day tomorrow,' she said. 'Spring is here.' And she set the rushes down by her feet and walked to where a dandelion grew, its fluffy head of seed nodding in the breeze.

'See?' Mary held the downy globe on its stalk above the boy and he looked up at it, his mouth opening. She blew at the clock of seeds and they scattered on the air. Micheál shrieked, his hands suddenly aloft, clutching at the sailing down.

'There was no cure in that foxglove.'

Mary turned. Nóra stood in the doorway, staring at them.

'Look at it! As it was before. All the trembling is all gone out of it. The struggle is all gone.'

'He does seem better.'

'Better!' Nóra ran a hand over her face. 'It screamed in the night again.'

'I know.'

''Tis not better if 'tis back to screaming. 'Tis not better if the changeling has fought the foxglove and won! 'Tis not better if the fitting and the sickening is all out of it, after we've spent the time with Nance, after the way we thought 'twas working.'

'But surely, missus, 'tis better to have a child with air in his lungs than shaking as he was.' Mary's lip trembled. 'It put the fear on me, to see him like that.'

'The fear on you? Girl, you should be afraid to see the fairy strong. You should be afraid to have one of Them amongst us.' She blinked rapidly. 'There's no knowing but that one, himself, there, blinked my man and my daughter. And there you are, playing with it. Doting on it. Cutting its hair and biting its nails and feeding it as though 'twas your own.'

'He likes the dandelion clocks,' Mary whispered.

'As well it might, fairy-child.' Nóra made to go back inside but paused, turning again. Her eyes were full of tears. 'I thought 'twas working,' she whispered, and she gave Mary a look of such wretched sadness that the girl fought a compulsion to go to her, to lay her palms against the widow's cheeks and stroke her face, and comfort her as she sometimes comforted her mother.

But just as quickly as the impulse arrived, it faded, and Mary remained kneeling beside Micheál. She said nothing, and after some silence Nóra turned back into the cabin, her head hung like the dead Christ.

Mary woke early on St Brigid's Day to the muted sound of rain falling outside. Gently rolling the boy and checking that his rags were not soiled, she rose and peered at the hearth. At home she and her brothers and sisters had always fought each other for the first peek at the smothered fire, to look for the mark of St Brigid's passing.

'There 'tis,' the little ones would cry, and they would see a soft crescent in the powdered ash that was surely the print of the saint's holy heel. 'She has come and blessed us.'

Mary sat on her haunches in the widow's cabin and examined the raked hearth. Nothing. The soot was as she had left it.

Homesick, Mary walked to the yard door, unlatched the upper half and pushed it out. She leant on the fixed lower barrier, breathing in the smell of rain. A rough day, she thought. A pelting day. Drops stammered in the puddles of the yard.

There was a soft clattering behind her and Mary turned, expecting to see Micheál – woken, fractious, wild.

The St Brigid's cross. It had fallen from where she had fastened it above the door.

Mary stared at the woven legs of reeds. It was not right. She had fixed the cross tightly, anxious to have its protection, its familiar eye to watch over her at night, to keep the fire from the thatch, to be assured of healing should she need it. To keep the fairies from the house.

Fear dried her mouth. She pressed herself flat against the door and called for Nóra. Nothing. She called again.

There was a low creaking from the next room and the widow emerged, her face soft with sleep. She held her head in her hands.

'What is it? What's the matter? You'll let the rain in. Look, 'tis coming down.'

Mary pointed to the lintel.

'What?'

'St Brigid's cross. Gone.'

Nóra bent and picked up the cross from where it had skittered across the floor.

'I fastened it, so I did,' Mary swallowed. 'What do you think the meaning is in it falling? I never heard of a cross falling. The protection . . .'

Nóra turned the rushes in her fingers, then brushed the dirt from the cross with her shawl and handed it back to Mary. 'Put it up. It means nothing. 'Twas the wind. The charm is still in it.'

Mary accepted the cross silently. For all the widow's dismissive words, she knew from the queer look on Nóra's face that she shared Mary's hollow nagging that all was not right. There was no wind. None at all.

Something had moved the cross. Something had cast it to the floor.

Nóra stood over the sleeping boy, her face grey. 'Did it shake last night? Was it sick and vomiting?'

'No, missus.'

'Is it after soiling itself?'

'Not as he was. None of the running and watering out of him. And no fever.'

A pained expression came over Nóra's face and her eyes glazed. 'We will never be rid of it with herbs.'

Mary blanched at Nóra's expression.

'I've been thinking, Mary. Fairies do not like fire. Or iron.' Nóra's eyes glanced to the smoored hearth. 'In the stories they threaten them with it. Tell them to leave or you'll bring the eye out of them with a reddened poker. Hold them over a shovel.'

'We held him over a shovel,' Mary whispered.

'We hold it over a *hot* shovel.'

'No.'

Nóra looked at Mary in surprise and some of the strangeness went out of her manner.

'No, I don't think we should be doing that.'

'We wouldn't burn it. Just threaten it.' Nóra bit at the skin around her nails.

'I think there's sin in that, missus. I don't want to.'

'It won't leave if we keep giving it herbs, Mary. Micheál will never come back if 'tis just foxglove and mint.'

'Please, missus. Don't be burning it up.'

Nóra ripped the skin from her nail, glanced down and smudged the blood. 'Just the threat would do,' she muttered to herself. 'Iron and fire. That is what it surely takes.'

'Nance. How are you getting on?'

'Musha, a good day and a bad day, thanks be to God. I was wondering when you might visit me.' Nance nodded at the straw-seated stool beside the fire and Áine sat down, smoothing her skirts in front of her.

'I think I am caught on the chest.'

'Your chest, Áine?'

'I feel a rattle.' The woman brought a slender hand up to her throat and blushed. 'I think 'tis the cold.'

'A bad chest, is it? And how long have you been caught?'

Áine glanced around the cabin. 'Oh, a while now. Since the new year. We threw the door open to let the old year out and the new one in, and I think a sickness was in its company.' She attempted a laugh. 'Now there's a catch on me. I cough, sometimes.'

'How is the damp with you?'

'The damp?'

'How have you and your man John stood the cold and the wet? Is the floor of your home dry?'

Áine absently pulled at a loose thread in her shawl. 'The storms last year disturbed the thatch. And the blackbirds pick it apart. A little rain comes in. We'll thatch again this year.'

'And have you enough to eat?'

'God provides plenty, though the butter's not coming thick at all. The profit is not in the milk.'

'Faith,' Nance said. 'There's no profit to be found in the whole valley, as I hear it. But I'm pleased to hear you've enough to eat. You deserve it all and more. Will you let me feel for the rattle?'

Áine nodded and Nance placed her hand flat against the woman's chest. She closed her eyes and searched for the clag on her lungs. She could sense nothing. Áine's breath seemed normal, although her heart was beating rapidly.

'Can you feel it?'

'Hush now. Close your eyes for me, Áine. Take a deep breath.'

Nance felt her hand grow warm against the woman's clothes. She felt Áine's desire for a child. She felt how she wanted it more than anything. How when Áine bled, bent double by the pain of it, the woman imagined her body was breaking faith with her, punishing her for its emptiness.

Nance saw Áine forcing herself to rise from bed and set the water to boil on the fire for John's breakfast. She saw her sweeping the cabin floor while her body knotted and unknotted itself in aimless ferocity. She saw how Áine hated the visitors who came on night-rambling, the men with greasy fiddles in hand, saw how she hated the way the women took up the precious warmth of the fire, how the men threw pieces of potato to the corner of the room for the fairies that she, cramped, falling out of herself, would have to kneel and sweep up when they left.

Nance saw Áine creeping to the ditch behind the house to replace her rags, marvelling at the violence of her womanhood. The bloody reminder of her unmothering.

There was a cough. Nance opened her eyes. Áine was looking at her, frightened.

'What?' she asked, her voice trembling.

Nance removed her hand and pulled her stool closer. 'You're a good woman, Áine. Faith, God knows we all have our troubles to bear. And God knows there are enough people in this world who turn their anger onto those around them. But some, I think, turn their anger against themselves. I think perhaps your body is sickening because you are sad.'

'Faith, I'm not, Nance.'

'The mind is a powerful thing, Áine. A mighty thing.'

'Sure, what reason have I to be sad?'

Nance waited. Silence settled.

Áine pulled at the tasselled ends of her shawl. 'I know what you're thinking, Nance.'

''Tis about a child.'

The woman hesitated, then nodded, miserable. ''Twas shameful for me. The night Brigid's baby died. 'Twas shame in being taken out of there like I was no help at all. Like I was no woman at all.'

Nance said nothing.

'Sure, I know what they say about us,' Áine whispered. '"A stick of yew in a bundle of kindling."'

'You want a child. There is no shame in that.'

'There is shame in a wife not being able to give her man what he wants.' Áine looked up, pained. 'John is a good man, but his family think ill of me. They suspect me because I am barren. They blame poor crops on me. They say the potatoes are in sympathy with me. The cow . . .' She clenched her jaw and shook her head. 'All the women here in this valley, they come to my house on *cuaird*, and . . . sometimes they bring their weans and the children dig holes in my floor and chase my chickens. They make me feel my childlessness. Nance, I think they mock me. One of the women! Her daughter refused to take food from my hand because the girl thought I had been away with Them and that was the reason for my having no children!' Áine choked back a strange laugh. ''Tis not though, is it? 'Tis not the Good People who have had a hand in my . . .' She brought her hands to her stomach.

'Would it frighten you to think so?'

''Twould give reason to it. But I never did anything against Them. I've a mighty respect for the Good People.' She hesitated. 'Kate Lynch told me of a woman whose own man struck her with a band of elm to fix a child in her.'

Nance gave a wan smile. 'Áine, are you asking after a beating of elm?'

'I don't know.'

''Tis right for you to visit me. Don't be blaming yourself. There is a natural sympathy in this world. For every ill thing that can come upon us, there's a remedy to lift it. All cures are within our reach.' Nance stood and offered Áine her hand. 'Here, follow me.'

The two women walked out of the *bothán* and into the cool calm of the evening. Everything was still except for a fog slipping down into the valley from the mountains.

''Tis a queer place here,' Áine whispered. 'I forget what silence is, married to a blacksmith.'

'Sure, 'tis quiet. Even the birds are silent in the mist.'

As they drew closer to the woods, Áine fell back. 'Perhaps I'll wait for you at the cabin, Nance. Perhaps I'll come another time. John might be wondering where I'm to.'

'I'll let no harm come to you.'

'How can you see the way? There's such a fog.'

'All the better. No one will see us.'

They walked into the trees. The ground was soft with leaf litter and the oak and alder, appearing out of the mist as they walked, sent a slow dripping from the branches above. Áine lifted her face, letting the drops dash onto her forehead, the water trickling down her nose and chin.

'It has been a long time since I wandered in this way.'

'Sure, a woman with a husband shares her marriage with the hearth.'

'Did you never get married yourself, Nance?'

Nance smiled. 'Ah, 'twas never a one would have me. I spent all my time as a girl in the mountains. I went courting with the sun.'

'I used to go walking up the mountains as a girl. To the west.'

'Did you now?'

'The wind up there always smelt sweeter.'

'Sure, I know it.' Nance crouched down and began to rummage amongst a tangle of ferns and ivy. 'Do you know what plant this is?'

'*Dearna Mhuire.*'

Nance plucked the soft, pleated leaves of lady's mantle, setting them on the ground beside her. When she had a neat pile she crossed herself, and Áine helped her to her feet.

'What are they for?'

'You'll see now.'

Back inside the warmth of the *bothán*, Nance quickened the fire with dried furze and set her crock, filled with river water, on the flames.

'Could you know this plant in the wild? Pick it safely?'

Áine nodded. 'I picked lady's mantle for my mother.'

'When the air grows warmer, the leaves will have a dew on them, and the best way to fix a child in you would be to mix that dew with water and bathe in it. Until then, we can hope for the same with an infusion.' She passed the leaves to Áine. 'Now. Boil these in a little clean water and drink of it for twenty mornings.'

'What is that pot there for, then?'

'Tansy.' Nance plucked several withered leaves off a dried plant hanging from the rafter and crumbled them into the water. 'If you cannot go far from the house for the *dearna Mhuire*, tansy leaves brewed as a tea will also help you.'

The boiling water became aromatic and Nance poured off the steaming liquid, handing a piggin to Áine.

She hesitated. 'There's no word of truth in what they're saying, is there, Nance?'

'What's that? What are they saying?'

'The bittersweet berries. Brigid.'

Nance felt her heart drop, but she kept her face calm. 'What do you believe, Áine?'

The blacksmith's wife looked at the cup in her hands, and then, as if deciding, took a long draught. ''Tis bitter.'

Nance was relieved. 'So is life. Make it to your taste, but take care not to use too much. Drink it for seven days. Today will be the first of your seven.'

Áine held her nose and drained the piggin.

'Will you remember, Áine?'

'I will.'

'Distilled lady's mantle for twenty days and a tea of tansy leaf for seven. And there is something else you must do.'

Áine paused. 'What is that?'

'When you turn your cow out to grass, let her eat the flowers of the field and then catch her water. 'Tis all-flowers water. All the good of the herbs she has eaten will be in it, and if you bathe in it you will have their cure.'

'Thank you, Nance.'

'And I will hold the charm for you in my mind, Áine O'Donoghue. Know you that. Boil the herbs on a hot turf fire, and all the while I will be holding the charm for you, and we will see you with a child before this year is out.' Nance gripped her hand. 'And then you may tell them that there was no harm in that bittersweet.'

*

Long after Áine had left, Nance sat brooding in front of her fire. For the first time since she had moved to the valley, she felt a threat against her, a summons to prove her ability. When she was younger it had been enough for people to know that she was the niece of Mad Maggie, that she had been taught the cure, shown the ways of the Good People. Then, when she was on the road, they saw the fact of her ability in her loneliness, in the absence of a husband, her crooked hands, her habit of smoking, of drinking like a man. They placed their faith in her because she was different from them.

But now Nance sensed doubt. Suspicion.

I must get this child back, Nance thought. If I can restore Micheál to Nóra, then they will see that there is no word of a lie in my dealings with Them. If I give Áine O'Donoghue a child, and return Micheál Kelliher to his grandmother, they will all return to me.

Nance shivered, thinking of the foxglove treatment. She had not had another visit from Nóra Leahy, and she guessed that this meant the changeling was still in the house. It had not worked to return her mother either, although they had tried. Maggie had made Nance sit on Mary Roche's chest to pin her arms to her side, and they had poured the foxglove down her throat while she spluttered and cursed them, while she spat it back in Nance's face. It had taken a long struggle before the fairy woman had swallowed the liquid, but when she did the change had been unsettling. The heart of the changeling had slowed to an erratic pumping. She had grown listless, then foamed at the mouth with her eyes wide and rolled, had vomited throughout the night. But the *lus mór* made her docile. Made her quiet when she had been screaming. Made her placid and waxen when she had been red-faced and scratching.

Her da had not liked to see the change, for all he was desperate for his wife to return. He had taken Maggie's gifts of *poitín* and gone on rambling, and had not returned some nights at all.

'Your da only needs a bit of time to himself,' Maggie had said. ''Tis no easy thing to see your wife swept and the violence needed to bring her back.'

Nance, older then, had struggled to remember her mother as she had been before the Good People took her. She had grown used to the fairy woman left in her place.

'What will you do if there's no restoring Mam through *lus mór*?'

'There are other ways.'

Nance was silent for a moment. 'Maggie? I want to ask you something.'

'What is it?'

'How did you get that mark on your face? You never told me.'

'I don't like to be talking of it.'

'I heard a man saying you got it after your mam was hit in the face with a blackberry. When she was carrying, like.'

Maggie rolled her eyes, began to fuss with her pipe. ''Twas not that at all.'

'Were you born with it?'

Plumes of blue smoke in the evening air. The whirring of a summer night.

'I was swept. Once. Just like your mam. They brought me back to myself with a poker reddened in the fire.'

'They burnt you?'

'I was away. The fire brought me round to myself.'

'You never said.'

''Twas when I was away that I got the knowledge.'

'Maggie, you never said. All these years you've been living here with us and you never told me you were swept.'

Her aunt shrugged and absently touched the mark on her face.

'Does Da know?'

Her aunt nodded.

'We should do that to Mam.'

Maggie drew on her pipe and let out a shuddering breath. 'Never on my life.'

'But it worked!'

'Nance, we'll not be putting the fairy out of her with fire.'

Silence between them then. Corncrakes rasping their pattern outside.

'Did it hurt?'

But Maggie never answered. There was a knock on the door, and there stood the boatmen of the lough, holding the body of her father aloft. Drowned, they said. Under before they could fish him out. Terrible accident. Terrible misfortune for the family. For Nance. Her mam gone soft in the head, and how would she and her aunt keep up with rent? How to stop the crowbars breaking down the door and pulling the thatch apart? They would do what they could but they had families of their own. Terrible misfortune. God be with them.

In her cabin Nance closed her eyes and rested her head on her knees. All this time past, the years lived through, but the sight of Maggie kneeling over her da and the howling between them that night, a cry taken up by the fairy woman in the bed, her mother's shadow, all ringing in her ears as though she were in that room again with her father's lungs filled with water. That sound, the mourning of three women all touched by the fairies, all unmoored.

There was no one Maggie turned away afterwards, no matter the sickness upon them or the badness they were after. Her aunt never said, but Nance knew. When the ones with the glower on them came, asking for the tides of luck to be turned, Maggie began to send Nance on errands.

'Let them in.' Maggie's voice would rise from the gloom of the cabin. 'It may be that I can help them after all. And won't you go and pick the Devil's-bit? 'Tis all a-flower and I have need of it.'

Her aunt must have known that it could not last. That whatever wickedness was being worked for their praties and scraws, the canker would return upon them in time.

Piseógs are fires that flare in the face of those who set them.

Three months later and Nance had come home to a dead hearth, no fairy woman in the bed, no Maggie by her side. The cabin cold and empty. She had kindled the fire and waited for their return. Wound the hours with worry.

It was only when she noticed that Maggie's things were missing – her pipe, her stores of herbs and ointments, the *poitín* – that she knew she had gone. Nance had sat on the rushes and cried herself to sleep.

Returned to the fairies, they said later. And taken Mary Roche with her. Both of them as mad as the other, gone back to the Good People and no sight of them since. And that poor Nance, all alone and a young woman too. Not two coins to rub together and no kin neither. She'll be on the roads with nothing but herbs to her name.

Nance's stomach creased in hunger. All the years past, but this was how it would be for her again if they did not come for cures, if she did not banish the changeling. Hunger and hollow and cramping. She would be back to waiting in ditches and shadows to calm animals that had been turned out to pasture. Nicking their veins to tap their blood, plugging the wounds with fat and the blessed untoothed leaves of devil's-bit scabious. Picking turf from where it had tumbled off piles, only coming close to those houses where the families were still asleep, where the smoke was not yet rising. Retreating to the rough footing of hills when the stir of morning began and the milking girls emerged puffy-eyed, and the men began the long walk to cut turf or tend their animals and crops.

Nance remembered that life on the road. Gathering blackberries and *fraocháin*, and untangling stray wool from thorny thickets of furze, and cutting watercress and coltsfoot, three-cornered garlic and bogbean. Nights spent sleeping beneath the flowering black-thorn, the pale blossoms against the dark branches like faces in the night. Turning her knife to Mary's fern for bedding. She had cut the bracken and found the initials of God whorled within the inner working of the stem.

Maggie had taught her how to survive in the face of misfortune. Before she had vanished, she had told Nance how a hungry woman might gather a little blood to boil with grain. How she might best beg milk off a farmer's wife. How to trap and skin an eel, or catch a hare, or take a little turf where it would not be missed. How to scrape a scythe through a cow pat and summon the goodness of the butter to yourself, muttering, 'All for me. All for me. All for me.'

But she had never taught her how to sleep on the road when there was nothing left, and you had only yourself. Nance had learnt that alone.

CHAPTER
FOURTEEN

Hart's tongue

'**G**od's blessing on this place.'

Mary and Nóra looked out the open door of the cabin and saw Peg O'Shea making her way towards them, leaning on her blackthorn stick.

'Ah, the devils are into your thatch.' She paused and raised her crook at the birds that were wheeling about Nóra's roof. 'Stolen straw makes cosy nests.'

'Are you well, Peg?'

'I am. I've come to see how you're all getting on. My, Nóra, you look a grievance.'

Nóra stepped forward to help Peg into the house. ''Tis the changeling. Oh, Peg. 'Tis back to bawling and shrieking the whole night through. Not natural, the lungs on it. Begod, Peg, I don't get a wink, nor the maid either. We're beside ourselves with lack of sleep.'

Peg eased herself down by the fire and looked at the child lying in Mary's lap, arms juddering, mouth querulous. 'The poor lad. An empty vessel makes most noise.'

Nóra sat down beside her. 'Do you see any change in it? I thought I could, but . . .'

'Nance is curing him?'

Nóra nodded. 'Just concoctions of herbs so far.' She lowered her voice. 'You should have seen it a week ago, Peg. Like something going through. A shaking.'

Peg frowned. 'A shaking? Nance was shaking the fairy out of him? Shaking him back and forth, was she?'

'Not a shaking like that,' said Nóra. ''Twas a herb she gave it and a shaking rose up in the body, like. Froth in the mouth and all.'

They watched Mary as she spat on a corner of her apron and wiped the boy's chin.

'I never heard of such a thing.'

''Twas *lus mór*,' said Mary.

Peg looked apprehensive. 'Foxglove? Oh, that's some powerful plant.'

''Twas awful,' Mary said, her eyes not leaving Micheál. 'There was a bath of it, and then we set the juice of it on his tongue, and he was fitting like a mad dog with it all. Like he was dying.'

'Good God. The poor wretch.' Peg looked at the child, concerned. There was a damp, pinched look about his face.

'Only, the shaking and trembling's gone out of him now,' added Mary. 'He's not so sick with it, God be praised.'

'It hasn't worked,' Nóra said abruptly. She gripped Peg's shoulder. 'Peg, 'twas as though we came close to having the fairy gone out of it, and then . . . nothing. I'm in pieces over it.'

'Oh, Nóra,' Peg murmured. ''Tis no easy thing. As Nance was telling ye, sometimes 'tis better to care for the changeling in your grandson's place if you can't be getting rid of it.'

Nóra shook her head vehemently. 'I'll be getting rid of it. I could never forgive myself if I did not try to find my grandson, Peg. For

Martin's sake. For my daughter's. I'm going to get Micheál back. I'm after other ways.'

'And what ways might they be?' Peg asked, her tone careful. 'You're not after nettling him again, are you, Nóra Leahy? I tell you, 'tis best you follow the advice of Nance, although . . .' She stopped and sucked her teeth. 'There's a lot of talk about that one going round.'

'About Nance?'

'Surely you've heard. There's talk she's got some darkness working against Father Healy and those that would have her out. Seán Lynch. Kate Lynch. Éilís and her man. Aye, that woman has the word against her. And Brigid, all that talk of the berries spread by Kate. And now Seán has been fighting over her.'

'What's that now?'

'Well, I say fighting over her, though there's more to it than that. Seán Lynch was making trouble at the blacksmith's today. The son-in-law told me. There was some quarrel over a horse between Seán and Peter O'Connor, and Nance was mentioned.'

Mary picked the boy up and moved him to the unfolded settle bed.

'Seán's fault?' asked Nóra. 'Had he drink taken?'

'As like as not. The daughter's man was up with me now, and he says there was some scuffle in O'Donoghue's yard.'

'What happened?'

Peg raised an eyebrow. 'Seán had taken his share of Peter's horse to make up the team. That's how it began.'

Nóra grimaced. 'Martin always said Seán was a stingy sort when it came to horses. Keep his too long and he'll be calling you lazy. Bring his mare back sharp and he's in a fit and saying she's been worked like a devil. He takes care of his own, does Seán.'

'And by his own you mean he takes care of himself,' Peg snorted. 'As I heard it, Seán was feeding Peter's horse hay with the seed slapped out of it, and his own the better oats. So when Peter saw Seán at the smith's he asked him to give the horse the same feed as his own, and Seán . . . well. Gave him a look that would wither grass and told him he did as he saw fit, and there was no strength in the horse at all, and did he want to be robbing a neighbour with no money coming in? And Peter said the dry was on the whole valley and 'twas not his fault. And then . . .' Peg paused, licking her lips. 'Then your boy was mentioned.'

Nóra blanched. 'The changeling? What was said, Peg?'

'Seán said Kate's turned over in her mind about the changeling in Nóra Leahy's house, and he knows there's some malice being worked on the place by Nance. He said that's the true cause of the dry. Said Kate thinks the boy is one of Them summoned by Nance to blink us all in anger at Father Healy. Oh, and Seán was spitting and fitting over it, the lad was telling me. Spitting on the ground like he was putting out a fire. Says he's after finding what looks to be *piseógs* on his land. Says someone's working to curse him. The horses were getting nervous with his racket, and Peter put out an arm to calm them, like, to keep them from the panic, but Seán thought he was after him and grabbed Peter's shirt. Brought him eye to eye. "I know you walk to her den of an afternoon," says he. "I know you're awful great with that *cailleach*." Then he said . . .' Peg took a deep breath, shaking her head in disgust. 'He said, "Sure, 'tis a sad state of affairs when a man who can't get a wife will go after the Devil for his."'

'Well. You know Peter, quiet as a church mouse on a holy day, would soon as fight a man as a priest. You wouldn't believe it. Didn't the red come down over him, and didn't he grab Seán's own collar and say he had no right to be calling a poor honest woman such a thing when he's a devil himself.'

'A man's mouth often broke his nose.'

'But Peter O'Connor! Nóra, have you ever heard such a thing? Peter O'Connor giving Seán a hearing! He said to him: "You're a devil. Pissing on Nance and starving every man's horse but your own!" Then Peter started on about Kate. "And we all know you're beating the dust out of your woman again. Wonderful hard man to go after them that can't be fighting back." He was saying, "You're some man, Seán Lynch! Some hard man!"'

'And then what happened?'

'Seán knocked the feathers out of Peter. Punched him everywhere except the roof of his mouth and the soles of his feet, as I heard it. Brought him down into the mud and stomped the face of him so that, once the men had dragged Seán off – swinging all the while – the bellows boy was out in the yard, picking teeth like flowers.'

'Sweet Jesus. How is the face on Peter?'

'John and Áine took him in and patched him up as best they could, but if the man was a bachelor before, they say he'll be an ugly one his whole life long now, more's the pity. Mouth like a broken window. Nose broke. They'll be chalking his jacket for a laugh this shrove, you mark my words.'

'He's right,' Nóra said, rubbing her chin in thought. 'Seán Lynch is a devil.'

'My bet is that Peter will be straight for Nance's tonight. He'll have need of her.'

Nóra hesitated. 'I wanted to go and talk to Nance myself this day. About another cure for the changeling. How we might banish it for good.'

Peg gave the boy a long look. 'If it can wait until tomorrow, I'd not go, Nóra. Let Peter have his word with Nance. If Seán or one of them see you and the child together with Peter and the *bean feasa*, that'll get the tongues wagging faster than the tail of a butcher's dog. I don't like to be talking ill of others, but sure, there's trouble coming, and you don't want Kate Lynch or Seán up here and asking to see the changeling, or saying you're against them. You've no man now, Nóra. If you don't have your reputation, what will protect you?'

Nance walked the river's length, dragging a broken branch behind her. It was a rare day of February sunlight, and she could see that spring had sent its first flush through the world. Despite the cold, she could smell the change in season.

The trees would soon be tipping with green. In a month or two bluebells would rise to make hallow the forest floor. Bare branches were brimming with life, and there was a haze over the fields. Alder buds swelled, and the men had begun to prepare the ground for crops. Soon there would be movement in the soil, pollen in the water.

Nance staked out the waking earth and pulled the tender shoots of herbs before the dew dried. They were gifted to her. She knew the smell of their sap like a mother knows her children. She could have found them in the dark.

As she walked Nance thought of the changeling, remembering the long purple mark on Maggie's face. Would it be enough to wave the hot iron close to the skin? Would it be enough to tell the fairy child what they planned to do if he did not leave for good? Maggie had told her the other ways they might try to force the return of her abducted mother if the foxglove did not work. St John's wort. Measured doses of henbane. Boundary water.

But never the blistering poker. 'Not on my life,' Maggie had said. Even though it had brought her back from the fairies. Nance closed her eyes and pictured the scar tissue, the puckered skin tight against the cheek. She imagined the iron against it, the hiss and steam and the sticking burn at the touch of the red poker and shuddered.

A strange noise interrupted Nance's thoughts. A hard, ragged breathing repeating itself on the breeze. Putting down her makeshift sled she crept between the trees until she could see the smoke of her cabin. There was a figure making its way down the path. A man, coughing, almost running to her door. His arms were wrapped about his ribs as he jumped over exposed roots and fallen branches.

Peter O'Connor.

Nance stepped out from behind the alder and oak and into the clearing. Sensing movement, Peter turned and slowed to a walk.

'Nance,' he called throatily.

'What is it, Peter? What has happened to you?'

The man retched loudly, dropped to his knees and threw up. Hunched over on all fours, he vomited again, then wiped a long strand of saliva from his mouth and sat back on his heels.

Nance placed a gentle hand on his back. 'There now,' she said. 'Take it easy. Take a breath, now, Peter. Take a breath.'

Peter looked up at her, wiping his lips. One eye was purpled, swollen, the lashes squeezed between the puffed, bruised lids. His nostrils were crusted with blood, and he wore an expression of such abject anger that Nance crossed herself.

'Peter. Come inside.'

He nodded, unable to speak. She helped him rise and directed him towards her cabin. After glancing around to see if anyone was about, she shut the door and tied it fast with straw rope.

Peter stood, his head and arms hanging from his body like a man condemned.

'Sit down.' Nance tugged his arm and pointed to her pile of heather. 'Better yet, lie down. Let me get us a drink.' She fetched a bottle.

Peter's hand trembled as he pulled out the stopper and brought the lip to his mouth.

'And another. Now, when you can, tell me what has happened.'

'Seán Lynch,' Peter spat. He rummaged in his coat and pulled out his pipe and tobacco. Nance waited as he stuffed the bowl with a shaking thumb and kindled the dry leaf. 'He turned on me. He had the lend of a horse. Treated her ill. And when I went to have words with him about it, he nodded his fist at me.' He sucked deeply on his pipe, wincing as the stem brushed against his split lip. 'Sure, Seán is no easy man to get along with, but you should have seen him. He was in one. He would have killed me.'

'Is there no other grievance he has against you?'

Peter blew out a heavy lungful of smoke, shrugging. 'I mentioned his woman, Kate. That fired him up some.'

'They're not great with one another.'

He shook his head. 'She looks like a kicked dog these days.'

'He'll get what's coming to him.'

'Will he?' Peter squinted at Nance through the smoke. 'I'm worried for you, Nance. Seán is after telling Father Healy that you're against God. 'Tis a hard start to the year, Nance. Tomas O'Connor had a cow down and for no good reason. Found her dead and swollen by the river, and no knowing how she wandered there. Took five of us to haul the body out the water, and she in calf too. Daniel Lynch's woman. Brigid. The wee mite dead. I've no mind for hen talk, but didn't Old Hanna find all her chickens dead and laid out without their heads. Some say foxes, but to just take the head? The bleedin' women are in pieces over their churns. I was on rambling to O'Donoghue's, and there's a pack of them there, fussing John for nails and ironwork and charms to bring the profit back to the milk. There's a woman up the mountain, says she cracked one of her eggs the other day. 'Twas no yolk to be had in it. 'Twas filled with blood! Some say 'tis our Good Neighbours at mischief. Some say 'tis the Leahy boy.' He offered Nance the draw of his pipe. 'Some say 'tis you.'

Nance was silent. She accepted Peter's pipe, wiped the blood from the stem and let her mouth fill with the rough smoke.

'You have no hand in *piseógs*, do you, Nance? Seán's saying he's after finding the suggestion of *piseógs* on his land. Stones turned strangely. Flints pointing at the crop ground.'

'To lay a curse is to set it on your own head.'

Peter nodded. 'Faith, I knew you were a Christian woman. You've always been kind to me.'

'Would you tell them when you hear it, Peter? Tell them I have no hand in that badness.'

'Not even for Seán Lynch?' He cast her a sideways look.

'Seán Lynch has been against me for years. If I had it in for him, he'd have been pissing bees and coughing crickets long before now.'

Peter smiled and Nance saw that he was missing several teeth. He took another long draw. 'Do you think 'tis the Leahy changeling?'

'You tell them I will have that boy restored. I will have the fairy out and the boy returned.'

'Has he the evil eye, do you think? Only, it makes sense, Nance. The cratur comes to the valley and 'tis only grief we've known since. And a strange kind, too. Eggs of blood and men passing at cross-roads, and rumours of hares sucking the cows dry of milk.' He cast Nance a dark look. 'The dreams I told you about, Nance. I keep having them.'

'You dream you drown.'

'Aye. I'm all under water and there's hands holding me there. Holding me fast. There's a burning in my lungs and I have a yearning to breathe, but though I'm looking up and I can see the sun beyond the surface, and the trees, there is a face there too.'

'Who is murdering you?'

Peter shook his head. 'I can't make him out. But Nance . . .' He sat up on the heather, dropping his voice to a whisper. 'After today, I'm thinking it might be Seán.'

''Tis a dark thing to think of a man.'

Peter was insistent. 'I couldn't account for his belting me the way he did. Like he wanted to kill me, so I said. And then, I was sitting there with John and Áine, as battered as a *sliotar*, and I think of it. He knows I think well of you, Nance. Even mentioned it. And if he's thinking you're behind the badness in this place, the powerful mischief going on, well.' He leant back, raising his hand to his swollen eye. 'He might have a notion that I've a hand in it too.'

Nance sighed. 'Peter, bless you, no one thinks you've a hand in *piseógs*. No one gives in to that.'

'They might think you've taught me.'

Nance thought of Kate all those years ago. The flashing needle in her hem. Her talk of turning stones, of walking against the sun. 'If someone has it in for another, the *piseógs* come natural. God forgive them, they always think of something.'

Peter gave her a careful look, then tapped out the dead ash in his pipe. He was about to refill it when he paused, glancing at the door. 'Did you hear that?'

Nance listened. The sound came again and they looked at each other, eyes widening. Somewhere in the valley, a woman was screaming.

It seemed that everyone in the fields had heard. As Peter and Nance made their way from her cabin to the lane they saw men running from their work, throwing their tools down and dropping their reins. Women emerged from the cabins by the Macroom road, blinking in the sunlight, children gawping by their aprons.

'What's that?'

'Did you hear it?'

'Good God, do you think someone's after being killed?'

'Where's it coming from?'

A group of people gathered in the lane, fear on their faces. ''Tis not an eviction, surely,' they said. ''Tis not yet rent day.' Then one of the men pointed at the O'Donoghues' bellows boy, running full pelt up the road to where they stood. His face was wild, his dirty hair sticking to his forehead in sweat.

'Help!' he cried. He stumbled on a rock and went flying on the road, then picked himself up and continued to run, arms wheeling in panic, knees grazed. 'Help!'

'Tell us! What is it?' The men ran to meet him, grabbing his arm and the boy let out a yelp. ''Tis Áine O'Donoghue,' he shouted. 'She's caught herself on fire.'

There was a crowd of people in the blacksmith's yard by the time Peter and Nance arrived, their faces anxious and intent. They stared at Nance from lowered brows as Peter dragged her across the dirt and pebbles into the open door of the O'Donoghues' cabin.

'I've Nance Roche here! The doctress! I've brought her,' Peter cried, spitting blood and pulling Nance through the doorway. For a moment Nance could see nothing in the dark room. Then she saw two figures on the ground. Áine was writhing on the floor as her husband tried to calm her and hold her down.

There was an awful smell of burnt flesh. The bottom of Áine's dress was black and burnt, the cindered cloth sticking to her legs. Nance could see her skin through the weave, already blistered and gruesome in moist, pink shine. It looked as though she had been flayed across the shins. Áine's eyes were shut and her mouth was wide and issuing a hellish scream.

'God have mercy on her,' Nance whispered. There was the smell of vomit, and Nance saw that John was being sick on the ground. The sight of the retching blacksmith holding his wife's blistered ankles jolted her from horrified silence, and she found herself telling Peter to find some butter and *poitín*, and to get John a sip of water.

Nance dropped to her knees. 'Áine,' she said calmly. 'Áine, 'tis Nance. You are going to be alright. I'm here to help you.'

The woman kept thrashing on the ground. Nance caught hold of her arms. 'Áine, be still. Be still.'

There was a sudden silence and Áine stopped struggling and fell limp.

'Is she dead?' John gasped.

'Not dead,' Nance answered. ''Tis too much for her to bear. 'Tis a faint. John. John, listen to me. I need you to go outside and tell everyone there to leave. Tell them to go and pray for her. And then I need you to go and fetch me ivy leaves.'

John got up at once and left, lurching sideways across the yard in the disorientation of his horror.

The bellows boy was standing rigid against the wall. 'We heard her shouting. John and I. We were out in the forge and we heard a screaming. We thought she was being murdered and all. We came in and she was all aflame. John got the blanket from the bed and beat her with it until the fire was out.'

'He did well to think so quickly.'

Peter was silent for a moment. 'Look at the legs of her. Nance, will she die of it?'

Nance sat back on her heels. 'I'll tell you if there's need to send for the priest and the sacrament. But now we have to take her to the river. Can you carry her, do you think?'

Peter and the bellows boy lifted Áine from the floor and carried her out of the room. John had sent some of the people on their way, but many remained, watching with hands over mouths, as the men stumbled down the slope to where the river lay.

Peter and the boy held the unconscious woman in the flowing water by the neck and feet. The water was freezing and the men shivered, their jaws locked with cold, their clothes wet to the waist. John had his eyes closed and was praying on the bank, muttering to himself. Peter held Áine with gritted determination, gently lowering her legs into the water in an even, steady rhythm. Ashes lifted from the woman's dress and were swept away by the current, greasing the surface of the river.

Nance crouched on the bank, watching the men with a keen eye. 'You will not die,' she announced to Áine. 'You will not die.' She held the hem of her skirt to her waist and filled it with hart's tongue fern and ivy leaves, plucking them with John from where they grew at the feet of the oak and alder, ash and holly.

The crowd had not dispersed. Many of the valley people were still stubbornly standing in the blacksmith's yard when they returned from the river, dripping and shaking with the cold. The onlookers crossed themselves at the sight of Áine's burns, but none ventured inside the cabin with them. The hearth had grown cold, and the room was filled with smoke and the smell of burnt hair.

Peter and John placed Áine on the bed in the far corner of the room, and as they settled her on the blanket she murmured, the lid of one eye rising unsteadily before falling shut. Nance ordered Peter to return to the river for more water and asked John to build up the fire. It was only when the turf had been kindled and the flames threw an uneasy glow about the room that they saw the gifts and tokens lying on the cabin's table. Noggins of butter and a basket of turf and kindling. Someone had placed a small salted nugget of bacon next to some eggs. Yellow flowers for protection: sprays of gorse and a cross woven of reeds. And on the edge of the table, a small, clean folded cloth of dowry linen.

That night was as long as the howl of a dog. Nance sat hunched over Áine for the full, slow swing of the moon, dribbling water into her mouth as the ivy and hart's tongue boiled on the fire. She urged Peter to give John as much *poitín* as would send him into sleep on the rushes, and kept the hearth alive, getting up only to refill the piggin of well water, feed the flames with turf and, once, to scrub the blood and ashes off the stone. The woman had left a shadow of her own scorching on the flag.

Shortly before dawn Nance drained the ivy and fern leaves and pummelled their paste into softened butter. She stepped out into the brittle chill and let the rising fingers of sunlight touch the poultice. Then she returned inside and dressed Áine's raw skin, painting the woman's wounds with the herbed fat under prayer and a blessing of her own tongue, soothing her with a stream of words that carried in them no other meaning than a calm urgency to stay alive. She closed her eyes and thought of her da and Maggie, and Father O'Reilly, and all those who had seen in her hands a higher healing, who believed she carried a light. And she thought on her light, her knowledge and her cure, and felt her hands grow hot with it, until all suddenly spasmed, and there were rough fingers gripping her wrists and the sound of the clay vessel breaking on the floor, and when she opened her eyes it was Father Healy and Seán Lynch taking her outside, pulling her so hard that her muscles tightened with the pain of their grip, and her toes scraped against the cobbles, and there was the fresh morning air and mud, and she lay in it and there was Father Healy, pale-faced, mouth saying something to John, who argued in desperation, and above her the birds circled and the sun was rising bloody, rising red in night's slaughter.

CHAPTER
FIFTEEN

Oak

'You'd think nobody ever died, there were so many there!'

'Hearing the Mass!'

Peg nodded, glancing down to the wicker basket where the boy was concealed beside her. She and Nóra were sitting out in the yard knitting, taking in the rare sun of a thin-clouded day while Mary washed the child's soiled rags, steam rising from her barrel.

''Tis the fear,' Peg said. ''Tis a nervous time, what with the animals in foal and calf, and the potatoes about to be put into ground. Folk are vexed. They want reassurance that all will be well. They're praying for the strange happenings to stop. There are them that might not believe in such things but for what has been happening.'

'Áine.'

Peg crossed herself. 'God be with her. Yes, Áine, but also your Martin. Brigid. There's queer things happening up the mountains if you believe half of what goes round. And they're after finding patterns in it all. They're after finding reason for it.'

The boy emitted a loud shriek from his basket and the women exchanged glances.

''Tis back as it was,' murmured Nóra, nodding at the child. 'Pounding its head against the floor, pounding its fists. The *lus mór* took all the cross ways out of it, but now it's after screeching for milk again, and scratching the maid.' Nóra reached down and pushed the boy's extended arm back into the basket. 'Will she live, do you think?'

'Áine?'

'Aye.'

'I pray to God 'tis so. There's a Killarney doctor with her. The priest brought him himself. He's hard against Nance now, and her that had the knowledge to take Áine to the river.'

''Twas swift thinking.'

'Aye, and I say 'tis what saved her. But Father Healy will have none of it. Tossing her out into the yard like that! Now, I understand he has no time for a woman like Nance, that he does be thinking she's a wonder maker. But, sure, 'tis a sad day when a priest is pushing a woman into the mud, with a grand age on her too.'

''Tis shameful.'

'Throwing after her all the herbs brought in good faith.' Peg sniffed. 'John O'Donoghue asked him to let Nance treat the woman, but there's no arguing with a priest. Sure, Father Healy will have Nance out of this valley. He's already after turning minds against her. Nóra . . .' She stopped knitting and sat the needles on her lap. 'There are those that used to go to Nance for the cure and now they won't even look in her direction. A man came the other day asking for her. Said his mother told him of a woman who could take the jaundice out of his child. But would you know, the man he asked was Daniel Lynch, and your own Dan wouldn't be telling him where she lives. Told him to go on home and that no one with the charms was hereabouts.'

'Dan's gone with the shock of the child, may God protect him.'

'And Brigid too, I'm sure. 'Tis a sad thing for her to be waiting for the churching and no one to be talking with but her man, when what she surely needs is company.'

'Faith, I can't imagine Dan speaking out against anybody.'

'It may be he's after believing Father Healy. The man is preaching against Nance at the altar. At the Mass he was saying she's nothing more than a quackered hag, turned to the rot and meddling in lives to bring food to her mouth.'

'Sure, Kate Lynch was telling all about the bittersweet Nance gave to Brigid.' Nóra nodded at Mary. 'The girl heard it herself at the well. Talk of poisoning. I don't believe a word of it.'

Peg nodded. 'I don't believe it either. But Nóra, that's what folk are saying of Áine.' She reached out and placed her hand on Nóra's knee. 'Someone saw her go to Nance's. Alone, like. They found tansy and lady's mantle in the house.'

Nóra shook her head. 'Sure, Nance was healing Áine with herbs afore Father Healy threw her out. The night she was burnt. They were just for the healing.'

Peg dropped her voice. 'But that's not all they're saying. Nóra, how do you think Áine caught fire?'

'Her dress caught light. From the hearth.' Nóra brushed Peg's hand away and resumed knitting. 'How many women do you know with a smouldered apron? Begod, Peg, pity on her, but when a woman spends her hours by a fire, she's bound to be burnt. Áine was unlucky to have it so bad, and God love her and heal her from it.'

Peg took a deep breath. 'Nóra, I'm with you. I have no hard word against Nance. I believe she has the knowledge. But folk are saying 'twas no ordinary fire Áine was building that burnt her. They found the piss of a cow in the crock.'

'In the crock?'

'On the fire. The doctor found it and told the priest, and Father Healy asked John what Áine was doing, boiling potatoes in the water of a beast. John, bless his soul, told him then. 'Twas a cure told by Nance. All-flowers water.'

From across the yard Mary lifted her head and stared, open-mouthed.

'Áine went to Nance to fix a child in her, so says John, and Nance gave her the herbs. The tansy. The lady's mantle. She also told her to bathe in all-flowers water. 'Twas when Áine was fixing a bath of it that she caught alight. That's what the high fire was for. 'Twas when she was following Nance's charm.'

Nóra looked out past the yard across the valley. There was a soft-ness on the hill, rendering the distance into golden haze. She could hear the ringing of tools on the air. ''Twas an accident, sure. No one is to blame.'

'I know that, but Father Healy is saying the sin is on Nance. Muttering *piseógs* and the like. And Nóra, those that have a reluctance to trace it back to Nance's hand are finding reason elsewhere.'

Nóra noticed Peg's eyes flicker to the basket, and felt her stomach drop. 'They're saying 'tis the changeling?'

'They're scared, Nóra. There's a fear in them.' Peg sucked her teeth in thought. 'I don't tell you this to put the fright on you. But I thought you should know what's being said in case anyone comes to pay you a visit, like.'

'I'm going to Nance today, Peg. She will return my grandchild to me. She will bring back Micheál and they will not be able to lay blame at my door.'

'I pray 'tis so, Nóra. Sweet, sore-wounded Christ. But be careful of folk. I wouldn't let them see you go to her. I don't know what they'll think, but I can tell you, it won't be good.' Peg shuddered. 'Not now.

Anyone who still has a desire to go to Nance will be waiting for all this to blow over.'

'Nothing is working,' said Nóra. She stood before Nance's door, reluctantly holding the changeling on her hip. 'You said you could banish it, Nance. Why won't the Good People give me my grandson back? What have I done?' She was near weeping. She could feel the bones of the changeling's chest against her side, feel his bleating breath.

'It takes time,' Nance replied. She was standing within the dark mouth of her cabin, her white hair mussed, arms held out from her sides like a man preparing to fight. 'There's no forcing the sea.'

Nóra shook her head. 'You talk to Them. They gave you the knowledge. Why don't you ask Them where Micheál is? Ask Them to return him to me. Tell them to take back *this*.' She thrust the boy out in front of her, her hands gripping the rounded staves of his ribcage. His toes buttoned inwards, bare to the cold.

'I am working the cure for you,' Nance said, eyeing Nóra warily.

'You do nothing! All you've done is stuff it with herbs that make it shit and tremble. It was leaking with your herbs. The lips of it have split for all the water that passed through it.' Nóra heaved the changeling back upon the ridge of her hip and lowered her voice to a hiss. 'Please, Nance. What you've done with the herbs and the foxglove, 'tis not enough. All it's been doing is crying the louder and dirtying itself. It was all quiet and shaking, but now 'tis just as it was before. I asked you to make Them take back their own, not have it grow weak and sick, and then strong and well again. Sure, if it was a burden before, the changeling's a weight on me now.'

Nance closed her eyes, swaying a little on her feet. She did not reply.

There was a long silence.

'You're filthy with drink,' Nóra finally spat.

Nance opened her eyes. 'I'm not.'

'Look at the state of you.'

Nance sighed and took an unsteady step forward, lurching for the doorframe. She gripped the wood and pulled herself out over the doorstep. 'Nóra.'

'What? Look at you.'

'Sit down with me.'

'Here? I'm not sitting in the mud.'

'Sit with me there. On that log by there.'

Nóra reluctantly followed the stumbling woman to the rotting tree trunk that lay fleeced with moss on the border of the woods.

Nance eased herself down onto it. She took a deep breath and patted the space beside her. 'Sit you down, Nóra Leahy. Put the fairy on the ground. By there, on the grass. Under the oak.'

Nóra hesitated, lip curled, but her arms ached from carrying the changeling. Placing the child on a clump of new grass, she grudgingly sat beside Nance.

The old woman peered up at the oak's bare branches. '*When the ash comes out before the oak, you'll have a summer of dust and smoke.*'

'What?'

Nance sniffed. 'An old rhyme. Sure, the trees do be knowing what will come, long before it passes.'

Nóra grunted.

'Do you see that there?' Nance asked, pointing out beyond her cabin.

'The Piper's Grave.'

'That's it. The oak. The rowan. The whitethorn. That's where They be.'

''Tis no news to me, Nance Roche. We all know where the Good People make their home.'

'I've seen Them. I've heard Them.' Nance blinked slowly, letting her arm drop to her side. 'My mother was a great favourite of Theirs. They would come for her. On the fairy wind. They gave her a steed of ragwort and she went with them to the beautiful places. My aunt too. Faith, that's where they went. And they left me, but they left me with the knowledge.'

Nóra looked at the old woman. Her eyes were half shut and her hands scratched at the moss on the trunk. She looked deranged.

Nance suddenly opened her eyes and frowned. 'I know what you're thinking, Nóra Leahy. You think that the years have wormed into my mind and made tunnels of my sense. You think I am riddled with age.' She leant into Nóra's face, her breath hot. 'You are wrong.'

There was silence. Both women looked to the woods.

'I thought it might be enough to hear one such as yourself pronounce him fairy,' Nóra said eventually. 'Ever since my daughter passed, I've been thinking how it was that the boy was wasting. The thought that it might have been Johanna and Tadgh, the hunger . . .' Her voice cracked. 'I thought they might have caused it to their own son. Maybe they were neglecting him. Maybe my own girl was no mother at all to him. I was after asking, did I not teach her how to protect a child? When Martin died I was thinking to myself that there must have been something I did to bring all the bad luck upon myself. That the boy was not on Johanna's soul but on mine.'

''Tis no sin on you, Nóra.'

'But I felt somehow that 'twas. And people were talking! I was so ashamed of him. A cripple like that. When Peter and John brought Martin to me, my own man's body on their shoulders, the only thing I could think of was to get the boy out the house. The shame to have folk inside and peering at his crooked legs and wondering why 'twas so.

Thinking on what sin brought the sense out of him when I saw him well and thriving not two years ago. Thinking ill of me. Blaming me.'

'Nóra, listen now. That boy is not Johanna's son. 'Tis not your grandson. 'Tis fairy. You know that! The look of him, the wasting on him. I tell you now that the cratur is nothing more than an old, withered fairy, changed for Micheál. And why did they take away your daughter's boy?' Nance placed her hand over Nóra's. 'Because he was the dearest lad they could find.'

Nóra smiled, eyes watering. 'I saw Micheál once, before he was changed. He was beautiful. A bud.' She looked down at the changeling. 'Not like this false child.'

'We will return him to the Good People, Nóra. I knew a woman who was swept and returned.'

'You did?'

'I knew two women swept. One was not returned, but the other . . .' Nance frowned. 'They brought her back to herself through a reddened poker. They lay the hot iron in her face and that was enough to banish the fairy forever and for her to be restored.'

Nóra paused, thoughtful. 'Fire returned her?'

''Twas my own aunt, and 'tis how I know it to be true,' Nance said. 'I saw the mark of it on her face with my own eyes. The scar. Like a brand.'

'And it worked?'

Nance rubbed her eyes, swaying on the log. 'Aye. It worked.'

Nóra sat up sharply. 'Then we must try a reddened poker.'

'No.' Nance's voice was firm. 'No, we mustn't be doing that.'

'But it worked, so you say yourself!'

'My aunt told me she'd never have it done to another. "Never on my life," so said she, and I've a mind to heed her.' Nance paused.

Nóra's mouth twisted. 'It needn't be a scalding or a branding. It might be enough to threaten the cratur with the flames. To frighten the fairy back to its own kind.' She pointed to the spade which lay against the outer wall of Nance's *bothán*, next to the waste heap. 'To sit the cratur on that and make as if to shovel it into the fire.'

''Twould not be enough to threaten it.'

Nóra's lip trembled. 'Then we burn it. Just a wee burn. On the face.'

Nance stared at her. 'We'll not be doing that.'

'I want it gone.'

There was silence.

'Nóra, think of Áine. Did you not hear the screaming of her? The skin was clean burnt off her legs. To the bone. Blistered.' Nance folded her mouth into a grim line. 'Not through fire . . . I know you want to be rid of the cratur, but we can't be burning him.'

'Áine's no fairy.'

'I can't be going against the word of my aunt.'

'You say we cannot burn it, but what else would you have me do? Tell me! You are the one with the knowledge!'

Nance grew very still. Nóra saw that her eyes were closed again. Her sparse, pale lashes flat against her cheek. She is old, Nóra realised. There was a weariness that clung to her. A vulnerability. Nóra noticed the slow rise and fall of her chest, the tiny rounds of her shoulders. The woman wore so many layers that Nóra had never thought of Nance as frail before. But sitting this close to her, in daylight, she saw that the *bean feasa* was thin. She was weak.

Nance's eyes opened, muted, fog-soaked. 'There is another way. We can take the changeling to where the fairies do be and banish it there.'

'The Piper's Grave?'

Nance shook her head. 'Where the water greets itself. A place of power. Boundary water.'

'The river.'

'You, me and the girl. Three women at the place where three running rivers meet, for three mornings in a row. We will all of us fast. We take the changeling before sunrise to the Flesk. Three times before sunrise for three mornings, and when you return home on the last morning, the changeling will be gone. And perhaps you will find Micheál restored to you. Maybe it is that the Good People will have returned him to you. The fairy will be gone.'

'We'll be going to the water?'

'Boundary water. We'll duck the fairy in water with the power in it. A mighty power.'

Nóra stared at Nance, gaping. Then, as if deciding, she pressed her lips together and nodded hurriedly. 'When will we begin?'

Nance hesitated. ''Tis only now March; the water will be cold,' she muttered, as if to herself. 'The water will be cold and the current will be strong.' She looked at Nóra, her expression unreadable. ''Twould be better if it were closer to the approach of May Day. That is when the Good People will be changing abode. They will be restless. They will turn their eyes to us.'

'May Day? But that is a good while away.'

''Tis only that it will be cold.'

'But the days are warmer than they were. Sure, they say it will be a fine month. Nance, I can't be waiting until May Day.'

Nance paused, before nodding. 'Tomorrow morning, then. Before sunrise, in a state of hunger. Don't be eating a thing from sundown, nor let the girl take any. Not Mary, not yourself and don't be letting the change-child near water nor a bite of food. And I will be fasting too.' Nance looked down the slope to where the river ran. 'Meet me here. I will be waiting.'

It had rained during the night and the ground was soft and forgiving, relenting under Mary's bare feet. It was dark, and she walked awkwardly along the overgrown path, unable to push away the ferns and low branches with the boy in her arms. She carried him on her hipbone, his unmoving legs shifting loose against her thighs as she walked, eyes fixed on the dark blur of Nóra in front of her. Nance was leading them to the river, the white of her uncovered hair bobbing in the gloom like an apparition.

Mary felt light-bodied and hollowed with hunger. Her arms ached. 'Is it much further?' she whispered. Neither of the women answered. Her stomach dipped in trepidation.

The widow had returned from Nance's the evening before in a state of high excitement. She had burst through the cabin door and pushed the child roughly into Mary's arms, breathing hard, eyes shining. 'Tomorrow,' she had gasped. 'We're to be taking him to the water, to the river. Boundary water, says Nance. There's more power in that than the herbs. Boundaries where the fairies do be. They can't cross running water, she says. They gather there, but can't be crossing.'

Micheál had started crying. Mary laid a gentle hand on his soft hair and guided his head to her shoulder.

Nóra had paced the cabin floor. 'You're not to eat anything,' she said, pointing at Mary. 'And don't be feeding it. Fasting, there's a need for fasting.'

'What are we going to do by the river?'

The widow had sat down by the fire and then almost immediately rose to her feet again. She went to the open door and peered down the valley. 'We'll bathe it. In the river where the three waters meet.'

Mary had stroked Micheál's hair, felt his hot breath and tears against her neck. ''Twill be freezing.'

Nóra had seemed not to hear. She took a deep breath of the evening air and closed the door, latching it tight. 'Three mornings. Three women.'

'Are we to fast for three days?'

'Don't you eat a thing. Not a crumb.'

'We'll be starving for it.'

'I think, Mary, that I will soon have my daughter's child with me. And you –' she had pointed a long finger at the child in Mary's arms '– you will be gone.'

There was no morning breeze and the trees were still. The woods held their breath in the hours before daybreak, and there was a hush of waiting, the ringing silence of unsinging birds. Mary felt the air grow damp as they approached the river, in the darker shadows cast by elm trees. Then, suddenly, she heard the burble of water and the canopy opened up, revealing a paling sky. The moon and a few lingering stars glowered above them.

'Through here,' Nance said. She stopped to make sure that Mary and Nóra were still following her before continuing. The women pushed past long grass and the sound of the water changed, became softer. Here was deep-running water, Mary thought. Nance had told them there was a pool of the three boundaries, where the Flesk met its sisters and the water threaded in dark trinity. The ferns and undergrowth thinned and Mary paused to cast her eyes down at the river. The early-morning sky was held in its trembling skin.

'This is the place,' Nance whispered. She turned to Mary and reached for the boy. 'Give him to me now. You'll be going first. You'll be bathing him.'

Mary's stomach lurched. She looked at Nóra. The woman was staring at the water, her face drawn.

Nance beckoned her. 'Quickly now. We need to bathe him before the sun comes up.'

'Sure, won't the water be too cold for him?'

''Twill be quick enough. You can wrap him again after you've dipped him.'

Mary handed Micheál to Nance. He was waspish, groaning.

'That's it, that's a good girl.'

'Are the Good People here?' Nóra whispered. Her shoulders were tense, her neck arched like an unbroken horse, eyes darting the length of the swift-moving river.

Nance nodded. 'Oh, you'll know when They're here. You'll know when They've come to retrieve their own.' She pointed at the unflowering iris that grew low to the river's edge. 'Yellow flaggers in bloom are a sure sign that a changeling has been banished into the water. You'll see. He'll be turning into yellow flaggers the third morning, when he's back with his own kind.' She turned to Mary. 'You'll need to take your shawl off now.'

Mary's arms were weak from carrying the boy such a long way, and they shook as she unwrapped her shawl from her shoulders. She thought, briefly, of her family in Annamore, what they would say if they could see her now, about to bathe in the darkness of a March morning with a stricken child. *Piseógs*, they would call it. Mary folded her shawl and placed it on a mossed stone. She started to tremble.

'Do I have to be the one to do it?'

Nance was firm. 'We'll all have a turn with the bathing. One morning each.'

'It won't harm him?'

''Tis a fairy,' Nóra whispered. 'Mary, get in the water. Come on now with you, before the sun rises.'

Gripping a low-hanging branch for balance, Mary stepped down the bank to the water's edge, using the exposed roots of trees as steps.

'Not yet,' Nance called. She beckoned Mary back. 'You've to take off your outer things.'

Mary stood there in the gloom, her knuckles white around the branch and its green fur of moss. Her teeth chattered uncontrollably. 'Can I not go in with my clothes?'

'You need to be bare.'

Mary thought she would cry. 'I don't want to,' she whispered, but she climbed back up the bank and took off her skirt and blouse until she stood naked in the pre-dawn light, hunched in modesty and shivering. Mary watched as Nance undressed Micheál from his wrappings, then carefully leant out to take him. She gripped him fast to her ribs, his bare skin clammy against her own, and inched her way carefully down to the river.

How she wished she was back home. She thought of the girls she had seen that May morning, crawling naked through the briars.

God forgive me, she thought.

The river was deep cold, black with tannin. Its touch brought a peal of shock from her lips, and she looked up and saw both women staring at her. Nóra's fingers gripped the cloth of her apron. 'It won't take long,' Mary heard her say, as if to herself. 'It won't take long.'

Gasping in the shock of the bitter water, Mary could see the white of her skin mirrored on the surface. She held the child aloft, his legs dangling. 'What do I do?' She had to raise her voice over the rush of the current. It pushed against her hips, and she inched her toes into the mud of the riverbed to steady herself.

'Put him in the water three times,' Nance called. 'Put his head under. His whole body.'

Mary looked at the boy's face. His eyes canted in his head, sloping sideways as one arm fought the air.

He is full of fairy, she thought, and she lowered him into the river.

CHAPTER
SIXTEEN

Yellow iris

Dawn broke as **Nóra and Mary** trudged their way back
up the slope to the cabin after their trip to the river.
Mary's skin under her clothes felt numb with cold, and
she worried that Micheál, too, was freezing. The boy was quiet in
her grip, his face scrunched into her neck, his breathing slow.

'He's frightful chilled,' Mary muttered.

Nóra looked back at her, panting as she took long strides up the
path. 'Quickly now. We don't want anyone to be seeing us. Wondering
what we're after doing away from home at this early hour.'

'He's not moving at all. He's caught the cold.'

'We'll be inside soon enough.' She waved Mary on, clearly frustrated at her slow pace. 'Quickly!'

Inside the cabin, Nóra grabbed the pail and went to milk the cow,
leaving Mary to tend to the fire. The girl's stomach groaned as she
fed twigs to the crackling flames. Three days of fasting, she thought.
She already felt lightheaded.

Micheál lay on the settle bed, eyes slipping back and forth. Once
the fire was high, Mary picked up the shawl she had draped over his

body and held it to the hearth to warm the wool. Before she placed it over him, she peeked at his skin and saw that the boy's flesh was blue with cold. Without thinking, she picked up one of his hands and placed his icy fingers in her mouth to warm them.

He tasted of the river.

After the cow had been milked and the fire stoked to a rustling pile of embers, Nóra suggested to Mary that they return to their beds for a few hours' sleep. Mary, stomach rumbling and her eyes aching from the early morning, agreed. She folded her blanket over and tucked Micheál in with her shawl, where, finally warm, he surrendered to sleep. Mary lay down next to him and studied his face. She had never seen his features in such detail. It was usually dark when she lay beside him, and in Micheál's waking hours she was too busy dribbling water into his mouth, or feeding him, or scrubbing the caked mess from his skinny buttocks, or soothing his rash with tallow to stop and look at him carefully. But now, as the early-morning sunlight cut through the cracks in the door, she saw how his nose was lightly freckled, the crust in his nostrils flaking. His mouth had slipped open, and she could see that a lower tooth in the centre of his mouth was at a strange angle. Reaching gently, so as not to wake him, she placed her fingertip on its tiny, ridged edge. The tooth wobbled, and then, as she added more pressure, came away from his gum and fell onto the mattress.

Micheál stirred, eyelids creasing, but did not wake.

Mary picked up the tooth and held it up to the light. A pearl, she thought. A little pearl. She ran her finger over the rough hollow, briefly filled with wonderment that a fairy child could have something so ordinary, so like a human tooth.

Rising, Mary went to the door, pushed open the top half and – as she had done so many times with her own brothers and sisters – threw the first-fallen tooth over her right shoulder into the dirt of the yard.

That will help keep you safe, she thought, and she returned to the settle bed and fell into a deep and dreamless sleep.

'Mary, wake up. Wake up now.'

A rough hand was shaking her shoulder. Mary blearily opened her eyes and saw Nóra's face – pale, alarmed – above her.

'Mary!'

Suddenly afraid, she sat upright and looked for the boy. He lay sleeping beside her, his arms thrown above his head. She breathed out in relief. 'What time is it?'

'We've slept the day through. 'Tis well past noon.' Nóra was wearing her husband's greatcoat, its broad shoulders making her body seem small, fragile. Wisps of grey hair fell over her face. 'Mary, they've found a *piseóg*.'

'A *piseóg*?' She felt her stomach turn.

'I was outside passing my water, and I saw Peg coming over the way. She told me. She's after telling everyone on the mountain. There's a crowd going there to see it. 'Tis a nest of something. A charm. Something bad.'

Fear flapped in Mary's chest. 'Something bad?'

Nóra nodded, picking up the shawl from where it lay over the boy and throwing it at her. 'Up with you. I want you to go and see it and tell me what it is.'

Mary rubbed her eyes and began to wind the shawl about her head. 'Who set it?'

'They don't know. 'Tis what everyone wants to find out.'

'Where?'

'At the Lynches',' Nóra whispered. 'Kate and Seán Lynch.' She helped the girl to her feet. 'Go and find out what it is.'

*

Mary found her way to the Lynches' farm by following the crowd of people walking the fields. There was a sense of nervous excitement amongst them, of anxious gossip.

'He was at the scoreground when he saw it. Says he doesn't think 'tis the first set upon his land.'

'Musha, I heard him talking of others at the smith's.'

'Stones turned up on their edges, branches and plants tied to his gate.'

'Ah, but this is a right old dark *piseóg*. 'Tis a nest of straw and a bloody mess inside it. Rotting. None of your stones and plants. This is some new darkness. Meant to be found, too, by the looks of it.'

'Seán's saying 'twas left by Nance Roche.'

'The priest has been sent for. 'Tis that bad, that troubling.'

'Oh, I don't like any of it.'

They neared the smallholding, and Mary squeezed through the crowd to get a closer look at the *piseóg*. It lay on the ground behind the Lynches' whitewashed cabin, partly obscured by a dung pile. It was a small thing, a nest, but clearly made by a human hand. There was none of the twigging wrought by beak, but careful, deliberate weaving. In the nest's hollow was a dark mass of bloody matter in a state of decay. The smell of it seethed in Mary's nostrils.

The crowd stood around in horror, crossing themselves and whispering out of the corner of their mouths.

'There's no saying that's an accident.'

'Sure, there's malice in this. Terrible malice.'

'What do you think 'tis there? The rot in it?'

'Would it be a bit of meat, do you think?'

A male voice suddenly rang out amongst the murmuring. 'The priest is here! Father Healy is here!' There was a rush of movement as the people parted to let the priest through.

He has come in a hurry, thought Mary. His clothes were spattered with mud.

'Here 'tis, Father.' Crabbed hands pointed at the ground where the *piseóg* lay.

The priest stared at it for a moment, fingers pinching his nose. 'Who did this?'

There was silence.

'Who here has lost the run of his senses?' Father Healy glared at the crowd, his blue eyes sliding over excited, fearful faces.

'Father, there's none of us knows who set it.'

'Sure, we've just come to see it.'

'What will you do, Father?'

The priest's eyes watered at the stench. 'Bring me a spade.'

One of the labourers sent his son to fetch a tool, and as he waited the priest took out a small clear bottle of holy water, carefully drawing its cork. With an air of great ceremony, he poured a little on the *piseóg*.

'A drop more, would you, Father?' piped a voice. There were chuckles from the crowd.

Father Healy clenched his jaw but did as asked, and splashed the nest and the ground around it liberally. When the spade was brought, Father Healy snatched it from the boy and, with an expression of impatience, slid it under the *piseóg*, lifting it into the air. The crowd took several steps back as it teetered on the metal edge.

'Where is your nearest ditch, man?' he asked. Seán, face dark with outrage, pointed to a corner of his field. The priest immediately set off towards it, the crowd of people following behind. Mary walked with them, the blood hissing through her veins.

The ditch was wet-bottomed, filled with nettles. Father Healy carefully lowered the *piseóg* down on the drier part of the ditch wall, then wiped the spade on the grass.

'What now, Father?'

'Will you bless the spade, Father?'

'Should ye have not used a stick instead? Will the *piseóg* not poison the work of the spade?'

Father Healy rubbed his eyes, then took out his holy water and flicked a palmful on the blade, murmuring a prayer under his breath.

'Burn it, Father.'

'The spade?' The priest looked momentarily confused.

'The *piseóg*. Will ye not burn the *piseóg*?' A man stepped forward, cheerfully offering his smoking pipe.

Father Healy, suddenly understanding, shook his head. 'The ground is too wet. Seán, will you fetch some dry fuel? Hay, furze. Whatever will burn. And a light.'

For some time there was a buzz of excited activity as the crowd followed Seán back to his cabin, helping themselves to his stores of kindling, furze and animal feed. Seán himself said nothing, although he seemed to smoulder with anger. Mary kept her distance from him, although at one point he caught her eye and held it, giving her a look of such disgust and hostility that she quickly averted her gaze and turned her attention to gathering sticks. Kate, she noticed, stood apart from the crowd, her shawl wrapped closely about her face. She seemed dazed, one eye purpled. At the sight of Mary she flinched, then took three careful steps backwards, spitting on the ground and crossing herself.

They burnt the *piseóg* in the cold, blue arm of twilight, under a pile of wood, turf, dried furze and straw. The fire blazed in the buckled air, the flames carrying a heart of violet. A sign of the perishing wickedness of the thing, Mary thought. It gave her a strange feeling, watching the bloody nest burn, while the priest climbed back on his donkey and the people remained, standing sentry around the fire.

Her mind crawled with uneasy thoughts. Who had plaited that nest of straw? What kind of devilment was abroad?

The smell of rot stayed with her long after the fire had died and the people walked back to their cabins, numb with the evening's chill. For all the priest's holy water she could still smell the moulding bloodiness of the *piseóg* on her hair long after she returned to Nóra's cabin.

⚓

Men gathered outside Nance Roche's hut that night, full of liquor, brandishing ashplants.

Nance heard them arrive. Their footsteps were loud as they crashed through the undergrowth, slashing at the bracken. Peering out of a gap in her wicker door, she saw Seán Lynch swaying at the head of the pack, stopping to unbutton his trousers. A few men cheered as he started to piss, aiming the dull splatter towards her hut.

There was the sound of something smashing. One of the men had thrown a *poitín* jug at the trunk of the oak tree.

'You're a black bitch!' Seán suddenly spat, a thick line of spittle flinging out of his mouth. The men grew silent at the fury in his voice. Through the chink in the door Nance could see five of them standing not ten yards away, their faces shining with sweat and drink.

Seán Lynch lurched to one side, waving his stick unsteadily in the air. 'You're a black bitch, Nance Roche, and may the Devil take you with him!'

There was silence. Nance held her breath. Her heart thudded like a man buried alive.

The men stood there for a long while, each of them staring at her hut. She knew it was dark, knew they could not make out the glisten of her eye in the gap of the woven door, but it seemed that each man looked directly at her. Five faces full of vim and cursing. Five walls of anger.

After what seemed like an hour's siege, the men finally turned and walked unsteadily back to the lane, talking amongst themselves.

When they had disappeared into the darkness and Nance could no longer hear anything but the sound of the wind moving through the woods and the light rush of the river, she sank back down against the wall, breathing hard, terrified. Her body trembled uncontrollably.

Men had broken into her cabin two days after she'd arrived home to find Maggie and the fairy woman gone. She found the room overturned, the delph smashed on the floor, the ashes of the fire kicked over as though someone had searched for something buried in the powder of the dead hearth.

It was dark when the men returned, boots knocking against the doorframe, fists on the whitewash.

'Where is she?'

Nance, scrambling to her feet, trying to open the back door to escape, finding it jammed against the clay.

'None of that, *cailín*. Where is she?'

'Who?'

'Where's the mad one? Your woman who sets the curses?'

'The cures?'

One of the men had spat, had glared at her for that. 'Mad Maggie of Mangerton.'

'She has no hand in *piseógs*.'

He had laughed. 'No hand in it, does she?'

Nance thought of what Maggie had taught her in the days before. Ways to gather the luck due to others and harvest it for yourself. Ways to strike a man barren. The things you might do with a dead man's hand should there be need for it.

'She's not here.'

'Not hiding out in yonder ditch?'

Nance shook her head. 'She's gone.' Tears then at the fear of the men standing in her dead father's cabin, the disappearance of the only kin she had left in the world.

The men had pointed their fingers in her face. 'If your mad whore of an aunt comes back, you tell her she'll get what's coming to her. Tell I know 'twas her that blasted my cows. Tell her I'll slit her throat same way I had to slit theirs.'

Now, slumped in her tiny *bothán*, Nance's hands were shaking just as they had shaken all night after the men had finally left her alone.

Virgin Mother save me, Nance thought. I am an ash tree in the face of a storm. Despite the woods, I alone court the lightning.

When Nóra woke the second morning, her stomach prickling in anticipation, Mary was already dressed and waiting by the lit fire with the changeling on her lap, hands firmly crossed over his stomach. The boy's head twitched on her shoulder. He was pining like a dog.

'Look at you, up and ready. You could have woken me. We could be halfway there.'

Mary gave Nóra an imploring look.

'What's the matter with you, then?'

'I don't want to go.'

'And why is that?' Nóra asked irritably. Her guts swooped in a thrill of excitement. She wanted to be by the river already. She wanted her turn at sinking the fairy child in the water. Wanted to feel its reluctance to leave.

'I'm scared,' said Mary.

'Scared of what? What fear is there in bathing in the river? You took your turn with it yesterday morning. You can watch this time.'

''Tis too cold for him. You saw how he was shivering and shaking, and how he turned blue with it. I'm afraid for him. And this morning he was yawping for his milk, missus. He's hungry!'

'So am I. So are you.'

'But with nothing in his belly I'm scared he won't stand the cold and he'll catch his death.'

'Mary, that's no child sitting on you there. And there's no saving Micheál unless we do as Nance says and put it in the water.'

The girl seemed on the brink of tears. 'I have an ill feeling about it,' she stammered.

Nóra took a sip of water from the dipper and splashed a little on her face. 'Enough, Mary.'

'I do. I have an ill feeling. I think of what the priest would say if he knew.'

'The priest had his chance to help me.'

'But missus, do you not think there's sin in it? I told you about the *piseóg* yesterday. This feels like we're having a hand in that same bad business. Getting up before dawn and baring ourselves in wild places. I don't want to be sinning. I don't want to be hurting the child.'

'You're only afraid because you saw the *piseóg* yesterday and it has turned your head.'

'They're saying 'twas Nance that set it!'

'That's a lie.'

'They're saying she wishes ill on the valley because Father Healy preached against her at Mass.'

'Gossip and hen talk!'

'But perhaps we can't be trusting her, missus. Perhaps she –'

'Mary!' Nóra rubbed her face with her apron and tied it around her waist. 'Would you have my daughter's son returned to me?'

The girl was silent. She pulled the boy closer to her.

'There is no sin in this,' Nóra said. 'There is no sin in returning to the Good People what was always theirs.'

Mary stared at the clay beneath Nóra's feet. 'Can I bring the blanket to warm him afterwards?'

''Tis yours to carry if you do.'

They walked to Nance's cabin under a clear black sky, the faint suggestion of pink to the east. Nóra noticed that Mary swayed on her feet as she carried the wrapped changeling. She must be hungry, she thought. The previous day's fasting had left Nóra feeling euphoric. Walking in the darkness, she felt as though her senses were sharper than usual. The cold air slipped into her lungs and left her nostrils ringing with the usual scents of earth, mud and smoke, but also the nearing damp of the river and the musty undergrowth of the forest. She felt thrillingly awake.

Nance was sitting up by her fire when they arrived. She started in surprise when they opened the door, and Nóra was dispirited to see that the old woman seemed distracted. Large bags hung under her eyes and her white hair, usually carefully knotted at the neck, was loose and tangled over her shoulders.

'Nance?'

'Is it time?' she asked, and when neither answered, she slowly rose to her feet. 'Let's to the boundaries, then.'

The silence, once they entered the woods, was oppressive. Nóra could hear nothing but the soft padding and rustle of their footsteps and the strain of Mary's breath as she wearied under the changeling's weight. The shadows under the trees seemed horribly still.

A sudden, shrill screeching carried along the valley, and all three women jumped at the sound.

A duck, thought Nóra. Just a fox killing a duck. But it left a prickling at the back of her neck.

'Did you hear the dreadful business at the Lynches'? The *piseóg*?' she whispered, trying to make her voice as steady as possible.

In the darkness Nance was silent.

'A *piseóg*,' Nóra repeated. 'The priest was sent for. He sprinkled the holy water upon it, and 'twas burnt, after. So said Mary.'

Mary's voice rang out in front of her. ''Twas a nest and some blood.'

'Sure, the girl told me it smelt like the Devil. 'Twas the way Seán found it. He smelt it out.'

'Trouble's coming,' Nance muttered. She seemed preoccupied. It wasn't until they had reached the same place in the river that she spoke again.

'Nóra, 'tis your turn.'

Nóra did not know whether the cramping in her guts was from excitement or fear. 'What have I to do, Nance?'

'The rite is the same as before. Do as the girl. Undress and take the wee fairy into the water with you. Be sure to place him all the way under three times. Every hair on his head under the surface. Let all parts of him under the power of the boundary. Let you don't slip. That river looks mighty high this morning.'

Nóra nodded, her mouth dry. She took off her clothes with shaking fingers.

'Perhaps I should do it again,' Mary said. She had crouched down on a tree root and was holding the boy close to her chest. He groaned at the sound of the water, his head thumping against her shoulder.

Nóra held out her arms for him. 'Enough of that, you know 'tis my turn. 'Tis how it must be. Give it to me, Mary.'

The maid hesitated. 'Will you be careful with him?'

'There's no harm intended,' Nance reassured her. 'We're only after sending the fairy child back to his own kind.'

'He was so cold yesterday. 'Tis terrible cold for him. And him being so little, so thin.'

'Give him to Nóra, Mary.'

'Quickly!' Nóra stepped over and took the child from Mary's arms. Letting the blanket drop from his shoulders she lay him on the ground and pulled the dress over his head.

'You've set him on a briar,' Mary protested. Nóra pretended she hadn't heard. She picked him up again and the boy suddenly grew angry, squawking, his fists swinging. Nóra felt his head smack against her collarbone.

'Into the river with you now, Nóra. That's it. Hold that branch there as Mary did yesterday. Don't slip now.'

The changeling, when Nóra first held him under the fast-flowing water, opened his mouth in surprise. But it was no more than a baptism, a rush of river into the mouth, and Nóra lifted him into the air before plunging him down again.

'In the name of God, are you or are you not Micheál Kelliher, son of my daughter?'

She had the sense that the changeling fixed her eye as the water flooded over his face for the third time, bubbles streaming from his mouth. She lifted him, dripping, and the sun broke across the surface. She had not noticed it grow light. Nóra clutched the fairy child against her bare chest and held him there until he burbled the river down her breasts and his lungs grew less ragged. She stood, shivering in the dappled water, and felt that it was true, in one day's time she would have her daughter's son restored to her, full-limbed and speaking. Standing in the river, she felt the promise of it in the current's quiet insistence and in the skylarks above, suddenly praising the sky with flight.

There was a dark knot of women at the well later that morning, cloaks drawn over their heads despite the clear March weather. Their voices were hot with conspiracy.

Mary glanced at them from where she stooped to let down her bucket and saw several pairs of eyes flick her way, some of them looking boldly. All at once the huddle of women moved towards her. Mary jerked upright, lifting her chin and staggering from sudden dizziness.

'You're a friend to Nance Roche, are you not, Mary Clifford?' It was Éilís O'Hare who spoke, a slant of accusation in her voice.

'We were talking here amongst ourselves, thinking on who might have set that *piseóg* on Seán's land.'

'Well, it wasn't me that did it, if that's what you're thinking.'

Éilís gave a high laugh. 'Isn't she a proud girl, thinking we were accusing her. Piss on nettles this morning, did you?'

The women laughed. Mary felt her spine run cold.

'Whoever did it was up and about while 'twas dark. Not even the dog was barking, so says Seán.'

'Might not have been so recent as that,' said another woman. 'Whoever set the *piseóg* might have put it down fresh, let it rot in time.'

'Kate did say she's been seeing Nance stealing about the fields in the blue of the morning when no one was about.'

'Sure, but my man is an early riser and he says he would swear on his mother's grave he saw an old woman accompanied by the Good People walking the lane in the dark. Near the Piper's Grave, out where 'tis wild. And his eyes are keen.'

'Keen enough to be seeing fairies now, is he?'

'Faith, many men see things through the bottom of a *poitín* bottle.'

There was laughter.

'It wasn't drink! He hasn't tasted a drop in his life.'

'Is he after thinking 'twas Nance and her spirits?'

'Ah well, they say she does be speaking with Them.'

'Begod, 'tis true. She *conspires* with Them. She's been asking them for the knowledge to steal butter and dry hens and burn up blacksmith's wives.'

'Terrible business.'

'I wonder what the blood was,' said one woman, eyes flicking nervously to Mary.

The women glanced at each other.

'Could be from an animal,' suggested one. 'Could be a hare, killed and bled.'

Mary looked at the ground. She thought she was going to be sick.

Éilís spoke again. 'If you see Nance, Mary, best tell her to watch who she's after setting curses on. There's none here who will be tolerating badness like that. Setting the fire against Áine. Bloodiness on Seán's farm.'

'Tell her to take to the road.'

'She has the cure,' Mary said feebly.

'Sure, I went to her for the cure in days past, didn't I?' Éilís smirked. 'And didn't she near poke my eye out with a gander beak. She's soft in the mind.'

'Is it soft in the mind or hard in the heart, Éilís?'

Mary saw that Hanna had wandered over, her forehead creased. 'You'd best get your story straight.'

'Only a fool would go to a herb hag such as she.'

'And are you still a fool, Éilís? Or did you leave that off when you married that great man of yours?'

Éilís scowled, but walked away, leaving Mary shaking.

Hanna reached over and placed a hand on her shoulder. 'Don't you mind her,' she said. 'You're after taking that Leahy boy to Nance, are you not?'

Mary nodded.

'You tell Nance Old Hanna knows that *piseóg* was none of her making.' She dropped her voice. 'Any woman could tell you what was in that nest. Sure, there's plenty blood amongst women, and God himself knows that business is beyond Nance these days. My own self too! No, 'twas a hand closer to home, so I think.'

Mary stared at her, horror-filled.

'Aye,' Hanna said, nodding to where Kate Lynch was drawing her water. 'Kicks her about the house. You mark my words, young Mary Clifford. She'll kill him one day. If anyone is soft in the mind, 'tis her. His fists have knocked it so.'

Nance stood in the dark, smoking coltsfoot and watching the lane. For three days she had eaten nothing and in her hunger she felt altered, alert. The flare of her pipe was painful bright, her ears pricked to every rustle, every suggestion of movement in the dark. Hunger had hollowed her until she felt like a *bodhrán*. Tight-skinned, every impression on her body amplified. She thrummed.

Nance heard it then. Cutting through on the still near-dawn, the fox cry of the changeling. She shuddered, sucked on her pipe. Several long minutes passed until Nóra and Mary reached her, following the tiny light of the burning leaf to where she stood in the doorway of her cabin. The widow was walking strangely, her hands curled into fists, her legs wooden. As she got closer Nance saw that the woman's jaw was chattering, although there was no frost on the ground. She seemed agitated.

'God's blessings on you both.'

'Faith but 'tis dark this morning.' Nóra's voice was high, saddled with expectation.

''Tis the last morning. 'Tis always darkest on the last morning.'

'Were it not for that slip of a moon, we'd be lost.'

'But you're here. And Mary, were you afraid to lose the way?'

The girl said nothing, only the white of her apron showing in the gloom. Nance reached for her shoulder and felt her flinch.

'There now. There's nothing to be afraid of. I'll be protecting you and 'twill be light soon.'

Mary sniffed, and the changeling cried out again, spooking them all.

Nance held her arms out. 'He knows we will return him to where he came from. Give him to me, Mary. I'll carry him down to the water.'

'He's too heavy.'

'I'm strong.'

'I want to take him. Let me hold him.'

Nance saw Nóra cuff the girl on the shoulder. 'Give it to Nance.' The widow turned and addressed her. 'You'd best be having words with the girl. She's been whimpering and carrying on all the night through.'

'Mary? Let me take the fairy.'

'He knows,' the girl whispered, as she reluctantly handed the boy over.

'What?'

'He knows where we're going,' she said, her voice plaintive. 'As soon as he saw we were on our way to your cabin he started up with the screaming.'

'Sure, the wee changeling doesn't want to be going back under hill! He has had you to care for him. But 'tis time to be changing him back for the widow's grandson.'

'What will happen to him?'

'He'll return to his own kind.'

'And it won't hurt him?'

'Musha, not at all,' Nance replied, but an image of Maggie crossed her mind. The long scar.

The journey to the river seemed impossibly long with the change-ling tight against her chest. The child, alarmed by Nance's strange hands, cried into the wrinkled skin of her throat as they walked, the dew-strung grass slapping against their skirts. She felt his piss seep through his linen, a spreading warmth against her hand.

The widow whispered excitedly to Nance as they walked.

'I had a dream last night. 'Twas no ordinary dream. Do you remember Peter O'Connor talking of lights at the Piper's Grave the night Martin died? I dreamt I was out walking the fields in the near dawn – 'twas a kind of blue as this – and as I neared the fairy place, I saw three lights under the whitethorn. At first I was afraid to see them, but my legs would not stop their walking, and sure, as they brought me closer, I saw the thorn in bloom and the petals were on the wind, and in the raining and fluttering of all that blossom, I saw that the lights were no lights at all, but Johanna and Martin and Micheál.' Her voice caught on their names. 'The three of them, Nance, standing under the tree. Waiting for me. And there was music playing of a kind you've never heard before.'

'Fairy music?'

'Like something the angels might play. Singing, too. And I could see the Good People dancing behind them. Such dancing.' There was fervency in the widow's voice. 'What do you think it means, Nance? Sure, 'tis a good omen. Do you not think 'tis a good omen?'

'We will find out soon, Nóra Leahy. So, we will find out.'

The valley grew lighter until it became clear enough to see the river, darkly brown and fringed with the green unfurl of bracken, tipping over the stones in high current. Nance, breathing hard, handed Micheál to Mary and undressed, pulling her many layers of felt and wool over her head and folding them on the ground.

Her breasts were moon-pale in the early light; the cold air tightened her skin.

''Tis the last time then,' Nance said. She looked at Nóra and saw
the widow standing stiffly upright, her arms tightly folded around
her chest, eyes wide. Her whole body was trembling.

'Mary, wait until I am in the river, then pass the boy to me.'

Mary stared at her, face white, saying nothing. She was on the
brink of tears.

The cold of the river ripped the breath from her lungs. Nance
waded in slowly, wheezing, stumbling as the mud of the bank gave
way under her weight, gasping as the waterline rushed over the slack
skin of her thighs and belly. God Almighty, it was fierce cold. The
current was strong. Her hips ached. She felt the river against her legs,
the way it stirred the small stones dislodged by her feet and turned
them silently over.

'Pass him to me now, then, Mary.' Her teeth chattered and Nance
wondered what would happen if she fell in the water. She felt old.
Suddenly fragile.

The girl didn't move. She crouched down on the bank and curled
the boy further into her chest.

Nóra took a step towards her. 'Mary, would you hand it to Nance!'

The girl pushed her face against the top of the boy's head, averting
her eyes. He let out a low groan.

'Give him to me.'

''Tis a sin to be doing this to him,' she whispered.

Nóra reached for the boy, who shrieked louder, but Mary held on
tightly, her arms locked about his chest. She began to cry. Furious,
Nóra plucked at her fingers, prying them from the child's ribcage.
'You're a bold girl to be doing this. Shame on you.' She slapped Mary
across the face and the girl cried out, releasing him. Nóra slung the
wailing boy over her shoulder, placed a hand over his screams, and

stepped directly into the water fully clothed. She waded towards Nance, bracing herself against the press of the river, and offered her the crying child.

'Please!' Mary shouted from the bank. 'Please! 'Tis a sin! 'Tis a sin to be doing this to him!'

Nance, shaking uncontrollably from the cold water, took the changeling and made the sign of the cross over his chest, the skin clinging to the bone. She looked at Nóra standing in the river, her back to Mary. The widow nodded and Nance plunged the screaming child under the water.

Mary collapsed onto the edge of the mossy bank, tears running down her face. ''Tis too cold for him!' she cried. Her hands scrabbled at the dirt and she began to choke on her tears. ''Tis a sin!'

'Whist, Mary,' Nóra muttered, nodding to Nance as she hauled him up.

'In the name of God, if you are a fairy, away with you!'

'Please, Nóra! Please don't be doing this to him!'

Nance thrust him into the river again, then lifted him clear of its surface, copper hair slick on his forehead, water gurgling from his mouth and eyes. Then finally, before he took a breath to cry again, she tightened her hands about his ribcage and pushed him into the rushing current for the third time. She glanced at Nóra and knew the woman could see the white thrashing of him under the foaming skin of the river, the flash of his hair like the quickening of a fish. Nóra met her eyes and nodded again and placed her hands on Micheál's chest as Mary wept. Nance locked her arms and looked to the willow, long-fingered with catkins, and the slip of watercress nuzzling the bank. She felt her hands grow painful numb in the racing water, and felt the nick of the boy's nails on her skin as he flailed, and she looked to the budding iris, their leaves clasped around their yellow flowers like hands folded in prayer, felt the wind in her hair as it suddenly embraced the trees and sent leaves and seed spinning onto the water's surface, now broken by the child as he raised his hand and clasped at the air above him. Nance closed her eyes and felt his struggles subside and she knew then, without looking at the fight gone out of him, at the eyes glassy, that the river had taken the fairy as one of its own; that the river had taken its due.

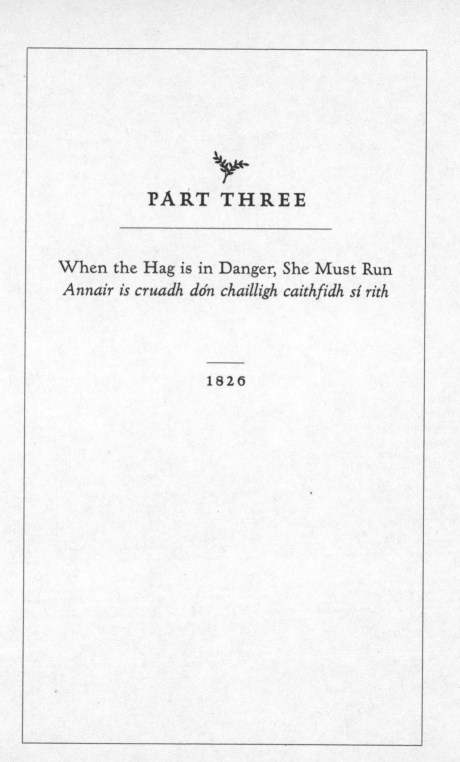

PART THREE

When the Hag is in Danger, She Must Run
Annair is cruadh dón chailligh caithfidh sí rith

1826

CHAPTER
SEVENTEEN

Bramble

Mary ran as though the Devil was after her. Splashing
through the puddles lying glossy in the fields, over the
lane and up the slope, with the flint of the hill studding
her feet, pain striking through her heels and dawn light flooding the
valley. She ran, her eyes blurred with tears, and her lungs hot and
tight, cramps tearing through her side. She ran. She ran with terror
pulling at her blood.

It wasn't until Mary saw the shape of Peg's cabin on the mountainside that she knew where she should go. Her instinct had been
only to flee, to leave the horror at the river and the sight of Micheál's
pale head lolling against the sag of Nance's body.

They had killed him.

Oh God in Heaven, they had murdered him and she had seen it,
had let it happen.

The stillness of that little body as he was lifted from the water,
ribs pressing against the skin of his torso, the drops slipping from
his feet, falling back into the river. The triumphant, happy crying
of Nóra, her skirt puffed about her, air trapped under the weave,

as she had turned and, exalted, pointed to a blooming flagger. The head hanging at an angle, throat exposed to the sky above. And the birds: the birds suddenly filling the trees so that Mary's shrieking was drowned out by their dawn chorus. All the birds, screaming at the light.

Mary ran until, tripping on a hidden stone, she fell, her hands immediately rising bloody from the scrape along the ground. She sat in the flint and soil and howled, bog-soaked, terrified.

It took an hour before Peg O'Shea could calm Mary and understand what it was she was saying.

The sound of the girl's screaming had woken the house, and her son-in-law had run out to see what had happened. He had returned, carrying Nóra's maid in his arms. She was in muddy hysterics, unable to talk, her breathing fast and rapid and her body shaking so hard that Peg had made her daughter swaddle the girl in a blanket and hold her fast.

'Mary, what has happened to you? Tell us what has happened.'

The girl wailed, her nose streaming, mouth open.

'Dear one, you're safe now. You're with friends. Tell us, Mary, what has happened to you?'

'I want to go home.' Her voice was notched with fear. 'I want to go home.'

'And so you will. But tell us first, Mary. Please, it vexes us to see you so.'

'They will hang me.'

Peg's family glanced at each other.

'Hang you?' asked Peg.

'She done him in,' the maid sobbed. 'He's dead.'

'Who?'

'Micheál!'

'Breathe easy, Mary. There you are, take a breath and talk to me now. Are you saying Micheál is dead?'

The girl fought her arms out of the blanket and grabbed at her hair, pulling it over her face. She rocked back and forth on the floor of Peg's cabin. 'Mam,' she whispered. 'I want Mam.'

'What did you see, Mary?'

'I want to go home,' the girl wept. 'I don't want to die. They'll hang me for it. They'll hang me for it.'

'Don't be thinking of hanging. Shhh. Tell me, Mary, what did you see? What has happened?'

Mary took a shuddering breath. ''Twas Nance,' she stammered. 'She drowned him and now he's dead.'

Peg found Nóra sitting alone by her hearth, gazing into the dead ashes. The widow was sitting very still, the greatcoat bulging around her, hands folded around a *poitín* bottle in her lap.

'Nóra? 'Tis Peg come to see you.'

The widow turned, her face blank. Peg saw that she had been crying: her eyes were red-rimmed and her nose wet.

'He's not here . . .' She gave a little shake, then quickly uncorked the bottle and drank, spluttering, wiping her mouth.

'Nóra. In God's name, what has happened?'

'I've looked for him, but . . .' She squeezed her eyes shut and shuddered. 'I came straight back, so I did. I ran here, Peg. I ran. I thought he might be frightened to be here alone.'

'Are you talking about the boy, Nóra?'

'He's not here,' she said in disbelief. 'I came back because I thought . . .'

Peg eased herself down onto a stool. 'You're soaked through. Your clothes are wet and dirtied.'

Nóra looked down, as if surprised to see her damp skirts covered in leaf litter and soil. Bramble thorns clung to her apron. 'I was in the river.'

'What were you doing in the river?'

'And then I came here. To see if Johanna's –'

'Nóra. Mary says that the change-child is dead. She's beside herself and saying that he was drowned in the river. Is that true?'

Nóra's expression darkened. 'Have you seen him?' She clutched at Peg's shoulders, bringing her face close. 'Mary. What did she say?'

'Nóra, you're frightening me.'

The widow's breath was sour with whiskey. 'Tell me what she said. Tell me what she said!'

Peg gently pushed Nóra away from her. 'Mary Clifford tells me that Micheál is dead. She is saying he is drowned.'

Nóra was silent, jaw clenched. 'No, Peg. Not Micheál.'

'She's saying she saw Nance drown the boy. Nóra, is that what happened? Did Nance drown the wee stricken child?'

''Twas fairy,' Nóra bleated.

'And did Nance drown the fairy?'

'Mary ran. We turned and saw her running away.'

'We? 'Twas you and Nance?'

'I thought Micheál would be here,' Nóra said. 'I thought he would be returned to me.'

Peg took a deep breath. 'Nóra. Is the wee cretin drowned?'

There was a knock and both women jumped. Father Healy stood in the open doorway, Peg's son-in-law standing behind him. The priest's face was grave, pouched with concern.

'Nóra Leahy? What have you done?'

Nóra shook her head, unable to speak.

'Your servant maid has just told me she witnessed the drowning of your grandson this morning.'

'No.'

'Nóra, is this the same lad you came to tell me about? The cripple boy? Have you gone and drowned him?'

'He was fairy.'

The priest stood over her, aghast. 'God forgive you. Where's the boy? What have you done with him?'

'He is not here.'

'Nóra, have you gone and murdered that child? Tell me the truth now, or . . . I tell you, God will condemn you for what you have done.'

Nóra pressed her lips together and remained silent.

The priest had turned white. 'Good God! Is she out of her mind?'

'She's had a shock,' Peg muttered. 'She's not herself.'

Father Healy put a hand over his mouth. 'You listen to me now. I've sent a man to the barracks. He is coming back with policemen. Do you understand me? Widow Leahy, listen to me. There are men coming to take an information from you. A sworn information. Do you hear me? Widow Leahy?' His eyes dropped to the *poitín* in her lap. 'Don't be telling me she's drunk. I'd not be taking any more of that, now.' He nodded to Peg, who eased the bottle out of Nóra's fingers.

'I . . .'

The priest bent down to Nóra. 'What's that? What are you saying?'

'I . . . I don't want to be leaving this place.'

'They'll be sending a constable to speak with you. And it might be that they will take you with them.'

'I won't be going. I can't be going.'

'Nóra, 'twill only be for a small while,' Peg cajoled. 'I'll look after your cow. Your hens.'

Nóra shook her head. 'No, I'll need to be staying. It might be that Micheál will be coming. If he's not come today, perhaps he'll be returned tomorrow. I'll need to be waiting for him.'

Father Healy's voice rose in exasperation. 'If your servant maid is saying he is dead, he'll not be coming back. Do you know where your grandson is? His body?'

'Micheál is with the Good People, but now he will be coming back. Now he will be returned to me. Nance said 'twill be so.'

The priest said nothing. He walked towards the open door, then paused and looked back at Nóra with a mixture of disgust and pity. 'If I were you, Nóra Leahy, I'd be praying.' He gestured to Peg. 'Make sure she doesn't leave this place until the constable arrives.'

By the time Nance had returned to her cabin, she was shivering help-lessly with cold. The river water had flooded her to the bone and she ached with it. The hunger she had felt so keenly over the past days had faded to nausea, and now that it was done, she wanted nothing more than sleep. Crawling to her bed of heather, Nance covered herself with her blanket and shut her eyes.

She dreamt then. She dreamt she was young and walking down the high street of Killarney, the mud of the road hardened by the heat of an early summer.

Suddenly, she was surrounded. Young women. Faces browned from their work outside. Baskets of fish on their backs, oozing scales. They called her name, mouths wide on the shape of it.

'Nance!'

'Nance, stop walking! We've a mind to talk to you.'

Her feet stopped. The ground warm on her soles.

The women crowded her.

'We thought we saw you May Eve. Up in the fields.'

'Aye, you were so. Walking alone, and in disguise.'

'I didn't do a thing like it.'

'But you were seen, Nance Roche.'

'Aye.'

'Aye, you were seen scrabbling through a briar.'

'I never.'

'But you were seen so. And the person who said he seen you swore it God's own truth.'

'Who says it?'

'He said you undressed and crawled through the bramble, and after he heard you saying some queer things too.'

'Tell me who said these lies.'

'I don't dare, Nance. You might curse him.'

'I never did such a thing.'

''Tis an awful sin, sure, Nance.'

'Is it true you've been away with the Good People?'

''Tis not. Never in my life.'

'We all know your mam's been swept.'

'Aye, and your aunt is Mad Maggie. She's in with Them. She's a grand one for curse work now.'

'They're all mad. Her mam too. 'Tis madness in the blood.'

'Aye, that's why your da drowned himself.'

''Twas an accident.'

'You're a liar, Nance. The madness turned him to it.'

'Or were it the fairies?'

'You'll be on the road soon. That's what happens to those who lay curses. Who do be in it.'

'Sure, there won't be any living for you in the cabin with your da gone.'

Anger swept through her until she felt that surely she was on fire. The women stood around her, and yet there she was, standing in the street, burning.

'You're mighty cruel,' she whispered.

And when they laughed, Nance dreamt she reached out and

touched each of them on the heart with her finger, burning like a wick. 'I curse you,' she said, and they screamed. 'May the grass grow high at your door, may you die without a priest in a town with no clergy, and may the crows have your carcass! *Imeacht gan teacht ort!* May you leave and never return!'

And they screamed. They screamed and they screamed, until the noise woke her and she sat up, panting.

Her cabin was gloomy with the low light of an overcast afternoon. She could hear footsteps and low conversation outside. There was the smell of crushed grass.

'Tis the Good People, Nance thought. They are coming to take me away.

For one long moment she could do nothing but stare at the smoking hearth and the streaks of soot on the whitewash, the rushes on the floor.

They are coming for me, she thought. As They came for Mam. As They came for Maggie.

'Nance Roche. Open the door.'

'Are you of the living or the dead?'

'Open the door.'

There was no time left to protect herself. No time to guard her life and soul with herbs or charms. Only the dead embers of her fire.

When the constable and his men shouldered in the wicker door, they found Nance on her hands and knees, stuffing her pockets with soot.

⁂

The arrival of two policemen from the Killarney barracks stirred the valley into speculation. People gathered on the road and watched the men on horseback as they rode to the small chapel, and then, with the priest in their company, along the slope, past the blacksmith's, past the well and its huddle of gaping women, to the foot of the hill beneath the cabins of Leahy and O'Shea. The crowd followed behind, staring as the police handed their reins to the priest and made their way up the pass on foot. One went into the O'Sheas' cabin, the other into Nóra Leahy's.

When they emerged several minutes later, holding the bewildered widow and her sobbing maid between them, an excited whispering broke out. They watched the men lead the women away up the road, back towards the chapel, before rushing up the hill to speak with the O'Sheas and learn of what had happened. Had the maid been caught stealing? Had the widow some hand in the death of her husband? When they spotted the police returning for Nance, they wondered whether all three had been in league with the fairies, blinking the valley and thinning the butter in the churns, killing animals for devilment. Setting *piseógs* against the priest.

It did not take long. By sunfall the valley was humming. An accusation had been brought against Nóra Leahy, Mary Clifford and Nance Roche. The fairy cretin Nóra had hidden from sight had been drowned in the river, and they were calling it murder.

CHAPTER
EIGHTEEN

Whitethorn

The police inspector was sweating, his neck pink against the dark green tunic of his uniform.

''Tis important you tell the truth to me now. Did you employ this woman –' he glanced down at a piece of paper in front of him '– *Anne Roche*, to kill your grandson?'

'Nance,' Nóra murmured.

The policeman looked down at the paper again. 'I have Anne.'

'She goes as Nance. Nance Roche.'

He looked up at her from under bushed eyebrows. His nostrils flared. ''Tis a simple question. Did you pay this woman money to have her kill your grandson, Micheál Kelliher?'

Nóra stared at the man's Adam's apple, bobbing above his tight collar. She brought a trembling hand to her own throat. 'I didn't pay her a thing.'

'Was it a favour then? Did you ask her to kill Micheál?'

Nóra shook her head. 'I did not. 'Twas nothing like that. She was going to cure it. To banish the fairy.'

The constable raised an eyebrow. 'The fairy?'

Nóra looked around the barracks room. It smelt of sweat and boot polish and bacon fat. Her stomach groaned. They had given her only one bowl of watery porridge each day since they'd brought her here from the valley. Four nights of hard sleeping on a damp straw mattress, locked in a room of stone. Four bowls of gruel delivered in silence. None of the men who brought her the food had answered her questions. No one would tell her if a small boy had been found in the valley. He would be looking for her, she'd told the officers who handed her the bowls. He has red hair. He is four years old.

'I need an answer from you, Mrs Leahy. Was that *fairy* you said?'

Nóra watched a fly drop from the chimney. It hovered over the dead grate, then smacked itself against the small, dirty window.

'Mrs Leahy?'

Nóra jumped.

'Your servant maid, Mary Clifford, is saying that this Anne Roche wanted to put your grandson in the river, on account of his being a cretin. Not her words. She called him "rickety".' He leant closer, his voice lowered. 'Sure, no easy thing to have a child like that in the home. Was it a kind of mercy you were after, Mrs Leahy?'

When Nóra didn't respond, he sat back and rolled a cigarette, licking the paper and eyeing her. 'I have a dog, you know. Every year that bitch has a litter. Eight pups, every year. I sell what I can, but sometimes, you know, Mrs Leahy, there's a runt.' He pushed back his chair with a squeak and fished in his pocket for some matches. 'Nobody wants a runt.'

Nóra watched as he lit the smoke, waved the match in the air until it expired.

He pointed the cigarette at her. 'So what do I do every year with the runts I can't sell? Do you know, Mrs Leahy?'

'I don't.'

He took a drag and blew the smoke into the air above him, his eyes still fixed on Nóra. 'I drown them. I take them down to the river, and I drown the wee things before they know any different. But Mrs Leahy . . .' He took another puff on his smoke, the dry paper catching on his lip. 'Mrs Leahy, a pup is no child.' He shook his head, his eyes never leaving hers. 'I don't care if that boy was no more than a runt to you. If you drowned him intentional you'll hang for it, so you will.'

Nóra closed her eyes and saw again the wan flicker of the changeling under the tan of river water. The dappled sprawl of first light on the bank. The branches filled with the witness of birds.

''Twas no boy.'

'How old was the child, Mrs Leahy?'

'It . . . He was four years old.'

'"It" you say again.' He wrote something down on the paper. 'And for how long was he in your care?'

'Ever since my daughter passed, God rest her soul.'

Nóra wished she could understand what the policeman was writing down. She wondered how a pattern of such slender markings could come from a hand so rough-fingered and calloused.

'And how long was that, Mrs Leahy?'

Nóra paused, eyelids fluttering. 'Since last harvest. August last.'

'Can you describe the state of Micheál?'

'The state?'

'His health, Mrs Leahy.'

'Can I please have some water?'

'Just answer the question.'

'It . . . He couldn't walk. Couldn't talk. Astray . . .'

'Pardon? You'll need to speak up.'

'Astray in his mind.'

The constable gave her a hard look, then slowly ground out his cigarette. He picked up the piece of paper. 'Mary Clifford has given us a sworn information. She –'

'Where is Mary? Where's Nance?'

The constable ran a hand around his collar, tugging at the starched cloth. 'For the present, the same charges have been brought against the three of you, Mrs Leahy. Arrested for wilful murder. It has been found that . . .' He hesitated and picked up another document from the table, examining the cursive. 'You have all been charged on the verdict of the coroner. "We find that the deceased, Michael Kelliher, came by his death in consequence of drowning in the river Flesk, on Monday, the sixth of March, 1826, by Anne Roche, and that Honora Leahy, the child's grandmother, and Mary Clifford were accessory to the same."'

Nóra sat up in confusion, aware of the sudden weighted knocking of her heart. 'Micheál? Did they find him? Did he come to the cabin?'

'Given the grave nature of these charges, Mrs Leahy, the case will be forwarded to the Summer Assizes in Tralee. You will be taken to Ballymullen gaol and tried with judge and jury. And unless the charges are dropped against them, so Mary and Anne will stand trial too.'

'Did you find Micheál?'

'Do you understand me now? Mrs Leahy?'

'Did you find my grandson? I was asking –'

'Your grandson's body was found at a location very near the residence of Anne Roche. The "Piper's Grave", as it is known locally.'

'The Piper's Grave?'

Nóra pictured the whitethorn in the deep blue of new morning, the dance of light about its branches.

'When Anne was confronted by the constabulary she led them to where she had left Micheál's body.'

'Micheál? Please, can I see him?'

The policeman gave her a long look. 'The three of you drowned Micheál Kelliher, Mrs Leahy, and 'twas Anne Roche that hid his body.' He glanced at the paper again. 'A shallow grave at that. Barely a grave at all. No more than ten inches deep.'

Nóra began to breathe rapidly, pressing her temples. 'I do not think 'twas Micheál.'

'Your grandson. Buried like a dog.'

'No. I do not think 'twas Micheál.'

She began to sob. A wail that filled the room.

'Mrs Leahy?'

'I do not think 'twas Micheál!'

'Come now.'

''Twas a fairy!' Nóra put her elbows on the table and cried into her hands.

'Mrs Leahy, 'tis important that you gain control of yourself and tell me what happened. Did Anne Roche tell you that your grandson, Micheál Kelliher, was a fairy?'

Nóra nodded, her face still hidden in her hands.

'And you are remorseful, for you understand that this was not the case?'

She wiped her nose on her sleeve and looked down at the shiny smear. ''Twas not Micheál they found then,' she whispered. 'That child was not my grandson.'

'Surely you would know your own grandson.'

She shook her head. 'No. He was changed. I saw him, and when he was brought to me, he was changed.'

'And this Anne told you that the change in him was because he was now a fairy?'

'She said that Micheál had surely been taken by the fairies. The cripple was one of Them. She told me she would have my grandson returned to me.'

318

The constable regarded Nóra carefully. Rolled another cigarette.

'Mrs Leahy. You, a woman of otherwise good repute, believed this woman when she told you your paralytic grandson was an otherworldly sprite?'

'Paralytic?'

'Had not the use of his legs.'

Nóra used her shawl to wipe her eyes. 'What? What is the word again?'

'Paralytic. 'Tis a medical term, used to describe children such as yours who have not the use of their legs, or arms, or anything at all. 'Tis a known affliction, Mrs Leahy. A disease of immobility. And 'tis what the coroner and his peers are saying Micheál suffered from.'

'No. 'Twas not a suffering. 'Twas not him at all.'

'Yes, it was, Mrs Leahy.' The man suddenly leant forward. 'All this talk of fairies. Sure, people will tell themselves anything to avert their eyes from the truth of a matter.'

'He will be waiting for me.' Nóra began to weep again. 'He'll be waiting for me, and no one there to welcome him home. Oh God in Heaven!'

'Mrs Leahy, did you tell yourself what you wanted to believe? Or was it some other understanding you were working towards? Give an old poor woman a chicken. Some fuel. And in return she'll deliver you of a runt, all the while gabbling about the fairies.'

'You're wrong.' Nóra drew her hands into fists. 'Micheál will be there, returned. And after all I've done, all to have him back with me. And you're keeping me here! 'Twas all I wanted, to have him back with me.'

The constable narrowed his eyes and took a long drag, watching her. The paper flared between his lips. 'Sure it was, Mrs Leahy. Sure it was.'

Nance looked up from where she sat on the cart rattling on the road through Killarney. Every rock and rut knocked through her bones, until she felt that her remaining teeth would shudder from their gums. She was unused to travelling so quickly. Unused to the rapid pull of a horse, its ears upright to the urging of the dark-coated man sitting in front, dirty collar about his ears.

She had lost track of time.

The widow was sitting across from her, pinned against the corner of the cart and the broad shoulder of a policeman. Nance could not tell if Nóra was awake – a shawl covered her face, and her head hung forward. When they had brought them out from the barracks and set them on the cart, the widow – pale, feeble-looking – had leant across and whispered to Nance. 'They will not believe me,' she'd breathed. But not a word since.

Nance looked past the bulk of the constable beside her and stared out into the streets of Killarney. The inns and lodgings, the fine line of the high street and the close, filthy lanes and yards that ran off it. Smoky, sunny Killarney with poxy children spitting in the alleys and men carrying baskets of scraw and sod. After five nights in her tiny barracks cell there was suddenly too much noise, too many dirty faces staring at them, noses wrinkling. She had fled this place twice. This unkind town. Mad Maggie, Mad Nance: one and the same. Father gone to the water, mother to the fairies, there's no knowing which way this one'll turn, but 'tis clear she goes with Them. She goes with Them that does be in it. She is of the Good People.

Nance shut her eyes tightly and braced herself against the jolt of the lane. When she opened them again the muck of the town had faded and they were on the old mail coach road to Tralee, between the mountains of rock and grass, a blessed distance from the towering horizon of trees, the lakes and hiving swarm of Killarney. Men were in the fields, seeding the eyes of cups, while other potato plants were stalking up and out of the earth. The world had finally flowered. Ditches starry in dog violet and gorse, sow thistle, dandelion and cuckoo flower creeping into the fields. The lone fairy whitethorns left to themselves amidst the cultivated ground, blossoming into thick curds of white. Her heart soared to see the bee-blown, petal-filled trees.

It will be May Eve in time, Nance thought. And she thought of how, in the valley, the people would soon pluck the yellow flowers for the goodness they drew from the sun, pulling primrose and marsh marigold and buttercups, rubbing them on the cows' udders to bless the butter in them, placing them on doorways and doorsteps, those thresholds where the unknown world could bleed into the known, flowers to seal the cracks from where luck could be leached, on that night of *Bealtaine* bonfire.

Twenty miles from Killarney to Tralee. Thirty from the valley. Even when she was younger and used to hard walking, a road like this would have taken her sun-up to sundown to tramp.

The light faded. The afternoon became quiet and the crickets began to chirp against the far-off call of a cuckoo singing down the dusk. Nóra had begun to weep quietly. The cart rattled the irons about their wrists.

Here is God, Nance thought. I see him still.

❧

Mary was sitting on the floor of the narrow Killarney barracks room with her head resting against the corner of stone, her fingers pinching the skin of her arm. Ever since the policeman had taken her from Peg O'Shea's cabin, a trembling had set up in her hands, and she had fallen into the habit of nipping her flesh to quell the shaking.

Her head ached. She had wept for the first two nights, sobbing into her hands, still dirty with the mud from the river, until her eyes swelled and she was dazed with exhaustion. The policeman who had questioned her had seemed uncomfortable at her distress. He had handed her his handkerchief, waited patiently until she could answer his questions.

But now Mary felt dry, tearless. She glanced down at the cloth, balled in her lap, and brought it to her face. It still smelt of shop soap, tobacco smoke.

The afternoon had darkened. There was a small square window high in the cell, and throughout the day Mary had focused on the sunlight falling across the wall, transfixed by its slow shifting. She closed her eyes. She could hear men speaking to one another outside in the barracks yard, and then the echo of footsteps walking down the long corridor beyond her cell.

There was a sudden clanking as the door was unlocked and opened, and Mary, expecting to see a constable, was surprised by the sight of a familiar face.

Father Healy waited until the door had been closed and locked behind him before speaking to her.

'Good afternoon, Mary Clifford.'

'Father.'

The priest looked around for somewhere to sit, then, seeing only the bare stone floor, stepped over to Mary and squatted on his haunches.

'This is a sorry business.'

'Yes, Father.'

He paused. 'I have been told that you swore an information.'

Mary nodded, tucking her knees up to her chest. She was aware of the grime on her feet, the muddy hem of her skirt.

'I have some good news for you. The Crown counsel would like you to be their chief witness.'

Mary felt her mouth dry in panic. 'Their chief witness?'

'Do you understand what that means?'

'No, Father.'

'It means that they are willing to drop the charge of wilful murder against you, if you turn witness. If you tell the court and the jury and the judge what you saw. What you did.'

'I did not mean for him to die, Father.' She glanced down at the handkerchief in her hands, the tiny bruises on the inner flesh of her wrist.

'Mary, look at me.' Father Healy's face was sombre. 'They are going to free you. All you will need to do is make your oath, and tell the court what you told the policemen. What you swore in your information. Answer their questions as best you can.'

Mary blinked at him.

'If you turn witness, they will not charge you. Do you understand? You will be able to return home to your mother and father.'

'I will not hang?'

'You will not hang.'

'And Nóra? Nance? Will they hang?'

'They are gone to Ballymullen today.' Father Healy shifted his weight, pulling at the cloth of his trousers. 'You understand that Micheál Kelliher was not a fairy child, don't you, Mary? He was a little boy suffering from cretinism. He was not taken by the fairies, but by the ignorance of his own grandmother and an old woman. He was not banished. He was *murdered*. You understand this, don't you?'

Mary clenched her teeth against the tears that suddenly threatened. She nodded.

Father Healy continued, his voice low. 'God has protected you, Mary. But let you find a lesson in the fall of Nóra Leahy and Nance Roche. Pray for their souls, and for the soul of Micheál Kelliher.'

'Can I go to Annamore?'

Father Healy rose, wincing. 'That's where you're from, is it?' He rubbed at a cramp in his leg. 'Not until the trial is over. You'll be coming with me to Tralee. The Crown counsel, the lawyers, will want to speak with you there. Do you have anywhere to stay in that town? Any kin?'

Mary shook her head.

The priest paused. 'Let me see if I can't arrange something for you. A place where you can work for your keep for the next few months, until the trial is over. Then you'll be on your own, do you understand?'

'Thank you, Father.'

He turned and knocked sharply on the door, and the sound of boots could be heard. As the key was turned in the lock, Father Healy glanced back. 'Give thanks to God for this, Mary. It is by His mercy alone that you are saved. I'll return for you tomorrow.' And then he was gone.

Mary looked down at her soiled hands, her heart pounding. I am free, she thought, and she waited for relief to sweep through her.

But it did not come. She sat, pinching her skin between her fingers.

Nipping the bread to let the Devil out, she thought.

They arrived in Tralee at dusk. Nance shrank into her seat at the sight of the town and its streets of business, at the fine houses along the promenade. Mail coaches, upright with gentlemen, clattered in the road amongst crowds of servants, tradespeople and the usual dregs of beggars. The widow briefly listed her head to gaze at the town, until they neared the limestone gates to Ballymullen gaol, when she glanced at Nance, terrified.

'We will never leave this place,' she whispered, eyes wide.

'No talking,' one of the policemen interrupted.

Nance became frightened then. They passed through the gates and immediately the air felt heavier, dank. Under the weight of the shadows thrown by the high walls, her body began to tremble.

Stone-silled, iron-grilled. The gaol was dark, and the constables moved them from the gate and into its passageways by lamplight. Nance's throat filled with bile and she thought back to her cabin and Mora, who would surely be waiting for her, udder heavy with milk.

The gaolers took Nóra and weighed her first, then after some discussion with the policemen they hauled the widow off into the dark corridor. Nóra looked back over her shoulder, her lips parting in terror before the shadows fell over her face, and Nance felt hands take her firmly about the arms and direct her to the scales.

'Anne Roche. Unknown age. Four feet eleven inches. Ninety-eight pounds. White hair. Blue eyes. Identifying marks include: tender eyes; enlarged joint, left and right thumbs; front teeth; cut mark on forehead. Catholic. Pauper. Charged with wilful murder.'

The women in the cell with Nance were mute and dirty. They lay on straw piled over the flagged floor, eyes large in the dark. One, her skin pocked like mountain soil, muttered to herself. Every now and then she shook her head, as if in disbelief at her imprisonment.

That night Nance woke to a piercing shriek, and when the guard came to see what the fuss was about, holding a lamp aloft, Nance saw that the mutterer had thrown herself at the wall, splitting her head on the rock. The guard took her away. When they had left and the cell was once more snuffed of light, a voice spoke from the corner of the room.

'I'm glad that one is away.'

There was a pause, then another voice replied. 'She's turned in the head.'

'Wantonly scalding with hot water,' said the first woman. 'That's what she's here for. Tried to boil her child like a pratie.'

'What did they pinch you for then?'

There was another pause. 'Begging. And yourself?'

'Borrowed some turf.'

'Drink.'

'And you, old biddy? Public nuisance was it?' There was a snide chortle at this.

Nance said nothing, her heart beating fast. She closed her eyes against the darkness and her ears against the faceless voices and imagined the river. The flowing river, in the height of summer. She thought of the green light cast by moss, and the berries on their brambles swelling with their sweetness, and the eggs in the hidden places breaking with tapping beaks. She thought of the life that thrust itself onwards outside the prison, and when she could see it there, see the unconquerable world, she finally fell into sleep.

Grey light slid down the wall like a stain. Nóra had been unable to rest in the close air of the cell with the suggestion of bodies around her, their coughing and weeping, and the scuttering sounds she could not place that filled her with terror. It was a relief to have respite from the pitch-black she had wept into all night. Rubbing her eyes, she saw that there were seven other women in the tiny cell with her, most of them asleep. Nance was not amongst them.

One girl, dark hair streaked with early grey, slept next to Nóra, her head resting on the wall. Another was sprawled by her feet, snoring. Both were thin, their feet black.

Only one other woman was awake. Mouse-haired, she sat with her legs tucked up beneath her, eyeing Nóra carefully. After catching

Nóra's glance she slid forward, crawling across the floor until she was beside her. Nóra sat up hurriedly.

'Mary Foley,' the woman said. 'Sleep well?'

Nóra drew the canvas dress she had been given about her. It was damp.

'I know what you're here for. You murdered a child.'

Nóra could smell the tang of the woman's breath.

'You'd best be after the priest. They're after hanging women that do be murdering now.' The woman tilted her head, examining Nóra with a cool eye. 'Johanna Lovett. They dropped her out the front of the gaol not a month ago for the murder of her man.' She winked. 'Like a fish on a line, she was. Bouncin' like a feckin' fish on a line.'

Nóra stared at her.

'I'm in and out of here more often than a sailor up a whore,' she said. 'I know everything.'

'I didn't murder him.'

Mary smiled. 'And I don't take the drink. But sure, the Devil manages to pour it down my throat anyway.' She sat back on her heels. 'Baby-dropper, are you?'

Nóra shook her head.

'How did he die then?'

''Twas no child at all.'

Mary Foley raised her eyebrows.

''Twas a changeling.'

Mary grinned. 'You're a mad one. Still, better to be mad than bad. That one there? Making an almighty racket?' She pointed to the snoring girl. 'Mary Walsh. Tried to conceal the birth of her baby. She'll be getting three months or so, unless they also decide to charge her with deserting her child. Then she'll be getting more. That's the badness in it.'

Nóra stared at the young girl and thought of Brigid Lynch, the blood rippling between her legs. The longed-for child in the *cillín*.

The changeling buried in the Piper's Grave. Ten inches of soil over that little body.

'Yer one there with the burn mark on her face? Moynihan. Attempted self-murder.' Mary sniffed, wiped her nose with the back of her hand. 'Tried to drown herself. Kept bobbing up like a cork so they fished her out.'

Nóra looked at the freckled girl Mary was pointing to, curled asleep in the corner, her hands tucked under her chin.

'Surprising, the amount of them here after a ducking. 'Tis stones you want, if you're after drowning yourself. 'Twould not be the way I'd go. Unless 'twas drowning in a bottle.' The woman nodded to herself. 'Sure. Only those who are born to hang are not afraid of the water.'

CHAPTER
NINETEEN

Mint

Mary's blouse was pinching under her armpits and she could feel sweat seeping through her collar. The Tralee courthouse was the finest, largest building she had ever stepped inside, but it teemed with people and Mary thought she might faint from the heat, from the stale air and the fear that lingered in the court from all those who had stood behind the spiked stand, protesting or accusing badness in the world. The violence in it. Beatings and burglary and theft and rape.

Mary searched the crowd for Father Healy. He had brought her to the courthouse from the home of the merchant family she had been placed with these past three months, but in the crush of the crowd she had lost sight of his face.

I have grown, Mary thought, running her fingers along the tight seams. 'Twill be the first thing I do when I return home. I will unpick these clothes and I will make room for myself.

She would have liked to burn them. Burn the skirt and the shift and the shawl and everything she had gone to the widow's with. Put them on the fire and burn them into nothing, and dress in new cloth that Micheál had never touched. Despite the hard scrubbing she had given her clothes on arriving in Tralee, she could still smell the boy on her. The piss and sourness of him. Smell the nights awake, the wet mouth of him screaming into her chest. The peck soap. The mint. The dark mud of the riverbank.

Mary cast a look at the men who had been sworn in as jury. Over twenty of them. A shoal of gentlemen, black clothes and beards trimmed, sitting placidly amongst the swarming, jostling horde of those who had come to hear the verdicts pronounced over the prisoners led to dock. It had taken Father Healy and Mary a long time to reach the front of the crowd. People collected in dense masses around the lawyers, pulling at their sleeves, asking for justice. Court reporters stood nearby, eagle-eyed, some of them sucking at pencils. Mary took a deep breath. Her hands were damp with nerves.

One of the jurymen caught her eye and gave her a kindly smile. Mary looked away, towards the chair where the judge sat. The Honourable Baron Pennefather. He looked tired.

At the end of this rope of words was Annamore. That was what she had to remember. She had to answer the questions and tell them of her fear, of the strange and sorry things they did to the boy. How frightened she was of all the fairy talk, how she did not understand what it was they were doing. That she was fearful of God and prayed that He would forgive her.

God forgive her. For saying nothing, for doing nothing, for not splashing through the river to slap the widow and take up the boy and carry him home to her brothers and sisters. They would have made a pet of him, she thought. They would not have minded that he screamed from hunger when they, too, were always crying from it. In a cabin of too many, one more would not have made a difference.

Mary started. A hush had fallen, although an undercurrent of babbling continued amongst the people still squeezing themselves into the room. There was a straining of necks and she saw that they were bringing Nance and Nóra into the room, their wrists in irons.

The women's months in gaol had changed them, had thinned them. Nance looked ancient. Dressed in the garb of the prison, she seemed to have shrunk ever smaller. Her white hair had taken on a yellow sheen in its unwashed state, and her shoulders were hunched. Nance's eyes, as fogged as ever, looked around her in confusion and fear. She seemed alarmed to see such a vast crowd of people.

Nóra, behind her, was weeping. Mary was struck by the difference in her appearance. Gone was the righteousness, the stubborn chin. Now Nóra's complexion was sallow and drawn, and she seemed to have aged several years. Her forehead was deeply lined. Despite the heat in the courtroom, she shivered uncontrollably.

Perhaps they will decide to hang them here, Mary thought, and fear creased through her stomach. It might have been her, standing there.

She wanted to leave the room. How could she speak in front of all these people? All these men in their fine clothes, and the judge come all the way from Dublin. She was only a girl from a bog. A girl of the rushes and the turf ground, where the soil oozed black and it was only ever grass and dust and clay underfoot, never the cobbles, never the lacquer of wood.

The counsel gave Mary a careful look. Smoothed his hair from his forehead, glossy with perspiration. She could feel her legs turn to water beneath her.

'Let the record state that in the case of wilful murder against Honora Leahy and Anne Roche the first witness called is Mary Clifford of Annamore.'

Mary stepped up to the witness box. They passed her the Bible and she kissed it, her fingers gripping the leather tightly.

'Mary Clifford, can you please identify the prisoners?'

Mary looked out at the sea of staring faces and saw, finally, the long forehead of the priest. He held her eye. Gave her a nod.

''Tis Nance Roche. And Nóra Leahy, who I served as maid to.'

'Mary, in your own words, please tell the court how you came to work for Mrs Leahy.'

''Twas Mrs Leahy who came for me when I was standing at the hiring fair last November in Killarney. She offered me work and said she had a grandson, and offered me money to help her care for him and help her with the washing and cooking and the milking. So I went with her.'

'Did she give any indication that the child was a cripple?'

Mary hesitated. 'Do you mean, did she say he was crippled?'

The lawyer gave her a tight smile. 'Yes. That is the question.'

Mary glanced at Nóra. She was staring, her mouth ajar. 'She did not, sir.'

'Can you please describe the state of Micheál Kelliher when you saw him?'

'He was in the cabin with a neighbour, and I was frightened to see him. I had never seen a child like it. "What ails him?" I asked, and Mrs Leahy said, "He is delicate, is all."'

'Can you please describe what she meant by "delicate"?'

Mary took a deep breath. Her hands were shaking. 'He was making a strange sound, and though old enough to be talking, he could not say a word. Mrs Leahy said, "There's no walking in him either." "Is it a catching sickness?" I asked, and she says, "No, he is delicate. There is no catching in it."'

'Did Mrs Leahy at any time describe the boy as anything other than her grandson?'

Mary looked again at Nóra. She was red-eyed.

'She said, "He is my daughter's boy."'

'In your sworn information you said that, although she had

introduced the child to you as her grandson, in time Honora Leahy believed that the child was not her grandson at all, but was –' the prosecutor paused, turning to face the jury '– a *changeling*. Is this correct?'

''Tis. She thought he was a changeling. There were others who also believed it.'

'Can you tell the court what you mean by "changeling"?'

Mary felt the eyes of the jury on her. She stood, faltering, suddenly aware of her hammering heartbeat.

'I mean a fairy.'

There was laughter in the crowd, and Mary was winded with shame. She could feel herself redden, feel the pricking of sweat under her arms. This was how they saw her, a stupid girl jumping at shadows, demented with fear. She remembered the mortification she had felt when the constable had asked her to sign the sworn information, and she had scratched a clumsy cross on the paper, fumbling the pen in her hand.

'When did Mrs Leahy begin to refer to her grandson, Micheál Kelliher, as a *fairy*?'

'She believed he was a changeling when Nance Roche pronounced him so.'

'And when was this?'

'In the new year. Or 'twas December. 'Twas the new year that we took the boy to Nance's for the first cure.'

Mary saw, with a horrible jolt of recognition, several men from the valley amongst the mass of faces. Daniel and Seán Lynch were there, stony-eyed.

'Mary, can you tell us why you went to Anne Roche?'

'She came to us.' Mary hesitated. ''Twas before Christmas. I was out milking and I came in and saw Mrs Leahy slapping Micheál. "The badness in you," she was saying. She was beating him.'

There was a murmur amongst the onlookers.

'She was beating him?'

'His hand had caught in her hair and it had pained her. "He can't help it," says I, and Mrs Leahy said she was going to get the priest for him. But when the widow returned 'twas not with the priest but with an apron of nettles. Then she got down on her hands and knees over the boy and stung him with the nettles. "That is hurting him," I said, but she did not listen to me. So I took the nettles and put them on the fire and I ran to Peg O'Shea for help.'

'Did Honora Leahy ever explain why she was "nettling" Micheál Kelliher? Do you think she meant to hurt him?'

Mary hesitated. The laughter had stopped, and there was now a silent tension in the room. 'I don't know.'

'Please speak up.'

'I don't know.'

'How did this incident lead to the involvement of Anne Roche?'

Mary licked her lips. Father Healy had not taken his eyes off her. 'Peg told me to go to the river and fetch dock for the boy, and so I went, but 'twas on my return that I hurt my ankle. I could not walk. There was a woman come up to me – 'twas Nance Roche. She took me to her cabin for the ankle cure, and 'twas there I told her what Mrs Leahy had done. "I have a right to be talking to that woman," she said, and then we returned to the cabin together and she saw Micheál.'

'What did Anne Roche say to Honora Leahy when she saw the boy?'

'"This cratur here might be fairy-born," says she.'

'And how did Mrs Leahy seem when Anne said this?'

'I thought she was relieved to hear it, sir.'

'Tell us, Mary, why do you think Honora Leahy, an established member of her community, a woman of good repute with a late husband of excellent standing, chose to listen to the opinion of Anne Roche – a woman who, as the court will hear, was impoverished, unmarried and, by all accounts sworn, an outsider with little to no financial, commercial or familial influence?'

Mary gaped at the lawyer, not understanding. She could feel sweat beading on her lip.

The counsel cleared his throat. 'Mary, please tell us why you think Mrs Leahy listened to someone like Anne.'

Mary looked over at Nance. She had been slumped against the dock, frowning. At the mention of her name, however, she straightened her back and gave Mary a wary look.

'Because she is a woman who goes with Them.'

'Them?'

'The Good People. The fairies.' Mary waited for more laughter, but none came. 'She has the knowledge of Them and their herbs. She told the widow that she could put the fairy out of him.'

Out of the corner of her eye, Mary noticed movement. A reporter stood, quickly writing something down.

'Mary, referring now to the information provided in your sworn testimony regarding the treatment of Micheál, can you please tell the court how these women attempted to "put the fairy out of him", and your own involvement, if any?'

Mary blanched. 'I only did what was asked of me. I did not want to lose my wages.'

The prosecutor smiled. 'That is understood. You are not on trial here.'

'They – we – tried to put the fairy out of him with herbs at first. There was mint put in his ears, and another herb rubbed on his feet.'

'Do you know the herb? Was it "lusmore"?'

'*Lus mór* was given in the next cure. When the mint did not work I was sent back to Nance by Mrs Leahy. "There is no change in the boy," I said, and so we were told to return and that is when they – we gave Micheál the foxglove.'

'And when was this?'

'January, sir.'

The prosecutor turned to the judge. 'Let the court note that foxglove, *Digitalis purpurea*, is poisonous.' He faced Mary. 'Do you believe that the prisoners knew, in giving Micheál Kelliher foxglove, that they were giving him a substance capable of causing death or illness?'

There was a stifled cry. Nóra had brought her hands to her face.

'I knew 'twas poisonous and I said so. But Nance said, "'Tis a powerful plant," and I knew that *lus mór* belongs to . . .' Mary stopped herself. 'They say *lus mór* belongs to the fairies and so I thought there would be a cure in it. But now I know 'tis only superstition.'

'Please describe how the foxglove was administered to Micheál Kelliher.'

"'Twas a bath of it. And the juice set on his tongue. And when he started up with a trembling, and his mouth was foaming, we were told to set him on a spade and make as if to shovel him out the door, saying, "Away with you!"'

There was another stirring amongst the crowd. The court reporter was writing furiously. Mary wiped her sweating palms against her skirt.

'In your information, Mary, you stated that the foxglove *did* have an ill effect on the child in the days after its application. You said that you were frightened for his life.'

She saw the boy again then, in the weak light of the cabin's dying fire. Saw him shudder ceaselessly against her, his head listless on the mattress. Remembered the feel of his tongue against her finger as she hooked the vomit from his mouth and made sure he would not choke.

'In the days afterwards I was scared he would die, so much water was coming from him, and he was unable to keep his food down.' She blinked away a sudden urge to cry. 'All the time he was shaking, sir. I thought he would die.'

'It must have been terrible to see. Was Mrs Leahy as upset as you?'

Nóra was weeping openly.

She is scared, Mary thought.

'Mrs Leahy was happy, sir. She thought she would have her true grandson returned to her. "'Tis no sin if 'tis fairy," she said. But when he did not die from it, she went to Nance herself and they decided to take Micheál to the river.'

'This was another "cure"?'

'Yes, sir. I was to take the boy the next morning down to Nance's with Mrs Leahy and together we would go to the river and put him in the boundary water. 'Tis the place where three streams meet. Nance said the power in the water would banish the fairy. "'Twill be cold," says I, but 'twas decided and, although I was afraid, I did as told. And I hope God forgives me for it.'

'What happened next?'

'We bathed him in the river for three mornings running.' Mary paused. Sweat trickled down her back. 'And . . . on the last morning Nance and Mrs Leahy kept him under the water for longer than usual.'

'And is that when Micheál Kelliher died?'

'Yes, sir.'

'What did you do when you saw the prisoners drowning the child?'

Nance was leaning forward in the dock, her mouth moving, muttering something under her breath.

'I was not sure then if the child was drowned. I thought only that the water was cold. I did not want him to catch cold. And then I saw that he was not moving, and I thought, "They have killed him," and 'twas then that I took fright.'

'Did you say anything to the prisoners when you realised that the child had, in fact, drowned?'

Mary paused. Her pulse jumped in her throat. 'I think so, sir.'

'You swore to it in your information.'

The boy lifted from the river. The water running from him, his skin pearled with it, the dripping from his fingers glittering in the light.

'What did you say, Mary?'

'I said, "How can you hope ever to see God after this?"'

A murmur immediately rose from the crowd.

'And did the prisoners reply to your question?'

Mary nodded. 'Nance said, "The sin is not on me."'

'Was anything else said?'

'I don't know, sir.'

'You don't know?'

'That was when the fear took me. I turned and ran to Peg O'Shea's and I told her that the boy was killed. I was frightened for myself.'

'Mary, before the defence examines you, could you please tell me what it was like to care for Micheál Kelliher? Do you believe he was burdensome to his grandmother?'

'He could not help it.'

'But was he a burden to your mistress? Was he a difficult and unloving child?'

The nights of wailing. The great, rasping screams. His head smacking against the clay, against her fingers as she tried to calm him, unplug his nose, ease his breathing.

Yes,' Mary whispered. 'Yes, he was a burden.'

'Did Honora Leahy wish to be rid of him?'

'She wished for the fairy to be gone. She wanted her grandson back, sir. A boy who would not scream and trouble her.'

The courtroom became noisy with conversation as soon as the counsel returned to his chair. Mary, relieved to have the gaze of the crowd off her, wiped the sweat from her neck with her sleeve. She looked at Father Healy, and he gave her a small nod of reassurance.

After one noisy minute, the defence lawyer rose. He introduced himself as Mr Walshe over the din, and waited several moments until the chatter subsided.

When there was absolute silence, he spoke. His voice was clipped, his words carrying across the room.

'Mary Clifford, do you believe that Honora Leahy and Anne Roche took Micheál to the Flesk because they intended to drown and kill him?'

Mary hesitated. 'Did I know he was to be killed?'

'Do you believe that the prisoners intended to drown the child from the time they decided to bathe him in the river?'

'I don't understand, sir.'

Mr Walshe gave her a cool look. 'Do you believe that murder was their thinking all along?'

Mary's heart flipped in her chest. 'I don't know.'

'You don't know if Mrs Leahy and Nance Roche intended to kill the boy?'

'I think they meant to be rid of the changeling.'

'Mary, forgive my insistence, but if they meant to be rid of the "changeling", as you call him, and you knew that would mean the boy would be drowned, why did you let them bathe him at all? Why not alert the neighbour you speak of, as you did when you saw Mrs Leahy "nettling" Micheál? Why not send word to the priest?'

'I did not think they meant to kill Micheál.' Mary could hear the uncertainty in her own voice. Her hands had begun to shake again, and she gripped her skirt.

'Then why take a small, helpless boy and bathe him in the river?'

Mary looked over at the dock. Both Nance and Nóra were staring at her, their hair lank and loose. Nóra was trembling, as though suffering from a fever.

Mary took a deep breath, the cloth pulling tight against her ribcage and the wild beating of her heart. ''Twas done with the intent to cure it, sir. To put the fairy out of it.'

Mr Walshe smiled. 'Thank you, Mary.'

CHAPTER
TWENTY

Elder

Nóra thought that she would never be warm again. She could see the glisten of sweat on the foreheads of the lawyers despite the early hour, could see people in the vast, shuffling crowd fan their faces and mop their brows with handkerchiefs, and yet she shivered as though she were standing in the snow against a high wind.

She wondered, not for the first time, if she was turning mad. Time no longer seemed to tread past in measured steps, but flung forward and back. The trial had bled from the previous day of the assizes into the next, but as Nóra stood, tense with the pressing threat of a full and painful bladder, she could not remember who had testified. As soon as one witness stepped forward to be examined, she looked and saw another in their place.

It was only Mary Clifford's testimony that she remembered in detail. She stood in the dock, shaking, and saw again the girl tilting from one foot to another under the pinch of questioning. Her gaze, when it met Nóra's, had seemed firm. For a brief moment Nóra could have sworn that it was her own redheaded daughter kissing the book, swearing an information against her.

My mother, who killed my son.

They are going to hang me, Nóra suddenly thought, and she gripped the fetters about her wrists. Beneath the droning of the Crown counsel, she thought she could hear the rattle of her teeth.

Nóra tried to focus on the new witness gesticulating to the court. She recognised him as the policeman who had arrested her in the cabin. He had shaved for the trial, she noticed, and she pictured him standing at a slip of mirror that morning, strop and razor in hand, while she had lain in her cell, picking at the skin of her feet. Nauseous. Sick with anxiety. Did he have a wife to boil the water for his shave? Had his breakfast been cooked for him? Nóra pictured the policeman carefully scraping the blade along his neck, until she felt a tightening around her own throat and, sickened, stared at the floor.

'And tell me,' the counsel was saying to the constable, 'what was the state of Anne Roche when you arrested her?'

'I went inside the house and saw the prisoner on her hands and knees. She was taking the ash from the hearth. I thought she was a woman out of her mind, and I said: "Anne Roche, do you know why I am here?" and she did not answer me. I told her I had a warrant for her arrest, and asked her if she knew where the body of Micheál Kelliher was, for she was accused of drowning him that morning. She answered me, "The Good People took Micheál and left a fairy in his place," and 'twas only when I asked her where the body of the *fairy* was that she took me to the deceased.'

'And where was the grave?'

'The grave was in an abandoned area known locally as the "Piper's Grave". It had not been dug deep, sir. The body was partly visible through the soil.'

'Did the prisoner seem distressed?'

The constable cleared his throat. 'She seemed surprised to hear that Mrs Leahy had been arrested also, and asked if there had not been a little boy with her. When asked which child she meant, Anne Roche replied, "Micheál Kelliher."'

'She said this despite having brought you to the grave and body of the deceased?'

'That is correct, sir.'

'Was there anything otherwise remarkable about the prisoners' appearance or attitude at the time you arrested them?'

'The clothes of Mrs Leahy were wet through. Sodden. We surmised that she had been in the river at some point that morning. There was the smell of river mud about her.'

'Were the clothes of Anne Roche also sodden?'

'No, sir. And I thought that was curious given both Mary Clifford and Mrs Leahy told me she had also been in the river, until the prisoner explained that she had bathed the child – the *changeling*, as she called him – in an undressed state.'

Nóra's body ached. Every night in the gaol she had pictured her empty cabin in the valley, imagining the creak of the door and Micheál entering the room, looking for her. She wondered what he would be wearing. What the fairies might have clothed him in. Perhaps he would be bare, and she imagined her grandson crawling under Martin's greatcoat, curling up on the cold straw mattress, or by the dead ashes of her fire, and waiting for her to return. Imagined the small round of his face peering out the window, imagined him standing in the yard as the wind tousled his hair, looking along the broad flank of the valley for the sight of his grandmother walking the lane.

He will be frightened, she thought. It may be that he has returned and is frightened. He is only a little boy.

What would happen if she were hanged? Would he stay in her

cabin until the grass grew long at her door? Would he leave and wander, lost, until he grew as thin as the one they had put in the water?

'Honora Leahy?'

Nóra started and lifted her face, biting down on her knuckle. The courtroom was staring at her.

The policeman who had been talking was no longer there. Instead, the lawyers and the judge were looking at her expectantly.

'Honora Leahy?'

She looked at Mr Walshe, who was urgently gesturing for her to move to the end of the dock.

'Yes?'

'Would you kiss the book and give your oath?'

Nóra did as they asked. She took the Bible into her trembling hands and felt the weight of its pages.

'Honora Leahy, can you please describe the state of Micheál Kelliher when you first took him into your care?'

Nóra gazed around the courtroom, her eyes landing on the faces of the jurymen. They were looking at her with interest, their foreheads wrinkled.

'Mrs Leahy, do you need me to repeat the question? How did you come to care for Micheál?'

Nóra turned to the lawyer. Someone in the crowd coughed. ''Twas me and my man both. My daughter, Johanna, had passed and 'twas her husband that brought him. He was all bones and we were worried for him. He looked starved. He was not walking, but I thought then maybe it was only a weakness.'

'And was this the first time you had seen your grandson?'

'I saw Micheál a time before. Two years ago. But he was a well boy then. He was talking and he had the use of his legs. I saw that he was well with my own eyes.'

'Mrs Leahy, your husband died shortly after Micheál was brought to you, is that not true?'

'He died in October.'

'It was surely a great misfortune for you to find yourself a widow and the sole support of a cripple boy?'

Martin, his eyes pennied, stomach offering up the plate of dried herbs, pinched and pushed into clay pipes and the smoke blown over his greying skin. Martin, smelling of the sky, of the valley, dropping to the earth with a hand over his chest while lights flared under the whitethorn.

'Mrs Leahy?' It was the judge who had spoken. 'Can you please answer the questions when addressed?'

The prosecutor frowned. 'Would you say it was difficult to be widowed and the sole support of a cripple?'

Nóra licked her lips. ''Twas a great sorrow to me.'

'Mary Clifford said that the boy was a burden to you without the assistance of your husband. Is that true?'

'Yes, he was a burden. That is why I hired her. For the extra pair of hands.'

'Mrs Leahy, Mary Clifford also said that, while she was in your service, you stopped referring to your grandson as Micheál, but called him a "fairy". She also said you referred to the child as "it". Can you please tell the court why you stopped referring to Micheál Kelliher as your grandson?'

Nóra hesitated. 'I had met my grandson before. There was no likeness between the one I had met and the one delivered to me. At first, I thought that he was only ill, and I tried to cure him, but the cures did not work and 'twas because the boy was a changeling.'

'Where did you believe your true grandson to be, if he were not with you under your care?'

'Swept. In the fairy fort. With the music and the dancing and the lights.'

There was a ripple of hushed conversation through the crowd.

Nóra closed her eyes. Under hill. Under whitethorn. On the fairy wind with a weed to carry you, to bring you to the boundary places, the threshold between this world and the other. Swept away from all anger, all suffering. Not good enough for Heaven and not bad enough for Hell. All places. In the air, in the soil, in the water.

'Mrs Leahy?'

Nóra felt lightheaded. She opened her eyes and suddenly recognised her nephew, Daniel, standing still and pale behind a sea of heads. She stared at him, her heart lifting, but he lowered his gaze.

'Mrs Leahy, having a cripple child in the home can be a terrible shame. A sorrowful burden. Your own servant maid has said that Micheál was forever crying, unable to feed or bathe himself, unable to speak or – indeed – love. He kept you from sleeping. And you, recently widowed and no doubt still in the grip of grief.' The man's tone changed. 'You were surely frustrated by Micheál's cretinism, Mrs Leahy. Angry, perhaps. So angry you saw nothing wrong in whipping a helpless boy with nettles you had *deliberately* and with intention picked for the purpose of applying to his skin.'

Nóra shook her head. ''Twas to restore the moving to his legs.'

'So you say. But to no avail, Mrs Leahy. And so, as Mary Clifford has said, you turned to the services of Anne Roche. Had you ever consulted Anne for her "cures" before this time?'

'Had I gone for the cure?'

'That is what I am asking, yes.'

'I had not, no.'

'And why was that?'

'I had no reason. My husband . . .'

She remembered the dead ember hidden in the pocket of Martin's greatcoat. Embers carried for protection. Where had it come from? From what hearth, what fire?

A glowing coal carried three times sunwise around the house for luck. An ember thrown into the potato field on St John's Eve. A coal drawn thrice over a nest in which birds are ready to hatch. A live coal placed in feet water to preserve a man during an absence from the home.

An ember to save against the trespass of evil spirits.

'Can you please repeat that, Mrs Leahy? The court cannot understand you.'

'My husband had gone to Nance. Once. For a hand.'

'A hand?'

''Twas ice. Ice cold and no moving in it. And she healed him.'

'So you knew who she was and were familiar with her position in the community as a quack doctress?'

'I knew she had the knowledge.' Nóra felt Nance looking at her then, and a sudden flare of uncertainty rose up in her. ''Twas her who said it was fairy, and 'twas her who offered to banish it!'

The prosecutor was thoughtful for a moment. 'It must have been a great relief to you, Mrs Leahy. A helpless, onerous child filling you with shame and grief and trouble, and lo – a woman who tells you he was no child at all, but a fairy. How relieved you must have felt to discover that you bore no duty towards him! How easy to have your own disgust and horror sanctioned with the knowledge that *it was not your grandson!*'

Nóra stared at the lawyer as he threw his hands up in the air, gesturing to the jury. They looked uncomfortable. She shook her head, unable to speak. They could not understand. They had not seen the great change in the child. There had been no human in the boy, in the bones brimming with fairy, the sour-skinned squall of him. If only she could return to her cabin and find her daughter's boy, show them the child returned to her.

'Will you tell the court, Mrs Leahy, if you agreed to pay Anne Roche for this great alleviation of guilt and trouble?'

'She does not take money.'

'Please speak up!'

'Nance does not take money. Eggs, chickens . . .'

'She takes payment in kind, is this what you are saying, Mrs Leahy? Was this the arrangement made between the two of you? That she would pronounce your crippled grandson a *fairy*, then work to *put the fairy out of it* through application of nostrums, herbal poison and, finally, *drowning*, and in kind you would supply her with the food and fuel she needed to survive?'

'I don't . . .'

'You must answer yes or no, Mrs Leahy.'

'I don't know. No.'

All Nóra could think of as she stood there, hearing the counsel repeat his questions, was that her body was failing her. She trembled uncontrollably, her bare feet curling in cramp on the floor as she attempted to keep up with his questions. Had she been glad to see the foxglove taking its effect on the child? Had she been saddened when it had not killed him? Had she been in the river the morning Micheál was drowned, and if Nance was in a state of undress, why had she been fully clothed? Why did she insist on referring to the child as a fairy when, as she had heard, Micheál's body had been found? Had she panicked and fled when she realised he had drowned, or had the drowning been her intention all along?

He was saying she had killed him. There was a pricking between her legs and, horrified, Nóra felt warm drops of urine roll down her thighs. She brought her hands to her face and began to weep in shame.

A hushed silence then. When Nóra opened her eyes she saw Mr Walshe rising out of his seat, his lips pursed in thought.

'Is it true that you wished the best for the boy in your care, Mrs Leahy?'

Nóra's tongue felt sluggish. She opened her mouth but no sound came out.

Mr Walshe repeated his question, as though he was speaking to an invalid. 'Mrs Leahy, is it not true that you nurtured the boy when he came into your care? That you sought assistance from a doctor?'

Nóra nodded. 'Yes. In September.'

'And what treatment did the doctor prescribe for your grandson?'

'Nothing. He said there was nothing to be done.'

'That must have caused you great distress, Mrs Leahy.'

'It did.'

'Mary Clifford, the Crown's witness, said that you sought assistance from your priest, Father Healy, also?'

'I did.'

'And what assistance did he offer you?'

'He said there was nothing to be done.'

'Mrs Leahy, am I correct in saying, then, that when the most careful nurture failed to restore the boy to health and strength, when neither doctor nor priest were able to avail you with medicine or help, you sought to find a cure via the only other means available to you? Through the local *doctress*, Anne Roche?'

Nóra's voice came out in a whisper. 'Yes.'

'And when Miss Roche told you that she believed she would be able to *restore* your grandchild to you, in full health and with all the capabilities and mobility you saw in him when you visited your daughter two years ago, you had *hope*?'

'I did.'

'And who could blame you for that, Mrs Leahy? Was it *hope* that led you to believe that the crippled boy we now understand to be Micheál Kelliher was *fairy*? Was it *hope* and a *longing* to preserve the life of your grandchild that led you to assist Anne Roche in her "cures"?'

'I . . . I don't understand.'

The lawyer hesitated, wiped his forehead. 'Mrs Leahy, did you hope to preserve the life of Micheál Kelliher?'

Nóra's head swam. She gripped the irons about her wrist. The fairies do not like iron, she thought. Fire, iron and salt. Cold embers and tongs over the cradle, and new milk spilt on Maytime earth.

'Mrs Leahy?' It was the judge, leaning forward, his blue eyes rheumy, voice deep and concerned. 'Mrs Leahy, the court is asking you if you have any further statement to make.'

Nóra brought a trembling hand up to her face. The iron was cool against her flushed cheeks. 'No, sir. None other than that I only wanted my grandson with me. None other than that.'

Nance listened as the man they called Coroner presented himself as a witness, his clipped red moustache uttering words she did not understand.

'Our inquest found that Micheál Kelliher came by his death following asphyxia, caused by inhalation of fluid and consequent obstruction of the air passages. Signs presented were consistent with drowning. The lungs were waterlogged, and there was evidence of river weed in the hair of the deceased.'

There was no mention of the yellow flaggers on the bank, the unfurling gold against the green and all the suggestion its blossom held. They did not mention the power in the boundary water, in the strange light that flooded the earth before the sun rose, in the actions of hungered hands.

'In your professional estimation, sir,' asked the counsel, 'how long would the deceased have been held under the water for drowning and death to occur?'

The coroner was thoughtful. 'Given that it seems the deceased was paralytic, either fully or in part, it may have taken less time than what may be deemed usual. I would venture to propose three minutes.'

'That is three minutes of sustained submersion?'

'That is correct, sir.'

'Are there any other findings you feel compelled to include in your statement today?'

The man sniffed, twitching his moustache. 'There were marks which indicate the possibility of struggle.'

'And by marks do you mean bruises?'

'Yes, sir. About the chest and neck. Inconclusive, but they did raise suspicions that the child was forcibly held under water.'

The counsel placed the tips of his fingers together, his eyes darting towards the jury. 'Mr McGillycuddy, in your professional opinion, do you believe that the findings of the coronial inquest indicate that the deceased was murdered with intent? That his was a violent death?'

The man looked at Nance and lifted his chin. He gave a brief, curt nod. 'I do, sir.'

Nance was ready when the court finally called for her statement. She had been waiting for the opportunity to tell her story, to reveal to the room the kernelled truth within the mass of stories and sworn informations and cross-examinations. She stood as Maggie would have done, straight-backed, eyes narrowed, and when they handed her the book to kiss, she did so with sincerity. They would not be able to fault her. She would show them the truth of her knowledge, her cure.

'Miss Roche, please tell the court how you make your living.'

'I give out the cure.'

'Speak up, please, the court cannot hear you.'

Nance took a deep breath and attempted to raise her voice. But the room was hot, and the air seemed to catch on her lungs, and when she spoke again there was a groaning from the crowd.

'Your worship, will you allow the prisoner to make her statement from the witness stand so that she may be heard?'

'I will.'

An officer of the court led Nance to the box where she had seen the various speakers give out against her. After a day and a half listing in the dock against the courtroom wall, it felt strange to now be standing at a different place in the room, so much closer to the dark-suited men sitting with their shined shoes catching the gleam from the glass windows. Before they had appeared shadowy, but now Nance could make out their features: their dry lips and greying eyebrows, the lines surrounding their eyes. Some, she saw, were surely her age, and she wondered if, as a girl, she had seen them and their gentle-blooded parents on excursion to Mangerton. Had her hands picked the strawberries that their mothers had bought and pressed into their pink mouths?

'Anne Roche, can you please tell the court how you make your living?'

'I help people with the knowledge that I have been given, and they give me gifts in return.'

The counsel glanced at the jurors, and Nance caught the suggestion of a smirk on his lips. 'And can you please explain what this "knowledge" is?'

'I have the knowledge to heal all manner of ills and sickness, both those of an ordinary kind and those wrought by the Good People.'

'Can you please describe the difference between the two?'

'There are those which are of a common kind, but there are some ills which are the mark of the Good People, and they call for a different cure.'

The counsel studied her for a moment. 'But, Miss Roche, what is the difference between the two?'

Nance paused, confused. She had already explained to him that she divined the mark of the Good People amongst the sick, that she administered to the ordinary bruise, the extraordinary swelling. 'It might be that a man has built his house on a fairy path, and it is that which brings the sickness to him, or it might be something else entirely.'

'So what you are saying is that people come to you with sickness, and it is only then that you *diagnose* whether their sickness was caused by *the Good People*, or otherwise?'

'That is the truth of it.'

'And how did you learn these things?'

''Twas taught to me by my own aunt when I was a girl and growing.'

'And where did your aunt learn these nostrums and mysteries?'

'When she was away with the Good People.'

The lawyer raised his eyebrows. 'And by Good People, you mean to say the fairies?'

'Yes, the Good People.'

'Forgive me for my *ignorance* –' there was a smattering of laughter from the crowd '– but why do you call the fairies *Good People*? It is my understanding that they are not people at all.'

'It is out of respect that I call them the Good People, for they do not like to be thinking of themselves as bad craturs. They have a desire to get into Heaven, same as you, sure, Counsel.'

'Miss Roche, I am acquainted with the fireside stories, but I must say that I do not give them credence. How do you know the fairies to be true?'

'Because they took my mother and my aunt. I know there is no word of a lie in Them, for didn't they lead me out of Killarney when I was poor and had no living at all, and didn't they show me the way to the valley where I have been living for these past twenty years?'

'You have seen them? How did they "show you the way"?'

'Oh, I have heard Them talking, and 'tis truth I see Them as lights coming to me and leading me, and there have been times I heard Them dancing or fighting.'

'They fight?'

'The Good People are fond of fighting and hurling and dancing and singing. And 'tis true that they sometimes cause mischief, and that is why the people come to me: because I have the knowledge of the ways in which to undo the damage they cause. I have the knowledge and the cure if the fairies do be striking you or taking the profit out of your animals or crops, or the power out of your legs.'

A rising murmur lifted from the crowd, and Nance could see several onlookers whisper to each other from behind their hands. They were listening to her. Relieved to finally be heard, she began to talk of the ways the Good People pressed up against the known world. She spoke of the power in saliva, in urine, in dung, in water from the holy wells, or that which held the leavings of iron. Of holed and hollowed stones, of soot and salt.

'The Good People have a mighty fear of fire and iron, and sure, 'tis the threat of these which will serve to banish Them, so they have no power against a reddened poker. And though they lay their claim to fairy plants and trees – elder, foxglove – if certain plants can be got without their interference, the power in them can be turned against those who lay claim to them. Sure, elder has a mighty mischief and *crostáil*, and the Good People ride its branches, but sure, I can wring the bad temper out of it. And there are a great many things aside, cures given to me by the Good People, which I may not say, for if the secret goes out of a cure, there will be no power in it at all.'

When she had finished, Nance took a deep breath and examined the jury. The men were looking at her with an expression she could not place. There was none of the lawyer's acid curl of the lip, none of the scowling or wariness she had experienced before. No anger, no fear. She realised, then, that they regarded her with the same expression of those she had begged from: pity, shadowed with disdain. Her stomach sank.

The lawyer was smiling to himself.

'Miss Roche, do you accept payment for your . . . services?'

'I don't be taking money, for I'd surely lose the knowledge and cure.'

'But it is true that you will accept gifts of fuel and food? Goods.'

'Sure, that is true.'

'Did you drown Micheál Kelliher in the Flesk on Monday, the sixth of March, in exchange for goods?'

Nance frowned. 'I'm not after drowning Micheál Kelliher, no.'

'Both Mary Clifford and Mrs Leahy have stated that you ordered them to bathe Micheál Kelliher in that pool of the river Flesk, where the boundaries of three rivers meet. They say they had so bathed him for three mornings running, and on the last morning you kept the child longer under the water than usual.'

''Twas to banish it. The fairy.'

'Not *it*, Miss Roche. Himself. Micheál Kelliher.'

''Twas no natural boy.'

'He was a paralytic, we hear. Could neither stand nor walk nor speak.'

''Twas the fairy of it.'

'He was your patient?'

'He was.'

355

'But you are not a doctor. You are ignorant of medical knowledge. Your training is only in *nostrums*. Old folk cures. Is that not so?'

Nance felt a kick of anger in her chest. Over and over they circled with their questions. Did she not make herself clear? 'I have the knowledge. Of the charms and the cures. Of the herbs.'

'Mrs Leahy has said you led her to believe that you were capable of curing the boy, Miss Roche. If you have the *knowledge*, then why is Micheál Kelliher dead? Why could you not cure him?'

Nance thought of Maggie, smoking by the warmth of the fire at night while the corncrakes filled the air outside with their long, scraping cries.

What is in the marrow is hard to take out of the bone.

''Tis not Micheál Kelliher who is dead,' she said finally.

'Do you truly believe that, Miss Roche?'

Nance brought her gaze level to that of the counsel. 'That child died a long time ago.'

There were exclamations from those listening in the court. Nance noticed the jurors shift in their chairs and exchange knowing looks.

'Is there any other statement you would like to make to the court?'

Nance hesitated. 'I have told you my truth.'

'That is all then, thank you.'

Nance was fetched down from the witness box and returned to her place in the dock next to Nóra. While the counsel made his closing remarks, Nance ran the pads of her fingers over her crooked thumbs, swollen sore in the heat of the courtroom. They throbbed, and she tucked them into her palms, balling her hands into fists.

There was a whimper beside her, and Nance saw that Nóra was shaking, staring as Mr Walshe raised a hand in an attempt to settle the crowd. An atmosphere of nervous excitement was issuing throughout the courtroom. She heard the judge wearily call for order, and one of the jurors sent a man to open the outer door of the court. There was a collective murmur of relief as fresh air fanned through the room.

Nance saw that, for all the defence lawyer's outward ease, Mr Walshe's face was shining with sweat, his shirt visibly damp beneath his suit. He regarded the sober-faced jury.

'Gentlemen, this case, although unusual and repugnant in the extreme, is not one of wilful murder. The Crown's chief witness, Mary Clifford, who was present at the time the accident occurred, who witnessed *firsthand* Micheál Kelliher's treatment not only at the Flesk on the morning of Monday, the sixth of March, but also in the months prior to his death, stood before you and – under oath – admitted that she did not believe the prisoners had deliberately drowned the child. Given her testimony, Anne Roche and Honora Leahy cannot be rightly convicted of wilful murder.

'Gentlemen, Micheál Kelliher lost his life through superstition. It is true that the circumstances surrounding his treatment at the hands of the accused are extraordinary. It is true that the gross delusion these women operated under is horrifying. The scale of their ignorance is appalling. But it cannot be discounted as incidental. The accused acted on the belief that the deceased child, Micheál Kelliher, was a fairy spirit. A *changeling*, in the words of the Crown's witness. Anne Roche selected a particular site of the river Flesk believed to be fairy-inhabited waters, and bathed him there with the assistance of Honora Leahy three mornings consecutively, contending that the falsely believed changeling would return to his supernatural realm.'

Nance remembered the wildness with which Nóra had hauled herself up the bank when they had lifted the banished changeling from the water.

'I will go to see if he is returned!' The widow's grey hair unfastening down her back as she grasped at tree roots and moss to drag herself from the river. 'I will see if he is there!' Lurching wildly through the ferns and bracken, branches swinging in her wake.

Burying the body of the changeling in the Piper's Grave, pimpled with cold.

'Neither of the accused can write, gentlemen. Anne Roche, particularly, is unlettered and ignorant of the modern world, and her statement that "the child died a long time ago" is evidence of her benighted belief that the boy she was curing was *fairy*. Again, let me remind you that even Mary Clifford, who was witness to the act, has stated under oath that the child was bathed not with intent to kill, but to *put the fairy out of it*. Given this testimony, and the pitiful intellectual and moral ignorance and the advanced age of the accused, I recommend to you an acquittal of this charge.'

Nance stared as the lawyer returned to his seat, fear rising in her throat. I have no ignorance upon me, she wanted to tell him. Don't be telling them that would have me hang that there is no knowledge about me.

Baron Pennefather cleared his throat. He waited until there was absolute silence before addressing the jury.

'Gentlemen. Let me impress upon you that while a charge of murder may be commuted to manslaughter where life was taken away under the influence of sudden passion, this cannot apply to the defence's argument that the life of Micheál Kelliher was taken as a result of superstitious belief.'

'We will hang,' Nóra whispered. 'They do not believe. They think it superstition.' Her voice shook, her tongue catching on the words. Nance's heart thudded in dread.

The judge took a moment to examine the waiting faces in the room. 'It is clear that the ignorant actions of the prisoners demonstrate their belonging to a caste derived from hereditary or progressive immorality. Yet, it is not a mark of wickedness we find in this case, but rather the overwhelming suggestion and likelihood of low intellectual power in combination with strongly developed passions of the lower nature.'

Nance began to breathe rapidly. What is he saying? she wondered. What is he saying about me?

'In short, while this is a case of suspicion, and requires to be thoroughly examined into, I encourage you to recognise the superstitious motives that are clearly, albeit disturbingly, evident. And I ask you to consider the problems of women of advanced age in prison, unfit for transportation, who demand much attention through infirmity. Thank you, gentlemen.'

Nance watched as the jurors rose together like a flock of grey-hooded crows and exited the room to decide their verdict. The noise in the courtroom was suddenly overwhelming.

I don't understand, thought Nance. I don't understand.

Looking down she saw that she still held her hands in fists.

The jury were gone less than half an hour before the clerk and officer of the court began to settle the crowd. Nance felt her heartbeat rise in apprehension as Justice Baron Pennefather entered the room and resumed his position in the chair, pressing his hands together as stragglers forced their way inside, fighting for a clear view of the prisoners.

Next to her, Nóra leant against the dock, her body slowly sinking towards the floor. Nance reached out to grasp her about the arm and Nóra's eyes flashed open.

'Don't touch me,' she hissed, before fear splayed through her expression and she clutched at Nance's retreating hands. 'I don't want to die,' she murmured. She lifted her fetters and attempted to cross herself. 'I don't want to hang. I don't want to hang.'

Nance felt the widow begin to shake again.

'Sore-wounded Christ. Oh, sore-wounded Christ, I don't want to hang. Oh, please, Lord.'

Nance began to rock on her feet, fear filling her stomach. She bit on her tongue until she could taste the iron of her blood.

'Sore-wounded Christ, Martin! Oh!'

'Quiet now.' An officer nudged Nóra and she gasped, suddenly gripping onto the wooden spikes in front of them to hold herself upright.

The atmosphere in the court was like that in the face of an approaching storm. An uneasy hush. A gathering tension in the air as the jurors were admitted back into the court and, faces solemn, returned to their chairs.

'I don't want to hang,' Nóra continued muttering next to Nance. 'I don't want to hang.'

The judge's voice carried across the room. 'Have you found your verdict?'

A white-haired man stood, hands carefully brushing down his trousers. 'We have, Your Worship.'

'What say you?'

Nance closed her eyes. Imagined the river, the peaceful unknotting of water.

She could feel Nóra shaking violently next to her.

'We agree with Your Worship that this is a case of suspicion, however, in the charge of wilful murder against Anne Roche and Honora Leahy, we find insufficient evidence for conviction. Our verdict is not guilty.'

There was a pause, and then the courtroom erupted in excited and furious reaction.

Nance sank to the floor, her legs collapsing in relief. Shutting her eyes, the clamour in the hot air around her sounded like nothing more than a sudden downpour of rain. Summer rain breaking over the pine needles hot-scented in the woods, crisping leaves browning in the oak, the alder, the torrential blessing of heavy cloud over the forest, and the sweet gurgle of water towards the river.

Nance only opened her eyes again when they hauled her to her feet to unlock the fetters. Blinking against the light, she was vaguely aware of Nóra, bent over, howling with relief, and beyond her, in the shifting, tidal crowd, Mary, staring at them with tears streaming down her pale cheeks.

'Mary!' Nance croaked. There was a heavy tug and the irons came off her wrists and in the sudden feel of lightness and freedom, she raised both palms to the sobbing girl. 'Mary!'

The girl spat on the ground. 'I curse you,' she mouthed. Then she turned and disappeared into the seething crowd.

CHAPTER
TWENTY-ONE

Heather

Mary stood in the crowded market street of Tralee, her eyes scanning the flocks of people that milled in the road. The day was hot, and she sweated in the new shift she had bought with the widow's shilling. She had wrapped the clothes still filled with Micheál's smell in a neat bundle and held this conspicuously at her hip, standing straight as a poker, her eyes meeting every casual and curious gaze that reached her. Let them see that she was for hire.

Pigs lay humped in the road, their squealing piglets in makeshift pens staked with pegs and string. Sheep, new-shorn, huddled under the eyes of boys and their fathers, capped, smoking, laughing at the women chasing a terrified chicken that had flown the straw coop.

Mary had asked Father Healy the road to Annamore after the trial. Had started walking the way, exultant, her heart thrilling in anticipation. She imagined the shouts of surprise as she rounded the corner, the little thumping feet hitting the dust as her brothers and sisters ran to her, wrapped their arms about her legs and waist and dragged her away to show her new-hatched chickens, scooping up the puffing, cheeping yellow. Her mam, lined and sombre as usual, but relieved to see her safe. Happy to have her home to work. And how she would work. She would tend the lazy beds until the stalks came thick and fast, and she would shake the soil from the clutch of lumpers, as yellow as butter, and no one would be hungry. They would boil them briefly, to eat them 'with the bones still in', as her da would say. And she would hold the little ones afterwards, or set them to sleep against the belly of the snoring pig in the corner, and all would be well.

She would forget Micheál. She would forget the strange boy bleating from the cold, who had curled into her neck for the warmth her body held there.

Mary had been thinking these thoughts, imagining her life back home, when she had stopped to drink from a well at the side of the road. A beggar woman was sleeping there, face heavily pocked. At first Mary thought she was alone, but at the splashing of the water something stirred under the woman's dirty cloak, and a small, naked child emerged. A little girl, her blonde hair greyed with dirt, holding her hand out to Mary in patient expectation. Mary stared at her, water still dripping down her chin, and then slowly unwrapped the food the priest had given her for the journey. Dried fish. A heel of stale, buttered bread.

The little girl took them from her hand, then crawled back under her mother's cloak to eat, the material quivering.

Mary had turned around then. The road back to Tralee seemed longer than the one she had taken from it, but a man and his wife heading into market on an open cart offered her a ride, and Mary took it, setting her bare feet on the spokes of the wheel and climbing up to the boards. She had set her eyes on the horizon, watching as the distance to Annamore lengthened with every step of the mule.

She would stand in the streets of Tralee all day if she had to. She would stand there until someone came and asked her, would she like to work a farm in summer, could she thresh and carry turf, and was she strong, and did she know how to churn?

I will take the first offer I get, Mary thought. There was no use in taking the measure of a face to gauge whether a place of work would be a safe one. It did not matter if the nose was red with drink taken, or if the eyes were webbed with the lines of laughter. There was no telling the shape of a heart from the face of the one who carried it.

The sun beat down on her. She was thirsty. Lifting the bundle up to her forehead to shield her eyes, she caught the scent of the fairy child in the old linen. Sour milk and stale potato. Hearth smoke and the cold night. All the witching hours awake with the changeling, all the wrapping of blankets and the fighting of his limbs, the sharp feel of his nails between her teeth as she carefully bit their lengths so he would not scratch himself in his dancing, in his fitting, in his strange reaching for the world around him. The hot feel of his tongue against her fingers as she fed him, the eyes sliding over her face and the feathers on his skin, the laughs dissolving into the air, and the screaming that pealed from him.

It knocked the breathing out of her.

Uncaring that people stared, Mary hid her face in the dirty bundle and wept.

After the trial, Nóra travelled back to the valley with Daniel. She had found her nephew waiting outside the courthouse, smoking in the sunshine and speaking with Father Healy. Both men had looked up as she approached, squinting in the glare of daylight.

'They freed you then,' Daniel had murmured, turning his pipe in his hands.

The expression on the priest's face had been one of ill-hidden aversion.

'You have much to thank God for,' he had remarked. 'You should have listened to me. I warned you, Nóra. I warned you that nothing good would happen for talk of fairies.' His face had pinked. 'Nance Roche did not stop with her nostrums, with her *piseógs*, with her heathen practices, and the Church will not stand for it, verdict or no. I can't be tolerating superstitious belief upheld over true faith. Nóra, blind yourself no longer to the sin of pagan delusion.'

Nóra had stared at the priest, unable to say a word. It wasn't until Daniel had placed a heavy hand on her shoulder and guided her away that she fully understood the meaning of the priest's words.

'He will excommunicate her,' she had whispered to Daniel.

Her nephew had sighed and gestured down the road. 'I'll take you home, Nóra.'

They travelled to Killarney by mail cart, neither of them speaking. The other passengers stared at her, and Nóra realised that her clothes, returned after the trial, were still covered in river mud. She covered her head and face with her shawl, despite the heat. Nóra was glad Daniel did not want to talk. There was a weight in her mouth, upon her tongue. She did not quite know what had happened. All she knew was that she must return home, must see if Micheál was returned.

When the cart stopped in Killarney, she and Daniel walked to the outskirts of the town, then stopped at the door of a cabin, asking for food and a night's lodging. They were hungry themselves, the woman of the house said. July was a mean month, a hungry month. God provide them with a fine crop and soon, or they would all be on the roads. Still, they were good people, she would feed them what she could and let them make beds out of straw and find a corner where they might sleep under cover, away from the night sky crawling with moonlight. Nóra fell asleep with straw scratching her cheek and woke before dawn. She washed her face in dew, and when Daniel woke, they walked the pale lane in the early-morning light as the robins swooped and the chitterling, waking animals rustled. As the day warmed and filled with people going about their business, carrying *sleánta* and creels, Nóra let her mind return to the child that would surely be waiting for her, saw her daughter's face echoed in his features, saw Johanna when she was young and all seemed light and full of possibility, until she barely saw the road in front of them.

It was only as they returned to the valley and its crib of mountains, clad with heather purpling in the twilight, that Daniel spoke to her.

'You'll be staying with us, then.'

They had crested a hill, and Nóra was breathing hard. She stopped and stared at Daniel. 'I'll be staying in my cabin.'

Daniel kept his eyes firmly on the road before them, maintaining an even stride. 'There was no rent paid on it.'

'I've been late with the rent before.' Panic rose in her chest. She ran to catch up with him. 'Sure, 'tis no uncommon thing, to be late with the rent.'

'You'll be in with me and the little woman, Nóra.'

'But Micheál will be waiting for me at my cabin.'

There was an uncomfortable silence. Daniel lit his pipe and clamped the stem between his teeth.

'And what about my belongings?' Nóra protested.

'You can fetch them. But there's a need to be selling the bed.'

Nóra cried then, wiping her face with dirty hands, until they rounded a corner and saw John O'Shea, face already browned with the summer, the shadow of a moustache lighting golden.

'Widow Leahy?' He was standing in the lane, his hands full of rocks he had been pelting at a bird's nest. 'They didn't hang you then.'

Daniel squinted against the setting sun. 'She can't stay to talk, John. Let her pass.'

'Do you know there's a rhyme about you?'

Nóra sniffed. 'A rhyme?'

The boy put his hands in his pockets and began to sing. '*Nóra Leahy, what have you done? You drowned your daughter's only son! The lad could neither speak nor stand. Did fairies take him, hand in hand? Or did you take him to the water, the only son of your only daughter?*'

Nóra stared at him, a sick feeling spreading through her chest. 'God forgive you.'

John's grin faded.

''Tis only a rhyme,' Daniel interjected. 'There's been worse said. John, go and tell Peg that the Widow Leahy's returned.'

The boy nodded and began to run down the lane.

Daniel turned to Nóra. 'Don't mind him. Go on with you to your old place and start collecting what you need. I'll fetch Brigid. She can help you carry your things. You'll be spending the night with us. She'll make you comfortable. I won't be in tonight. There's business to attend to.' He nodded to her, his face grim, then continued down the lane after John at a quickened pace.

When both men were mere specks in the distance Nóra sank to her knees in the dust of the road. The words of the boy ran through her head and she vomited, bile stringing in the summer wind.

The grass was high around her cabin. Nóra, gasping for air, pulled the door to and stood on the step. The room was musty. Dirt had blown in and the straw blocking the window was gone. Old rushes were eddied in the leavings of the wind.

'God bless all here,' Nóra cried, stomach heaving. She looked around the room, desperate for some sign of the boy, but all was still. The room was as she had left it, the hearth dead, the settle bed unfolded.

Nóra took a tentative step inside. 'Micheál?'

Nothing.

'Micheál? Dear one?'

Nóra shut the door behind her. Then a sudden noise sent her spirits soaring. She rushed into the bedroom, unable to breathe, hope mounting in her chest. She had been right! Micheál was here! He was under the greatcoat on her bed, here was the form of him, here he was sleeping.

But there was nothing under the coat except an unfolded blanket. Nóra clasped it, breathing quickly. There was a quiet murmur of a hen by her feet, and as her eyes adjusted to the dim light, Nóra saw that the chicken was broody, had settled on a nest scratched from old rushes and straw pulled from the mattress.

A slow uneasiness dripped through her.

Please God, she prayed, pulling back the blankets on her bed, growing frantic, more desperate. Please God, please Martin, please let him be here. 'Micheál!'

Nothing. No sound but the cluck of the disturbed hen.

Unsure of what she should do, Nóra pulled on Martin's greatcoat and staggered out into the main room, sinking onto a stool. Silence rang in her ears.

He wasn't there. He had not been returned.

She had been so certain she would find him, perhaps sitting by the fire, eyes looking up to her as she entered. Martin's face, Johanna's colour. She rubbed her cheek against the rough frieze, taking long breaths of her husband's remaining scent. Reaching into the pocket, she took out the dead ember and turned the char in her hands.

He was not there. She had been so sure.

Outside the birds sang down the sun.

*

'God and Mary to you.'

Nóra turned, her eyes swollen. Peg stood at the threshold of the cabin, leaning on her blackthorn, looking on in silence.

'He isn't here.'

The old woman offered her hand to Nóra. 'You've returned to us, God be praised.' She waited as Nóra wiped her face. 'What trouble,' she murmured. 'What sorrow. Come on with you, now. Sitting in the dark like this, and no fire lit. Well. At least the night is warm. I'll sit with you for a bit now, shall I?'

She eased herself down next to Nóra, and together they sat by the ashes in the orange light of the sunset.

Peg pointed to the table and Nóra saw that cream was rising in a clean crock.

''Twas the son's woman. She couldn't bear to hear the beast bawling. Your butter is with me. For the safe keeping.' Peg sucked her teeth. ''Tis back in the milk.'

Nóra nodded wearily. 'That's a blessing.'

'There's need of blessings in this valley.'

There was a sudden chorus of crickets. The women sat in silence, listening to the chirring.

'They buried him in the *cillín*,' Peg said finally. 'Father Healy said 'twas best.'

Nóra blinked, staring at the dead fire.

Peg leant closer. 'What in God's holy name happened to the cratur?'

'I was after being rid of the fairy, Peg,' Nóra murmured.

'When I saw you that morning, Nóra, you were soaked to the bone.' She placed a hand on her knee and lowered her voice. 'Did you give him a wee push?'

Nóra didn't know what to say. She gently nudged Peg's hand away before standing and rummaging for the bottle she'd left in the hearth nook. 'Where is it, Peg?'

'I'm not accusing you. 'Tis only, if you did, 'twould be –'

'Where is it?'

'Where is what?'

'The *poitín*.'

Peg sighed. 'Gone, Nóra. There was someone here . . .' She threw up her hands. 'I sent the boys down when I saw what they were about, but they took what they felt was theirs.'

'Seán Lynch.'

Peg shook her head. ''Twas Kate. 'Twas a fear on everyone after the *piseóg*. After Áine. Kate was here and looking all about your churn. She was thinking 'twas the boy that blinked the milk and brought the baby out of Brigid. She was looking for signs of cursing. Says she found a flint by the dash. She said Seán had laid claim to your goods, that you were sure to hang, and she was to take some things while he was up in Tralee.'

'What did she take, Peg?'

'Some things of Martin's. The *poitín*. The pipe. The coin you had. Clothes. What butter was here before, and some other food. The salt.'

Nóra looked up and saw that the wooden box was gone. ''Twas from my wedding.'

'She would have taken the cow only there were some of us told her to wait until we had news of the verdict.'

'I might have been hanged, Peg.'

'I know.'

Nóra felt like she would choke. She pulled at the loose skin of her throat, pressing her chin against her knuckles, and began to weep. Peg extended a hand to her and Nóra took it with the grip of the drowning, squeezing her fingers until the old woman grimaced in pain. Still, she let Nóra sink her nails into her skin.

'He isn't here,' she sobbed.

'I know,' Peg said softly. 'I know.'

It was some time before Nóra could speak again. She sat with her face streaming, chin slippery.

Peg crossed herself. 'Thank God in his infinite mercy you are saved.'

Nóra wiped her eyes. 'They thought us mad. The fairy talk. They didn't give in to it, but the girl said 'twas not done with the intent to kill and so they could not be calling it murder.'

'After the arrest Father Healy read to us from the *Chute's Western Herald*. It said you were of good character, Nóra. There's none here who can say you are anything other.'

'There's a rhyme about me that says otherwise.'

'You're a good woman, Nóra Leahy.'

'I wanted to be rid of the fairy.'

'He was a burden to you.'

'He was not Johanna's son. There was none of my blood in him.'

Peg brushed the hair out of Nóra's eyes. ''Tis a queer thing. For all the badness that has been in this place, folk are saying that with the changeling out of the valley there is peace again. That surely the boy was blinking the hens and the cows, for now the profit is back. Women who thought they might not have enough to keep shadow stitched to heel are calling for the egg man, purses filling again. Those who thought they might be on the road paid their rents after all.'

'Daniel says this place is lost to me.'

Peg clucked her tongue. ''Tis a shame, but sure, you'd be rattling around on your own.'

'Did they find who lay the *piseóg*?'

'They say 'twas surely Nance, but fortunate that 'twas found so soon and set to rights by the priest. There was no time for the curse to be sinking in the soil. Kate was spouting at the well, saying sure 'twas Nance, for don't curses come home to roost, and 'tis what happens to folk who wish others ill. Their wickedness catches up with them and they find themselves in Tralee with a nice rope collar.'

'Kate Lynch!' Nóra spat, growing tearful. 'Coming in here and taking what belongs to me after Seán's bidding. I'll be going over there and taking it all back. The salt box!'

'Nóra . . .'

'She believed it more than anyone. She believed it more than anyone! How dare she talk about rope collars. We're kin, after all.'

Peg tenderly wiped the tears from Nóra's face. 'Kate's gone.'

'What?'

'Kate Lynch. Seán returned from Tralee this morning to an empty cabin. She left some days ago, we think. Taken all she took from you, and all the egg and butter money. Seán says 'twas a small fortune gone missing from under the bed.'

Nóra gaped at her.

'Oh, he's in a fit over it. Went straight out today searching for her, saying she might have been taken.' Peg gave a small smile. 'Says the tinkers have been on the roads, might have stolen her. Oh, and there's the usual talk of the fairies at the biddy well. Some are saying she's been swept, others are telling Seán to go to the Piper's Grave on Sunday night and she'll be riding out on a white horse.'

'Kate's gone?'

Peg nodded. 'Aye. I'd bet my good leg and my bad that the poor woman won't be coming back.'

Nóra was thoughtful. 'And Áine?'

'She lives. I heard Brigid Lynch has been going in to care for her.'

'Thanks be to the Virgin.'

There was silence.

'Peg, I thought for a moment . . . When I came back, I thought I heard him in the bedroom.'

'Nóra . . .'

'I thought 'twas him. Peg, when I was up in Tralee, I kept dreaming of him. Dreaming I'd return and he'd be here, waiting. That perhaps there was some delay on him that morning in the river, that it would take time before he was restored to me.' She began to cry again. 'Peg, the fear was on me that I'd be hanged and he'd be here waiting for me!'

'Oh, Nóra.'

'Waiting for his grandmother, but she'd be lying in the pit at Ballymullen!'

'There, now. You're not to be hanged. You're back where you belong.'

'But he's not here!' Nóra shook her head. 'Oh, I can't stay in the valley.'

'Nóra, there's no place else for you to go.'

'Look!' She swept her arm around the empty cabin. 'This is all the home I had, and 'tis gone to me. I am all alone. All alone, and no choice but to go in with Daniel and Brigid when I was the woman of my own house.' She wiped her eyes. 'Martin is dead. Micheál . . . He's not here.' She clutched at her heart. 'I don't know . . . I don't know what has happened.'

Peg took up her hand and stroked it. 'Ara, you've got me, have you not? And 'tis a blessing to have your nephews, God protect them. You'll keep company with Brigid, and sure, 'tis no bad thing to be in a full house.'

'Full house or no, I am alone,' Nóra whispered.

'Come now, woman. Count your blessings! You're not alone – you have plenty kin in this world left to talk to and share the heat of a fire with. God knows it has been a terrible winter for you, and a terrible hardship it must have been sitting in gaol thinking you'd be gone to God. Nóra, there's none that envy you for that. But you've come home to hens in the roost and cream in the pot that you might be taking with you. And would you look next to you, Nóra, for don't you have old Peg too?'

Nóra squeezed Peg's hand. 'Do you think . . . Micheál, it might be that he'll come home to me. One day . . .'

Peg pursed her lips.

'He will. For that was no human child. Was it, Peg?'

'No,' murmured Peg eventually. She rubbed Nóra's hand. 'No, Nóra.'

'And it may be that he'll come back.'

Peg gave her a long look. 'But if it happens that he stays away under hill, with the Good People and the lights and the dancing . . . Well, 'tis worth knowing that there is always worse misfortune to be had.'

There was a sound at the door and Nóra looked over to see Brigid staring in at them, a large basket in her hands.

'God and Mary to you, Nóra Leahy.' Brigid blinked at her, unsmiling. She was pallid from her time indoors, and Nóra thought she seemed frail.

'Why, Brigid! 'Tis good to see you up and out,' said Peg, a note of forced cheerfulness in her voice. 'I've not seen you since your churching.'

'A lot has happened since I saw you last.' Brigid stepped over the threshold and stood by the dead fire, looking down at Nóra. Her face was blank. 'Daniel said they very nearly hanged you.'

Nóra nodded, her mouth dry.

Brigid's expression hardened. 'Dan said Nance deserved to hang. For what she did to Áine. For the *piseóg*. For the bittersweet.'

Nóra stared at her, unable to speak. It was Peg who answered.

'Brigid, come now. Let's have none of that. I'll tell you something. Nance was always a strange one amongst us, but 'tis no rhyme nor reason behind her murdering babies and catching women on fire, no matter the preaching Father Healy has against her. Áine's skirts caught as women's skirts sometimes do, and 'tis no use in blaming another for the fire's liking of a low apron. And did Nance not do her best to be with you in your time of need?'

Brigid paled, still looking down at Nóra. 'She did it, didn't she?'

'Did what?'

'She drowned that boy.'

Peg glanced between them, her beady eyes alert.

''Twas fairy,' Nóra croaked.

Brigid chewed her lip. 'Did you see her? After the trial?'

'No. I lost her in the crowd.'

'Do you know if she was thinking of returning to the valley?'

''Tis where she lives. She'll be wanting to get back to her cabin. 'Twas all I could think about on the road. Getting home.'

Brigid shook her head. 'She'll have no home here. Not now. Get what you need, Nóra. I can't be waiting all night. 'Tis near dark.'

Peg held out a hand. 'Brigid? What are you saying, child?'

''Tis her fault, after all. Come on, Nóra. You can't be staying here.'

'Brigid. What is happening?'

'Dan said I wasn't to tell. Nóra . . .'

'What?'

Brigid bit her lip. She was breathing quickly, gripping her basket so hard that her knuckles were white.

Peg was reaching for her blackthorn stick. 'Let's go, Nóra. To Nance's.' She shuffled towards the door, looking sickened.

Nóra started rising to her feet.

'There's nothing to be done,' Brigid burst out. ''Tis decided.' She shot a finger out to Nóra in warning. ''Twas decided when you were away. And you are lucky that 'twas not decided against you!'

Nóra's stomach swooped in fear. Slowly, her hands trembling, she took Brigid's proffered basket and silently began to collect her belongings.

❧

Nance stood by the woods, gazing at where her *bothán* had stood. Four days' slow walking on the road from Tralee, the long shuffle home on feet stippled with pain, and the cabin was gone.

They had burnt her out. All was ash.

She sank down in the long grass at the edge of the clearing, in the shadows where she would not be seen from the lane, and, exhausted, she slept. She curled into the sweet-smelling summer ground and let her fatigue overwhelm her, until the evening breeze began to blow. She sat up to a sky washed in red cloud.

They must have been careful about it, she thought, sitting up against a tree and looking out over the scorched ground. Had they heaped the roof with dried fuel? Maybe they had quickened the flames with *poitín*. The fire had been high – the uppermost leaves of the nearby trees were black, and half the trunk of the oak was burnt. She stood and walked to the tree and ran her hands carefully over the sooted bark. Charcoal crumbled away, leaving her fingers dirtied. Without thinking why, she brought her palm to her face and blessed herself with the ashes.

Nothing was left. Nance stepped over the crumbling lengths of cindered beams that lay on the ruined ground, poking amongst them for any belongings that might have survived. She found what remained of her gathered wool, once carefully combed and carded, and now a hairy clot upon the ground. The smell of smoke was thick. There were no herbs left. Her stools, the turf, even the clay pots of fat had been burnt to nothing.

It was only when she found the small iron clasp of her goat's lead that she felt the surge of grief, gutting her as swiftly as the swoop of a knife. She closed her eyes and folded her hands tightly about the flaking metal, and imagined Mora, the door shut against her, the fire rising about her. Crying, she began to dig in the ashes for bones, but the light was fading and she could not tell what might be the handle of her tin pail, and what might be the slender remains of her faithful goat.

The night fell starry. The moon rose thin-lipped. Nance sat down in the dead embers of her home, and dug with her hands until she felt the residual warmth of the fire in the soil. She lay in it and blanketed herself with ashes.

Nance gasped awake the next morning at the sound of footsteps. Hauling herself up out of the weight of soot, she looked wildly around her. It was not yet dawn, but the sky had paled to the blue of a robin's egg.

'Nance?'

She spun around. A man stood at the edge of the fire's dark stain, peering intently at her.

Peter O'Connor.

'I thought you were dead,' he said, covering his mouth. He stepped over and helped Nance to her feet. She noticed he was trembling.

'Peter. God bless you.'

He was staring at her, sucking his bottom lip. 'Praise God they freed you,' he stammered.

Nance placed her hand on his forearm, and he gripped it, overcome.

'I thought you were gone from me,' he choked out. 'There was so much talk of the trial. They were saying you'd be hanged or sent away. And you only trying to help.' He raised her fingers to his face and pressed them against his stubbled cheek, chin quivering. 'I was afraid for you.'

'They could not touch me.'

'I was afraid for you, Nance.' He turned away, wiping his eyes. When he turned around again, he was calmer.

'They have burnt me out,' Nance said.

'When the verdict was heard, 'twas decided.'

'Seán Lynch.'

'He came back and found his wife gone and his money with her, and he came here the night before last. He had an anger in him.'

'Kate Lynch is gone?'

'Swept. He was in a state, Nance. He thought you had a hand in it. I couldn't stop them.'

'I know.'

'I tried.' Peter placed a hand over his eyes. 'He had a party of hard men behind him. I'm sorry for it.'

''Tis not your fault.' She took him by the shoulder and he leant into her touch.

'You never did a thing against me. Against anyone.'

They sat in the ashes then, until rain appeared on the hilltops in the distance, and the lowing of animals filled the air.

'You can't stay here,' he said.

'No.'

'Come with me.'

He took her to his cabin, tucked on the raw face of the mountainside, helping her up the steep slope. As they approached he began to explain what had happened.

'They did it at night. All of the men except John O'Donoghue. He wouldn't have a part in it.'

'Daniel Lynch?'

Peter frowned. 'All but John and myself. But when I saw the pack of them going off after sundown, I followed.' He looked at Nance, disgusted, then motioned her inside the cabin.

Nance stood for a while in the darkness, then gasped.

Her goat stood in the corner of the room, tethered to a battered dresser, piles of droppings at her feet. The exhaustion and relief Nance had been suppressing since the trial suddenly overwhelmed her, and she staggered towards Mora, falling over and throwing her arms around the animal and her familiar warmth, her smell of hay and milk. She rubbed her face in Mora's coat, her eyes suddenly wet.

'My dear one. Oh, my dear one.'

'They were going to slit her throat.'

Nance stroked Mora while Peter stood aside, watching.

'I thought she was dead,' Nance murmured, finally releasing the goat and gingerly drying her eyes with her dirtied shawl. 'You took her.'

'I would not let them kill her like that. Now, Nance. Would you not lie down and close your eyes for a small minute? You must be dead tired from the road. 'Tis a long way you've come.'

Nance slept in the quiet cool of Peter's cabin that day. From time to time she woke and saw him sitting in the doorway, squinting out across the rain-soaked valley, or walking softly about indoors, setting the room to rights. At dusk he woke her and handed her a piggin of warm goat's milk, a cold potato. He watched her as she ate. 'You're looking mighty thin on it, Nance.'

''Twas little feasting to be had in Ballymullen.'

'I was meaning to tell you. You're welcome here, Nance. With me. 'Tis not much, what I have, but there's no kin of mine left in the valley and . . .' He flushed. 'What I'm trying to say is that I could marry you. There's nothing they could do then. Against you.'

'I'm an old woman, Peter.'

'You've always been kind to me, Nance.'

She smiled. 'An old woman without a man is the next thing to a ghost. No one needs her, folk are afraid of her, but mostly she isn't seen.'

'Will you think it over? I'm an able man.'

'I will, Peter. Thank you, I will.'

They said little else that evening. Peter sat by the hearth while Nance rested on the heather, and occasionally they looked at one another and smiled. When night had finally wrapped itself around the cabin, Peter said the rosary, and they washed their feet and lay down to rest by the smoored fire.

Nance rose before dawn. Peter was still asleep, snoring softly where he lay by the raked hearth, sprawled, arms above his head. He looked older in sleep, Nance thought.

Quietly, so as not to wake him, she unraked the embers on the hearthstone and selected a fat lump of charcoal. She let it cool as she milked Mora, and when she had the pail filled, she placed the drink and the dead ember on the dresser and blessed them both.

Then she untied the goat and silently left Peter's cabin.

Her bones ached. Nance set out towards the lane, the goat's rope loose in her hand, limping from the soreness in her hip.

When did I become so old? she wondered.

The air was sweet and damp. A morning mist rolled down off the mountains and their purple skins. Hares moved lightly through the heather, white tails scuttling through the dark tangle of brambles before the rowan trees, blossom-white, the clover. The lane was empty before her, and there was no movement in the waiting valley, no wind. Only the birds above her and, in the slow unpeeling of darkness, a divinity of sky.

AUTHOR'S NOTE

This novel is a work of fiction, although it takes as its inspiration a true event of infanticide. In 1826, an 'old woman of very advanced age' known as Anne/Nance Roche was indicted for the wilful murder of Michael Kelliher/Leahy (newspaper accounts list different names) at the summer Tralee Assizes in Co. Kerry. Michael had been drowned in the river Flesk on Monday, 12 June 1826, and had reportedly been unable to stand, walk or speak.

At her trial, Nance Roche claimed that she had been attempting to cure the boy, not kill him. The boy had been brought to the river in an attempt to 'put the fairy' out of him. Nance was acquitted on these grounds.

There have been several recorded cases of death and injury suffered as a consequence of people attempting to banish changelings and recover those believed to be lost to them. The most famous of these cases is that of twenty-five-year-old Bridget Cleary, who was tortured, then burnt to death by her husband and relatives in 1895, in Co. Tipperary. Angela Bourke's *The Burning of Bridget Cleary* (1999) is an outstanding account of this case, and I recommend it to anyone curious to discover more about how and why such tragedies have occurred in Ireland and abroad. *The Good People: New Fairylore Essays*, edited by Peter Narváez (1991), also provides modern-day considerations of the medical afflictions possibly suffered by those considered to be changelings.

Irish fairy lore was (and remains) a deeply complex, ambiguous system of folk belief – there is little that is twee or childish about it. As Bourke mentions in her preface to *Burning*, 'A large part of this book is concerned with considering fairy belief as the products of rational minds, operating in circumstances that are outside the experience of most people in modern, literate societies.' In writing this work of fiction I have sought to portray fairy and folk belief as part of the fabric of everyday rural nineteenth-century Irish life, rather than as anomalous.

In creating the fictional character of Nance, I drew heavily on the stories and accounts mentioned in Gearóid Ó Crualaoich's *The Book of the Cailleach: Stories of the Wise-Woman Healer* (2003), and the fairy stories of Lady Augusta Gregory, Thomas Crofton Croker, and Eddie Lenihan and Carolyn Eve Green's *Meeting the Other Crowd: The Fairy Stories of Hidden Ireland* (2004). Nance's use of and reference to herbal medicine was informed by Patrick Logan's *Making the Cure: A Look at Irish Folk Medicine* (1972), Niall Mac Coitir's books *Irish Trees: Myths, Legends and Folklore* (2003) and *Irish Wild Plants: Myths, Legends and Folklore* (2006), as well as the work of John Windele, James Mooney and W.R. Wilde on superstitions and popular practices relating to medicine and midwifery, much of which was published in the mid-nineteenth century.

My depictions of Irish rural life in the pre-famine days of the nineteenth century were informed by many sources, including but not limited to the work of Kevin Danaher (Caoimhin Ó Danachair), E. Estyn Evans' *Irish Folk Ways* (1957) and the scholarship and publications of Claudia Kinmoth, Jonathan Bell and Mervyn Watson, Patricia O'Hare, Anne O'Connor and – the 'bible' (as I so often heard it called) – Seán Ó Súilleabháin's extraordinary *A Handbook of Irish Folklore* (1942).

ACKNOWLEDGEMENTS

While researching this book I was blessed to have the opportunity to meet and speak with many erudite historians, curators and academics who generously gave up their time to answer my sometimes strange (and often ignorant) questions about Irish folklife. Thank you to the National Folklore Collection at University College Dublin for its vast specialist library on folklore and ethnology, and to Bairbre Ní Fhloinn for her assistance, suggestions and time. Thank you to Clodagh Doyle, curator at the Folklife Division of the National Museum of Ireland, for the tour and for offering me access to the division's research library. Immense gratitude to Stiofán Ó Cadhla from the Department of Folklore and Ethnology at University College Cork for his correspondence and for providing me with much invaluable research material. Thank you to Sarah O'Farrell and Helen O'Carroll from Kerry County Museum in Tralee for their assistance and kindness, and for allowing me to borrow the 'treasure chest' of information from the Poor Inquiry. Thank you to Patricia O'Hare from Muckross House Library for generously giving me a private tour of the grounds and permitting me access to the library records.

Any inconsistencies or fallibility found in my depiction of Irish folklore, folklife and fairy belief in this novel are my own, and should bear no reflection on those who so kindly sought to inform and support my work.

Thanks must also go to Seán O Donoghue from Salmon Leap Farm in Co. Kerry for showing me the old *cillín* on his property next to the original 'Piper's Grave', and for allowing me to wander over his farm to see the Flesk. Thank you to Michael Leane for giving me a tour of the river, and for telling me of times past. Thank you to Chris and James Keane, and to James's mother, Mary, for their hospitality and for so patiently letting me step on everyone's toes at the *ceilidh*.

Thank you to the staff of Flinders University and my colleagues at *Kill Your Darlings* for their ongoing support. Thank you to the friends who shared their various stories and ideas with me, and who may recognise, in this novel, traces of past conversations.

I am indebted to the support and passion of my publishers, editors and early readers. Heartfelt thanks to the marvellous Alex Craig, Judy Clain, Paul Baggaley, Sophie Jonathan, Mathilda Imlah, Gillian Fitzgerald-Kelly, Natalie McCourt, Cate Paterson, Geordie Williamson and Ali Lavau. Thank you to my incredible agents: Pippa Masson at Curtis Brown Australia; Gordon Wise, Kate Cooper and colleagues at Curtis Brown UK; Dan Lazar at Writers House; and Jerry Kalajian at the Intellectual Property Group. It is an honour to work with you all.

Finally, love and gratitude to dearest Heidi, and to Pam, Alan and my sister, Briony, to whom this novel is dedicated.